A Blossom of
Bright Light

Also by Suzanne Chazin

*Land of Careful Shadows**
A Jimmy Vega Mystery

The Fourth Angel

Flashover

Fireplay

A Blossom of Bright Light

SUZANNE CHAZIN

KENSINGTON BOOKS

KENSINGTON BOOKS are published by
Kensington Publishing Corp.
119 West 40th Street
New York, NY 10018

ISBN-13: 978-1-61773-635-3

Printed in the United States of America

For Janis—
With all my thanks for being there through
good times and bad.

Tiny Feet

A child's tiny feet,
Blue, blue with cold,
How can they see and not protect you?
Oh, my God!

Tiny wounded feet,
Bruised all over by pebbles,
Abused by snow and soil!

Man, being blind, ignores
that where you step, you leave
A blossom of bright light,
that where you have placed
your bleeding little soles
a redolent tuberose grows.

Since, however, you walk
through the streets so straight,
you are courageous, without fault.

Child's tiny feet,
Two suffering little gems,
How can the people pass, unseeing.

By Gabriela Mistral
(Translated from Spanish by Mary Gallwey)

Chapter 1

There are decisions you make in life without realizing you are making them. They don't even seem like decisions at all until you're suddenly bounding along, breathless as a husky in the snow, farther and farther from some elusive fork in the road where it all could have been different.

Had he seen the fork or even had an inkling it was there, Jimmy Vega could have saved so many things that night. His relationship. His conscience. A life. Had he thought with his head instead of points considerably farther south, he would have chosen far differently. It would have changed everything—because it wouldn't have changed anything at all.

It was a Saturday evening in late October, a time when the trees flame with color and the leaf peepers form conga lines on the highways heading north from New York City. There was talk of a dusting of snow in the forecast. Lights flicked on early from windows decorated with carved pumpkins and paper ghosts cut by children itching for Halloween.

Normally Vega would have clocked in at work by now, but he'd switched tours with Teddy Dolan so Dolan could take his kids to their adoption agency's fall dinner tomorrow. Normally Vega's girlfriend of five months, Adele Figueroa, would be fetching her nine-year-old daughter from gymnastics, but Sophia's best friend had begged the girl to sleep over. As a result, a rare and beautiful thing opened up on their calendars: a whole fourteen hours to spend together. Alone.

They knew how they were going to spend it, too. A log in Adele's fireplace. Chinese takeout. Coronas and limes. Marc Anthony and Shakira on the stereo. The evening stretched out before them like a vast blue ocean waiting to be explored.

One minute, Adele was sitting with Vega in her funky, adobe-colored dining room, holding a fortune cookie playfully out of his reach, breaking off bits of it and rolling them around oh-so-suggestively on her tongue. The next, her phone was ringing in the kitchen, harsh and insistent. It was eight p.m. They'd been together just over an hour.

"*Puñeta!*" Vega slumped in his chair, the air suddenly gone out of him. He always fell into the Puerto Rican street vernacular of his youth when he got frustrated.

Adele rose and shot him a warning look. "It could be Sophia, you know." Vega had to remind himself that they were on different sides of the parenting divide. Vega's daughter, Joy, was eighteen, a freshman at the community college. He'd have fallen off his chair if she'd called him on a Saturday night.

It wasn't Sophia. It was Rafael, the evening manager at La Casa, the Latino community center Adele had founded ten years ago and given up a promising law career to keep afloat. Not to mention her waste of a Harvard degree.

Vega could hear Rafael's panicked, rapid-fire Spanish through the receiver. Something about Jazmin, his six-year-old daughter. It sounded like she'd gotten hurt.

"Oh my goodness," said Adele. "Do you think the thumb is broken? Can she move it?"

Vega already had an idea where this conversation was headed. He blocked the doorway of the kitchen and waved furiously at her like she was standing on a cliff, about to jump.

"You're not covering Rafael's shift tonight, Adele. Tell him to close the center early if he has to take Jazmin to the emergency room."

Adele ducked under Vega's arms and walked back into the dining room. The table was littered with half-empty takeout cartons and palm-sized packages of soy sauce. Two brightly painted Mexican candlesticks sat among the ruins, their tapered candles still glowing with promise. She leaned over and blew them out. Ribbons of smoke curled from their snuffed wicks. Just like Vega's evening—up in smoke.

She spoke into the phone. "Did you try Luis? Is he available to take the shift?"

More panicked words from Rafael. Adele turned her back. "Of course you have to go. Can he speak to me tomorrow?" Vega had a sense this wasn't just about Jazmin anymore.

"Close the center," he said again.

Adele ignored him. "So is Zambo there now?"

Zambo. That was all Vega needed to hear.

"Oh no. No way, Adele. You're not going in for that drunk." All the cops and social workers in the area had Zambo stories, and as a county detective, Vega had heard every one. Zambo wasn't his real name. Vega didn't even know his real name. Everyone just called him Zambo, short for *patizambo*—"bowlegged"—in Spanish. He was a homeless alcoholic from someplace in Central America with a penchant for religious delusions and a long string of petty misdemeanors that never quite rose to the level of deportable offenses. Vega was betting he'd just walked into La Casa with some new claim that God had personally singled him out for something other than an extra case of communion wine.

More chatter from Rafael.

"Zambo says he just saw Jesus." Adele listened, then

corrected herself. "The baby Jesus. In the arms of the Virgin Mary. In the woods behind La Casa."

"*Coño!*" Vega cursed loudly enough for Rafael to hear. "Every time that mutt gets a couple of drinks in him, he thinks God's sending him an Instagram." Some of the local cops took bets on where Zambo would have a religious delusion next. Once he claimed the Virgin Mary spoke to him from behind the Slurpee dispenser at the Subway on Main Street. Another time, he saw Her at the Laundromat over on Sunset. He considered the Mobil gas station owned by two turbaned Sikhs to be sacred property because he saw the head of Jesus in an oil stain there.

Oddly, Zambo never seemed to see Jesus or Mary in church. Then again, Vega had spent years as an altar boy, and he'd never had anything that would qualify as a religious experience in church either.

"Tell him to lay off the extra-strength lagers," Vega called out.

Adele's mouth went slack. She slid a glance in Vega's direction. He expected annoyance. He was behaving like a child. If she chewed him out later, he'd take his lumps without complaint. But what he saw instead stopped him cold. Not anger. Or frustration. Or any emotion with a shred of heat in it. No. There was something more tepid and sad in the watery set of her big, chestnut-colored eyes, the slight downturn in her full lips, the slow exhale from her chest. This was disappointment. And it sliced right through him because he understood that this was not the first time lately she'd given him that look. It had been building. Somewhere in the dim recesses of his subconscious, he knew that. But he hadn't realized it fully until now.

Nothing had been said, of course. It was telegraphed in her shortened embraces, the way she no longer sent little "thinking of you" texts, or returned his with only *x*s or smiley faces at the bottom. Sometimes he'd catch her lost in thought. He'd tense and wait, but the words never came. People brought their troubles to Adele. Adele brought her troubles to no one—sadly, not even to him. Maybe because he was the source.

She cradled the phone to her ear and grabbed some plates off the dining table. Then she walked the stack past Vega into the kitchen and dumped them into her deep, cast-iron sink. Vega grabbed the cups and bowls and followed. Adele had a dishwasher, but the sink was so big, she and Vega always did their dishes by hand. Vega loved the routine. It reminded him of when he was a little boy in the Bronx, watching his mother and grandmother in the kitchen. Just thinking about his mother brought an ache to his heart. She'd been gone eighteen months now, murdered in a botched robbery in the Bronx. The police had yet to arrest a suspect. Every month, he called the station house for an update on the case, and every month, the only thing that changed was the name of the detective in charge.

"So I take it Zambo wants to show me the spot behind La Casa where he had his vision," Adele said to Rafael over the clatter.

La Casa was only a five-minute drive from Adele's house. Taking her there was no trouble at all. But Adele wouldn't walk behind the center and come right back. She'd chat with clients and restock the copier and clean out the refrigerator and answer the half dozen e-mails that seemed to come in every hour at that place. And she'd be there until midnight. She might as well have kept her promising Wall Street law career for all the hours she put into that place.

Vega came up behind her and wrapped his arms around her waist. He pressed himself into her body and breathed in the scent of her—vanilla and limes and something entirely her own. He massaged the muscles on either side of her spine, then brushed her silky black hair away from her neck and ran his lips down the contours. She shivered in response. He wanted more than anything to make love to her in front of the fireplace tonight. He wanted to buy sweet rolls and strawberries in the morning and dip them in whipped cream that they'd lick off each other's lips.

He wanted her to look at him like she used to.

"Don't go, Nena," he whispered. He was the only man she'd ever let call her "baby" in Spanish. "Tonight belongs to us."

She closed her eyes and exhaled a prayer over the phone that was disguised as a question.

"You think this is just another one of his hallucinations?" she asked Rafael.

Vega wanted to tell Rafael to do what he should have done in the first place and kick Zambo out. That mutt was probably only at La Casa because it was cold out tonight. Too cold to make trouble and chance having the Lake Holly police pick him up and dump him in neighboring Wickford like they always did when he got on their nerves.

"You can talk to Zambo tomorrow," Vega whispered into her neck, his breath hot and moist on her skin.

Vega untucked Adele's blouse from her jeans and snaked a hand inside, letting his fingers tease at the elastic of her underwear. Her body grew sweaty and liquid to the touch. There was a catch in her breathing, a moment when he had her, really had her, the way he used to. He could sense the wave breaking over her. Soon she would be bobbing in the current, her thoughts pulled out with the tide. He could feel them receding in the foam, a mere blip on the horizon. In an hour, they would lie in the afterglow of their lovemaking and forget they'd ever harbored any other thoughts.

Going . . . going . . .

She pushed his hand away.

"Fine." Vega raised his arms in a gesture of surrender. "Some drunk means more to you than I do." He stomped to the door.

"Rafael? Can you hold for just one moment? One moment, I promise." Adele put the phone down and followed Vega to the front hallway. "Jimmy, please. Something's wrong."

"No kidding."

"No, I mean with what Rafael's telling me. Zambo's never said anything quite so specific before. He called the woman he saw in the woods 'the Lady of Sorrows,' like the Catholic church in town."

"It's just another term for the Virgin Mary, Adele."

"I know that. But this doesn't sound like one of his usual rants. I feel like I should check it out."

"How 'bout what I feel? That place has got you on a chain, Nena. Every time somebody over there needs you, you go running back. I'm tired of it."

Vega grabbed his jacket from the coat tree. It was a bluff. He wasn't leaving. Not really. He'd drive her over to La Casa and sit in a corner, hunched and sulky, checking his e-mail and playing games on his iPhone until she was ready to leave. He knew when they'd started dating last May that her life wasn't her own. He'd tried hard to be happy with whatever part she gave him. God, he'd tried. But he was a man, after all. And he wanted her. Just this once, couldn't *he* be the focus of her attentions?

Adele blinked at him. There was no disappointment for once in her gaze. Only longing. She walked over to the table and picked up the phone.

"Listen, Rafael? I—can't come in tonight. I'm sorry—I just can't. Close down the center. Tell Zambo I'll speak to him another time. I hope Jazmin's thumb isn't broken. I'll call you tomorrow, okay?"

Vega tossed his jacket back on the coat tree and scooped

up Adele the moment she clicked off the call. He could barely contain his excitement as he buried his head in her chest and felt the pleasing give of her flesh. He was seventeen again, awash with the thrill of a woman's body. Awash with the thrill of Adele. "You won't regret it, Nena," he breathed into her hair, his voice husky with yearning.

Never in his life had he been more wrong.

Chapter 2

It was the last good night's sleep Jimmy Vega would have for a long time. At seven the next morning, his cell phone rang by Adele's bedside. Both he and Adele sat up, certain they'd overslept. God forbid Sophia should come home and find them in bed together. Vega and Adele were careful to keep their relationship strictly platonic when the child was around.

The caller ID was blocked, and for Vega at least, that usually meant it was coming from a cop's cell. Vega tried to wring the hoarseness out of his voice before he answered.

"Vega? Captain Waring."

His boss. Commander of the county police department's detective division. Vega wasn't due at work until four p.m. He was about to protest that he'd changed shifts with Teddy Dolan, but Waring was ex-Navy SEAL. Police work to him was like the military, a 24/7 calling. Plus, you never contradicted a superior officer.

"How far are you from Lake Holly at the moment, Vega?"

"Umm," Vega grinned. "Pretty close by." He stroked a hand down Adele's thigh and avoided her quizzical gaze. His own house was forty-five minutes north of Lake Holly, a little two-bedroom lakeside cabin he was still in the process of winterizing nearly six years after his divorce. He couldn't afford to live anywhere in the county on a cop's salary. He was on the promotional list for sergeant, but the list moved slowly and the pay raise wasn't huge.

"We've got a situation near the Lake Holly turnoff to the parkway. The local PD is there now, but it falls under our jurisdiction. I want you to take the lead if you can get there within the next half hour."

There would be no sweet rolls from the bakery this morning, no strawberries with whipped cream. Vega tried to swallow back his disappointment. He was looking forward to another couple of hours with Adele. The sheets felt so buttery, her flesh so cuddly. He loved the way her lemon-yellow walls caught the early morning sun and warmed it. He loved the two paintings hanging behind her mission-style bed, one of women washing clothes in a mountain stream, the other of people picking crops on a bright green terraced hillside—both gifts from clients who mythologized their birthplaces even as they ran from them.

He could lie to Waring and say he was tied up, but there was no denying that the familiar adrenaline rush was kicking in. Somebody was dead, and he was enough of a homicide detective to want to know why. Although he'd backed into being a cop when his girlfriend—later wife, later *ex*-wife—got pregnant and he couldn't support a baby as a rock-band guitarist, the job had grown on him. Or perhaps more accurately, he'd grown into the job.

He'd worked at an insurance agency after college but couldn't stomach being cooped up all day behind mountains of meaningless forms and spreadsheets. He liked the pureness of police work, the way it divided the world into right and wrong. True, he saw people at their worst. And, no doubt, it had colored his view of human nature. But he still believed in the essential goodness of what he was doing. He was there to make things better. If he'd wanted predictability, he should have stayed in insurance. Just the thought of it made him want to put a bullet through his brain.

"I can be there in ten minutes, Captain." Vega felt Adele's body shift to the other side of the bed. There was a coolness to the sheets where a moment before they had felt so warm and welcoming. He had a sense she would see a double standard in his willingness to work this morning when he'd given her so much grief about doing the same thing last night. Already, he was marshaling an argument in his head. *This is a matter of life and death—not babysitting a social club and listening to some drunk yammer on about his hallucinations.*

Wait. Scratch that. If he uttered even one word of what he was thinking, Adele would have his head. No matter how he phrased it, the subtext would be the same: *My job is more important than yours.* And yeah—he felt that. Deep down, if he was honest, he did. But if he'd learned one thing in thirteen years of marriage to Wendy, it was this: the more logic you bring to an argument, the more likely you are to spend the night on the couch.

Vega and Adele's clash of careers had been a sore point in their relationship from the moment they started dating five months ago. He was a police officer who believed in upholding the law whether he agreed with it or not. She worked primarily with undocumented immigrants who were lawbreakers by their mere presence in the country. And then there were the myriad of smaller differences between them. He worked shifts, often stripping down to a T-shirt and jeans as soon as they were over. She worked all the time, moving from the day-to-day of running a nonprofit to the cocktail-hour dinner jacket schmoozing that got it funded. He tried hard not to take his work home with him. She filled their time together with stories of her clients and their troubles. He hated politics—left or right, it didn't matter. She lived for it.

Some weeks, the only way he could see her was to suffer through some benefit dinner full of earnest, gray-haired patrons who asked what Latin American country he was from (*Does the Bronx qualify?*) and activists who considered a Puerto Rican cop at best a paperweight in a tie and at worst a sellout to his people. He and Adele were supposed to attend a fund-raiser for county supervisor Steve Schulman this coming Saturday night. Schulman was expected to win a seat in the U.S. Senate next month by a wide margin over his Republican opponent. Adele was a big supporter. She couldn't wait. Vega was dreading the event—the dull pleasantries, the handshakes that felt more like hand-offs, the obsession with inside-the-Beltway politics that wouldn't make one whit of difference in real people's lives. Adele had been nagging Vega for at least a month to secure a rental tux for the event. He'd yet to do it.

He tried to push these thoughts from his head and concentrate on the case at hand. "Can you give me an idea what I'm walking into?" he asked Waring.

"A couple of day laborers went to relieve themselves in the woods behind La Casa," said Waring. "They found a dead newborn in a pile of leaves, umbilical cord still attached."

"A—*baby?* In the woods behind La Casa?" The words came out soft as a prayer. All the sunlight seemed to drain from the room. Vega felt the mattress shift as Adele leaned in closer. A prickly static filled the air. They both sensed that if they touched one another, the shock might kill them.

"A female," Waring added. "The first officers on the

scene said she appeared to be full-term. Possibly Hispanic. She wasn't wearing any clothes or blankets. Only a disposable diaper."

A baby. The baby—

"Jesus," said Vega softly, echoing Adele's conversation last night.

"Keep it together, Detective, all right?"

"Yessir. I didn't mean—" *No. Not now. Not until he knew more.* Already his insides were curdling like he'd drunk too much coffee on an empty stomach. This had to be what Zambo claimed he saw last night. A baby. In the arms of the mother who likely abandoned her. There had been a window of opportunity to save this little life perhaps—and Vega had talked Adele out of it. He'd failed that child. He'd failed himself. He'd failed Adele.

Vega shot a glance at Adele now. She turned away from him and got out of bed. She was wearing one of his old denim shirts folded across her. The sleeves came past her fingernails. She shivered as she looked out the window at the sugarcoating of frost glistening on the grass and the swirl of dead leaves dancing across the driveway. Temperatures had dipped into the freezing range last night. The wind had picked up. The promise of winter was already on the horizon.

"Did the local PD find any trauma to the body?" Vega was hoping for something to convince himself he wasn't to blame.

"Not that I'm aware of," said Waring. "Are you going or not?"

"Uh, yessir. I'm headed over right away." Vega disconnected the call.

"I'm going with you," said Adele.

"Oh no you're not."

Adele yanked a pair of pants out of a drawer and

slammed the drawer shut with more force than she needed to. "A dead baby was found behind La Casa. *My* building!"

Vega grabbed his jeans off the back of her bedroom chair, stuffed his legs into them, and zipped them up.

"This is a potential homicide investigation, Adele. You can't go anywhere near that crime scene."

"Well, it wouldn't *be* a homicide investigation if you hadn't—if I hadn't—"

Vega walked over to her and held her firmly by her shoulders. She tried to fight him off, slapping at his bare chest. He absorbed the blows without letting go.

"Nena, look at me." She wouldn't. She was ashamed of him. What was he thinking last night, carrying on like some hormone-addled teenager? They'd had the *whole* night. An hour or two wasn't going to make any difference.

"Zambo's a crazy drunk who's always telling stories. Did you rush out to that Subway store when he heard the Virgin Mary behind the Slurpee machine?"

"This is different, and you know it, Jimmy. I had a duty to check on this one, and I let you talk me out of it. I let that baby die."

Vega released her and grabbed the rest of his clothes he'd slung carelessly across her bedroom chair last night in a rush of passion. He yanked his undershirt over his head and mismatched the buttons on his shirt three times before he got them right. He looked like the mess he felt, but it would have to do. "*You* didn't let her die. *I* didn't let her die. Her *mother* let her die."

"Is that how you rationalize things? Is that how you sleep at night? I never should have trusted you!"

The words sliced right through him. He stopped buttoning his shirt and sank down on the unmade bed. She sat down beside him. He felt the heat of her hand hover over his back. Then it retreated. It was the retreat that hurt more than anything, that sense that she was already weighing her actions, weighing him.

He pushed himself off the bed. "I've got to go." He shoved his wallet, keys, and Swiss Army knife in his jeans, then tucked his gun in his duty holster and belted it around his waist.

"Go, then," she said. It sounded like a curse.

Chapter 3

The Lake Holly police had already cordoned off the area behind La Casa by the time Jimmy Vega arrived. Save for one patrol car and a single unmarked, there was nothing on the street. All the businesses in this industrial neighborhood were closed on Sundays, all except for Adele's community center, which didn't open until the churches let out after noon. So the normal bustle was muted. The propane company's red and white trucks sat idle. The gate around the auto body shop was locked up tight, the smashed cars on the other side of the razor wire huddled like defendants awaiting bail.

Vega didn't want to waste time fetching a county police car, so he drove up in his own black Ford pickup and parked it behind the unmarked. He always kept a gym bag full of investigation essentials in his backseat. He started rummaging through the bag now for white coveralls, booties, a notebook, and a pen. The officer standing at the entrance to the cordoned-off area started walking over, all swagger and authority. Whatever the police said to the contrary, they all profiled. Vega never kidded himself into thinking that he was anything to them out of uniform but a toffee-skinned Puerto Rican with a gun.

The cop must have recognized Vega halfway over though, because his step relaxed.

"Hey, Detective." His breath came out soft and cottony in the cold air. "You catching?"

"Affirmative," Vega grunted as he pulled out a package of white coveralls to zip over his clothes. He wished he could remember the officer's name without squinting at his nametag. Something Irish. *Murphy? McNulty?* He had skin like a radish—white except for the ears, which were bright red from the cold.

Vega did a quick inventory of what he needed to bring with him: radio, iPhone, disposable gloves, notebook. "Who's doing the initial in your department?"

"Detective Greco. He's up there now. You've worked with him before, right?"

On the hillside, Vega spotted a set of white coveralls through the canopy of orange and gold trees. From this distance, Greco looked like a Macy's Thanksgiving parade float. Perhaps more than one.

"Yeah. Not sure if that's a blessing or a curse."

"Funny. He said the same about you."

Vega picked his way up the gentle slope, careful to disturb as little as possible. Leaves crunched like potato chips underfoot. A crow cawed overhead. In an hour or less, the hillside would be overrun by an army of crime-scene techs and personnel from the medical examiner's office. But right now, the ground felt as pure and unblemished as the little life it once held.

Vega found Louis Greco standing very still in a patch of yellow maple leaves so iridescent they looked as if they carried their own light source. With his wine cask of a body and fringe of graying hair, he brought to mind a medieval monk. Vega had run into the man periodically since they'd last worked together. Their relationship was built on slinging jibes at one another and their respective departments. But none of that had any place here. This death was different, the stain so much greater. No one knew that more than Vega.

Greco tucked a cross inside his pocket. His voice was phlegm-choked when he spoke.

"Just saying a little prayer for her."

Vega set his gym bag down on the root of a maple tree. He wished he felt the power and presence of God the way people like Greco did—the way his mother had. When Vega looked around, he felt only a void stripped of weight and meaning. What meaning could there be in bringing a child into the world only to take her out of it right away? And what if he were to blame for it all? Maybe he wasn't enough of a Catholic to feel God, but he was still enough of one to feel guilt.

"Our guys, they've dubbed her Baby Mercy," said Greco. "They figured she deserves some mercy, even if it's only in death."

Vega slipped on a pair of light blue nonlatex gloves and approached the body. She was lying on her back, her lavender-tinged umbilical cord curled to one side of her. Vega had forgotten how small newborns were. It had been a long time since he'd held one. She barely compacted the leaves beneath her. She wouldn't have extended from his fingertips to his elbow.

She was full-term, though. And perfect. She had a beautiful, melon-shaped head with a fine dusting of black hair. There were dimples on her chubby limbs. She hadn't been dead long. Her skin still had a milky tea color, and her eyes caught and held the light in their glassy, dark blue irises.

Vega squatted beside her. He saw no lividity marks—those purplish stains on skin when the heart stops pumping and the blood begins to settle. If her blood had begun to pool at all, it was pooling beneath her, which meant she had died in this position—on her back, faceup, staring in her unfocused newborn way at the trees that towered over her, regally indifferent.

"Two day laborers found her at six thirty this morning," said Greco.

"In the open? Like this?" She was naked except for a baggy disposable diaper that looked huge and tentlike on her tiny bottom. On the front of the diaper was an imprint of Winnie the Pooh chasing a butterfly. Vega felt the urge to pick her up and warm her the way he hadn't last night.

"She apparently had a few leaves covering her, but McCaffrey, the first-due officer, said the men saw her feet poking out and pushed everything to one side. They thought she was still alive." Greco gestured to some broken branches and leaves on the far side of the body. "Not much of a covering, as you can see. Whoever left her here did so in a hurry."

Vega didn't touch her. His department's crime-scene techs hated when detectives messed with a "virgin" scene. But even without touching her, Vega could see that her color was good and rigor mortis hadn't yet set in. He was no medical examiner, but if he had to guess, he'd say she'd been dead less than four hours. Which meant she'd died sometime after three thirty a.m., at least seven and a half hours *after* Adele got that call from Rafael. Vega felt like he'd swallowed a roll of pennies. There was a coppery taste at the back of his mouth, a foreign weight pressing on his gut.

"Hey, Vega—you okay, man?" Greco stepped closer and put a meaty paw on his shoulder. "Maybe you wanna see if somebody else can take this one?"

"No." Vega took a deep breath and pushed himself to his feet. He walked over to his gym bag and pulled out his iPhone. The crime-scene techs would take hundreds of pictures from every angle, but in a case like this, with so little obvious evidence, he liked a few shots of his own.

"Make sure you get some pictures of the bruises on her face." Greco bent over and pointed out one on each side of her skull and another beneath her nose. The shadow of his hand was big enough to eclipse her entire body. "These look like broken capillaries to me. Like somebody put a hand over her face to smother her. A small hand, I'd wager, judging from where the bruises are."

Vega took a close-up shot. Greco didn't have to state what they both knew from experience: In these sorts of cases, the killer is almost always the mother.

"I'm thinking she was smothered and dumped as quickly as possible sometime before dawn," said Greco. "Probably not long before those day laborers showed up."

A shaft of morning light angled through the trees. It lit up the mist on the fallen leaves and made them sparkle like they'd been dipped in honey. A spiderweb, pearled with dew and cocooned insects, dangled between two fallen trunks, brocaded in a rich emerald moss. Death was all around him. Some of it beautiful. Some of it unbearable. Vega took a deep breath. He had to tell. He just had to.

"What if she didn't die right away? What if it took a while?"

"You mean, like, she survived the smothering?" Greco shrugged. "No way to tell until the ME takes a look at her. It's possible, I guess."

A sudden gust of wind rained down a shower of fresh leaves from sixty-foot-tall maples and oaks that had probably been on this earth as long as they had, perhaps longer. It made Vega feel small and insignificant. He closed his eyes and stood very still like a young child convinced that if he just confessed his sins, they might all disappear.

"Around eight last night," he began, "Adele got a call

from Rafael Lozano, the evening manager at La Casa. Zambo came in, claiming he'd just seen the Virgin Mary in the woods with the baby Jesus in her arms."

"*What?*"

"Zambo claimed he saw a woman and baby in these woods last night."

"You think Zambo saw *this* baby?"

"I don't want to think so," said Vega. "But yeah, it's possible. According to Adele, Zambo called the woman the Lady of Sorrows—"

"That's the name of the big Catholic church in town—"

"I know. It's also one of the names we called the Virgin Mary when I was an altar boy. We called her Lady of the Seven Sorrows and Mother of Sorrows too." Vega couldn't believe how much of that rigmarole came back to him, whether he wanted it to or not. Only the words and rituals, though. Never the faith. He could have used a little faith right now.

"Did Adele check out Zambo's story?"

"No. I told her not to. I thought it was bullshit."

"She called you about it?"

"She didn't have to call." Vega held his gaze.

Greco's jaw set to one side. "Uh-huh. Right." He'd been a detective long enough to recognize a confession when he heard one. "So you're figuring this baby died so you could get laid."

"The thought's crossed my mind."

Greco let out a slow breath of air, resigned as always to the human condition. "Didn't think you two would last this long."

Vega didn't respond.

"Are you looking for absolution, Vega? Because you don't need it here. It's like they say: hindsight's twenty-twenty. How could you have known?"

"I guess."

"I mean, it's not like Adele *knew* Zambo was reporting on something real for a change."

Vega turned away. He didn't want to feed the lie. To outside eyes, it might look like an honest mistake. Only Vega knew how hard Adele had pleaded with him to check out Zambo's story. And what did he do? He brushed her aside. He treated her concerns like one more petty annoyance. Everything she cared about was unimportant and insignificant to him. That was his real sin. And he couldn't take it back. "I'm sorry" just didn't cut it here.

"So at this point our chief witness," said Greco, "whom we can't yet rule out as a suspect, is a homeless, delusional drunk who may or may not have seen or done something that would impact this investigation."

"He should be easy to find, at least. He's always around."

"Except when he isn't. He likes to disappear every now and then. I'll call it in to my guys and see if they can track him down." Greco pulled out his radio and paused. "Any other disclosures you care to share before we start working together again?"

"I'm not holding anything back."

"Sounds like you never do." Greco raised an eyebrow. "Might be a strategy to consider on the home front sometime."

Greco radioed his patrol officers. Then he and Vega split up and scoured the area, searching for footprints, discarded chewing gum wrappers—anything that would give them a clue as to who dumped this baby and why. They found beer cans—lots of beer cans, and cheap plastic bottles of vodka, a favorite of the hard-core drunks in the area. Vega and Greco didn't really believe the alcohol containers had anything to do with the person who dumped the baby here. But they were hoping against hope that perhaps

Zambo wasn't the only witness in these woods last night. Two drunks were better than one—at least in this case—if only to compare stories.

The two men worked silently, taking notes of things they wanted the crime-scene techs to bag and remove. Vega made a sketch for himself of where the body was found in relation to the community center. Through the trees, he could see the parking lot at the back of the center. At the far end of the lot was a Dumpster.

"We know the baby was probably abandoned before it got light out, right?" asked Vega.

Greco nodded. "At this stage anyway."

"You're looking to get rid of a baby quickly. Why walk all the way into the woods? Why not just throw the body in the Dumpster?"

"Too great a chance of being spotted at the community center," said Greco. "Remember, if you're right about Zambo, the baby was placed out here alive before eight last night. La Casa was still open."

"But if the killer walked into the woods via the community center, they had to walk past La Casa anyway. Not to mention that Dumpster."

"Even a mom who wanted to get rid of her baby might feel a twinge of guilt throwing her in a Dumpster."

"Maybe," said Vega. "Then again, maybe she came from another direction." He scanned the hillside behind them. There was a vague path through the trees. In summer, it would be completely overgrown with nettles, porcelain berry vines, and barberry bushes. But this time of year, most of the underbrush had already died off, leaving just a few skeletal branches of red berries and thorns.

"The parkway's up this way, right?"

Greco nodded. "You think she parked on the side of the road and walked the baby into the woods from there?"

"It's worth checking out."

They trudged up the hill past clusters of bright red viburnum bushes and feathery groupings of hemlocks. Acorns rolled beneath their shoes, and chunks of rotting bark littered the path like fallen plaster. Brambles caught on their coveralls and scratched angry white lines across the skin on Vega's wrists. He'd had a deep coffee tan all summer. It was fading now.

"It's a hell of a schlep through this in daylight," said Greco between breaths. Perspiration beaded the top of his scalp. "Still think a woman who just gave birth is gonna walk through here in the dark with a baby in her arms?"

"Half the pregnant women in Lake Holly are in better shape than you, Grec."

They heard the highway up ahead, marked by an intermittent *whoosh* of cars. They followed the sound until they found themselves on a flat, six-foot-wide clearing next to the northbound side of the parkway. It was a Depression-era road—narrow, quaint, and twisting—certainly never meant for the volume of traffic that zigzagged along it now. It was still early on a Sunday, so traffic was light, which was good because neither of them was wearing a reflective vest.

"I don't know," said Greco. He wiped a sleeve of his coveralls across his forehead and kept one eye on oncoming traffic. "It's hard to imagine anyone stopping here unless they broke down and had no choice."

Vega studied the ground. The weedy thatch was shot through with stones—hardly ideal turf for any tire impressions. And yet a car had been here recently. He could tell by the way the weeds were lying flat or broken along two parallel troughs. Vega pointed this out to Greco.

"Yeah. Okay. I'll buy that it happened at *some* point."

"If she brought the baby by car, she was traveling northbound," said Vega. "We should check the exit just south of here and the one just north for all recorded vehicle activity in the past twenty-four hours."

"Will do," said Greco. The first time Vega told Adele about all the automated license plate readers in the area that could spew out specific car locations with a click of a button, she railed against police invasion of privacy. Vega wondered if she'd change her mind about the technology if it caught the person who did this.

Greco, of course, pointed out the obvious hole: "We'll have plenty of raw travel footage. But nothing to tie it to."

"By the time you pull it all together, we may."

An SUV whizzed by, sucking the air as it passed, nearly knocking them both over. Vega stepped back near the guardrail. He noticed it was scuffed. There were a few chips of paint at his feet and a small, triangular piece of red plastic that appeared to be from the covering of a vehicle indicator light. He pointed out the paint chips and plastic to Greco.

"We should get the techs to tag and bag this stuff. Maybe it will give us a make and model of car to match up against the license plate reader data."

Greco frowned at the red plastic. "I don't get it."

Vega straightened. "Get what?"

"Why someone would sentence a baby to death out here when, under the Safe Haven Law, all they had to do was walk her into Lake Holly Hospital. Or our police station. Or any manned firehouse, no questions asked. Didn't even have to be the mother who walked the baby in. Didn't even have to be in Lake Holly."

Vega studied Greco in the bright light of the clearing. His jowls had gotten more pronounced. His shoulders sagged in on themselves like an old pillow. Vega could tell he'd have preferred to spend the rest of his days until retirement filling out theft reports and putting a few more dealers out of commission. He didn't need the burden of this baby on his conscience.

Greco opened his mouth and gave voice to what they were both thinking: "What sort of person would choose this instead?"

Vega offered up the only answer he could think of: "Someone who didn't see a baby. They saw a problem. And they wanted it to disappear forever."

Chapter 4

The assembly hall was packed for Sunday services. Luna Serrano ushered her younger brother and sister into folding chairs near the back. Papi took the aisle. Luna was glad they'd arrived late. It made it easier to avoid all the small talk and questions. "There's no point in talking anymore," Papi had told them this morning, as they were getting ready for church. "It's in God's hands now. He'll listen. Or He won't."

God hadn't been listening much lately, thought Luna. But she didn't say this to her father.

The stage in front was strung with white lights. In the center, an empty lectern awaited the booming, sweaty presence of Pastor Ray. Dulce scratched at the crinoline in her pink dress. Mateo played with his tie.

"Sit still," Luna hissed at her siblings. Dulce stuck out her tongue in response. Papi hunched forward in his folding chair, ignoring all of them, and studied an address on a slip of paper in his hands. He shoved it into his pocket as soon as Pastor Ray bounded onto the stage and an electric guitarist and drummer began playing, *"Dios Está Aquí"*— "God Is Here." The congregation immediately got to their feet, singing and swaying to the music. For a minute, the joyful beat swept Luna away, made her feel almost like a normal fifteen-year-old again.

Almost.

"We must be open to the miraculous," Pastor Ray urged in Spanish as the congregation took their seats. "We must be open, as Paul and Silas in the Bible were open." Pastor Ray paced the stage and spoke about how Paul and Silas were shackled in a prison cell. Instead of bemoaning their fate, they praised God. In response, God sent an earthquake to free them.

Papi sank down in his seat and tugged his pant cuff over his right ankle. Señor Ortega leaned forward and patted Papi on the shoulder. Señora Aguilar turned in the seat in front of Luna and whispered a promise to drop off a casserole of tamales and beans at their apartment later. It felt like when Mami died all over again.

My father's alive and healthy! Luna wanted to stand up and scream to all the people who were giving them pitying looks. *He's not going anywhere!*

She prayed that that was true.

The rest of the service was a blur. Luna stood up when she was supposed to stand up and prayed when she was supposed to pray. Finally, Señora Gomez sang *"Fe"*— "Faith," a signal that the service was ending and everyone could head to the back of the hall, where cookies and cake were being spread out on a long folding table.

Her father rose from his chair as soon as Pastor Ray stepped off the stage. "We need to leave."

"But Papi," Dulce whined, "I want cookies."

"We don't have time."

"But Papi—"

"No!"

Luna grabbed her seven-year-old sister's hand. "Come." She led Dulce and her nine-year-old brother, Mateo, out into the sunshine. Their car, an old brown Chevy, sat on the other side of the gravel parking lot.

"I wish we were going to La Bella Vita," said Mateo.

"Me too," said Dulce. La Bella Vita was the Italian

restaurant where their father used to work as a cook. On Sundays after church, he used to let them sit in a corner of the kitchen and sample the dishes before the restaurant opened for dinner. Luna could still see him in his white chef's hat and tunic, the cuffs of his black-and-white check- ered uniform pants curling over his sneakers. Everything he made tasted so good. But he couldn't work now. The gov- ernment wouldn't let him.

Luna walked Dulce and Mateo across the parking lot. She thought her father would be close behind them. But when they got to their car, he was nowhere in sight. A mo- ment later, he emerged from the church, walking with that awkward limp he had nowadays. He was carrying a paper plate with a napkin over it. Dulce knew what was under- neath before he even lifted it. She bobbed up and down on her toes like someone was pulling her shoulders with a string. Luna saw a smile curl beneath her father's mus- tache. Papi never said it, but Luna knew he was worried that Dulce's last memories of him might be reduced to some moment like this. Her little sister wasn't yet six when Mami died of meningitis. It was only a year and a half ago, but there was already so much about her that the child had forgotten.

Dulce reached for the plate as soon as their father walked over. She grabbed a cookie in each hand.

"One at a time," said Luna.

"You're not my mother," Dulce shot back in English with a mouth full of mashed Oreos. Luna flinched. Papi kept his head down and said nothing.

Mateo's hand hovered over the remaining cookies, mov- ing first to one and then to another.

"Come on, Mijo," their father urged gently. "We need to get moving." Mateo finally settled on a chocolate chip cookie, and both children climbed in back.

Papi then held the plate out to Luna. She shook her head, no.

"But you like chocolate chip."

"I'm not hungry," she lied. Last week at school, a girl in Luna's gym class called her "fat." Papi said she was pretty. But Anglo girls at Lake Holly High had a different definition of pretty. Pretty was straight pale hair that spilled like water down your back. Pretty was size two jeans and a boy's chest.

What Luna felt was not "pretty," but something more shameful, something she didn't have words for. Sometimes when she bent down at her locker, boys grabbed her rear end. She didn't want a body that made boys do that. She wished Mami were still alive to talk to about these things. Papi was great to talk to about practical stuff. He was proud of her success in school and encouraged her dreams of becoming a doctor. But he was too traditional and Mexican to talk to about more personal matters. It would embarrass them both.

Her father wrapped up the last two cookies and shoved them under the backseat for later. Then he slid behind the wheel while Luna got into the front passenger seat. When he lifted his right leg, she saw the rectangular outline of that horrible black box beneath his sock. He'd had to wear it for four months now. Twenty-four hours a day. They all tried to pretend it wasn't there. He kept a sock over it most of the time except for the two hours every day he had to charge it.

In the car, her father handed Luna the slip of paper with the address scribbled across it. The address was in Broad Plains, about twenty-five minutes south of Lake Holly. He tilted his rearview mirror and eyed Mateo and Dulce, arguing in the backseat over whose arm was taking up more room.

"We're visiting an important man this afternoon," he told them. "He's putting time aside to try to help us, so you need to be on your best behavior."

Luna didn't think Papi knew any important men, but

she didn't say this. Instead she asked, "How do you know him?"

"Señora Figueroa knows him. He's also from southern Mexico, from a village in Chiapas not far from where Mami and I grew up. Señora Figueroa told me if anyone can help us, he can."

Papi touched a big fat envelope tucked down beside his seat. It was old and worn, stuffed thick with paperwork her father had kept over the years to prove that he'd always held a job in this country and paid his taxes. He didn't have a Social Security number, but he had a TIN—a tax identification number—that he faithfully filed under every year. Her mother had been convinced that if the family did everything right, in time she, Papi, and Luna would become American citizens—just like Mateo and Dulce, who were born here. Then Luna could study to become a doctor and help the family buy a little place of their own, with enough room for a garden.

It was all Norma Serrano had ever wanted. She used to come home from her housecleaning jobs with old copies of magazines her employers gave her: *Family Circle, Good Housekeeping, Better Homes and Gardens*. She'd spread pictures of houses with front porches and white picket fences across the kitchen table and fill her children's heads with visions of what it would be like to live in a place where there was no landlord who'd let himself into your apartment while you were out and rifle through your belongings to check on what kind of person you were or pound on your door at odd hours to make sure extra tenants weren't staying with you.

She kept a potted garden on their kitchen windowsill where she grew basil, cilantro, and mint. In third grade, Luna's class planted begonias for Mother's Day. Luna gave her mother a pink one that they still had on their kitchen windowsill in a terra-cotta pot Luna had painted. The herbs, however, were gone—destroyed when the family had to leave their old apartment after a neighbor's place caught fire. Most of her mother's magazines were destroyed in that blaze too. Only one stack of *Better Homes and Gardens* was left. They sat in a dusty pile under Luna's bed. She couldn't bear to look at them, and she couldn't throw them away.

"Luna—" Papi held her gaze in the windshield as they headed south. The trees had thinned out, and a couple of tall office buildings took their place. "You understand what has to happen if—if we can't change things?" Papi never said the word "deported." It was like the word "cancer." To say it was to make it true.

"It's not going to happen," she answered firmly.

"Please, Mija. You need to face the possibility. How can Dulce and Mateo be strong if you fall apart?"

"Umm." Luna turned her head away and gazed out at other vehicles whizzing along the highway. She imagined herself traveling in a different car, with people who never had to worry about the things her family had had to worry about for practically her entire existence.

"Alirio and Maria José have talked it over. It will be tight, but . . ." His voice drifted off. Luna didn't want to talk about Papi's cousins. She'd met them maybe half a dozen times in her life. They lived in Queens in a two-bedroom apartment with their three children, all under the age of eight. How long could she, Dulce, and Mateo realistically stay with them?

"We don't have a choice, at least for now," said her father. "You can still go to high school in Queens. And Dulce and Mateo can continue their educations." He gripped the steering wheel tighter as though they were having an argument. Maybe he was having one with himself. "If I take them back to Mexico with me, what future would they have?"

"It won't come to that." Luna laced her fingers on her lap to keep them from shaking. Fortunately, Dulce and

Mateo were fighting again, so they weren't really listening. They understood, but they didn't. It was a blessing really.

In Broad Plains, Luna helped her father locate the address. It was a tall gray office building on a street of other tall gray office buildings. Papi parked the car, grabbed his thick envelope of papers, and herded all of them onto the sidewalk. He straightened Mateo's tie and smoothed the braids Luna had put into Dulce's hair that morning. By the time they walked into the building, Papi was sweating heavily.

The lobby was empty except for a bored-looking security guard. Her father showed the man a dog-eared business card that read: BRODY, KATZ, O'CONNOR AND SCHULMAN— ATTORNEYS AT LAW. The guard directed them to a bank of elevators that let them off on the fifteenth floor. Dulce and Mateo were silent on the way up. Luna wondered if even they understood that their family's very existence might depend on the man they were about to see.

On the fifteenth floor, they got off and wandered around until they found the office door. Papi knocked hesitantly and then pushed the door open. On the other side was a large room with black leather furniture and framed diplomas on the walls. A short, balding Mexican-looking man with a big nose and a fat belly stepped out of an office and greeted Luna's father in Spanish. He was dressed in an expensive-looking sweater and casual slacks that made their overdressed church clothes look desperate.

"Señor Gonzalez," Papi bowed. "I'm very honored that you have agreed to speak with me today." He used his most polite and formal Spanish. Luna wondered if this was how he addressed the *patrón* who owned his family's land when he was a boy. She had no memory of their life there. Her parents left when she was only three.

Señor Gonzalez seemed to appreciate her father's deferential tone. He shook Papi's hand and smiled warmly at Dulce and Mateo. He didn't look at Luna. She wasn't sure why.

"Señor Serrano, I'm pleased to make your acquaintance," he said. "Adele Figueroa has told me so much about you. Why don't you leave the children out here in the waiting area? It's perfectly safe. And you can come and sit with my lawyer, Adam Katz."

Papi shot Luna a nervous look. His English was passable, but Luna knew he would have preferred her to be in the office with him to help if Mr. Katz didn't speak Spanish. But Mateo and Dulce would get wild without her, and in truth, Luna had been through all the events of that terrible day so many times, she had no wish to go through them again. The front window of their apartment still had tape across it from where the police broke the glass and forced their way in. The police turned everything in the apartment upside down. They broke the clay bird Luna had made in second grade for her mother's birthday. Her grade-school graduation photograph had disappeared entirely. In her dreams, she could still hear the police screaming in English and Spanish at her father: "Where are the drugs?" as Papi lay on the floor, hands cuffed behind his back, his eyes wide with incomprehension and fear.

The Lake Holly police never admitted they'd messed up the address and raided the wrong apartment. Not that an admission or even an apology would have helped them now anyway. The raid turned out to be the least of their problems.

Luna heard the three men's voices from the waiting area. She picked out her father's soft tenor, which rose and fell in fits and starts of English peppered with Spanish. She pictured him spilling out the contents of his envelope, the history of his thirteen years of life in the United States written on faded pay stubs and copies of money orders and handwritten receipts.

Señor Gonzalez and Mr. Katz would have had to look more closely to see the real price her father had paid to work in this country. When Luna was six, a meat slicer took off the tip of his middle left finger at a food processing plant where he worked in New York City. He'd had to hail a cab and get himself to the emergency room after his boss told him to just "put a Band-Aid on it" and then docked him two days' pay for his "carelessness." To Luna, at least, her father's scars were stronger proof of how hard he'd worked to make it here than any piece of paper.

She wandered the waiting area while Dulce and Mateo played some sort of game where the black leather couch was a school bus. Along one wall were head shots of all the firm's lawyers. One of them she recognized from ads on TV: Steve Schulman. He was running for Congress. Her father was right: these *were* important men. She hoped they could help him.

"This must be very hard for you."

Luna turned to find Señor Gonzalez standing behind her, holding out a glass of water. She hadn't heard him enter the room.

She took the water to be polite and mumbled her thanks. She didn't want to say anything that could get her father into more trouble.

Señor Gonzalez swept a hand toward the window. "Quite a view, yes?"

"It's very nice," said Luna. Actually, she preferred Lake Holly, with its wooded hills and green lawns. All she could see here were flat concrete boulevards and a jagged collection of steel and glass buildings.

"You're—in high school?"

"Yes. I'm in the tenth grade."

"The tenth grade. I see. So you are only fifteen?"

Luna didn't know what to make of the word "only," so she stuck with the facts. "I turned fifteen in July."

"And did you have a quinceañera?"

She shook her head, no. How could she think of asking

Papi for a big fancy party in the middle of all they were going through?

"I had a cake. My family put up streamers and sang 'Las Mañanitas.'" Papi loved to wake them up on their birthdays singing the traditional Mexican birthday song.

"How nice," said Señor Gonzalez. "I'll bet you're a smart girl. You look very smart. Very—mature." He put a palm on Luna's back and directed her closer to the window. She could feel the sweaty heat of his touch right through her dress—right along her bra strap.

"Here," he said. "If you look out from this angle, you can see the Hudson River."

The señor's touch felt greasy and unclean—even through her dress—though Luna couldn't say why. She pretended to be annoyed by something Mateo and Dulce were doing and used it as an excuse to break away. *How much longer is my father going to be?*

Papi emerged from the office a few minutes later, shaking Mr. Katz's hand. He looked pleased, if a little unsure.

"What do you think, Adam?" Señor Gonzalez asked the lawyer.

Mr. Katz took off his gold wire-rimmed glasses and massaged the bridge of his nose. He seesawed his head back and forth.

"Look, even a continuance at this point would help. It would buy Mr. Serrano some time at least." The lawyer smiled at Papi and gave him a thumbs-up like he was a kid at a baseball game praying for a homer. "Hey, if my partner Steve Schulman gets elected in November, who knows?"

Afterward, Papi bought two slices of pizza at a pizzeria down the street and cut each in half for the four of them to share. He looked happier than he had in many weeks.

"The señor, he complimented all of you," said Papi. "He told me I had a nice family. Especially you, Luna. He said you were a lovely girl."

Luna fingered the spot along the back of her bra strap where Señor Gonzalez had placed his sweaty palm. She would scrub the spot as soon as she got home. But for now, she forced a smile.

"How nice."

Chapter 5

Jimmy Vega pressed his hands against the display window at the Lake Holly Hospital nursery. He counted nine babies: two preemies in special incubators and seven others swaddled on their sides in open bassinets. Most were napping: fists curled, eyes shut, their little mouths sucking furiously. They all looked so—animated. Like little surprise packages of stored energy and talent just waiting to explode on the world. Vega thought of Baby Mercy, the package that would never get to be opened. His heart felt like someone was scraping sandpaper across it.

"Sir? Can I help you?" asked a nurse in Winnie the Pooh scrubs. "Visiting hours aren't until after two on Sundays."

"Oh. Sorry. Is Marc Feldman around? They said he was on call today." Vega pulled out his badge. He'd forgotten the hospital had recently beefed up its maternity ward security.

"I'm afraid Dr. Feldman just went into the OR. An emergency C-section. It's likely to be a while."

"How about Joy Vega? Is she in?"

"His intern? I think she may have left already." The nurse read his badge. "Vega—are you related?"

"She's my daughter."

"Why don't you have a seat in the visitor's lounge," said the nurse. "I'll check if she's still here."

Vega sat down on an orange vinyl couch and thumbed the magazines spread across the coffee table. No *Sports Illustrated*s here. Only *American Baby* and *Babytalk* and *Pregnancy & Newborn*. Everywhere Vega looked, he saw babies. Even on his iPhone, Mercy was there, staring back at him like some darling new family addition. There was no escaping the ghost of what he'd done.

He tried to remember what Joy was like as a newborn, but the images were fuzzy, bathed in the sleepless stupor and panic of being a brand-new cop, husband, and father all at once. He was barely twenty-four at the time. Too young, he realized now. Too immature on every front. It took him about three years to get the hang of being a cop. Wendy would argue that he'd never gotten the hang of being a husband. As for the father part, well—he'd done a hell of a lot better than his old man. At the very least, he'd stuck around.

And now Joy was all grown up. A college freshman. Vega had seen her exactly four times since she'd started classes seven weeks ago—which wouldn't have been so bad except it was a commuter college and she was still living at home here in Lake Holly with Wendy and her second husband. The investment banker. He got to see more of Joy than Vega did.

The door to the maternity ward opened, and Joy stepped out. She had a distinctive walk—that little bounce to her stiletto boot heels, those bangles she always wore that jingled like sleigh bells. There was still the kid about her—the way she experimented with too much eyeliner. That little tug she gave to her ponytail after she removed her hospital ID from around her neck.

She was always underdressed by one season, so it was not surprising she was wearing a lightweight shirt jacket belted over knit pants. The jacket was a leopard print that shimmered slightly under the fluorescent lights. Even in the overheated hospital, Joy looked cold. Vega had the urge to take off his own insulated jacket and drape it around her shoulders, but he knew he would embarrass her.

"Hey, Dad. What's up?" She looked happy to see him at least. She even let him kiss her hello. She felt the side of his face as he bent over. "You're scratchy."

She used to say that as a kid, right before the two of them would line up in front of the bathroom mirror—him with his razor, her on a princess stool with a Popsicle stick in hand, both of them with a face full of shaving cream. It seemed like yesterday.

"Sorry. I didn't have time to shave this morning." Vega nodded to her jacket. "Where are you off to already?"

"I've got a seventh-grader on the other side of town waiting for me to teach him the wonders of quadratic equations." Joy's side job. She was a natural at math. It beat waiting tables.

"Better him than me." Vega grinned.

Joy's face clouded over. "Were we—uh—supposed to have lunch or something?"

"Nah." She looked relieved. He felt deflated. "I'm here to talk to Dr. Feldman about a case I'm working on. But can I at least walk you to your car?" Joy's car was Wendy's hand-me-down white Volvo. A "mommy car," was how Joy described it. She'd wanted Vega to buy her a shiny red MINI Cooper, but between helping her with tuition and installing a new transmission on his truck, he was strapped for cash. Besides, the Volvo seemed like a safer choice.

"My car's in the shop getting new tires for the winter," said Joy.

"Ah. Good idea," said Vega. "You can't be too careful now that you're commuting to school."

"If I was any more careful, I'd be driving a snowplow."

Vega walked her to the elevator and pressed the down button. "You want me to drop you at this kid's house?"

"Um"—she pulled out her iPhone and checked her messages—"I'm getting a ride."

"Friend picking you up?"

"No"—she kept her eyes on the screen—"Alan."

"Oh." The investment banker. The father of the twin cannonballs that forever sank his marriage.

When he and Wendy divorced, they'd both agreed not to snipe at each other through their daughter. It was a point of pride to Vega that he'd been able to make good on this pledge—no easy feat given that Wendy had been two-timing him with Alan while they were still married. And she had the souvenirs to prove it: *Ben and Sam. Sam and Ben.* Wall Street may have screwed over the rest of the country. Alan just did it with Vega's wife.

Joy knew the raw facts of her parents' breakup. She could do the math well enough to recognize what had transpired—if not back when she was twelve, then certainly now. But like all children, she was the star in her own universe. Her parents' dramas were background noise. She loved her mother from a child's perspective, and hard as that might be for Vega to swallow, he had to. And so he did. For Joy. Because for all the terrible wrongs he felt Wendy had done to him, she'd done something truly wonderful when she'd given him his daughter.

The elevator dinged and the doors opened. They stepped in. "Since I'm already here," said Vega, "why don't I drive you instead?"

"Alan's on his way."

That was debatable. Alan was late to everything. More than once, Vega had driven up to their sprawling Georgian colonial for a scheduled visit with his daughter only to find that Alan hadn't gotten around to bringing her back from some family outing yet.

When they got to the lobby—surprise, surprise—Alan's

black Mercedes wasn't parked in the circle out front. Joy flopped down in one of the lobby chairs and tapped out a message on her iPhone, presumably to Mr. Reliable. Vega took a seat across from her and drummed his fingers on the armrests. He wasn't going anywhere until that jerk showed up. He wasn't about to leave Joy without a way to get to her tutoring gig.

"What did you want to see Dr. Feldman about?" asked Joy.

"He's still running that study, right? The one that looks at the effects of dietary education on low-income pregnant women?"

"Of course, Dad. I've been helping him with it for two years." It was a good first step if Joy wanted to get into medical school. Vega assumed that was still her long-term goal.

"Do you deal at all with the study participants?"

"Every week."

"Have any of them ever seemed—I don't know—overwhelmed? Maybe depressed to the point that they would abandon their babies?"

That stopped her in mid-text. She put down her phone. "*What?* Why would you ask that?"

"I'm trying to locate the mother of a newborn the Lake Holly police found earlier today."

"*Found?* As in 'found alive?' Or 'found dead'?"

"That information hasn't been released yet."

Joy rolled her eyes. "Really, Dad. Sometimes, you're such a cop."

"I've been called worse. And I'm still asking here: can you think of a patient of Dr. Feldman's who might be capable of abandoning her newborn?"

Joy picked at her manicure. Her nails were aqua today with white polka dots. They ran the whole gamut of shades and designs. Vega wondered how much Joy paid for such nonsense. Or was it Wendy and Alan who were paying? Were they bribing Joy with the things he wouldn't or couldn't buy for her?

Joy noticed her father scrutinizing her and tucked her fingers under her thighs. She muttered something. It sounded like "Sunday" in Spanish.

"Did you say *Domingo?*" It was Vega's fault entirely that his daughter spoke only a smattering of high school Spanish. It would have been so easy to speak it to her when she was little. Now, it was too late.

Joy hesitated. "I'd be breaking patient confidentiality."

"C'mon, Joy." Vega pulled a face. "Cops ask these sorts of questions all the time. I need a lead here. You're not going on a witness stand."

She let out a slow exhale. "I don't even know if she's had her baby yet. She hasn't shown up in a while."

"Give me a name. Dominga—?"

"Flores. Dominga Flores. She's a live-in nanny here in town. At least she was when I saw her. The family she was working for said she couldn't stay with them once the baby was born, so I don't know whether she's moved on. She was definitely very distraught over the situation."

"Who's the family?"

"Their name is Reilly, I believe." Joy looked down at her phone. "Alan just texted me that he's caught in traffic. He'll be here in five minutes."

"*Traffic?* On a *Sunday?* What? Three soccer moms in minivans?"

"Daaad." Joy put a hand on his knee. "He's coming, okay?"

Vega sank back in his chair. "If I were late, you wouldn't be so forgiving."

"You wouldn't *be* late. You'd be early—and then complain when I . . . Oh, forget it."

They were both silent for a moment. Vega tapped the armrest of the chair to a beat only he could hear. He tried to return to the topic at hand. "This Dominga, how old is she? What's she like?"

"Midtwenties, I guess. Quiet. She's very sweet. Just really—stressed. She's from Honduras, and the baby's father—he's Guatemalan, I believe. I think he's married back in his country. He doesn't want to have anything to do with the baby."

"Did *she* say she didn't want the baby?"

"No. She just acted—I don't know—scared. I guess she's afraid of how she's going to support herself and her child." Joy frowned. "If the baby turns out to be Dominga's, she won't go to prison for abandoning it, will she?"

"A judge and jury make those decisions, Joy. Not me."

"But she may not have had that many options."

"The Safe Haven Law gives her options. If she ignored them, she has to face the consequences."

"Come on, Dad. It's not always that simple. Sometimes every choice a person has is bound to cause someone pain."

"I disagree."

"Just look at Adele's situation. What's the painless choice there?"

"Adele?" Vega leaned forward in his chair. He felt a kernel of something frozen and black settle in his stomach. "What's Adele got to do with this?"

"You know," Joy stumbled. "That job. In D.C. The one Steve Schulman offered her if he gets elected."

"Job?" Vega felt like he was staring at the headlights of an oncoming train. He couldn't move. All he could do was stand frozen in their glare. "Schulman didn't offer her any job."

"I tutor Charlie Gonzalez's son in math. He's one of Schulman's chief campaign advisers and a neighbor of ours. I heard him talking about it like it was a done deal."

"Adele would have told me."

"I guess." Joy stared at her hands. "You should probably ask Adele."

A sleek black Mercedes whipped around the hospital's front circle. The driver beeped his horn. It was Alan, impatient as ever. Joy rose from her seat, seemingly grateful for the reprieve.

"Listen, Dad—maybe I'm wrong."

Joy wasn't wrong. Vega knew that already. All he had to do was replay the last few weeks in his head. The silences. The unanswered text messages. The disappointment in Adele's eyes last night and this morning.

"I'm sorry, Dad. I've gotta go. I'll talk to you soon, okay?" She kissed him on the cheek. "See you."

"Yeah. See you."

Chapter 6

"Okay, Sophia. Let's try this again. Which number is smaller? Negative six or negative one?"

"I told you, Mommy! One! One is smaller than six."

"No, Mija," said Adele. "One *is* smaller than six. But *negative* one is larger than *negative* six."

"But that makes no sense!" Sophia shoved the worksheet across the dining table and folded her arms across her chest. She was getting near the breaking point. They both were. Sophia was dog-tired from being up late at the sleepover—a misnomer if ever there was one. Adele felt beaten down by the events of this morning. How come Peter got to do all the fun stuff with their daughter, like taking her ice-skating and Adele ended up with fourth-grade math?

She retrieved the worksheet and laid it gently in front of her daughter. "What you need to remember is that negative numbers work in reverse. The bigger the negative, the smaller the amount. So negative six is *smaller* than negative one."

"But six is bigger."

"When it's a positive number."

"But if you owed somebody six dollars, you'd owe *more* than if you only owed them one. So it's bigger."

Ay caray! Adele's head was pounding. Her nerves were shot. Every time the phone rang, it was someone else telling her about the dead newborn found behind La Casa—everyone but Jimmy. He had yet to call since he'd stormed out of the house at seven-thirty this morning.

She was in the process of drawing a number line for Sophia when the phone rang again. She checked the caller ID. It wasn't Jimmy. But it was a call she knew she had to take: Steve Schulman, the county supervisor, who, if the polls were correct, would soon become the next Democratic U.S. senator from New York.

"I have to answer this," Adele told her daughter. "Fill in the numbers on the number line, and I'll check them when I get off the phone."

The little girl groaned and rolled her eyes. She was nine going on thirteen. Rhinestone jeans. Sequined shirts. All sparkle and high drama. Adele took the phone upstairs. She hadn't told Sophia anything about Schulman's offer yet. She hadn't told anyone.

She walked into her bedroom and shut the door. "Hey, Steve." She feigned a brightness she didn't feel.

"You're busier than I am, Adele, and that's saying something. I've been trying to reach you for two days." He had no idea she'd been dodging his calls. And why would he? Most people would give their right arm for the opportunity Schulman was offering her. What was her problem?

"It's just been crazy at work lately," said Adele. That was one way to describe a homicide investigation behind her community center.

"So—you're coming to the gala Saturday night, right?"

"I wouldn't miss it for the world." Adele wondered again if Jimmy had gotten around to renting a tuxedo. She'd been asking him for a month to do it. He kept putting it off, like a lot of things in their relationship. Then again, the same could be said of her.

"You know," said Schulman, "I would love to be able to introduce you on Saturday as my new Hispanic Affairs appointee."

The words hung on the line a half beat too long. Adele knew she was supposed to say something.

"I'm flattered, Steve. More than flattered. Honored—"

"You *are* going to accept, aren't you?" He had an airline pilot's voice. Quietly confident under the most harrowing of circumstances. More than once Adele had relied on Schulman for his reassuring demeanor, not to mention his political savvy and sway with community leaders.

She'd first met Steve Schulman ten years ago when he was an up-and-coming state senator for the district and she was a former Wall Street lawyer who'd just won a class-action discrimination suit against the town of Lake Holly on behalf of a group of day laborers. As part of the settlement, she'd been granted the resources to start La Casa. It was not a politically popular decision. Overnight, picket lines formed across from the center. Adele was deluged with hate mail, even at her home, telling her to "Go back to Mexico"—despite the fact that she was born in the United States and her parents were from Ecuador.

Every week, there were angry letters in the local newspaper decrying the death of their bucolic little village at the hands of "alien invaders." All the local politicians walked a fine line with Adele, on the one hand extolling the "American melting pot" and, on the other, reassuring their voters that they did not support "lawbreakers."

Only Schulman was able to step above the fray and see the bigger picture. A real estate lawyer and small-time developer, he quickly rounded up local civic and business leaders and community activists and forced them to sit in the same room with one another. He charmed the Hispanic community with his stilted, gringo-accented Spanish and willingness to partake in their culture. And he rightly pointed out to business leaders that Latinos were reinvigorating a downtown that had been slowly dying as middle-class residents took their business to the malls.

He could not change everyone's heart, but he changed enough of them, and Lake Holly—unlike so many other towns faced with the same challenges—managed to emerge from the crisis stronger and, at least in Adele's mind, better than it had been before.

She admired him. She owed him. And so she stumbled about now for an answer. "I haven't spoken to my daughter about the position yet. Moving to D.C., leaving La Casa, those are big decisions—"

"As opposed to what, Adele? Organizing mitten drives and English classes? Figuring out how to squeeze another year's worth of life from your copier? God knows, I'm your biggest fan. And, God knows, I appreciate the work you've done at La Casa, the contributions it has made to the community. To the county. But it's time to move on. You're a Harvard-educated lawyer, a woman with the vision and courage to change the lives of a much broader group of Latinos than you could ever hope to staying in Lake Holly."

"I know. It's just that—"

"I'm sure you could find someone else to take over the reins there."

Yes, she could. She had several highly competent people working there now. They could keep the place running and take over the fund-raising. But who would handle all the little details? Who would remember to give the Serrano children extra snacks when they came for tutoring because their mom was dead and their dad was overwhelmed with the fact that he was facing deportation? Who would scavenge garage sales for old SAT prep books so that maybe—just maybe—Orestes Pilar had a shot at going to college? Who would buy a cake for Nataly Mejia, who was too proud to tell anyone her tenth birthday was coming up and her family couldn't afford a celebration?

But no. Even those weren't the biggest reasons. The biggest reason didn't *know* he was the biggest reason. She hadn't told him.

"I just need some more time, Steve. I mean, the election's still several weeks away. And you won't be taking office until January, and—"

"I recognize a stall when I hear one, Adele. What are you afraid of?"

"Nothing—"

"Because this is a once-in-a-lifetime opportunity. It's not every day you get the chance to shape policy on a national level."

Oh God. What wouldn't she have given for a chance like this straight out of law school? Or even a couple of years ago, right after her divorce? And then *he* came along. And overnight, everything changed. No man had ever made her laugh harder or caused her body to tingle from head to toe when he entered a room. Was that what happened when you fell in love? Did you rearrange the evidence to suit the verdict like some small-town judge fixing speeding tickets?

They didn't belong together. Anyone could see that. He loved predictability. She craved excitement. He didn't like his opinions scrutinized. She relished a good debate. He was methodical and practical. She preferred to think big and fill in the gaps later.

He didn't understand her job or why it mattered so much to her. He'd deny that if she said it. But she knew it in the way he sometimes drifted off when she was sharing some dilemma about a client, the way he'd grow restless at functions, jiggling his legs, jangling his keys, playing with his phone or his Swiss Army knife. He viewed work—any work, even his own—through a blue-collar lens. It was something he did, not something he was. You gave it your best shot, and then you went home.

She'd tried to see things his way. She'd tried to compromise. And look what it had cost—a child's life.

"Look," said Schulman, "if you don't want to be my Hispanic Affairs adviser, just say so."

"I do want it."

"Then you're accepting?"

"Probably. That is—look, Steve, a terrible thing happened this morning. A newborn was found dead behind La Casa. I'm having a hard time processing anything today."

"Did they find the mother?"

"Not yet, as far as I know. I'm going to be asking around."

"A word of advice? Stay out of any controversy right now. Let the police handle it. You need to be squeaky clean if you're going to work for me. Which brings us back to the big question."

They were both silent for a moment. Adele didn't know what to say.

"Look, Adele, I really, really want you for this position. I know you'd be terrific at it. But I need *you* to want it."

"I do. I just—I need a little more time to get things in order."

"How about you give me your answer at the gala Saturday night? Deal?"

"Yes. Deal. Thank you, Steve."

"You come to D.C., I'll be the one thanking you."

Adele hung up the phone. She'd just bought herself six more days before she had to come up with a decision. So why didn't she feel any better?

Because I still have to tell Jimmy. Every bad thing Adele had faced in her life she'd handled by avoiding the issue and bottling it inside: her childhood traumas growing up with undocumented parents, her financial struggles at Harvard, her failing marriage. Adele had dealt with each by not dealing with it. She could do that largely because she was the recipient of the pain, not the instigator. But here finally was a problem she couldn't pretend away. She was going to have to face him squarely when she delivered the news. Six days, six weeks—it didn't matter.

What mattered was—this time she was the one inflicting the pain.

Chapter 7

Adele needed to clear her head. So did Sophia. They'd been working on math problems long enough. Outside, the late-afternoon sun had settled like butterscotch over the landscape, and the air carried the scent of cinnamon and fresh-cut wood. The days were getting shorter. Autumn was slipping through their fingers.

Adele hauled Sophia's bike out of the garage and pumped some air into the tires. Just a few blocks from their house was a small bodega that sold Good Humor ice cream. Adele and Sophia were both suckers for their Candy Center Crunch Bars.

Walking into Claudia's bodega was like stepping into another country. Light filtered through the stalks of green and yellow plantains that dangled from ropes on the ceiling. The air smelled like ripe fruit and strong coffee. There was a sense of treasure and mystery on every shelf, from the colorful peppers shriveled like old lady's fingers to the rows of strange herbs that traditional healers—*curanderos*—used to treat a variety of ailments from diabetes to colic.

There were items one could only find here: cartons of the cinnamon-rice drink *horchata*. Jars of cashew apple jam. Bins of squash seeds that the Guatemalan women ground up to make a nutty-tasting stew. And there were

things one could find elsewhere but that had more meaning in a place like this: dried and salted codfish. Votive
candles with the Virgin of Guadalupe etched across them.
Beans in every shape and variety. Burlap sacks of rice.
Cans of Café Bustelo, the old Cuban-style espresso. Jars of
Vicks VapoRub, a staple in every Latin American's medi-
cine chest. Claudia Aguilar's store was more than a bodega;
it was a safe harbor for people who might never see their
home port again.

Adele tried to imagine herself shopping in a place like
this in Washington, D.C. Would she even *find* such a
store? Every time she traveled there, she was struck by the
cookie-cutter sprawl of the surrounding suburbs. All the
town houses and shopping malls looked the same. Bland.
Brick-veneered. Soulless. People always seemed in flux and
on the move. Oh sure, there were plenty of immigrants in
D.C. But how could she form real relationships if her for-
tunes were tied to an electoral calendar? In Lake Holly, she
knew everyone. Leaving would feel like a betrayal. And yet—

"Doña Adele! *Que bueno verte!*" Claudia called out
from behind the counter. Claudia was a short, energetic
Salvadoran with a body like a Russian nesting doll and
hair the color of a used chalkboard eraser. She worked
seven days a week and carried herself like she was everyone's mother—something the young men in the area, so
far from home, really appreciated. Like a lot of the immigrants in Lake Holly, Claudia still used "Don" and "Doña"
as signs of respect.

Adele lifted her hand in greeting. Usually Claudia's daughter, Inés, was behind the counter helping her. But today there
were only two people in the store besides Claudia: a customer
at the front counter and Claudia's mildly retarded grandson,
Neto, who was unloading crates of guavas and habañero peppers while his miniature dachshund, Chicha, danced around
his legs.

Chicha rolled over for a belly rub the moment she spotted Sophia. While the girl was scratching the dog, Neto grabbed a habañero pepper from the crate he'd just unloaded and held it out to Sophia between his stubby fingers.

"This? Don't eat," he said in Spanish, then laughed in his thick, nasal way. "You eat this?" He fanned his mouth. "Ay, it's hot!"

"Don't be silly, Neto!" Claudia chided from behind the counter. "She doesn't want that." Claudia reached behind the register and held out a tamarind-flavored Mexican candy to Sophia. The child hesitated.

"Go take the candy and say thank you to Doña Claudia," Adele instructed her daughter in Spanish.

Sophia gave her mother a smoldering look, then took the candy and sputtered out a shy *gracias*. The child understood Spanish, but getting her to speak it was another matter. Adele hoped that that would change as Sophia got older, but with a last name like Kessler, her ties to her Latin roots already seemed like a thing of the past. Sophia didn't even like tamarind.

"We were just talking about you," said Claudia. She nodded to the woman whose order she was ringing up.

"Me?" Adele stepped closer. The woman at the counter was dressed in a tailored black wool jacket with a poufy, furlike collar. Her nails sported a French manicure, and her handbag looked expensive. Claudia had only one customer Adele knew of who could afford such things.

"Doña Esme, *cómo está?*"

Esmeralda Gonzalez ran a hand through her high, tight ponytail and mumbled a shy greeting in return. For some reason Adele could never fathom, she made Charlie Gonzalez's wife nervous—which struck her as odd since she and Gonzalez got along well. Carlos "Charlie" Gonzalez was something of a legend in Lake Holly, a man who crossed the border from Mexico thirty years ago with nothing but the clothes on his back and rose to become the owner of a multimillion-dollar string of car washes as well as a political force in the state Democratic Party. He was a big supporter of La Casa and one of Schulman's chief campaign advisers. Yet for all the years Adele had known Gonzalez, she could count on one hand the number of times she'd said more than hello to his wife.

"We were talking about that terrible situation," said Claudia.

Adele thought for a moment that Claudia was referring to the infant behind La Casa. But it was too soon for anyone in the community to know about that.

"I was just telling Doña Esme that I saw him in church this morning. With his two little ones. And the older girl, the one you like so much. Such a beauty."

Manuel Serrano. Claudia was talking about the cook who used to work at La Bella Vita. His situation concerned all the Latinos in Lake Holly—even the ones who had green cards and the ones born here—because all of them had relatives who didn't and weren't.

Serrano had become the biblical Job of Lake Holly. Eighteen months ago, his wife died suddenly of meningitis. Then a fire in a neighbor's apartment caused Serrano and his three children to have to relocate. Then the local police kicked down the door of his new apartment, ransacked his belongings, and arrested him in a case of mistaken identity. And finally, instead of apologizing and letting Serrano go, they discovered a fourteen-year-old deportation order against him from a labor raid at a California garment factory when he was twenty-two.

For four months now, Adele had been helping Serrano fight deportation. He had a final hearing coming up a week from Monday. If his lawyer couldn't convince a federal immigration judge to stay the order on the grounds that he was the sole support of his children—two of whom were American-born citizens—he'd be deported back to

Mexico, separated from his kids for the rest of their childhood, if not forever.

"Do you have any news on the situation?" Claudia asked Adele.

"I think Doña Esme probably knows more than I do at this point," said Adele, "seeing as her husband arranged for Manuel's lawyer."

"I don't know anything," said Esme. "My husband does not talk to me about such things."

"Really?" The word came out sharper than Adele had intended. She had to remind herself that Esme had married Gonzalez when she was a teenager and he was in his thirties. Gonzalez liked to tell the story of returning back to his village, where he fell hopelessly in love with his wife on the eve of her taking her vows as a nun and begged her on bended knee to marry him. Adele couldn't picture Vega or her ex doing something so corny—or so romantic, for that matter. Then again, there wasn't a man on earth she'd have let slip a ring on her finger in her teens.

"I'm sure Don Charlie and Steve Schulman's old law partner are doing all they can for Manuel," said Adele.

"So he'll be free soon?" asked Claudia.

"That's hard to predict." Adele didn't have a magic wand she could wave and stay Serrano's order of deportation. People always attributed to her more power than she possessed—and then got annoyed when she couldn't come through.

Take Serrano's ankle monitor. When he first got arrested, Immigration and Customs Enforcement, the federal agency that handles deportations, wanted to ship him off to a detention center in some distant part of the country and expedite his removal. Adele worked an all-nighter to convince a judge to release him on humanitarian grounds and monitor him at home while he fought deportation.

It was a huge victory. And although Serrano was forbidden to work under the conditions of his release, he was extremely grateful for the chance to remain with his children. But as far as the rest of the community was concerned, Adele had slapped an electronic ball and chain on an innocent man and gotten him kicked off his job.

She couldn't even begin to explain to Esme and Claudia what Serrano was up against now: federal policy, judicial expedience, the whims of Washington on any given day. Steve Schulman might—*might*—have the influence to get a judge to issue Serrano a stay of deportation. Not legal residency, mind you. Just a promise not to deport him *right now.* But it would be political suicide for a candidate not yet in office to intercede publicly or try to call in those sorts of favors right before an election. Also, it could backfire. A judge could decide to spite a politician who tried to exert that sort of pressure. People got deported for a variety of reasons, not all of them logical.

Adele couldn't give Esme and Claudia the news they wanted, so she tried to change the subject. She gestured to the huge pile of food Claudia was ringing up and sorting into various bags and boxes. Esme appeared to be buying for an army.

"I'll bet three growing boys must eat you out of house and home," said Adele.

"These things aren't for me."

"Doña Esme buys groceries for many people in town," said Claudia. "Especially the ones who are too proud or too sick to visit the food pantry."

"How wonderful," said Adele. "I had no idea." The Gonzalezes already gave generously to La Casa as well as to the medical clinic, the town's food pantry, and a scholarship program at Lake Holly High School.

Adele noticed packages of hand warmers among the items Esme was buying. "Are you taking these to Mano Amiga?" Adele knew that, in addition to all their other charities, Esme ran Mano Amiga—Helping Hand—at her church. It was an outreach program for the homeless.

Esme nodded. "Winter is coming."

"When are you going again?"

"Tomorrow. Why?"

"Zambo came to see me last night at La Casa," said Adele. "I wasn't there. I know he goes to Mano Amiga a lot, especially when it gets cold outside. If you see him, can you tell him to come by La Casa as soon as he can? I really need to talk to him."

Esme took out her checkbook and began writing a check for the groceries. Claudia didn't take credit cards—the overhead was too steep. And besides, her customers mostly paid in cash.

"I don't think I'll be seeing him again," said Esme.

"Why?"

Esme tore off her check and handed it to Claudia. "The last time I spoke to him, he told me he was going back to Guatemala."

"He always says that. Every time the weather gets cold and the Lake Holly police dump him in Wickford."

"He was serious this time, I believe." Esme stuffed her checkbook back into her handbag. She looked down as she spoke. She often looked down when she spoke. Adele suspected it had something to do with her teeth. They were straight and white, but according to Gonzalez, when he first married her they were very crooked. The dental implants came later—late enough, Adele suspected, that Esme never got used to looking people straight in the eye when she was talking.

"Does he understand that if he leaves, he might not be able to come back?"

"I only know what he told me," said Esme. "He seemed very certain. Maybe he wanted to see you to say good-bye."

"Huh." Adele felt like she'd just had the wind knocked

out of her. Here was Manuel Serrano doing everything he could do *not* to get deported. And here was Zambo, heading back by choice. People were nothing if not surprising.

"Mom! Can we go?" asked Sophia in English. Her ice cream was beginning to melt. Chicha the dachshund was looking up hopefully in case any of it dropped. Neto was reciting his favorite flavors, but he couldn't get much beyond chocolate and vanilla.

"One minute, Mija." Adele turned to Esme. "If it turns out Zambo was just bluffing and you *do* run into him, can you tell him to come see me at La Casa?"

"Of course," said Esme. She kept her head slightly bent and didn't meet Adele's gaze. "I send everybody to you, Doña Adele. I'm sure you always try your best to help people."

There was something in the way Esme spoke the words, the way Claudia kept her own gaze on the scuffed counter, that made Adele feel the weight of their expectations and the sense that already, she'd failed.

Chapter 8

The Reillys' house sat in the middle of a block of modest capes and split-levels all evenly laid out like a set of dominoes, all yellowing under the sodium glare of streetlights. Behind the pulled shades of picture windows, televisions flickered and dogs barked. People stumbled about taking out the trash, half hidden in the shadows of bushes hyper-pruned to the shape of cannonballs or Chinese takeout containers.

It was not the sort of neighborhood where Vega expected to find a live-in nanny. He'd expected something more, well, *upscale*. Still, Dominga Flores was the best lead he had so far as a potential mother of Baby Mercy. According to Dr. Feldman's records, she'd skipped her last three prenatal checkups and hadn't been in to see him in almost six weeks. Her cell phone number—likely one of those pay-as-you-go varieties—was out of service. Her employers offered his best hope of tracking her down.

Vega parked in the street and walked up to a front door with a plaque beside it. The family name was burnished into the plaque, the dot over the "i" replaced by a shamrock. The Gaelic words ERIN GO BRAGH were etched beneath. Vega smiled to himself. When he was a boy growing up in the South Bronx, every fire escape and bodega in his neighborhood sported a Puerto Rican flag, a symbol of pride that people outside his culture—particularly Anglos—tended to regard with suspicion. But really, how was this any different?

A woman answered the door with a baby on her hip. She was dressed in oversized gray sweatpants and a sweatshirt with an assortment of pale splatters and stains across it. Her blond hair was carelessly gathered into a loose bun. Strands hung down the sides like she was a piece of corn in the process of being shucked. Vega wasn't sure if she was the babysitter or the mom.

"Sorry to bother you, ma'am. My name is James Vega. I'm a detective with the county police." Vega showed her his badge and ID. "I'm looking to talk to Mr. or Mrs. Reilly. Are either of them home?"

"I'm Mrs. Reilly." The baby fussed on her hip. A boy, judging by the square heft of his body. He had blue eyes and a pale down of wispy hair that stood straight up on his head. He was making those low-level whines that promised to detonate at any moment. It was a long time ago now, but Vega could still remember how he and Wendy were always handling Joy like a grenade with a pulled pin.

"May I come in?"

"Um, sure."

Vega stepped in the doorway. A toddler ran past his feet with a push toy in hand—some sort of fire truck with bells and whistles. From the kitchen, he could hear a man's voice trying to coax another child into eating one more bite of carrot. The child was screaming like the man was sticking needles into her flesh.

"Have I got you at a bad time?" asked Vega.

"Actually, this is about as good as it gets."

She gestured to what Vega assumed was a living room on her left. It had no grown-up furniture, only a scattering of beanbags on the wall-to-wall beige carpet surrounded by piles of dolls, trucks, and blocks. On a single low table with padded corners sat a collection of sippy cups and spilled Cheerios. A flat-screen television blared cartoons.

"How many children do you have?" asked Vega.

"Three. It's looks like more, I know. But with my three, it always does." She nodded to the baby on her hip. "C.J. is eight months. Brody, who just ran past, is two and a half, and my daughter, Kayla," she gestured to the kitchen, "is five."

A big bear of a man with receding reddish-blond hair walked into the living room. He had the shell-shocked demeanor of a soldier just off the battlefield.

"This is my husband, Bob."

Vega identified himself again and shook the startled man's hand. Vega wasn't sure what was startling him, having a cop in his house or having all these kids. Vega realized he'd never gotten the woman's first name.

"And you are?"

She seemed stumped by the question for a moment, as if she couldn't recall any name except "Mom."

"Oh, sorry. I'm Karen."

The five-year-old must have realized her tantrum over carrots wasn't having the desired effect. Her parents were preoccupied. So she walked into the living room and began screaming at the top of her lungs. The two-year-old made another pass through the room pushing his fire truck. The baby's fussing seemed positively blissful by comparison.

"Is Dominga here?" asked Vega. At the mention of her name, the five-year-old stopped screaming.

"Do-ga? Do-ga? Where's Do-ga? I want Do-ga!" Her two-and-a-half-year-old brother took up the cry while he smacked his truck into a wall.

Karen smoothed her daughter's blond hair. "She's not here, sweetheart." She turned to Vega. "I'm afraid Dominga doesn't work for us anymore, much to my children's disappointment."

The little girl kept up her chant. Vega wasn't sure what was more annoying, her previous tantrum or her new fixation.

"Sounds like your children really miss her."

"Oh my goodness, they do! We all do."

"Do you know where I can find her?"

Karen gave Vega a wary look. "What is this about?"

Vega studied the living room. There was nowhere to sit but on the beanbags, no way to talk over those cartoons and the screech of kids.

"Is there someplace we can sit and talk? Perhaps the kitchen?" He knew he could never hope to catch the complete attention of both parents in this house, so he decided to settle on Karen. Women were more perceptive and often more accommodating in his presence. "Mr. Reilly?" he turned to the husband. "Could you keep an eye on your children, sir, while I chat with your wife?"

"Um. Okay." Bob Reilly looked like he hadn't quite recovered from the last episode when Karen handed off the baby to him.

"You can start C.J. and Brody's bath," she told her husband.

Vega felt sorry for the guy.

The kitchen was small and frilly, with flowery curtains across a window and school calendars and snapshots on the refrigerator. Tiny sneakers lay in a jumble by the back door. The table still had dinner plates across it. Kayla's carrots sat in a congealed lump on her plate.

Karen looked embarrassed by the mess and started clearing everything. "Can I get you some coffee?"

"No thank you, ma'am. I'm fine. And you don't need to clear anything on my account."

"I don't really know how to sit still anymore," she admitted. "Would you mind?"

"Do whatever you feel comfortable with."

She grabbed a stack of plates and began scraping the remnants into the garbage. "You still haven't told me why you want to find Dominga. She's a wonderful young woman. I don't want to get her in trouble or anything."

"This has nothing to do with her immigration status, if that's what you're concerned about. I just need to know whether or not she's had her baby. Do you know if she's given birth yet?"

"No. I don't. The hospital might know."

"Her due date was two weeks ago, but there's no record she gave birth."

Karen stacked the plates in the sink and ran water over them. Upstairs, Vega could hear Bob Reilly trying to maintain order with an army in revolt. The tears and tantrums seemed endless.

"I thought she'd stay in touch with the kids," said Karen. "You saw Kayla. She *adored* Dominga. But Dominga just—left—and never looked back. I don't understand how she could just abandon them like that."

"I was under the impression you *let* her go."

"We did. But not because we didn't love her. We have a tiny au-pair suite downstairs. A room just big enough for one person. Look at this place," Karen unfolded her hands, more prayer for divine guidance than any invitation to poke around. "We can't manage with three children underfoot. How could we add Dominga's baby to the mix? Where would we keep the child? How would we cope? I'm a third-grade teacher, Detective. My husband travels around the country selling data-processing equipment. We chose a live-in nanny because it was cheaper and afforded more flexibility than putting three kids in day care. We're not rich. We're at our breaking point already. As much as I love Dominga, we simply couldn't do it."

"So you fired her."

"*Fired* her? We gave her a month's severance and great recommendations. Plus *I* was the one who found her another job. At a beautiful estate in Wickford caring for an elderly woman who was absolutely delighted at the prospect that she'd have a little baby in her great big house."

"Is that where she is now?"

Karen opened her dishwasher and began stacking plates inside. "I assume so. She left here about six weeks ago and promised she'd keep in touch. She promised *Kayla*. And then—nothing. She even disconnected her cell phone. I have a ton of stuff here that she was helping me sell on eBay. And she hasn't even called me about that."

"Do you know if she's all right?"

"I called her employer's house after she disconnected her cell phone. She was very cold on the line. Just 'yeses' and 'nos.' I called back and got her employer's son, who was visiting. He told me Dominga didn't want to speak to us anymore and hung up. I cried after that call, Detective. Dominga was with us for five years. She was like family. She *raised* Kayla. I'm starting to wonder if it was all an act, you know? Like maybe she never cared about my kids at all."

"So you never found out if she had the baby?"

"At that point, she hadn't. That much I know."

"And how long ago was that?"

"Maybe—four weeks ago?"

"You said you got her the job. Was this a family friend?"

"At an estate in Wickford?" Karen Reilly laughed. Lake Holly had a wide range of income levels. Neighboring Wickford had just two: rich and richer.

"I found the job for her through Craigslist," said Karen.

"Do you still have the address and phone number?"

"I have everything."

"Can you show me?"

Karen hesitated. "I'm sad that she didn't stay in touch, Detective. But that doesn't mean I want to cost her her job."

"I have no intention of making trouble for her outside of confirming whether or not she had her baby."

"Why do you need to know?"

Vega put on his best cop voice. "I'm afraid I can't divulge the specifics of an ongoing police investigation."

Karen sighed. "Okay. Come with me."

The Reilly house was a split-level with gates on both the upper and lower portions of the stairs. Karen unlatched the lower gate now and led Vega down a short flight of stairs into a room with boxes of clothes and children's toys, all neatly arranged next to a desk with a computer and a printer.

"My sideline business," Karen explained. "I sell stuff for people on eBay. Clothes. Toys. Bric-a-brac. You'd be surprised how much money you can make on commission doing this."

"You mentioned that Dominga helped you?"

"She was terrific. She couldn't open an eBay account herself because of her, uh, immigration status. But she was great at acquiring and selling things. I split everything with her, fifty-fifty."

Vega's eye was drawn to a fuzzy zip-up jacket, the color of Pepto-Bismol, that lay neatly folded on top of a stack of clothes for sale. Joy owned a jacket just like that. It was impractical as all hell. Too short in the midsection, too long in the sleeves. When she reached for anything, it rode halfway up her chest. Maybe that was the point.

"Where do you get all this stuff?" asked Vega.

"From people I know, from people Dominga knew. Dominga knew all the nannies and housekeepers in town. They get a lot of stuff from their employers."

"And do you sell everything?"

"What we don't sell, we give to charity, so it's all good."

Karen led Vega through a short hallway to a small bedroom with an adjoining bathroom. It was indeed as tiny as Karen had said. But the walls were papered in pretty floral paper. The bed looked comfortable. There was a chest of drawers, a closet, and a flat-screen TV with a remote. Vega didn't know much about live-in nannies, but the situation looked decent.

"You haven't hired another nanny yet?"

"We'd like to find someone," said Karen. "But it's so hard to find anyone we feel comfortable leaving our children with. Right now, we're getting by with part-time sitters and my mom filling in, but we can't go on much longer like this."

"Do you mind my asking how much you paid her a week?"

Karen opened the top drawer on the dresser and began rummaging inside. "Dominga got room and board plus $400 a week in cash and two weeks paid vacation. She worked seven a.m. until seven p.m. weekdays, which is long, I know. But she only worked every other Saturday night for us and a very occasional weekend day. Plus, whenever she had the time, she did the eBay sales, and she made half the cash she brought in on that as well."

"Still," said Vega. "That's sixty-plus hours a week. Which comes out to"—Vega, the accounting major, did the math in his head—"well under seven dollars an hour. For three kids."

"We're not rolling in money here, Detective. Why do you think I got into eBay sales? We're middle-class people doing the best we can. We treated Dominga like family. She was with us for five years, and she seemed happy here."

Karen pulled a book out of the top dresser drawer and handed it to Vega. "Here. See for yourself."

It was one of those "make your own book" photo albums. On the laminated cover was a picture of a young, brown-skinned woman with the blond baby on her lap and the two other Reilly children on each side. The girl, Kayla, was giggling, and the woman looked like she was about to start giggling herself. Vega could see from the look on both their faces that this wasn't scripted. He thumbed through the pages and saw dozens of similar shots that showed the progression of time through Dominga's ever-increasing pregnancy and the children's growth. But in all the shots, Dominga looked happy. So what happened?

"You didn't give this to her?"

"I'd planned to send it once she settled in. I was hoping to bring the kids to visit her sometime. After that call—I didn't know what to do."

Karen handed Vega something else from inside the drawer: a printout of the original Craigslist ad with an address and phone number scrawled at the bottom. The ad read: *Seeking live-in companion/caregiver for elderly woman in Wickford. Some light housekeeping and cooking. References required. Competitive salary.*

"Out of curiosity, do you know how competitive the salary was?" asked Vega.

"A thousand a week. A big jump from what I could pay her," Karen admitted. "But Dominga was pretty much expected to be available to Mrs. Davies around the clock except for Sunday afternoons, when her son visited. Dominga said that was fine right now because she'd be tied down with the baby anyway. Also, the um—baby's father—was out of her life."

"He dumped her?"

"He was married. In Guatemala. I don't think he was looking to start another family up here. Bob and I wanted to help her get some money from this guy through the courts, but she seemed uncomfortable with the idea, so we just backed off. She was almost twenty-six. We didn't want to meddle in her affairs."

"You know the father's name?"

"Esteban. Esteban Ovillo. He's a mechanic over at the muffler dealership."

Vega copied down Ovillo's name. "Mind if I keep this ad and contact information for Mrs. Davies?"

"Are you going to visit Dominga?"

"Yes, ma'am."

Karen pressed the picture book into Vega's hands. "Can you give her this? *Please?* Maybe she might just—I don't know—call us sometime?"

Vega took the book. "I'll see what I can do."

Vega checked his cell phone as soon as he left the Reillys. He had a text from Adele.

Call me. I REALLY need to talk to you. XXX

If it was about the investigation, he couldn't talk. If it was about anything else, he wasn't sure he wanted to. What was he supposed to say? *Sure, leave me and go off to D.C.?*

Adele was his first real relationship since Wendy, perhaps his first real relationship as an adult if you consider that he was barely twenty-three when Wendy came into his life. Adele was more than a girlfriend; she was his best friend. She knew all the names and quirks of the guys he worked with. She could sing (badly, but he never told her that) all the songs he performed with his band. She'd heard every story of his childhood in the South Bronx, from the foul-mouthed parrot that lived in the tenement apartment above him to the time he and Henry Lopez stole and ate Mrs. Clemente's *arroz con gandules* from her fire escape. (Vega swore he still had the rubber-sandal marks from the beating his grandmother administered with her *chancletas* afterward.)

Vega and Adele shared a whole arsenal of inside jokes that often sent them into hysterics with one word or look.

When he made love to her, it was with his heart and soul, not just his body. He looked at no other woman. He desired no other woman. How could she throw all that away?

He put the call through and waited for her breathy hello.

"Hey," he choked out. His throat felt tight. His palms began to sweat. He couldn't even say her name.

"I was wondering when you'd call me back," she said. "The phone's been ringing off the hook."

"I'll bet."

"So what's going on?"

You first, he was thinking. But instead he said, "You know I can't tell you anything about the investigation."

"Not anything?"

"Adele—"

"It's just that—God, Jimmy—I feel terrible."

He didn't know what to say to that, so he said nothing.

"You don't feel bad?" she asked him.

"Of course I feel bad."

"You never show it."

"You never show things, either."

They were both silent for a moment, each waiting for the other to speak. "Where are you?" she asked finally.

"Still in Lake Holly."

"You want to stop by?"

No. Better to deal with this over the phone. Quick and dirty. Wendy broke the news that she was leaving him over dinner at their favorite restaurant. He never ate there again.

"I'm beat, Adele. I've got a forty-five-minute drive ahead of me. If there's something you want to say to me, say it now."

She sighed. "I wanted to tell you in person."

He waited, acutely aware of every sensation: the way his truck's vinyl seats felt like cold, dead skin to the touch, the jarring rattle of someone fitting a tin lid on their trash can. Life went on all around him. He wrapped a hand around the steering wheel and studied the cold spill of streetlight through his windshield, the way it cast shadows on his knuckles. He flexed and unflexed his hand. If there was something—or someone—he could hit right now, he would.

"Okay. Look, Jimmy," Adele said slowly. "Since you won't come over, there's something you should know."

Chapter 9

Vega waited. He could feel his breath balling up in his chest with anticipation. *Steve Schulman has offered me a job. I'm moving to D.C.* Two sentences and it would all be over. Other guys, they'd go out afterward and drown their sorrows over a beer with friends. But how do you do that when your girl is also your best friend?

Maybe it was because his dad walked out when he was two, but Vega never felt the burning urge for male companionship that other men did. As a small child, he loved hanging out in his mother's kitchen, watching her deep-fry *alcapurrias*—meat fritters—while his grandmother taught him how to salsa to the scratchy eight-tracks she used to pick up over on Tremont Avenue.

After his grandmother died when he was eleven, Vega and his mother moved north to suburban Lake Holly, where he stuck out as the token minority in a sea of Irish and Italian faces. He was a good baseball player—always a litmus test of friendship among boys—and his skills earned him a degree of acceptance and respect from other boys in town. But he never hungered to compete and ended up more comfortable behind a guitar than in a dugout.

His career as a police officer should have remedied all that. Most cops had a truckload of fellow-cop buddies.

But Vega wasn't the sort who spent his off hours drinking or fishing or watching ball games with other men. And even though he loved getting together with his band, Armado (Spanish for "armed"—they were all in law enforcement), his relationships with the men never went deeper than their shared love of playing music. Adele was the one he told his troubles to, the one whose advice he sought. She was his gravitational center. Without her, he felt weightless and out of kilter. And so he braced himself like a condemned man before a judge for whatever she had to say now.

"Have you found Zambo yet?" she asked him.

"Uh, no." He couldn't see what this had to do with her going to D.C. "The Lake Holly PD is still looking for him."

"I was in Claudia's today," she began. "You know Claudia Aguilar? The lady who owns the little bodega around the corner from me?"

"Uh-huh." She'd lost him. Completely. He could follow any map but a woman's train of thought.

"I ran into Esmeralda Gonzalez, Charlie's wife? She works with the homeless in town through her church, so I asked her if she'd seen Zambo. She said Zambo told her he was going back to Guatemala. She thinks he already left."

Vega waited for more.

"Did you hear what I just said, Jimmy?"

"I heard."

"You seem—I don't know—distracted."

No shit. "Esme Gonzalez thinks Zambo's in Guatemala. So?"

"But if he is—"

"If he is, then I'm the pope."

"It's worth checking out."

"Checking out how, Adele? Calling the Guatemalan Embassy? The guy's probably passed out in Michael Park somewhere. The PD will find him."

Silence. She sucked in her breath. "You're always so sure."

"Now you're going to tell me how to do my job?"

"You tell me often enough how to do mine!"

Vega flicked the heater vents in the truck. Should he ask about Schulman? *No.* Pride wouldn't let him. So he said simply, "Is that it?"

"What do you mean, 'Is that it?' "

"Is that all you wanted to tell me?"

"Boy, you're just the soul of compassion this evening. Do you realize that not once—*not once*—have you said you're sorry for talking me out of going to see Zambo last night?"

"And what would that change? Would that change *anything?*"

"Maybe just . . ." Her voice trailed off. Vega waited. "You never rented that tuxedo."

They were talking about a dead baby, and now she wants to talk about a freakin' suit? Vega would never understand women.

"I've been busy."

"Umm." There was a heaviness to her voice, a slow grind of gears. Vega felt her weighing what she should say and what she could hold off on until another day. And that's when it hit him: she'd been doing the same thing for weeks now. He'd been a fool not to see it coming.

"Get some sleep, all right?" Adele said finally. "We're both exhausted." She hung up, and all the way home Vega's words echoed in his head: *What would that change? Would that change anything?* And he knew what he should have said—what he should have realized weeks ago. The obvious answer:

Us.

*   *   *

Monday morning. Valley Formal Wear. The empty waiting area had benches tufted in black velvet and a three-
paneled mirror that made Jimmy Vega feel like he was
staring at his reflection in a fun-house arcade and every
angle was bad. He had thirty-five minutes before he had to
meet with the medical examiner. That should be enough
time, shouldn't it?

"What sort of tuxedo would you like to rent?" asked
the blond salesman with the prep-school accent. "Single-
breasted? Double-breasted?"

"Single-breasted, I guess."

"Peaked lapels? Or notched?"

"I wouldn't know a peak from a notch," Vega admitted.
"Whatever's black, basic, and reasonable."

"When do you need it by?"

"Uh, Saturday, I guess."

"You *guess?*"

"I'm not sure I'm still going."

"Please tell me you're not getting married."

Vega allowed a smile. "No. Nothing like that. It's a political fund-raiser. I just don't know if I want to go at this
point or if I'm even still invited."

The man raked his fingers through a spray of stiff bangs
and ran his eyes across Vega's faded black polo shirt, off-
the-rack sports jacket, and chinos. They seemed to tell him
everything he needed to know about Vega's fashion sense.
"You're cutting it close as it is. We charge a twenty-dollar
rush fee if you want to rent in under fourteen days, plus an
additional twenty-dollar deposit that you'll forfeit if you
cancel."

"So it's gonna cost me forty bucks if I don't go?"

"I'm afraid so."

"And what's the fare if I do?"

"That depends on what you choose, but something in
the neighborhood of a hundred and fifty."

"How fast can you pull an outfit together?" Vega checked his watch. "I'm kind of in a hurry."

"Then perhaps you should consider painting tails on a T-shirt, hmmm?"

Maybe it was the smolder in Vega's eyes or the holstered gun that was apparent as Vega slipped out of his jacket, but the salesman's accent went from Harvard to Hoboken in seconds flat. "Let me take some measurements and see what I can do," he mumbled.

The salesman took his measurements and left Vega in a dressing cubicle while he disappeared in back to see what he could find. Vega's phone dinged with a text. Louis Greco. Vega had passed along Adele's information about Zambo to Greco last night. Vega was hoping she was wrong.

Still looking for Zambo, texted Greco. *Nobody saw him around last night. Could Adele be right?*

Keep looking, Vega texted back. *$50 says he's not in Guatemala.*

The salesman emerged from the back room and inserted something wrapped in plastic through the curtain. He seemed to have relocated his New England boarding school accent in the back room as well.

"I'm afraid we don't have any black tuxedos available in your size right now. But we have a very fashionable royal blue one with a shawl collar."

Vega held up the garment bag. "What's a shawl collar?" He pictured one of those granny square blankets that people drape over couches. It didn't sound flattering.

"A style lots of celebrities wear. Ryan Gosling wore a tux very similar to this at the Academy Awards last year."

Vega didn't want to admit he didn't know who Ryan Gosling was and never watched the Academy Awards, so he just grunted as he unwrapped the tuxedo from the plastic. The blue was less Hollywood and more Sesame Street.

Vega could have doubled as Cookie Monster's well-dressed brother.

"You don't have anything else?"

"Nothing that's remotely in your size on such short notice."

Vega was five-foot-ten and a hundred and sixty pounds, lean and muscular. So much for all the stuff he kept hearing about Americans getting fatter. The guys renting tuxedos definitely weren't.

"But I need a black tuxedo."

"It has a black satin collar and a black stripe down each leg."

The stripe looked silly to Vega, like he was a doorman or the tuba player in a high school marching band. He started to try it on and then stopped. *No.* This was ridiculous. Who was he kidding? Adele was leaving him, and he was renting a tux for the occasion? He wrapped the tuxedo back in the plastic and handed it through the curtain.

"I can't do this. I'm sorry," said Vega.

"You're not renting the tux?"

"I'm not attending the event." He was going to have to start getting used to a life without Adele. Might as well start now.

The medical examiner's office was a small and unassuming building tucked away in a corner of the state medical college's campus. Outside, the building looked like a maintenance facility. The windows were cut high into the beige concrete. A curtain of asphalt surrounded it. On the roof, there was a collection of tall vents, shafts, and air systems that added to the sense that the building's purpose was purely to power other facilities on campus.

Inside, however, was another matter. The waiting area resembled the lobby of a Holiday Inn. There were skylights, greenhouse plants, and a cheerful receptionist who welcomed Vega as if she had no idea that the only people who checked into this place didn't do so of their own accord.

As a cop, Vega had seen so many gruesome deaths, most no longer bothered him. But a baby or young child's always stayed with him. He could never be objective when it came to children. He didn't know if that made him better at his job—or worse.

The only thing that made the experience manageable was Dr. Gupta. Anjali Gupta had been the ME for as long as Vega could remember, and for someone who dealt with the most unappreciative patients a doctor could ask for, she had one of the best bedside manners around. In Vega's opinion, her talents were being wasted.

"Detective Vega. Good to see you." She stopped in front of him, erect and proper as always, and gave a small nod of the head. She was dressed in her usual white lab coat over a loose flowery skirt that came nearly down to her ankles. Her hair, graying at the temples, was pulled back haphazardly into a bun behind her head. Her feet were clad in fluorescent pink sneakers. She looked like someone's color-blind grandmother on vacation.

"Good to see you too, Doc. Wish the circumstances were better."

"They never are, are they?"

Dr. Gupta buzzed them through a doorway. The walls were tiled an industrial green. The floors were painted cement. Everyone was in scrubs.

"I performed the autopsy yesterday," said Gupta. "I understand your department and the Lake Holly police are conducting a DNA dragnet?" Her voice had the soft singsong of an Indian childhood tinged with the rising inflections of a British education. It made Vega's mangled Bronx vowels sound barbaric by comparison.

"Yes," he said. "We've got uniforms going door to door in Lake Holly trying to get people to do cheek swabs." A swab from even one distant blood relative would be enough for the police to map a trail to the baby's mother.

Gupta handed Vega a set of surgical gloves as they stepped inside the forty-five-degree room at the end of the hall. A loud ventilation system kept the smells to a minimum, but it was impossible not to detect an overlay of something greasy and humid in the air.

"How's the dragnet progressing?"

Vega made a face. "It would be progressing a lot better if the Lake Holly PD hadn't screwed up royally four months ago and erased any goodwill they'd built up in the Latino community."

"What happened?"

"They were supposed to serve a warrant to some gang-banger but mixed up the address and ended up arresting this fry cook instead."

"The cook is suing?"

"He wishes," said Vega. "No. It's bigger than that. ICE slapped a detainer on the guy because he had a prior deportation order from a labor raid years ago in California. Now he's facing a one-way trip back to Mexico. His wife's dead, and he's the sole support of his three kids. The community's pretty upset and not in a mood to cooperate with the police."

"Maybe you'll get lucky with the dragnet."

Vega sighed. "One can only hope. Any surprises I should know about from the autopsy?"

"Always," said Gupta.

Along one wall was a bank of steel lockers. On the other were charts detailing their contents. Gupta pulled a chart off the wall and walked over to a locker with the corresponding number. She opened the door and slid out the tray. The little white body bag barely took up a tenth of the space on the tray. Gupta zipped it open. On Sunday, Mercy had looked capable of being cuddled back to life. Today, her skin was the color of spoiled meat, her facial muscles seemed to have melted, her pupils had dilated, and there was a blue-white haze in the center of them that made her look doll-like. She wasn't a person anymore. But that didn't make Vega's job any easier.

"It's all in the report," Gupta explained. "But I wanted to show you a couple of things I think you should see." Gupta raised her hand over the child's face and gently lined up her fingers with bruise marks on either side of the baby's eye sockets. The heel of her palm rested directly over the bruises beneath the baby's nose.

"What does this tell you?" she asked Vega.

"Well, I know *you* didn't smother her. So I'm guessing someone with your size hand did."

"Which would likely be a woman's hand."

"A woman. Yes," Vega agreed. "Greco and I figured as much."

"Detective Louis Greco," said Gupta. "He hasn't retired yet, I take it?" Vega was always amazed at her recall of names and specifics. Another reason she should have ministered to live patients. The dead don't care what you call them.

"He says his wife would work him harder."

Gupta allowed a small smile. "I don't doubt it."

"So the cause of death was asphyxiation?"

"No," she said. "The cause of death was hypothermia. There was tissue damage consistent with hypothermia. Plus, there were high catecholamine concentrations in her urine."

"Catecholamine?"

"Hormones made by the adrenal glands," said Gupta. "To put it bluntly, the baby died of shock from the cold."

"Not asphyxiation?"

"Not asphyxiation. Her lungs show all the earmarks of normal respiration. It certainly appears someone tried to smother her. But it was the cold that killed her."

Vega closed his eyes. This was not what he wanted to hear. "And the time of death?" He tried to ask the question casually. But so much was riding on the answer.

"Approximately five a.m. It appears she died only about ninety minutes before she was discovered. But certainly, she'd been there a while."

Five a.m. Eight hours *after* Rafael's call. Vega could've flown to Puerto Rico and back with Adele and still had a chance to save this baby. It was his fault entirely that she died. Whether he was willing to admit it or not.

He took a deep breath and tried to remind himself he had a job to do here. "Any idea how long she was alive? Or when she might have been abandoned?"

"Judging from the condition of the umbilical cord blood, I'd estimate that the baby was born ten to twelve hours prior to her death," said Gupta. "So that would put her birth at anywhere from five to seven p.m. on Saturday. I took some skin samples of the bruises to see if they were proximate to the time of death or possibly administered soon after her birth. Newborns bruise easily, which is good news here, because I had more to work with. I did a histological exam and it appears that there was some healing of the vessels already going on by the time of death."

Vega's head was spinning. He had no idea what Gupta was trying to tell him.

"Doc, I took maybe two basic science courses in all my four years in college. I can tell you how to read a spreadsheet or calculate the future value of an annuity. But I have no idea what you're telling me."

"I'm saying the person who attempted to smother the baby did so several hours before she died."

"I have a line on someone who claims to have seen a mother and baby in those woods around eight the night before. Possible?"

"Entirely possible," said Gupta.

"The one time that drunk gets anything right . . ."

"Pardon?"

"Nothing. It's just that—my only witness is this bow-legged alcoholic everyone calls Zambo. No one ever takes him seriously. Except this time, I should have. And now I can't find him."

"Let's hope you do."

Back in her office, Vega went over her report. He took some notes, and Gupta corrected his medical misspellings.

"And the baby? She was full-term?" asked Vega. "Basically healthy?"

"No congenital abnormalities," said Gupta. "Do you have any leads at this point?"

"One, possibly. I'll know more later today." Vega gathered up his papers and stuffed them into a folder along with the autopsy report. Gupta regarded him over the tops of her glasses.

"So you were a finance major in college?"

"Worse, accounting. The subject should be registered as a lethal weapon. I nearly died from it."

She laughed. "I'll bet your parents made you study it."

Well, not parents. Just mother. But as far as Vega was concerned, she was the only one entitled to call herself a "parent" anyway.

"How'd you guess?"

"We Indians know something about parental pressure. My parents wanted me to be a surgeon."

"So what happened?"

"I preferred having no hand in my patients' demise. An advantage in my line of work. Yours too, in homicide, I expect."

Vega looked down at the envelope in his hands, heavy with the autopsy report. *Hypothermia. She died of hypothermia.* What the hell was he thinking Saturday night?

"Yeah," said Vega. "Most of the time."

Chapter 10

Luna Serrano sat in her global studies class and listened to Mr. Murphy drone on about the Russian Empire under Catherine the Great.

"The Russian serfs were just like slaves," he told the class. "They had no legal rights. They could be separated from their families and sent to distant estates if their masters chose."

Luna kept her head down and pretended to take notes. She didn't want to think about how much the serfs and she had in common.

This may be my last Monday ever at Lake Holly High.

She'd told only three friends about her situation. There was nothing anyone could do, and it got exhausting repeating herself all the time. Lindsay offered for Luna to come live with her family. But they didn't have room for all three Serrano children, and Luna could never leave Dulce and Mateo. Natasha and Grace each lived with their moms and siblings, so there were too few adults and too many kids in their homes already. Nobody knew what to say, so they just stepped around the subject like it was this big fart in the room they were all pretending not to smell. Instead they talked about homework and crushes and television shows on TeenNick. The school talent show auditions were coming up on Thursday. Natasha was going to do a hip-hop dance. Lindsay was too shy to go on stage. Grace and Luna were supposed to sing a Beyoncé duet together.

At dismissal time, Grace walked up to Luna's locker while Luna was gathering her books to make the school bus to La Casa. Dulce and Mateo got tutoring at La Casa after school while Luna did her homework and helped younger children.

"So, about the talent show auditions," said Grace. She sounded out of breath, like she'd been running even though she was standing still. She played with her hair. It used to be long and black like Luna's, though recently she'd put an auburn rinse on it. Now it was the color of an eggplant. Grace was also Mexican, but she was born in the United States, and her parents had gotten their green cards long ago. They were separated now. Grace complained a lot about how her father always spied on her and was worried she had a boyfriend. "I wish he'd just leave me alone!" she'd say to Luna. Luna never knew how to answer.

"The auditions are Thursday, right?" asked Grace.

"Yes," said Luna. "Right after school."

"See, I was wondering—since you may not be able to uh—you know—be in the show in December? I was thinking of asking Marly Lugo if she could do the duet with me? Is that okay?"

Grace spilled out the request like Luna had a choice in the matter. But there were no choices. Marly Lugo had already been asked and had already accepted. Telling Luna was just the awkward finale. Luna kept her head in her locker and pretended to be figuring out whether she needed to take both her math and her English notebook to La Casa. "Yeah. Sure," she mumbled.

"Thanks, Luna! I knew you'd understand!" And just like that, Grace was gone. Luna saw her at the far end of the hallway, pulling her cell phone out of her backpack. She was sure Grace was dialing Marly to let her know it had all been settled.

It doesn't matter, Luna told herself. If she ended up in Queens, there wouldn't be time for talent shows anyway. She'd need an after-school job. She'd need to look after Dulce and Mateo. Her father's cousins would be giving them a roof over their heads. They couldn't be expected to support them too, and Papi wouldn't be able to do much from Mexico. Besides, the talent show was the least of the things Luna would be missing. In her locker was an application for Lake Holly's summer science honors program. The kids who completed that program usually went on to get Intel and Westinghouse college scholarships. Luna had straight As in biology. Her science teacher, Mr. Ulrich, kept urging her to apply. The deadline was November 1. Luna could tell he was frustrated that she hadn't submitted her paperwork. It was too exhausting and embarrassing to explain why.

The hallway had started to thin out by the time Luna grabbed her backpack and made her way to the buses. It was an odd feeling to be in your childhood and aware that it was almost over. She wasn't ready for it to end.

She'd been going to school in Lake Holly since she was in second grade. She knew it wasn't cool to say you liked school, but she really did. She liked the way her principal, Dr. Larkin, greeted all the kids by name in the mornings and announced everyone's birthdays over the PA. She liked the way the gym floors gleamed when the sun struck them at just the right angle. She liked going out with her friends at recess and sitting under the three enormous maple trees by the soccer field. Lake Holly High was built in 1957 when those trees were much smaller. The original builder had nailed the school's chain-link fence to their trunks. Now those trunks were so huge, they encased the fence.

Luna was sure there were nice schools in Queens. But they'd never have trees like those—and her friends would never be sitting under them at recess, waiting for her.

She'd really wanted to sing that Beyoncé duet with Grace in the talent show.

She'd really wanted to get into that summer science honors program.

Outside, Luna hefted her backpack over her shoulder and scanned the row of yellow school buses for the one that would take her to La Casa. She heard her brother calling her name.

"Mateo. What are you doing here?" Mateo and Dulce were in the elementary school about a mile down the road.

"Papi's in the car," Mateo said breathlessly. "He wants us to come with him."

"Is something wrong?" Luna felt a panicked squeeze in her gut.

"Papi's court date has been moved to Thursday."

"*This* Thursday?" *Three days more as a family. Three days!* She felt light-headed and queasy.

"Papi spoke to Mr. Gonzalez, and he told him to come over right away," said Mateo. "Papi didn't want to have to worry about picking us up later from La Casa, so we're going with him."

Luna's father looked pale and hunched when she got into the car.

"I'm hungry," Dulce whined in back. Papi hadn't thought to bring anything to eat. He probably ran out of the house in a panic when he got the news. His hair was still wet from a shower. Luna fished around in her backpack for half a roll of Life Savers that Lindsay had given her earlier in the day. She tossed them in back to Dulce.

"Suck them, don't chew them. They'll stick to your teeth and give you cavities." She sounded like Mami.

Her father eased his brown Chevy past the school buses and out of the parking lot.

"Why did they move up the court date?" asked Luna.

"I don't know," he said. "Mr. Katz called me, and I called Señor Gonzalez and Señora Figueroa about it right away. The señor was working from home today. He told me to drive to his house and Mr. Katz would be there too."

"Do you think they can do anything?"

Papi looked straight ahead without answering. Lately he'd been wrapping their possessions in newspaper and packing them into cardboard cartons. His stuff mostly. But some of theirs as well. Luna knew that's what he did all day when they were in school.

"Maybe we should point the car to California and just keep going." Luna said the words half-jokingly, though she couldn't deny that the possibility had crossed her mind.

"I have the ankle monitor, Mija. I wouldn't get ten miles. And they'd lock me up for certain after that." From the way Papi said it, Luna knew that the idea had occurred to him too.

He shot a glance at Dulce and Mateo in the rearview mirror. "How was school today?"

"Mateo got sent to the principal's office," announced Dulce.

"*What?*" Papi put his foot on the brake and steered to the curb. Two cars honked behind them. He turned and glared at Mateo. "What were you doing?"

"Nothing." Mateo stared at his lap.

"Were you disrespectful to a teacher?"

"No."

"He was fighting," said Dulce. "With a boy on the playground who said all immigrants should be deported."

The words shot through the car like a hot knife. Papi swallowed hard and combed his fingers through his damp hair. "Mateo. You can't worry about what other people say. Do you understand me?"

Mateo nodded but kept his eyes on his lap.

"When you fight a person like that, you go down to his level. Then he wins and you lose. This is not how I want you to behave if I'm . . . If I'm . . ."

Papi's voice dropped away. Mateo wiped the back of his hand across his eyes. Papi's voice softened. He reached behind and chucked Mateo on the knee. "It's okay, Mijo. You learned, yes? It doesn't matter what a boy like that thinks. You are as American as he is—okay?"

"Okay."

Papi edged back into traffic and handed Luna directions to Señor Gonzalez's house. The Gonzalezes lived outside of the main part of town in a development called The Farms. When Luna's mother was alive, she cleaned a lot of houses in The Farms. Sometimes, when Luna was little, she'd tag along, so the big houses didn't have the same effect on her that they had on her father and siblings. All three of them gaped as they drove by houses so big, her father joked that he'd need a map to find his way to the bathroom. Luna said nothing. All she could think about was her mother's dream of a little house with a garden. Luna had always assumed that one day, they'd get it. Now she'd just be happy if all of them could be together again in their three-and-a-half-room apartment.

Luna read the directions. "Take a right," she told her father.

He turned onto a short, dead-end street. Mateo was the first to match up the house to the address.

"That's the one." Mateo pointed to a huge white mansion with a separate three-car garage. "Wow," he said. "Can you imagine living here?"

"He's rich, rich, rich!" chimed Dulce. Papi shot Dulce a look in the rearview mirror, but it was what they were all thinking.

Papi parked on the street, and they all got out of the car, unsure which door on the house they should walk up to. The front entrance looked imposing, and they hardly felt like invited guests. Yet the side entrance felt a bit too familiar. Dulce skipped across the grass, and Papi called her back, though in truth, it looked so lush, Luna felt like kicking off her shoes and doing the same thing.

They all stood like lawn ornaments for a moment. Then a side door opened and a young Latina in dark jeans and a ponytail stuck her head out.

"Señor Serrano? My husband is expecting you," she said in Spanish. "Welcome."

"Señora." Papi bowed. "Many thanks to you and your husband for seeing us."

"This is *your* house?" Dulce blurted out.

"Dulce!" Papi scolded. But Luna understood what her little sister meant. Señor Gonzalez was old and fat and balding. Señora Gonzalez looked more like his daughter than his wife. She wore bright pink lipstick and smoky eyeliner, and her ponytail was swept high off her neck like a schoolgirl. She covered her lips when she smiled as if there was something wrong with her teeth, which was odd because they were as straight and white as a TV reporter's.

"My apologies," said Papi, shooting a dark look at Dulce. "My daughter needs to learn her manners."

"No apology necessary." Señora Gonzalez allowed a little bit of her perfect white-tooth smile to flash at Dulce and Mateo. "My three boys are having snacks in the kitchen. Would you like to join them?"

"Yes!" said Dulce. She started to run into the kitchen. Papi put a firm hand on her shoulder.

"Please, señora. That's not necessary. You are busy. We will not impose."

"It's not an imposition. I think my middle son, Alex, knows Mateo from school."

Mateo, Luna noticed, was hanging back. Now she understood why. He was embarrassed that somebody from school might know their circumstances.

"We can wait outside," Luna offered.

"Don't be silly," said Señora Gonzalez. "There's plenty of room in the kitchen to eat and get your homework done."

It was clear they had no choice but to accept her hospitality, so they followed Señora Gonzalez into a passageway, where she hung all their coats on hangers in a closet. Then they walked their backpacks up a short flight of stairs to a massive kitchen with gleaming steel appliances. There were no school bulletins tacked to the refrigerator, no cereal boxes left on the counters, no random knickknacks on the windowsills. At a long counter in the center of the kitchen sat three boys with their books spread out, doing homework. They all had their mother's square chin, deepset eyes, and thin upper lip. The youngest looked about six and the oldest about eleven. The middle boy had to be Alex. He and Mateo offered each other a husky hello. It felt awkward.

"Make our guests welcome," Señora Gonzalez told them, which of course made everyone feel even more awkward. She introduced Christian, her oldest, Alex, and the little one, David. Then she poured milk for the three Serrano children and gave them each plates for cookies.

"I will supervise the homework," she told Papi. "Let me get you settled with the men."

Papi followed the señora down a long hallway with polished wood floors that reminded Luna of her high school gym. Their footsteps receded until the Serrano children were alone with the three Gonzalez boys. There was a tense moment when they all stared at one another. It was Dulce, as usual, who broke the silence.

"Bet you can't lick your elbow," she challenged the Gonzalez boys.

"Can too," said Alex. He rolled up his sleeve, and of course he couldn't. It was physically impossible. But the Gonzalez boys didn't know this, and pretty soon they were all trying to do it. Luna too.

That was her little sister for you.

Within minutes, the homework was forgotten. Mateo, Alex, and David were talking about game one of the World Series, Christian was asking Luna what high school was like, and Dulce was asking if the Gonzalez boys had a trampoline (they did).

Señora Gonzalez returned and ordered everyone to get back to their homework. Luna asked to use the bathroom, and the señora directed her to a room with gold faucets and towels that were so perfectly straight and dry, she was afraid to wipe her hands on them, so she wiped them on her jeans instead. On her way back to the kitchen, she shot a quick glance into the living room. It had a two-story ceiling, a black leather sofa, a white rug, and a crystal chandelier. For all the beautiful furniture, the house felt vacant somehow. Luna couldn't put her finger on why, and then she did: there were no pictures or personal items. No family photos. No school art projects. Her own parents had crossed the border from Mexico with only the clothes on their backs. Her family had lost a lot of their possessions in that fire last year. And yet they still had pictures and drawings and homemade stuff all over their tiny apartment.

Luna walked back into the kitchen. The others had finished their homework already. She had a lot more than they did, but she could finish it later. Señora Gonzalez suggested the children go outside and play. Dulce was itching to try their trampoline.

Outside, Luna double-knotted Mateo's shoelaces and tucked a strand of Dulce's hair back into one of her braids.

"You take good care of your brother and sister," said the señora as the children scampered off.

"Thank you," said Luna, though the words sounded less like a compliment and more like an accusation.

"It always falls to the oldest girl, doesn't it?" asked the señora.

Luna cupped a hand over her eyes and stared out at the trampoline. She wasn't sure what the right response was so she said nothing.

"My mother died when I was twelve," the señora continued. "I was the oldest girl too. So I know: the world is a cruel place when you don't have a mother to look out for you anymore."

"My father takes good care of us."

"Perhaps," said Señora Gonzalez. "But he's a man. A good man, I can tell. But still a man."

Luna wanted to defend Papi, but she quickly realized that nothing she said would help her father's situation, so she remained silent. The señora moved on to more standard topics, asking what Luna liked to do in school and how she spent her free time. Luna tried to answer, but with their lives in limbo, even the simplest conversations felt like an effort. Both of them quickly lapsed into silence, and soon the señora went back inside, leaving Luna in charge of the rest of the children.

Dulce began to tire of the trampoline. She was now up on the jungle gym with the boys. She asked them something and then ran over to Luna. "David says there's a Hula-Hoop in the garage. Can you get it?"

"Dulce!" Luna scolded. "This isn't a play date."

"It's okay," Christian shouted. "I told her if she wants to find it in the garage, she can play with it."

"Can you find it for me?" Dulce pleaded. Luna could see her little sister was having a good time, so she agreed to go look.

The three-car garage was around the side of the house. The doors to the garage bays were closed, but there was a side entrance that was unlocked. Luna let herself in and flicked on a light. The Gonzalezes had a car in each bay: a Mercedes sedan, an Escalade, and a Corvette convertible. Papi had told her that Señor Gonzalez owned a chain of car washes. Luna guessed it made sense he would like cars.

Unlike the house, the garage had a certain lived-in quality to it. There were shelves of tools and canisters of paints and solvents. There were baskets full of baseballs and soccer balls and a corner taken up with bicycles and sleds. Luna didn't see a Hula-Hoop.

She wandered around until she spotted a big red hoop hanging from a high hook on the far wall. She stood on tiptoes and tried to nudge it off the hook. Her first attempt barely moved the hoop, but the second one pushed it off the hook and onto the floor. Not just the hoop, unfortunately. Too late, she saw that a carton had been resting on a plank above the hoop. It too fell down, nearly landing on her head.

Magazines, DVDs, and flash drives scattered across the cement floor. Luna prayed she hadn't broken anything. That was all Papi needed right now.

Luna turned the carton right side up and began hastily trying to shove everything back inside. The DVDs and flash drives were unlabeled. The magazines all had women on the cover dressed in their underwear in embarrassing poses. There was no way she could return the carton back to that high shelf. She wasn't tall enough. If she left the box here, someone might think she was snooping.

Luna started to fold down the cardboard flaps, hoping at least to make it appear that the box was never opened. A photograph on top of one of the magazines stopped her.

It was a snapshot of a young Latina, maybe fourteen or fifteen, with long black hair and a curvy body. She was wearing only a bathing suit top and very short bright pink shorts. She was turned away from the camera, hands on her hips, looking back over one shoulder. In this position, her shorts rode up until you could see the crack of her behind, and her butt cheeks stuck out like two loaves of whole-wheat bread. Her face was blank and glazed. Her lips, smeared in bright red lipstick, were pursed ever so slightly. There was a stiffness in her bearing, a masklike quality. The pose was not her own. Luna could see it in her dark eyes, the hint of something sad and pleading. She followed the length of the young woman's sturdy legs to the bare floor and recognized the baskets of baseballs and soccer balls behind her, the same baskets Luna saw in the garage now.

Her neck turned clammy. The garage walls felt like they were closing in. She smelled gasoline and solvents, hot tires and damp wood. Dulce was outside, calling her name, saying they were ready to leave. Luna pushed the box into a corner behind a pogo stick and sprinted out of the garage. She was the first one in the car. She lied and told Dulce she never found the Hula-Hoop. She'd never tell her what she did find. She'd never tell anyone. But she couldn't forget, either. When Luna looked in the mirror, there was no mistaking.

That girl looked an awful lot like her.

Chapter 11

Vega had hoped to locate Dominga Flores while it was still light out. But he ended up spending the rest of the afternoon chasing down a witness in another case involving two teenage boys nicknamed Flaco and Lil and a girl named Ruby, who thought she liked Flaco, then thought she liked Lil. Now Lil was dead, Flaco was in jail, charged with his murder, and Ruby was pregnant by a different boy altogether. Hormones and handguns. Three-quarters of Vega's caseload was made up of variants on this.

He flicked on his high beams and studied the navigation system on his dashboard computer one more time. This was supposed to be Barnes Lane. There were no street signs to mark it—just stone walls and woods and pinpricks of light behind electronic gates. His suspension told him he'd left asphalt behind at least a quarter mile back. He'd already had two close calls with kamikaze deer. He wished he'd thought to use the latrine before he'd left his office. He could feel a gallon of coffee sloshing around inside of him, and he didn't dare relieve himself by the side of the road. That was all he needed—to have one of Wickford's finest catching him pissing on some Fortune 500 CEO's front lawn. He'd never live it down.

Vega had spent his teenage years just twenty minutes

west of here, but he could count on one hand the number of times he'd done more than drive through Wickford, with its whitewashed storefronts and Revolutionary Era churches. Lake Holly and Wickford were almost like different countries. Lake Holly was Little League and burgers on the grill. Wickford was horse farms and sushi by the pool. When Vega and Wendy were married, she took him to a few parties out this way. The women were all blond and leggy with anorexic builds and vampire smiles. Their husbands did exotic things with money that Vega, even with his accounting degree, couldn't understand. They all golfed and played tennis and discussed the turbos on their Saabs and the titanium on their bikes. Wendy's second husband, Alan, was originally from Wickford. And a cycling fanatic. It figured.

Vega was almost ready to double back when his GPS indicated that the two stone pillars he was parked beside were the entrance to 17 Barnes Lane. A six-foot-high slatted fence enclosed the property. Through the wrought-iron gate, he saw a copse of tall pines. Up the hill from the pines, Vega saw the upper floors of a stately Tudor. Lights glowed amber through prisms of glass.

He turned down his police radio and buzzed the security intercom on a console by the front gate. A gust of wind scattered dead leaves across the Belgian block driveway. There was a total absence of other noise here in the woods. No highway noise. No road noise. Not even a jet plane overhead.

Then Vega did hear a sound. A pitter-patter like someone was throwing uncooked rice kernels across the driveway. Not rice. Nails. Animal nails.

A slash of moonlight picked up something sleek and muscular in the pines on the other side of the gate. He counted two dark forms. Pointed ears. Long snouts. A metallic glint in their ink-colored eyes.

Doberman pinschers.

They hung back in the trees, pacing like sentries. Every now and then their mouths opened and Vega saw a flash of canines. He was glad he was in his unmarked Impala with a six-foot-high gate between them.

A man's voice answered the intercom.

"If it's a package, just leave it by the entrance."

"Sir? This is Detective James Vega with the county police. I'm looking for a Mrs. Violet Davies."

"What's this about?"

"If I can speak to Mrs. Davies, I'd be happy to explain."

"That's my mother. She's resting at the moment."

"Then perhaps I can come up and speak to you."

"Concerning?"

"A routine matter. Having to do with some unclaimed property." That was true enough. Vega had a photo book in his car that Karen Reilly had made for Dominga. Dominga had yet to claim it. But Vega decided to leave Dominga's name out of it for the moment. It would be easier to ask about her face-to-face.

"This isn't a good time."

"Sir?" Vega's voice got flat and steely. His cop voice. "It will only take a few minutes." Vega had no legal grounds to compel the man to talk to him, but the threat of authority was usually enough. Cops banked on it.

"Make it quick. I have things to do."

Vega eyed the Dobermans pacing in the trees. "I'm going to have to ask you to restrain your dogs while I'm on the premises."

"Drive up to the circle and park. I'll put them in their pen when you get here."

"Thank you." Vega opened his glove compartment and retrieved some dog treats and a can of pepper spray. He tucked the treats in one pocket and the pepper spray in the other. Using lethal force on people's pets was a big no-no these days. Not that Vega ever wanted to shoot an animal anyway. But now especially, dog owners sued, and in places like Wickford they sued big. Vega was on the sergeant's list. He'd chance a bite before he'd chance doing something that would get him passed over for a promotion.

The gates slowly opened, and Vega nosed the Impala up the driveway toward a stone and stucco Tudor, probably built in the 1920s, with a slate tile roof and windows set with diamond panes of leaded glass. Beyond the glow, the lawn turned velvety, trailing off into a smudge print of woods. Vega followed the semicircle of driveway and parked in front of a three-car attached garage next to a dark green Land Rover with a dog cage in the rear compartment.

The two Dobermans raced after Vega's car and leapt at its doors, their nails clawing at the paint as they pressed their muzzles to the glass. Vega reminded himself that he had several thousand pounds of steel between him and these creatures. But still. Even the smears on the windows from their saliva felt terrifying.

A side door to the house opened and a bearded white man with glasses whistled for the dogs. They broke contact with Vega's car and ran inside. Vega counted to ten before he moved a muscle. He wasn't taking any chances. He even clipped his heavy-duty flashlight to his belt before he got out of the car. That flashlight was heavy enough to coldcock a suspect. It could certainly do the same to a dog. He left the picture book Karen Reilly had given him behind on the passenger seat. He wasn't sure how he was going to play that yet.

He walked up to the front door and rang the bell, expecting the bearded white man again. Instead, a young Latina opened the door and stood before him, head slightly bent, eyes on the floor. Vega recognized her from the picture book: *Dominga*. She had the same round face and high cheekbones, the same long, glossy black hair pulled into a ponytail at the nape of her neck. Except in all of Karen Reilly's pictures, she was smiling.

"Señorita Flores?"

Dominga lifted her head and tried to place his face. "I don't know you," she whispered through chapped lips. She was wearing a loose, flowery dress, so it was hard to tell whether or not she'd had the baby. There was no baby in sight. Not even the sound of a baby.

"May I come in?"

Dominga looked over her shoulder. She was standing in a foyer paneled in rich dark beadboard. In the corner, Vega could make out the balustrade of a sweeping staircase. Somber portraits hung on the walls, the people pasty-faced and constipated-looking. Through an archway, Vega could see what appeared to be a living room. There were heavy brocade couches, a black baby grand piano, and a bay window with a stained-glass crest of a lion in the center.

The bearded man walked up behind Dominga, towering over her compact frame. Vega guessed him to be in his early fifties. He had small blue eyes behind black-framed glasses and one of those stringy comb-overs that made him look like someone had parked a loom on his head. He was thin except for a slight paunch beneath his dark blue wool sweater. He looked like a college professor. Dominga broke eye contact with Vega the moment the man entered the foyer.

"What's this all about?" he demanded.

"Just a routine matter, sir. Is it Mr. Davies?"

"Yes."

"And do you live at this address?"

Davies hesitated. Vega wondered why. "On and off," he said after a moment.

"As I said on the intercom, Mr. Davies, the county police recently recovered some property. We have reason to believe it belonged to your mother's housekeeper here."

"*Stolen* property?"

"No, sir. Nothing of the sort." A cop showing up and demanding to speak to a housekeeper could easily get that housekeeper fired. Vega didn't want to cost Dominga her job if she was an innocent in all of this. "This is just unclaimed property that we believe might belong to Ms. Flores. I have it in my car if she can come out and take a look."

"Both of us will come."

"No. That's not necessary." Vega wondered if this guy was always so overbearing. "It will just take a minute." Vega turned to Dominga. "You'll need a coat. It's cold outside."

Dominga spoke to the floor. "I don't have a coat."

Vega noticed her feet for the first time. She was wearing rubber beach sandals. His grandmother's *chancletas*. In late October. In the photo book, there were shots of Dominga playing with the children in the snow. She had a coat then. And winter boots. Didn't this young woman ever venture outdoors anymore?

"Do you have a coat she can borrow?" Vega asked Davies.

"Can't you just bring whatever it is inside?"

"I'm afraid that's impossible." Whatever was going on here, he was unlikely to get a clear picture of it with Davies around.

Davies rummaged through a closet in the foyer until he found a shapeless brown tweed coat with a velvet collar. It had a Bergdorf Goodman label inside and looked at least twenty years out of date. Violet Davies's coat, no doubt. Davies also managed to dig up a pair of sensible black calf-length rubber boots. They were too large for Dominga's tiny feet, but she wasn't walking far.

"You're just going to your car, correct?" he asked Vega.

"Yessir. She'll be back in a few minutes."

Dominga shuffled out of the house with her head down and her hands tucked under her arms. She didn't speak. Davies remained on the doorstep, eyeing them.

"Does he always watch you this closely?" Vega asked her in Spanish. He was betting Davies didn't speak more than a few words.

Dominga mumbled into the velvet collar. "*No quiero problemas.*" I don't want any trouble.

"Trouble from him?" Vega continued in Spanish. "Or trouble from me?"

She licked her chapped lips. "Trouble from anyone."

Vega nodded to her belly. "Have you had your baby, miss?"

"Yes."

"Boy? Girl?"

"A boy."

"When?"

She looked confused. "Almost three weeks ago."

"Where is he?"

"Upstairs. Sleeping."

"Where did you give birth to him?"

"Here."

"In the house?"

Dominga looked over her shoulder. Davies was still standing at the doorway watching them, arms folded across his chest.

"Yes."

"By yourself?"

"No."

"Who helped you?"

"A woman."

"You mean a midwife?"

"Yes, a midwife."

"What was her name?"

Dominga hesitated. "I don't know."

"Was she Spanish?"

"Yes. Spanish."

Vega put on his gloves. The temperature had dropped. He could feel the cold bite right through his jacket and khaki slacks. "Why didn't you go to the hospital?"

Dominga shook her head and looked down again. She didn't answer.

"I'm asking, miss, if you or your baby have seen a doctor?"

"No."

"No, you don't want to? Or no, he won't let you?" Vega jerked his head in Davies's direction. Davies called from the step again.

"How long is this going to take, Detective?"

Dominga shot a nervous glance at the step.

"Sir? The less you interrupt, the faster it will go." Vega used his command voice. That usually kept civilians at bay. He turned back to Dominga.

"Are you telling me that you aren't free to leave?"

Dominga met his eyes. She looked nothing like the Dominga in Karen Reilly's photographs. The skin beneath her eyes was bruised-looking from lack of sleep. Her face was gaunt. She started to tear up. "Please, officer. I can't lose my job. I don't want to get into any trouble."

Coño! This was not a situation he wanted to get into tonight, either. And yet something was very wrong in this house. Even if Dominga was telling the truth and her baby was upstairs, not dead in the woods, there was still the matter of her cowed and frightened demeanor and the fact that mother and child had never seen a doctor or received proper medical attention.

First things first, however: he had to make sure the child was alive.

"Miss—if we go back into the house right now and I ask you to show me your baby, can you?"

"Of course."

"His name is—?"

"Emilio."

Vega popped the Impala's trunk and lifted the hood to shield him and Dominga from Davies's gaze.

"I need you to pretend you're looking at some items in the trunk of my car," he instructed her.

"Why?"

"Because I want to give you something. And I don't want your employer watching us while I do it."

He walked to the passenger seat and grabbed the envelope with Karen Reilly's photo book. Then he walked back to the trunk and slipped it into Dominga's hands.

"What's this?" she asked.

"Open it."

She undid the clasp and slid out the contents. Her mouth formed a little "oh" at the picture on the cover. It was a summer shot of Dominga and the Reilly children at what looked like a playground. All of them were in sleeveless tops, and they were seated at the bottom of a slide. The baby was in Dominga's lap with an oversized sunhat on his head. The toddler boy was curled by her side running a Matchbox car across her thigh, and the girl was hugging her from behind, her mouth stained red, probably from a cherry snow cone. All of them were tanned and smiling. Dominga pushed a palm against her eyes and clutched the book to her chest as if it were the children themselves.

"Oh God. I miss them. Mr. Neil won't let me call."

At the sound of his name, Neil Davies started walking over. "Can she go now, Detective? She really needs to get back to work."

Vega stepped away from the trunk and stuck out his hand. "Sir? I will *not* ask again. If you cannot be patient, then I suggest you wait inside."

Davies huffed his way across the driveway and slammed the door. When Vega returned to the trunk, he found Dominga shaking—from fear or cold, he couldn't tell.

"Easy," said Vega. "He can't hurt you while you're with me." He stared back at the house. "Karen Reilly told me Mrs. Davies lived alone."

"When I first came, yes. But then after a few days, Mr. Neil came with the dogs. He told me he was here to help his mother until after I had the baby. But then—he just stayed." She swallowed hard. "He is not a good man."

"Why is that?"

Dominga flicked her eyes at the doorway.

"He's inside. He can't see you," Vega assured her.

Dominga pushed up the sleeve of her dress beneath the coat. There were bruise marks in various stages of healing up and down her arm.

"Neil Davies did that?"

Dominga nodded.

"Do you have other injuries?"

"On my backside. The back of my legs. Sometimes my face. Anything I do wrong, he hits me. If I don't cook the meal fast enough. If I don't fold his laundry the right way. If the baby cries when he's trying to sleep. One day, to punish me, he made me eat the dogs' food."

"Does he do anything to you sexually?"

She looked down at her feet, embarrassed by the question. "No. But I fear—in time—when I've recovered from

Emilio . . ." She shook her head. "I don't know what to do."

"Has he hurt the baby?"

"No. Not the baby. Or the missus. Only me."

"And he doesn't let you leave the property?"

"No. I leave. I go to the supermarket and the dry cleaners."

"He drives?"

"Sometimes I take a taxi."

"But he makes you leave the baby here?"

"No. I take Emilio with me. I would never leave my baby."

Vega frowned in confusion. "Wait. If he's giving you taxi fare and letting you take your baby, why don't you just leave?"

"And go where? I have no money, no pa—" She suddenly realized who she was talking to. "I cannot get work with a newborn. How can I take care of Emilio?"

"There are agencies that would help you. Karen Reilly would've helped you."

"She told me I had to leave because of my baby. I could not go back and put this burden on her."

"Did you tell anyone about the beatings?"

"No."

"But people must have seen you? Seen your bruises? The midwife, surely."

Dominga shrugged. "People see, but they don't see. You pass gardeners mowing lawns, nannies pushing carriages. You go to a diner and a busboy takes away your dishes—do you really look at their faces? Do you stop to ever wonder what's happening to them? Whether they're well-treated?"

"I suppose not," Vega admitted.

"What could I do? What can I do now?"

A gust of wind bit into Vega. He shivered. Here, on this estate, set off from the world by a six-foot-high fence and a dirt road, how could Dominga not feel trapped? In every direction, the rolling lawn ended in choked woods. At night, under a gauzy wash of moonlight, it looked dark and impenetrable, but Vega was willing to bet it didn't look much more welcoming during the day, either.

"Okay." Vega took a deep breath. "What I want you to do is pretend you're examining something in the trunk of my car. I'll call this into the Wickford Police."

"But they'll call immigration. They'll take my baby!"

"No they won't, miss. You just need to trust me on this."

Vega left Dominga at the trunk and got into his car. He punched the license plate number of the dark green Land Rover next to him into his dashboard computer. The owner came up as Neil Davies with an address in Lower Manhattan.

Vega pulled Davies's driver's license and Social Security number off his motor vehicle records and fed those into the computer, looking for priors. Up came two DUIs over the past six years and a charge two years ago for soliciting sex from a fifteen-year-old on the Internet. The sex charge got plea-bargained to a misdemeanor. But regardless of whether Neil Davies got probation or not, he was still considered a convicted sex offender. Which meant he was required to register with the state sex-offender registry and notify the registry and the police every time he moved. If Neil Davies was living here all these weeks, as Dominga claimed, he was not only looking at charges from assault to unlawful imprisonment, he was looking at immediate jail time for being in violation of his probation.

Vega radioed the county dispatcher that he needed two cars to respond from the Wickford PD: one to sit on the house until a relative or other caretaker could be found to look after Violet Davies, the other to process the arrest of her son. Dominga he would take care of himself. He'd take her statement and drive her and her baby to the hospital to get checked out. After that, Dominga would need a referral to a social services agency to help get her safely settled.

Vega pulled out his cell phone to dial Adele. She was the person he always called for these sorts of placements and referrals. He started dialing her number—

—and stopped.

She wasn't the only person he could call on for a referral. There were other ways to get help for a woman in Dominga's situation. He'd grown too dependent on Adele. That had to change. Starting now. He scrolled down his list of contacts until he came to Jenny Rojas. She was a social worker at the Sisters of Mercy down in Port Carroll. She was reliable. She'd be around to help Dominga as her case moved through the courts.

Adele wouldn't. Not for Dominga. Not for him.

Vega walked back to the trunk of the Impala. "Okay. We're going back to the house. I want you to get the baby and show him to me. Don't tell Davies what you're doing. Let me handle that. Then I want you to gather your things and the baby's things, and once I call for backup, we'll go down to the Wickford police station and you can swear out a complaint—"

"But where will my baby and I go?"

"We'll get you checked out at the hospital, and then I'll put you in touch with someone who can help you, don't worry."

Vega started to walk Dominga to the house. He looked down toward the front gate, half expecting to see the light bars of a couple of Wickford police cruisers ricocheting off the trees. He saw nothing. He listened for the crunch and pop of stones under tires or the squawk of police radios. He heard only the lazy creak of a loose shutter and the slow hiss of a storm door slowly shutting somewhere behind the house. He wondered if that's how things were done here—nothing to alert the neighbors or disturb the cloak of civility.

A bush beside the garage rustled. And then Vega heard a noise that sucked up all the breath in his lungs.

A growl.

Vega took out his flashlight and shined it in the direction of the sound. Staring back at him were two ropy, muscular black shapes with phosphorescent eyes and pointed ears. Their huge jaws opened. Their canine teeth gleamed in the moonlight. A low rumble emanated from their chest cavities. It sounded like distant thunder.

Vega forced himself to breathe and remember his training. *Don't run. Don't show your backside.* His limbs went cold. The night air felt like buckshot to his lungs.

"Get behind me," he ordered Dominga. "I want you to slowly walk around the back of my car and get into the front passenger seat. Can you do that?"

"Yes," she said in a tiny voice.

"Okay. Do it. Now."

Vega reached into his pocket for the dog treats and threw them across the lawn away from the car, hoping the dogs would follow. It was a miscalculation. The dogs had no idea what he'd thrown and didn't follow. Now he was out of dog treats and their white-orbed eyes were locked on Dominga.

"*Carajo, no!*" yelled Vega. His gun was too dangerous to even think of using out here in the dark with Dominga moving around. So he swung his heavy-duty flashlight overhead and stepped closer to the dogs, offering himself as bait. The bigger one lunged for Vega but connected with the casing of his flashlight instead. The dog's teeth latched on tight, and Vega felt ninety pounds of pure muscle trying to wrestle him to the ground.

Sweat poured off Vega's body as he fought to stay on his feet, fought to get a grip on the pepper spray in his pocket.

He aimed it at the animal's eyes and pushed down on the nozzle. A stream of aerosol whooshed from the container. The dog let go of the flashlight, yelping as it retreated across the lawn, where it began sliding its face against the grass. Vega knew that pain. At the police academy, instructors sprayed it in new cadets' eyes so they would never forget the sting. But it was temporary, and more importantly, it was the only way to ensure Dominga's safety. Behind him, his car door slammed. Dominga was safe inside. He breathed a sigh of relief.

The smaller Doberman retreated to a safe distance, where it continued to bark and growl. Vega lowered his pepper spray, convinced he was getting control of the situation. A light flicked on at the side of the house. Davies stuck his head out the door.

"Hey! What did you do to my dogs?"

Vega dropped his flashlight to his side. "Get your dogs secured now! Right now! Where I can see them!"

Out of the corner of his eye, Vega picked up a shadow of movement. A second later, a white-hot pain tore through his left calf muscle. He danced backward with the weight of the second dog on his leg and swung wildly with his flashlight. The dog yelped and ran away. Something warm and sticky began to ooze down his leg and into his sock. Blood.

"Your fucking dog just bit me!" he shouted at Davies. "Get them secured now!"

Where were the Wickford police? Vega was a good twenty minutes from Lake Holly Hospital, with no cop cars in sight. If this stupid dog had pierced an artery, he'd bleed out before help arrived. He pulled out his radio.

"Ten-seventy-eight, ten-eleven," said Vega, giving the police codes for an injured officer and a dog bite incident. "Need an ambulance and animal control dispatched to 17 Barnes Lane."

Vega opened the driver's side door and sat on the seat to examine his leg. His left sock was saturated with blood. His beige khakis were ripped and stained where the dog had bit into his flesh. He was afraid to separate the fabric from his skin. It seemed to be stemming the blood flow at the moment.

"How bad is it?" asked Dominga.

"I'll live," said Vega. He pushed himself to his feet. At least he could still put weight on it. That was a good sign. "We need to get your baby, miss." He limped to the door with Dominga in tow. Davies was waiting for them in the foyer.

"My dogs never bite," said Davies. "You must have done something."

If Vega had a dime for every dog owner who said that. He ignored Davies and spoke to Dominga in Spanish. "Show me your baby."

Dominga disappeared up the stairs. "What did you just say to her?" Davies demanded.

Vega raised a hand for Davies to be silent. He didn't have to be nice anymore. He was on solid legal ground now.

"Time to go, detectiveDetective," said Davies. "You've caused enough trouble for one night."

Vega gave Davies his flat I-don't-give-a-shit gaze. "Does your mother have anyone who stays with her when you aren't here?"

"You mean, besides Dominga?"

"Yes."

"My cousin Laurie. Why?"

Dominga appeared on the landing cradling an infant boy with a tuft of black hair that stood straight up from his scalp, like a miniature Don King. He had the pruney, flattened face and glazed, unfocused eyes of a newborn, but at this distance at least, he looked reasonably healthy. Either way, Dominga wasn't the mother of Baby Mercy.

Vega turned now to Davies and focused his full attention on the man for the first time.

"Turn around, sir. Place your hands on the wall, feet spread apart."

"What? You're arresting me because my dog bit you?"

Vega began patting him down. "Trust me. That's the least of your problems."

Chapter 12

Adele glanced at the clock on the wall of her office. She had forty minutes to make it to Sophia's school for this afternoon's International Day. She would've gladly spent the next two hours with Charlie Gonzalez and Adam Katz exploring every option to fight Manuel Serrano's deportation. But forty minutes would have to do.

"Thank you both for coming today," said Adele as she handed Gonzalez and Katz their coffees and drew a faded blind over a wall of glass. It wouldn't stop the smack and rumble of pool games that clients were playing on the other side, but it would give them the illusion of privacy. "Whatever happens, Manuel and I are both grateful that you are trying to help him." Katz had given up a ton of billable hours for this case, and Gonzalez had a business to run, so their contributions weren't chump change.

Adele took a seat behind her desk. Nearly every available inch of it was covered with stacks of papers. No matter how hard she worked, she never caught up. She blew on her coffee. Gonzalez put his down at his feet and walked over to her outside window. "Do you mind if I open it a little wider?" he asked. "It's warm today, no?"

"Of course. Be my guest."

The sky was the color of cigarette ash and pregnant

with rain that drifted on a damp current of cold air. Gonzalez's request had nothing to do with the temperature,
and they both knew it. Over the summer La Casa had lost
its lease on its old building and relocated to a former fish
market. On humid days like this, the place smelled like a
wharf at low tide. Adele's clients had done their best to
make it nice. They'd cleared debris. They'd scrubbed the
walls and floors with bleach. They'd painted it in cheerful
colors. The smell was still there. Adele imagined it was
better, but maybe she'd just gotten used to it. Steve Schulman would shake his head if he were here and remind her
that this was why she needed to leave La Casa. She'd developed a tolerance for low expectations.

"So," said Katz, opening his briefcase and balancing it
on his lap. There was nowhere else to put it. "The good
news is that we've gotten the Board of Immigration Appeals to agree to consider a review of the case."

"Adam, that's wonderful!" said Adele. The Board of
Immigration Appeals was the highest federal body for immigration matters in the country and the one court that
could halt Serrano's order of removal.

"Not so fast," said Katz. "The bad news is that their
first available review date is three weeks from now—
which will do Serrano absolutely no good."

"But can't you get a continuance on his upcoming court
date this Thursday?"

"Serrano has already had several continuances." There
was a loud crack on the other side of the wall as someone
broke for a new game. The old center had insulation. This
new one had nothing. It was like trying to concentrate inside a tin of marbles. Katz moved his chair closer to
Adele's desk and tried to ignore the noise. "I didn't realize
he'd had those continuances when I first looked at the file.
The feds won't delay him any longer—not unless some
judge on the board of appeals intercedes on his behalf."

"Can we get someone to intercede?" Adele bounced a look from Gonzalez to Katz. They both shifted uncomfortably in their seats. They all knew what Adele was asking: *can Steve Schulman call in some favors?*

Gonzalez put a thick-knuckled hand on the knee of his dress slacks. He was a broad, burly man, short in stature, with a weathered face and dark, hooded eyes. If not for his expensive-looking gold watch and the cut of his white dress shirt, he could have passed for one of his car wash employees.

"This is not something Steve can do right before an election," said Gonzalez. "He would be helping *one* man—maybe. But it might be at the expense of many."

"But Steve wouldn't be asking for favors from politicians or supporters," said Adele. "He'd just be talking to a few judges at the Board of Immigration Appeals. He wouldn't even be asking them to rule in favor of Manuel, only to speed up a consideration of his case."

"Adele." It was Katz's turn to speak now. "If Steve goes shopping like that, it's bound to get back to John Sawyer's people. The Republicans would have a field day with this. It has all the appearances of pulling strings."

"A judge is going to tattle to Sawyer's people?"

"One sympathetic judge—maybe not," said Katz. "But Steve would have to shop it around, and that could turn out badly."

Adele sat back in her chair and offered up a few more suggestions. One by one, Katz or Gonzalez shot them down. The men had done their homework. And Katz knew far more about immigration law than Adele did. After a few more attempts at a resolution, Adele gave up. "So it sounds as if there's nothing anyone can do."

"*Nothing* is a big word." It was Gonzalez who spoke now. He had a soft voice. Adele had to lean in over the noise from the pool tables to hear him.

"The problem, as I see it, has two parts." Gonzalez tended to speak slowly and consider his words—a good quality in business and politics, both of which he was very savvy in. But Adele couldn't help looking at the clock. The meeting had gone on longer than she'd anticipated. Sophia would be furious if she were late to International Day. Sophia had volunteered her to represent Ecuador. Adele's original idea had been to hand out chocolate, a major Ecuadorian export. Nobody told her until yesterday that Lake Holly Elementary was a "nut-free zone," so nut-tainted foods like chocolate were forbidden on school grounds. Instead, Adele was up until two this morning putting together a Power-Point presentation on the Galapagos Islands, the one place in Ecuador she knew nothing about. If Adele showed up late today after the chocolate fiasco, Sophia would probably disown her.

Gonzalez held up a finger, oblivious to Adele's clock-watching. Being a man, he would never understand the tyranny a nine-year-old could exert on her divorced, guilt-ridden mother. "One, Serrano is afraid that if he leaves the U.S., he will never be able to return. That is a risk, yes. But if Steve wins the election, we may be able to solve that in time."

"Okay," said Adele.

"His other problem," said Gonzalez, "is his three children. If Serrano is deported, the children are going to have to move into his cousins' apartment in Queens. I understand it's a small two-bedroom apartment and the cousin already lives there with his wife and three small children, so there is very little room."

"Yes," said Adele. "I've asked around Lake Holly, and no one is able to take in all three children for an indefinite period of time, especially since Manuel may not be able to support them adequately from that distance."

"That is no longer a problem," said Gonzalez. "I have

found a family in Lake Holly who is willing to take in all three children for as long as is necessary and support them until Serrano can return."

"You have? Oh my goodness, that's wonderful," said Adele. "I'm forever in your debt. Who's the family?"

Gonzalez tented his fingers beneath his square chin and shook his head. "I cannot reveal their name until I've spoken with Serrano about the offer and he has accepted. It would be wrong to presume before asking, no?"

"Of course," Adele agreed. "You should ask Manuel first. And maybe it won't come to that."

Katz and Gonzalez traded glances. Today was Tuesday. Serrano was going before a judge in less than forty-eight hours. Adele was sticking her head in the sand if she thought Serrano had a prayer of staying.

Katz gathered up his papers and rose from his chair. Gonzalez followed suit. The men had other business to attend to. Adele knew in her heart that nothing more could be done. And besides, she would be late to Sophia's school if she delayed any longer.

"Thank you both so much," she said. She grabbed her purse and offered to walk the men out. If she left with them, she might still be able to make it to Sophia's school on schedule. For once, things were falling into place.

She'd spoken too soon.

By the tiny front office stood two Latinas, both in their mid-twenties. One was totally Americanized: blond streaks in her dark hair, eyeliner, a knit skirt, and leggings stuffed into high leather boots. Adele recognized her from the few times they'd met at conferences and symposiums. She was a social worker for the Sisters of Mercy over in Adele's hometown of Port Carroll in the southern part of the county. Jenny something.

The woman next to her appeared to be a client. She was cradling a newborn and was dressed far more down-market: a pair of pink sweatpants and a sweatshirt. Off-brand sneakers. No makeup. Her hair pulled back carelessly into a ponytail. By her feet sat a lumpy diaper bag with Winnie the Pooh emblazoned across it. Her eyes followed Adele as Adele walked toward the front door. There was a silent plea in them.

Oh God. Not now.

"Hola, Adele! Cómo estás?" Jenny smiled as if Adele had been expecting her. Gonzalez and Katz nodded but kept walking. Adele saw her chances of escape narrowing by the minute. But she couldn't ignore the woman. Jenny—

Rojas. The name came to her in the same minute the baby began to fuss.

"I was wondering if I could have a moment of your time?" asked Jenny in Spanish.

"Could we do it tomorrow perhaps? I have to be at my daughter's school."

The baby fussed more loudly. "My client really needs your help now, Adele. You're the only one who can give it to her."

"What's the matter?"

Jenny switched to English, probably to limit the number of eavesdroppers. "She lived in Lake Holly until six weeks ago. Since then, she's undergone a pretty serious trauma. A criminal trauma. The police rescued her and her baby last night and assigned her care to my agency down in Port Carroll. But all her connections are here in Lake Holly. I felt I should see you personally about this. I thought maybe you could help. But if you can't right now—"

The baby began to holler, clearly hungry. The mother began to sob. *Ay caray!* This wasn't happening. Adele checked her watch. She was now officially late.

"Okay. Look. How about we do this?" Adele nodded to the mother and switched to Spanish. "What is your name, señora?"

"Dominga."

"Dominga? How about you and Jenny head back to my

office. It's past the pool tables on the right. You can breast-
feed your baby there. The shades are drawn. You'll have
total privacy. I'll send my assistant, Ramona, to get the ba-
sics about your situation, and I'll be back as soon as I
can."

"Gracias," both women replied.

Adele turned toward the front door. She was going to
have to walk a tightrope this afternoon to balance all her
obligations. Why hadn't the police just sent this woman to
her in the first place? Everyone in Lake Holly and the surrounding towns knew Adele was the go-to person for this
kind of thing.

"Hey Jenny?" asked Adele. "Who referred Dominga to
you? It wasn't a Lake Holly police officer, was it?"

"No. It was the detective who rescued her last night.
He's from the county police, I believe."

Adele stood very still. She felt as if she were watching
herself from a great distance. "You don't happen to remember his name, do you?"

"I have his card somewhere. He's Puerto Rican. Nice
build. Good-looking—"

"Vega? James Vega?"

"Yeah. That's him. He didn't call you on this?"

He didn't call her on anything anymore, it seemed.

Chapter 13

"So, you guys—you're like *CSI?* The TV show?"

Jimmy Vega tried to look interested in the student standing before him with a North Face backpack slung over one shoulder. He was all of nineteen, bored and entitled-looking, with a pierced nose, orange-dyed hair, and a skateboard under one arm. He was interchangeable with half the community college's student body milling about the campus on Career Day.

"I'm a homicide detective," Vega explained to the kid. "I personally don't handle the processing of evidence like the people in *CSI.* But we have an excellent forensics unit that does. We also have one of the leading digital evidence labs in the country."

Vega eased himself into a folding chair behind a table with county police recruitment flyers and refrigerator magnets fanned across it and tried not to look as pissed as he felt about Captain Waring volunteering him for this assignment. Vega wondered if it had anything to do with that time back in September when a couple of the uniforms put up the new *Picture Yourself Here* county recruitment posters above the men's room urinals and Vega laughed about it at the morning meeting. Well, he wasn't laughing anymore.

The kid before him scratched at a straggle of chin hairs

that were probably meant to pass for a beard. His backpack looked big enough to transport a bong. Vega was being unfair, he knew. But with Joy here now, he saw the campus through a father's eyes.

"Your department examines digital evidence?" asked the kid.

"That's right."

"So you guys—you, like, snoop on people's computers and stuff?"

"We only snoop on the bad guys."

"So, like, how do you know if someone's a bad guy?"

"The police have to show probable cause and then go before a judge to get a warrant."

"But you have to snoop to, like, know all that, don't you? So it's, like, you're invading someone's privacy to prove you have the right to invade their privacy."

Carajo! Vega didn't need this kind of grief this afternoon. His left calf throbbed from the five stitches he'd had to get last night in the emergency room after that damn dog bit him. He was tired from all the paperwork he'd had to do this morning, from writing up Dominga Flores's statement to filing forms to increase the size of the DNA dragnet for the mother of Baby Mercy. They were no closer to finding her or Zambo. He hadn't even seen Joy yet today and she *went* to this school.

He grabbed a promotional magnet off the table and held it out to the kid. "Why don't you take one of these and go visit the Greenpeace booth, huh?"

The magnet read: *Stay alive! Don't text and drive!* The exclamation points were a little over the top in Vega's opinion. Like being yelled at before you did anything. He knew from experience that this was not a good position to take with teenagers.

The kid turned up his lip and reared back like Vega was proffering a pair of used athletic socks. "Don't need a magnet. Keep it." He dropped his skateboard to the sidewalk and flipped it right side up with his sneaker. Then he pushed off. "Fascist," he mumbled as he rolled into the crowd.

Fascist? He was a fascist? He wished the stoners in his old garage band, Straight Money, could hear that. Or his *corillo*—his childhood friends—back in the South Bronx. When did he become a poster boy for all the things he used to distrust? Eighteen months ago, he was still walking around undercover with a diamond chip in his ear, a five o'clock shadow, and the nervous hustle of a narc who just hoped his fellow officers knew enough not to fire on him. Now he wore sports jackets with dark blue polo shirts and laughed too loud in the presence of other cops. Inside, he felt the same.

Some things he got right—like putting that creep Neil Davies out of commission last night and getting Dominga Flores and her baby the help they needed.

Some things he didn't. He could no longer close his eyes without seeing that patch of bright yellow maple leaves and feeling the leaden weight of what he'd done. He still had those pictures of Mercy on his iPhone. He couldn't bring himself to delete them even though his guys in crime scene had taken more evidence photos than any of them would need.

Vega texted Joy again. He wondered if she'd gotten hung up at a tutoring gig. He'd been here for over an hour and hadn't seen her yet. She hadn't even returned any of his texts. In forty-five minutes, all the companies and agencies would be closing down the fair. And not a minute too soon. The forecast called for rain. It had held off most of the afternoon, but the sky now looked like it had been shaded in with a pencil. A strong breeze billowed the pop-up tents lining the quad. Vega massaged his calf. He wanted to go home and put his feet up.

He propped his leg as best he could and stared out at the throngs of students milling about the quad. He'd been to this campus many times over the years as a police officer for training and routine callouts. It was part of the county police's response area. He wished it were prettier. It backed up to a low-rent shopping center off a four-lane highway. Even now, surrounded by a curtain of orange and gold trees that hid the shopping center, the Band-Aid-colored buildings looked like giant shoe boxes. Their glass entrance doors were pockmarked with dozens of faded flyers for concerts and fund-raisers, chemistry tutors and roommates. A sculpture in the middle of the quad looked like a collision between a shopping cart and the innards of a '57 Chevy. Add in the collective tattoo markings and piercings of the student body and the whole scene rivaled a Burning Man Festival. Vega had hoped for a more prestigious start for Joy—something better than the commuter experience he'd had—but she seemed happy here at least. All things considered, Vega couldn't complain.

The career fair attracted plenty of employers at least, from major corporations to various government agencies and nonprofits. The booth organized by the New York State Police in particular had attracted a pretty big crowd all afternoon. Vega could see why. A female trooper had brought along a big tawny German shepherd to show off the dog's search-and-rescue skills. Here was Vega, trying to get students interested in the joys of forensic accounting and the state police had brought a dog. Game over.

"Hey, stranger."

Vega had been so focused on finding Joy that he didn't see Adele until she was standing in front of him.

"What are you doing here?" His words came out sharper than he'd intended. He could never be neutral with her. He just hoped she wouldn't pull that "let's be friends" crap when she ditched him. His heart was too bound up with hers not to be scarred by any attempt to cut it away.

"I called your office. They said you were instructing coeds on the joys of police work."

"Who said that?"

"Teddy Dolan. Actually he said you were on punishment detail for illegal possession of a sense of humor."

"Huh. You got that right."

He wished some student would come by right now and ask a bunch of dopey questions. He'd even settle for Mr. Fascist again. Anything to divert his attention. He supposed that's what happened when two people built up a layer of unspoken resentment between them. It had been the same with him and Wendy at the end. He jerked a thumb across the quad at the female trooper and the shepherd. The dog had sad puppy eyes and a tongue like bubble gum that lolled to one side. It looked as eager as a new cadet.

"Goddamn ham," said Vega. "Now everybody's gonna want to work K-9."

"You should bring horses next time."

"I would—if we had 'em. The department sold them off four years ago in the budget cutbacks. Only the state police have dog and pony shows now."

"You don't have anything fun."

"I'll bring that up at the next meeting. Should be good for another punishment detail."

Adele played with one of the magnets on the table. Vega had managed to give very few away. They were black and white with exclamation points. What did his department expect?

"Sophia's going to be at Peter's this evening," said Adele. "Are you free for dinner?"

He couldn't handle a big emotional talk right now—not with his workload and sore leg.

"I can't, Adele. Not tonight."

"Are you having dinner with Joy?"

"Dunno." Was he? With Joy, he never knew.

Vega straightened his left leg to take some pressure off of it and looked across the quad to the state police booth.

The female trooper was hiding a package inside a box for the dog to find. It was like a giant three-card monte game. That's when he saw her. She was standing near the front of the demonstration dressed in that same shimmering leopard-print shirt jacket. It was too flimsy for the weather and almost made him long for that gaudy Pepto-Bismol pink one she owned, if only because it was a little warmer. She looked over her shoulder, and their eyes met. She lifted an arm full of bangles and gave her father a wave. Vega waved back. Okay, so he wasn't the center of her universe. But at least she knew he was here. At least she seemed happy about it.

"How bad is it?" asked Adele.

"Huh?"

"Your leg. I understand you got bitten by a dog last night."

"Who told you? Dolan?"

"No. It's not important who told me. Why didn't you call me from the emergency room?"

Vega shrugged. "It was late. You couldn't have come anyway. You have Sophia."

"I'd still want to know. I *always* want to know."

He folded his arms across his chest and kept his gaze on the dog demonstration.

"Jimmy? What's going on? You don't call. You don't tell me you got hurt on the job. You do this heroic thing—rescue a mother and her baby—and don't share it with me. You don't even send her to me afterward. You send her to Jenny Rojas, who brought her to me anyway."

"Aha!" He unfolded his arms and looked at her for the first time. He could do in anger what he could no longer do in love. "So that's what this is about. You're pissed that I didn't bring Dominga to you."

"I'm not *pissed*. I'm hurt. And confused."

"Well, that makes two of us."

Two students started to approach his table, then caught

the vibe and thought better of it. He was in a very public place having a very private argument. *Puñeta!* He didn't want this. But the juices were flowing and he felt powerless to stop them.

"I took Dominga to Jenny Rojas because I know in a month Jenny will still be here to stay on top of her situation. Can you say that? *Can* you?"

Adele blinked at him. A slow dawning worked through the muscles of her face.

"I thought not," said Vega. He slumped in his chair. "You want to go wine and dine the power brokers in D.C., be my guest, Adele. But you can't have it both ways. I didn't send Dominga to Jenny out of spite. I sent her there for her own good. Because I know what Jenny doesn't."

There. He'd said it. It was out. The helium balloon inside of him sputtered and died. You can only fight when there's something still at stake. And he'd just told her there wasn't. He knew. It was over.

She was quiet for a long moment.

"How did you find out?" she asked finally.

"Like you say, it's not important who told me."

"Nothing's been decided."

"Right," he said without conviction. "That's why you included me in the whole decision-making process."

"If I had, you'd have told me not to go."

"Damn straight, I would've. You're needed here. Your clients need you."

Vega watched Joy maneuvering through the crowd, shouldering a backpack as she ran across the quad toward his booth.

"And what about you, Jimmy? Do *you* need me?" Adele asked so softly, neither of them was sure she'd asked it at all.

Joy ran up to his table before he could answer. She wasn't wearing her jacket anymore, only a short-sleeved sweater and paper-thin bleached jeans tucked into high, rust-colored leather boots with stiletto heels. His ex-wife's, if he'd had to guess. She always favored the good stuff.

"Hi, Dad. Hi, Adele," Joy panted. "Can you hide me?"

"*What?*"

"I'm supposed to hide so Daisy, the dog, can't find me."

"Where's your jacket?" asked Vega. There were goose bumps up and down Joy's arms.

"With Trooper Sorenson. Daisy needs my scent in order to track me."

Vega slouched off his sports coat and wrapped it around her.

"Daaad. I'm okay."

"Indulge me." The coat skimmed her thighs. The shoulders stuck out like football pads. She looked like she was five again, playing dress-up. She nodded to Vega's hip holster. "Now everyone can see you're carrying."

"The trooper's carrying, too. What's the big deal?"

"You're my father."

"Didn't know that was a federal offense."

Joy crouched beneath the table and dropped her backpack beside her. "Do you see Daisy?"

"The trooper's letting her out of her crate and putting a harness on her now," said Adele. She was still standing by the table as if frozen in some sort of time warp, their argument unfinished, the heat gone, but not the heartache.

The trooper held Joy's leopard-print jacket under the animal's nose. "*Jowww,*" she said to the dog.

"What's *jowww*?" Vega asked Joy.

"*Jowww* means 'find' in Chinese. The trooper said many handlers give their dogs commands in lesser-known foreign languages. A lot use Czech and Dutch. She chose Chinese. That way, no criminal can ever control the animal."

"Unless he wants to order sweet and sour pork."

The dog's tail was curled tightly. She lowered her head and kept her nose close to the ground, pulling the trooper along by the leash. The dog seemed headed in a straight line for Joy.

"What will Daisy do when she finds me?" asked Joy.

"Usually they're taught to sit at attention and bark," said Vega.

"She won't attack or anything?"

Vega felt the throb in his calf and winced. He hadn't told Joy about getting bitten last night. And this certainly wasn't the time to discuss it. "She won't attack. Not unless the trooper gives the command to bite. But hey, she'll probably want chopsticks and a fortune cookie first."

"Not funny, Dad."

Daisy was halfway to Joy when a gust of wind blew through the quad. The dog stopped in her tracks and lifted her snout in the air. Then she turned in a circle like she was chasing her tail. When she came out of the spin, she began heading north of Joy's location, maneuvering between legs and bicycles and skateboards with such single-minded determination, the trooper had to jog to keep hold of the leash.

"What the—?" said Vega, cupping a hand over his eyes.

"Where does that dog think it's going?" asked Adele.

"What is it?" Joy asked from beneath the table.

Vega was no dog handler, but he'd been around a fair number of police dogs through the years. He'd seen dogs fail to track a scent. He'd seen dogs give up. But he'd never seen a dog so focused and so entirely wrong.

"The dog is heading north," he said. "I haven't been on campus in a while. I thought there was just woods back there."

"Until you hit the shopping center," said Joy. "But there's a fence in between."

Vega expected the trooper to tug on the dog's leash and shove Joy's jacket in the animal's face again. But the trooper continued to let the dog take control. She was either some sort of dog whisperer or she was too embarrassed to admit that her dog had screwed up.

The dog stopped at the far end of the quad and circled again. There was something in the German shepherd's posture that felt like alarm, something eerily human in the way the animal kept doubling back and rechecking herself. None of the students seemed to register the change in the atmosphere. But Vega felt it. Like static electricity. It pricked his skin and revved up his senses like he'd just mainlined a double espresso. It was the same sharp bite he used to feel in uniform when he made a traffic stop that he sensed was going to turn into anything but routine. Daisy was, after all, a search-and-rescue dog. Some SAR dogs are also cadaver dogs. He didn't want to alarm Adele or Joy, but he didn't think this dog was just plain incompetent, either.

"Should I get up?" asked Joy.

"Yeah. All right," said Vega. Dogs have terrible eyesight. If Daisy couldn't smell Joy, she definitely wasn't going to be able to see her at this distance.

"Maybe there are too many students in the quad," Adele suggested. "All those different smells."

"Dogs smell like we see," said Vega. "They don't combine scents. Each one is distinct. That's why you can't wrap cocaine in fabric softener sheets and expect to sneak it past a trained police dog." And Daisy *was* trained, Vega reminded himself. A dog like that was too smart to make such a big mistake. Then again, maybe this wasn't a mistake. Maybe Daisy had a bigger mission in mind.

"Wait here," Vega told both of them. "I want to see what's going on."

He caught up to the trooper and Daisy on a pathway north of the quad. Daisy was pulling hard and fast on her harness and panting as she tracked and then circled, lifting her snout into the air before zeroing in on the pavement again. Swear to God, Vega would kill that dog if all she was following was some kid's discarded meatball hero in a Dumpster behind the shopping center.

"So much for tracking my daughter," Vega huffed as he trotted alongside the trooper. The trooper was young and fair-haired, with the sort of sinewy build and even, unassuming features that separately promised beauty but together added up to bland. "Pioneer stock" was the way Vega might have described her. Of course the uniform didn't help, with its Smokey-the-Bear hat and Gestapo-tailored gray jacket and pants.

"That was your daughter?"

"She's a freshman here."

The trooper flung Joy's leopard-print jacket at him. "Then you might as well take this."

He caught the jacket and kept up his stride.

She regarded Vega from the corner of her eye. "You're welcome to go back to your daughter."

"Think I'll tag along."

"I'm perfectly capable of working my dog."

"Well, *your* dog is in *my* jurisdiction, so you're stuck with me until we figure out whether Daisy's got a bead on something, or she just has a Jones for some shrimp fried rice."

"She *responds* to Chinese, Detective. She doesn't eat it."

"Yeah? Well, maybe next year, the state police can just bring pens like everyone else. In China, she'd be a menu item."

The trooper gave Vega an appalled look but stopped suggesting he stay behind. *Good.* Beyond the path, the campus trailed off into untended woods and thickets of brambles. Clouds swirled overhead like ink stirred into water. The wind picked up. Vega felt the first drops of rain. *Shit.* He didn't even have a jacket on now.

Daisy hopped over a fallen log and into the woods. Vega and the trooper followed. Thick gray stalks of maples and oaks obscured their field of vision. A lot of the leaves back here had already fallen, and the ground was blanketed with moldering acorns. Vega felt the first insistent drops of rain. His calf hurt. The gauze bandage scraped against the fabric of his pants every time he swung his leg.

"We'll be at the shopping center in a minute at this rate," he panted.

"There's a shopping center back here?"

"That's why you need a cop who knows the terrain, Trooper—?"

"Sorenson. Becca Sorenson."

"Jimmy Vega." Vega nodded to the dog's harness. It kept getting snagged on low-lying branches. The sooner they got this over with, the sooner they could take cover before the rain came down in earnest. "Is your dog trained to search off harness?"

"Yes." Sorenson unhooked the animal and shouted, "*Chooo!*" Daisy bounded ahead.

"That a sneeze? Or did you just tell the dog something?"

"*Chooo* is the command to fetch in Chinese."

"A Chinese German shepherd," huffed Vega. "You couldn't have at least taught it German?"

"The dog doesn't know she's a German shepherd," said Sorenson.

"Well, she better know she's a search-and-rescue dog or she's gonna be retired after this."

Thirty feet in front of them, the dog stopped and began pacing back and forth in front of a dark, moss-covered tree limb that was lying across a pile of wet fallen leaves. Vega would have passed right by the spot. It looked identical to the rest of the woods except for the chain-link fence ten feet ahead that had been cut open at the pole and curled back like peeling wallpaper. It was the sort of small-time delinquency that might have gone unnoticed for months, especially with winter closing in. It felt ominous now.

"You see the strip mall?" Vega asked Sorenson. It sat just beyond the fence, an acre of asphalt anchored by a long rectangle of stores with a KFC and a Payless shoe outlet at one end and a Staples office store at the other. Rain darkened the curtain of asphalt surrounding the building and beaded the windows of cars parked in tidy rows close to the stores.

The dog sat in front of the tree limb and barked.

Sorenson hooked the dog back onto her leash. Vega yanked the limb to one side and used his foot to feel around beneath the slick pile of leaves. His shoe brushed against something weighty and solid. He sprang back as if on fire—and he knew. He patted his pockets for a pair of disposable gloves. He always kept a spare pair on him, but they were in his sports coat and his sports coat was wrapped around Joy.

This was awkward.

"Um—Trooper? Do you happen to have an extra pair of gloves on you?"

Sorenson blew out a slow breath of air as she reached on her duty belt and extracted a sealed pair of gloves. "Maybe the state police should bring gloves instead of pens next year, hmmm?"

Vega ignored the dig and slipped into the gloves. Then he squatted down and brushed aside a few of the leaves. Daisy whimpered. Sorenson stroked the shepherd to calm her and fed her a treat.

Vega saw the gray-tinged skin first, followed by a fan of long black hair threaded with bits of leaves and twigs. A woman. No, scratch that. She looked more like a teenager. A Hispanic teenager. She was lying faceup, her body preserved enough for Vega to think she hadn't been here more than a couple of days. She was wearing a pair of baggy gray sweatpants and a black hoodie that was unzipped to reveal a faded yellow T-shirt beneath. There were no obvious gunshot or knife wounds. She could have died of a drug overdose and been covered up by a panicked companion. Or she could be a murder victim. It was impossible to tell at this point. With the breach in the fence, there was no way to even know if she was a student at the college or from somewhere else, via the shopping center.

"I'm going to call this in to my people," said Vega. "Do me a favor? Get campus security on your radio and let them know about this as well. This girl could be a student here. Tell 'em she's Hispanic, maybe five-one, slight build. Maybe someone at the college can identify her—"

"Your daughter can."

"Excuse me?"

"Your daughter can identify her," said Sorenson. "Daisy's a search-and-rescue dog, Detective. She's trained to go after scents she detects on the bait I give her, not look for bodies whenever the urge strikes her. If Daisy tracked us to this body, she did it by picking up the scent on your daughter's jacket."

No. Impossible. Sorenson had to be mistaken. "My daughter's very particular about her clothes," said Vega. "She wouldn't lend them out."

"The victim didn't have to be wearing your daughter's jacket, Detective. Your daughter just had to be in close contact with her."

"You mean"—Vega corrected—"the jacket had to be in close contact with her." That distinction was everything, at least to Vega.

"The jacket. Yes," said Sorenson. She held Vega's gaze for a moment and he looked away. He didn't want to dwell on the implications.

The rain was coming down steadily now, darkening the shoulders of Vega's blue polo shirt. The heat from his jog into the woods had worn off. Sweat congealed on his skin. He shivered, not just from the cold, but from something deeper. He stared at the teenager's body. She was surrounded by a glossy frame of wet orange and yellow leaves. With her

Hispanic features and long black hair, she reminded him of those statues of the Virgin of Guadalupe, the patron saint of Mexico—the ones encircled by golden rays of light.

Vega held Joy's leopard-print jacket away from his body. Its shimmer felt cheesy and tainted suddenly, like it belonged to someone he didn't recognize.

Or worse, someone he used to.

Chapter 14

Joy stared at the head shot on her father's cell phone. "I swear, Daddy, I don't know her. I mean, maybe I passed her on the street somewhere. But honest, I don't know her."

They were sitting in Vega's car, rain drumming hard on the roof, waiting for the crime-scene techs to show up. Joy was hunkered down in Vega's sports coat since her own leopard-print jacket had been bagged as evidence. Vega had sent Adele home without telling her anything except that they'd found a body in the woods. Then Vega called Wendy and told her to cancel Joy's evening tutoring engagements. He didn't explain why. Nor did he elaborate when he ordered Joy into his car. She stopped protesting when he thrust that picture of the dead girl's face at her. He'd hoped Joy would know the girl and have a ready, innocuous explanation for the jacket fiasco. She didn't. That worried him more.

"Think, Joy. *Think*. You were wearing the jacket when I saw you at the hospital on Sunday. When did you last get it cleaned?"

"I don't know. I don't take it to the dry cleaners every week."

"Did you loan it to anyone? Did you leave it behind somewhere?"

"I don't remember."

"Well, you've got to. You've goddamn well got to!"

Vega punched the dashboard and let out a stream of Spanish invectives. Joy started to cry. That made him feel worse. "Chispita," he pleaded, using her childhood nickname, "Little Spark" in Spanish. "Don't you understand? That girl was covered up. Somebody covered her. Even if she just died of a drug overdose, at the very least someone is guilty of failing to get her medical attention and trying to hide her body. She might even have been murdered. We don't know yet. And right now, whatever happened to her, you're the prime suspect."

"But I don't know her!"

"That's not a defense. Better that you *did* know her and could explain the situation. Maybe she was in a class?"

"Not that I remember."

"How about at Dr. Feldman's? Maybe she was one of the participants in his study?"

"It's possible." Joy sighed. "I hang my jacket on a coat tree in the waiting area."

"Okay." Vega felt like he was finally breathing again. He flicked the heater vents to deliver a blast of warm air in his direction. He was going to have to make do tonight with a rain slicker over his short-sleeved polo shirt. He couldn't let Joy go home without a jacket. "That's good. That's a start. I'm going to send this photo over to Dr. Feldman's e-mail right away so we can try to get a positive ID."

Through the fogged-up windows, Vega saw the pulse of red lights in the parking lot. The campus police had cordoned off the woods. A couple of uniformed officers from his department had joined them on site protection. Sorenson had signed out with her dog, her job more or less done except for submitting a statement to the county police. But a whole new army was about to descend. Vega rubbed the sleeve of his vinyl rain slicker against the window to clear it. He made out four vehicles: the county crime-scene van, the medical examiner's van, and two detectives' cars. It was going to be another long night. He needed to change the dressing on his stitches. It would have to wait. He turned to his daughter.

"Listen, I want you to go home and stay home tonight. Don't talk to anybody about this right now. Let's see what Dr. Feldman has to say, okay?"

"Okay." She started to shrug out of her father's sports coat.

"No, Chispita. Take it. You can give it back to me to-morrow."

"But you'll be cold."

"I'll be all right."

"Thanks, Dad." She kissed him. "Thanks for always looking out for me."

"I hope I always can."

Vega watched Joy get into her own car and leave. Then he drew the hood of his rain slicker tight around him and got out of his county police car. He hoped crime scene had brought the extra pair of Tyvek coveralls he'd requested, along with some tents to keep the immediate scene dry and preserve evidence.

He recognized a detective getting out of one of the other county cars. Vega didn't have to see the blond walrus mustache. Or the shaved head. He could pick Detective Teddy Dolan out anywhere by the way he stood, feet spread apart, like the Jolly Green Giant surveying his territory.

"Yo, Teddy," Vega walked over. "You working this one with me tonight?"

"Actually—" Dolan ran a finger back and forth across his mustache. There was something guarded in his eyes. "—Captain Waring—he, uh, he thought maybe you should sit this one out. Go home and rest that leg."

Vega stared at Dolan and watched the big man squirm. Cops were lousy liars with other cops.

"Don't piss on my shoes and tell me it's raining, Teddy."

"What? You need the overtime that badly?" Dolan spread his big, fleshy pink palms.

"This isn't about overtime, and you know it," said Vega. "This is about that state trooper—what's her name—making a call to Captain Waring about my daughter. She's a *dog handler,* man." He wanted to be angry at the trooper. Her and that stupid Chinese-speaking mutt. But the rational side of his brain knew it wasn't personal. If he were in her shoes, he'd have done the same thing.

"Let it go, Jimmy, okay? You can't do anything about it, anyway. The decision's been made from on high. Conflict of interest and all. C'mon man, you don't think I'll watch your back? If there's anything you need to know, I'll tell you."

Vega wiped a wet sleeve across his face. He could taste acid bile at the back of his throat. This couldn't be happening. "It's a jacket, Teddy. A freakin' jacket. It could have been in contact with the victim anywhere. It doesn't mean anything."

"Of course not. I hear ya."

Vega's phone dinged with an e-mail. He cupped a palm over the screen to shield it from the rain and checked his messages. Dolan turned to leave.

"Hold up," said Vega. "This message is from that doctor Joy works with. I asked him if he recognized our Jane Doe. That could be the point of contact."

Vega opened the message: *I'm sorry, Detective. I don't recognize her. She's not one of my clients. I'd know if she were.*

Dolan nodded at the screen. Vega noticed he wasn't quite as reassuring as before.

"Hey, no sweat. I'm sure there's a logical explanation for all of this." He put a paw on the sleeve of Vega's rain slicker. It felt just like the hold Vega put on suspects when he was trying to wear them down. Part paternal. Part threatening.

Dolan gave Vega's arm a quick squeeze and then released him. "Just tell your daughter maybe at some point we can sit down and talk, okay?"

Like hell I will.

Chapter 15

It was dark when Luna woke up. Daylight saving time was still two weeks away.

She wondered where they'd be by then.

The apartment felt drafty and muted, weighted down with cardboard cartons stacked on top of one another where their things used to be. She hustled Dulce and Mateo out of bed and into their clothes for school. She braided Dulce's long, shiny black hair. Above them, feet pounded the creaky floors and water rushed through the pipes. All their neighbors woke up early too. Luna heard the trill of Spanish through the walls drowned out by the scrapes of pots and pans in their own kitchen as Papi prepared breakfast.

It was Wednesday morning. Papi's court date was tomorrow.

Luna, Dulce, and Mateo drifted into their tiny kitchen one by one. Mateo was always last. He hated getting up, but he rose as soon as he smelled onions and peppers frying. These days, the family could afford only hot cornmeal for breakfast. This morning, however, Papi had made omelets. Luna saw him in the kitchen expertly flipping one in a pan. She didn't think he'd cooked at all in Mexico. Cooking was women's work. But he was a good cook now. He put the first omelet, all sizzling and golden brown, on

Dulce's plate and cut it in half for Dulce and Mateo to share. It smelled good. The cheese oozed out of the sides like warm sunshine.

"And now for yours," he said to Luna. "With just a little onion and cheese, the way you like it." He smiled at her, his mustache turning up at the edges just below his prominent cheekbones. He was dressed in a T-shirt and jeans, but he was freshly shaved and showered. Luna wondered if he had another meeting with the lawyers this morning.

He turned his back to his daughter and cracked the eggs. Luna felt a bit like a condemned prisoner facing her last meal. She wanted to savor this moment with her father in the kitchen cooking for her, knowing just how she liked her food—how much salt and hot sauce to add, dicing the onions extra fine, skipping the green peppers.

She had lived with her father every moment of her life save for about ten months when she was a baby and he went to California to find work. They knew all those little things about each other that you could only learn over long periods of time. She knew how he hummed to himself when he thought no one could hear. How he hated the taste of avocados and the smell of peanut butter. His favorite soccer team was Chivas because all their players were Mexican. He danced just like a little kid when they won.

Her father was always the one who chased the monsters out of her room at night when she was small. He worked the factory's graveyard shift when they lived in Queens, but he stayed awake every morning to walk her to school after a boy on their block tried to bully her. He once spent a whole day turning a refrigerator carton into a playhouse for her, complete with doors and shelves. Luna knew he was proud of her. He'd always encouraged her dream of becoming a doctor. And she knew that she was his support too. She was probably the only other person in the world beside Mami who had ever seen him cry.

She couldn't imagine her life without him in it.

Mateo scraped a chair across the floor and slid his body between it and the table. Luna tried to remember whether he or Dulce had a spelling test today. One of them did, she was sure. Then she remembered that she'd left her geometry homework in Dulce's math workbook while she was helping her last night. She walked over to her sister's backpack and began pawing through it.

"What are you doing?" Dulce demanded. "Get out of my backpack!"

"I left my geometry homework in your math book."

"No, you didn't!"

"Yes, I did. Remember? When I was helping you with your addition last night?"

"You took it out. I saw you."

"Where did I put it then?"

"I don't know."

Luna pulled out Dulce's math workbook and rifled through the pages. The homework wasn't there. She shoved Dulce's workbook back into her backpack.

"Hey!" Dulce yelled. "You smushed all my stuff!"

"Luna," Papi said gently. "Eat your omelet. It's getting cold."

Luna didn't listen. She raced into their bedroom. She opened drawers and tossed out their contents. She pulled apart the blankets on her bed. She yanked boxes out of her closet and began ripping open the carefully sealed packing tape. Luna knew she had a solid A in the class. One misplaced worksheet wouldn't change that. But she couldn't stop tearing things apart. She'd packed all those boxes so carefully, and now everything was in one big trash pile on the floor. She stared at the heap—the huge, confusing jumbled heap that represented her life. Her baby pictures. Her school mementos. Pictures of Mami. It was all a mess. She sank to her knees and began to cry.

Papi walked into the room and gathered Luna in his big

strong arms like she was five again. She'd been trying to hold everything in, but she couldn't anymore. She sobbed like someone holding onto a jackhammer. Her whole body shook with it. Dulce and Mateo stared open-mouthed from the doorway. They'd cried often. Luna suspected it scared them that she'd finally succumbed as well.

"Don't cry, Mija," Papi said softly, stroking her hair. "I'm not dead. It's just for a little while. Not forever."

"I don't want you to go," Luna sobbed.

"I know. And I don't want to go." His voice caught and he swallowed hard. He was trying to be strong. She had to be strong too. She took a deep breath and palmed her eyes. Papi knelt down and started helping her put everything back into the boxes. Luna had no idea where her geometry homework had gone. She didn't care.

"Listen," he beckoned Dulce and Mateo next to them on the floor. The black box on his right ankle made a soft thud as it hit the bare wood. "I wanted to tell you this over breakfast. But I will tell you now."

"You're staying?" Mateo piped up hopefully. Papi stared at his hands.

"I wish, Mijo. I pray for that more than anything." He took a deep breath. "But this? This is good news even if it's not the news we hoped for. You will not have to move to Queens. All of you will be able to stay together here in Lake Holly."

Dulce and Mateo looked at Luna. She was the mami now. Her reaction would be their reaction. Luna could tell they were relieved to be staying in Lake Holly. She was relieved too. But it was a muted sort of relief because wherever they were, they wouldn't all be together, and that was the only part that mattered. Still, she tried to act happy. She knew that was what her father wanted.

"That's wonderful, Papi." She forced her voice to sound confident. "Are we going to stay with a family?"

"Yes," he nodded. "A good family. They are willing to

provide for you until I can pay them back." Luna was sure the "payback" arrangement was her father's idea. He'd have never consented otherwise. "You won't have to move schools or change friends." Papi leveled his gaze at Luna. "And you, Mija—you'll be able to apply for the science program this summer and audition for the talent show."

Luna didn't think her father even knew about these things. She'd been trying not to burden him. Dulce probably told. She was such a bigmouth. Still, something warm and pleasing bubbled up inside her chest, a sensation Luna recognized as excitement. She was a teenager again. She could do teenager things. She could gossip with her friends at recess under those big maple trees by the school fence. She could dream. She could hope.

And then Luna felt guilty because of course Papi could do none of these. He'd be two thousand miles away in rural Mexico.

Luna wondered if he'd read her mind. Her father put a hand on her forearm. "It's not forever, Mija. We have friends—important friends now. They will help me come back. You'll see. This is not good-bye. This is—a vacation, yes?"

"Señora Figueroa arranged this?" asked Luna.

"She helped, yes."

"Is the family Spanish?" Luna had no idea why she asked that. She had Spanish friends and non-Spanish friends. She supposed she was searching for comfort and familiarity.

"Yes," said Papi.

"Do they have children?" asked Dulce.

"Yes. Children. And a backyard with a playground—and a trampoline." Her father's eyes twinkled. Mateo guessed right away.

"Is it Alex Gonzalez's family?"

Her father sat back and smiled like he'd just presented them with a wonderful gift.

Dulce got up from the floor and began jumping up and

down. "Yes! Yes! Yes! I'm going to live in a mansion." She was like Papi. She embraced each moment and tried to squeeze as much pleasure from it as possible. Mateo, however, was like Luna—like Mami. He was careful not to judge things too hastily. He offered a cautious smile.

"It will be nice to have someone to kick a ball with." He'd always wished for brothers. Papi had four, all in Mexico.

Luna said nothing. She looked at the floor. She couldn't face her father's searching gaze.

"Luna? How do you feel about this?" he asked softly.

She looked at Dulce's flushed face, all lit up like she'd just won a trip to Disney World. She saw Mateo's cautious yet secretly pleased curl of the lips. And there was her father's eagerness and yearning. What could she say? Her fears were vague and unformed. She had no reason to speak against this decision. Anything she said would only fill her father with worry. That's not what Papi deserved right now.

She forced a smile. "If we stick together, I'm sure we'll be fine until you return."

Luna wondered if those words were for him or for herself.

Chapter 16

Vega arranged to retrieve his sports coat from Joy on campus Wednesday morning before either of them started classes or work. She had foundations of sociology at nine a.m. in Field Hall, a building off the quad with all the charm of a Soviet-era bunker. Vega pushed through the throng of teenagers and followed the under-lit and dingy halls until he came to the right doorway.

When he got there, Joy was standing in the hallway outside her classroom with Teddy Dolan. Dolan had one arm braced against the cement-block wall next to Joy and his feet positioned directly in front. Cop body language, all of it designed to overpower and intimidate. Vega had done the same thing to suspects. There was no mistaking how Dolan perceived his daughter.

"What the—?" Vega called out as he hustled over.

Dolan turned and poured on the Irish charm. "Hey, Jimmy. Just saying hi to your daughter seeing as I'm working on campus right now—"

"Save it for some street mutt." Vega inserted himself between Dolan and Joy. Dolan took a step to one side and opened his arms like a priest about to give a benediction.

"C'mon, Jimmy. I'm gonna have to talk to her at some point—"

"Says who?" Vega backed Dolan against the wall. It made no difference that Dolan was four inches taller and probably sixty pounds heavier. If being a kid in the South Bronx had taught him anything, it was that size only deterred a fight. It didn't necessarily determine the outcome. He pointed a finger at the big man's chest. "You have something to say to Joy, you say it to me first, got that?"

"Hey, man, don't make this adversarial."

"Dad, you're embarrassing me—" Joy tugged on his arm. "—It's okay if he talks to me. I didn't do anything. I told him that already."

Vega knew what every cop knew, what Teddy Dolan was banking on right now: the next best thing to a suspect who admits his guilt is a suspect who swears he's innocent. Life is full of half-truths. The longer you talk, the more likely they are to come out.

"Shut *up!*" Vega snapped at her. Joy looked aghast. Her father never spoke to her that way. But this was like pushing someone out of the path of an oncoming train. You don't have time to be delicate about it.

Vega turned to Dolan. "What happened to watching my back, Teddy? Is the captain leaning on you? 'Cause Joy's only link to this girl is a jacket—a jacket that could have been anywhere."

"It's way more than a jacket at this point." Dolan brushed a finger across his thick blond mustache and rocked back and forth on the balls of his feet. With his shaved pink head and wall of flesh just muscular enough to do some damage, Teddy Dolan looked like every black and Spanish person's nightmare image of a cop—right down to his laser-blue eyes and the Harley Davidson tattoo on his forearm. When Vega first met him, he took Dolan for the sort who might shoot first and ask questions later or take a cheap shot when no one was looking.

But Dolan wasn't like that at all. He never lost his temper during an arrest. He was quick to mediate situations where other guys might try to assert authority. Five years ago, while still in uniform, Dolan rescued two toddlers from a crack house. He and his wife, Cathy, a teacher, became their foster parents. Two years ago, the Dolans finally got to adopt Andre, now six, and Keisha, who was seven. Dolan's cubicle at work was plastered with photos of Andre in his beloved Yankees baseball cap and Keisha in cornrows.

Students were filing into Joy's classroom, scraping chairs across the floor, unloading laptops onto desks. Joy shifted her backpack and looked at the doorway.

"I've got to go," she told them.

"Wait," Vega held an arm in front of Joy, blocking her. He could read the hesitation in Dolan's eyes. Dolan wanted to tell Vega what he knew, but he was afraid to at the same time. Vega decided to lean on him a little.

"C'mon, Teddy—if you know something, spit it out, man. Look, maybe we can straighten this whole thing out, the three of us, right here and now." It was the sort of thing Vega often said to suspects to get them to confess: *Let's straighten this out.* He wasn't sure whether Dolan would take the bait. But he absolutely needed to know what sort of evidence the cops had on his daughter.

Dolan turned to Joy. "You know a quiet place where the three of us can talk?"

"But my class is starting," Joy protested.

"*Ay, puñeta!* Will you forget the class?" said Vega. "*This,* Joy—*this* is what matters right now. Nothing else! You are in no position to bargain with the law."

She got that hooded, sulky look she sometimes got when she thought her father was being heavy-handed with her. Vega didn't care. He meant what he said. Nothing was more important than figuring out who this girl in the woods was and how Joy knew her.

"The cafeteria's usually empty at this hour," Joy muttered. "Kids with morning classes are in them already and everyone else is sleeping."

Vega and Dolan traded looks. *College students.* They would've liked a schedule like that.

Joy was right about the cafeteria. Except for a man mopping the floor and a woman at the register, the place was empty. Vega bought two coffees for him and Dolan and an herbal tea for Joy. They sat at a small table by a large bank of windows overlooking the shopping cart sculpture in the middle of the quad. Dolan parked himself at the small end of the table, and Vega sat cater-corner to him with Joy on the other side. Vega was determined to stay between his daughter and the police at all times.

"So what have you got?" Vega asked Dolan.

Dolan sipped his coffee, made a face, and added more sugar. "I know what we haven't got: an ID for her."

Dolan rolled up his sleeves. Vega could see the red-and-black Harley Davidson eagle tattoo on his forearm. Vega was never into tattoos. He was squeamish about needles. He had a piercing in his left ear that he got back in his early twenties when he still thought he was going to make it as a guitarist. He nearly fainted from that. Joy kept begging for a tattoo. Vega wouldn't allow it. He wondered how long it would be before she did it anyway. For all he knew, she'd done it already.

"She's not a student here," Dolan continued. "She isn't an employee of the shopping center behind the campus. We've run her prints, and she's not showing up on any missing persons' registries. She has no criminal record—"

"Immigration?" asked Vega.

"I checked with ICE," said Dolan. "No matches."

"That would lead me to believe her connection to Joy is accidental."

"I'd say you're right," said Dolan. "Except for this." He pulled out his cell phone and brought up a photo on the screen. He slid the picture in front of Vega and Joy. It was a scan of a credit card receipt from Tony's Pizza, a popular takeout place in Lake Holly. The receipt was for two plain slices and a Snapple. It was dated July 12, a little over three months ago.

"I don't understand," said Vega.

Dolan focused on Joy. "Recognize the receipt?"

Joy blinked at him. Vega noticed her looking a little pale and scared for the first time. "I don't know," she said finally.

"I traced the card last night," said Dolan. "It's your credit card, Joy. Your mother is the cosigner. It wasn't reported stolen. Is it still in your possession?"

Joy opened her backpack and pulled out her wallet. The card was inside. She made a small burbling sound in her throat. "I guess maybe I bought some pizza and a Snapple there in July?" She sounded unsure.

"Somebody at Tony's Pizza knows the girl?" asked Vega.

"Nobody at Tony's Pizza knows the girl," said Dolan. "But that receipt? For food bought on a credit card in your daughter's possession? It was inside a pocket of the black zippered hoodie the victim was wearing last night."

Vega sat up straighter. His fingers tingled with pins and needles. He folded them over each other to try to staunch the sensation. He couldn't meet Dolan's gaze. The implications were clear: Joy knew this girl, at least since mid-July. Joy had bought her pizza, perhaps. And she'd lied to the cops—lied to *him*—about all of it. Dolan had kept them talking long enough for Joy to produce the credit card and admit it hadn't been stolen. Vega had thought he was playing Dolan. But Dolan, it turned out, was playing him. And he'd fallen for it.

Vega took a deep breath and tried to think. He was so deep in thought, he almost missed his daughter's next words.

"What hoodie?"

"The hoodie the girl was wearing when the dog found her yesterday," said Dolan. "Didn't your dad show you a picture of her?"

"He only showed me her face."

Dolan scrolled down his screen and put another image in front of her. "That's her, head to toe."

Joy squinted at the screen. The light was bad. It was raining. She asked, "Do you have any other pictures?"

Dolan clicked through several more close-ups and long shots from every position. Joy pointed to something on one of the pictures. Her fingers were steady. She didn't try to backtrack or qualify her statements the way most suspects did when they were caught out in lies.

"Does that hoodie have a pink lining?" asked Joy. "And black piping around the pockets?"

"What's piping?" asked Dolan.

"Trim. A satiny black trim," said Joy.

Dolan frowned at Vega. Vega shrugged. They were homicide cops, not fashion designers. They noticed blood spatter and bullet holes. "Piping" to them was a hollow piece of steel, very effective in bashing in someone's brains.

Dolan stroked his mustache. "What's it matter whether it's got 'piping,' as you say?"

"Because I used to own a zippered black hoodie with a pink lining and black satin trim on the pockets. My mother asked me to clean out my closets over the summer, and I gave her a bunch of stuff to give to Goodwill, including that hoodie. This sort of looks like the same one. I probably left the pizza receipt in the pocket."

Vega reared back. He saw the implications even before Dolan. He turned to Joy, his pulse racing. "So if you gave the hoodie away and nobody had it cleaned, your scent would still be on it."

"I guess," said Joy.

"So conceivably, you might never have had any contact with this girl. She just happened to be in possession of a hoodie you'd given away."

"That's all I can think of." Joy shrugged.

Dolan placed his palms flat on the table and leaned forward. "I'm not casting aspersions, Joy. You understand? But to make that story stick, you gotta be able to prove your mom gave that hoodie away."

"Well, she'll tell you it's true," said Joy.

"That's a start," said Dolan. But a weak one, as Dolan and Vega both knew. Parents will often lie for their kids. Vega wouldn't, but his ex-wife was another matter. Hell, she'd lied to him often enough.

"What would be better," Dolan continued, "is if your mother can give me a sworn statement to that effect and produce a donation receipt from the particular Goodwill store she donated the stuff to that would allow me to track the probability that what you're telling me is true. Otherwise—you understand—it's just a theory."

Dolan's tactful way of calling Joy a liar.

"*Theory* or not," said Vega, leaning on the word. He wanted Dolan to know he didn't appreciate the insinuation. "It can't hurt to figure out if the hoodie the girl was wearing is the same one Joy's describing."

"Yeah. You're right. Let me call Dr. Gupta. I think her clothes are still over at the ME's office."

Dolan excused himself and walked out of earshot to make the call. Vega laced a hand into Joy's. His was sweaty. Hers was cool. She disengaged.

"You didn't have to be so rude to me earlier, Dad. I told you I didn't know that girl. Do you think I'm lying?"

"Maybe you're protecting someone."

"Is that *your* way of calling me a liar too?"

"No. It's just that—this is a very serious situation, Chispita. I don't think you get that. If I'm being rude, as you say, it's to protect you."

"I can protect myself."

"Famous last words."

A teenager with multiple tattoos and piercings shot past the cafeteria window on a skateboard. Vega nodded at the boy.

"What's with all the tattoos on campus? I see more ink here than at the county jail."

"I know him, Dad. His name's Tosh and he's a pre-med like me."

"Huh. Looks like he's had plenty of meds already."

Joy rolled her eyes. "You are such a cop sometimes." She pulled her phone out of her backpack to check her messages. "I saw Adele with you at the career fair yesterday. Have you patched things up?"

Vega folded his arms across his chest and looked out the window. Just hearing Adele's name made him heartsick all over again. "You were right about the job in D.C.," he said. "She's leaving."

"She told you that?"

"She didn't have to. I can see that's where things are headed."

"So?" Joy shrugged. "What's the big deal? You can't date her long distance?"

"I barely see her as it is!"

"Well, you'll see her even less if you break up."

Vega didn't answer.

"If I got a job offer like that, you'd be encouraging me," Joy pointed out.

"That's different."

"It shouldn't be. If you love her, you should want what's best for her—whatever that is."

Dolan got off the phone and walked back to their table.

There was a deliberateness in his step that Vega couldn't read. He wasn't breaking out the handcuffs, but he wasn't breaking out the champagne, either.

"Well?" asked Vega. "Does the hoodie have a pink lining?"

"It does," said Dolan. "In all likelihood, it's the same one Joy is describing."

"Good." Vega felt like he could breathe again. "Talk to my ex, get a statement, and then you can focus the investigation in a different direction." Vega began to rise from the table. "I gotta get to work."

Dolan put a hand out to stay him. He turned to Joy. "You should probably get back to class. Your dad or I will be in touch if we need anything."

"Okay. Thanks." She kissed her father on the cheek, a surprise. "See you later, Dad." She didn't look worried in the least. *Should she be?* Vega felt like his insides were going through the spin cycle. He waited until Joy had left the cafeteria to speak.

"Spit it out, Teddy. What did Gupta tell you?"

"Some good news and some bad." Dolan sighed like even the good news wasn't all that good. "The teenager— and Gupta says she's definitely a teenager—wasn't murdered. She died of an internal hemorrhage. From a rupture to her uterus in childbirth. She died elsewhere and was moved to that location."

From somewhere just outside the cafeteria, Vega could hear voices and the sound of someone putting change in a vending machine. He understood before Dolan could even get the words out what the bad news was. He understood too that he was going to be part of this case after all. Whether he wanted to or not.

"The bad news," said Dolan, "is that Gupta tested her DNA as part of your dragnet. It came back positive. I think you just found the mother of Baby Mercy."

Chapter 17

Dr. Gupta had Baby Mercy's DNA. She had her mother's DNA. By process of elimination, the police now had a complete DNA profile of the baby's father as well. Unfortunately, the profile didn't match anyone in the police database. So until they could find and question the baby's father, Joy would remain on everyone's radar.

Captain Waring's first instinct was to remove Vega from the Baby Mercy end of the investigation since it was now related to the dead teenager on campus. But Vega pointed out that for another detective to step into the case at this juncture would entail a lot of overtime—perhaps even a handoff to the state police. Waring was loath to assign more overtime and even more loath to hand over jurisdiction. So for the time being at least, Dolan and Vega were working opposite ends of the investigation, with support from Louis Greco and the Lake Holly police in between. For Vega, it felt like waking up a Red Sox and being traded to the Yankees. But at least now he could get his hands on the teenager's autopsy report.

Not that it told him much. Dr. Gupta put the girl's age at between fifteen and seventeen, given that only some of her bones had completely ossified and her wisdom teeth had only started to erupt. She had no tattoos or obvious scars. Her teeth in general were in poor condition, which

Gupta noted would be expected if she grew up in a place that lacked water fluoridation—a situation common in Latin America. She was small in general—just under five feet tall. At death, she weighed only 115 pounds, and that was after having given birth to a full-term baby.

Dolan made up a flyer in English and Spanish listing the dead teenager's height, weight, and approximate age and where her body was found. The flyer also contained front and side photographs of her face—eyes closed—and a description of her clothing. What Dolan didn't disclose was any mention of her pregnancy or that her baby was the one found in Lake Holly. They would leave that to a suspect to reveal. Right now, the key to the whole case was putting a name to this girl. And Vega knew the first place he needed to visit.

The block surrounding La Casa was a lot busier on a Wednesday afternoon than it had been on Sunday morning. The auto body shop was open, hydraulic saws squealing from the dim recesses of the garage. There was a sandwich truck in front of the propane company where several workers in dark blue uniforms were lined up, placing their orders.

Vega parked his unmarked Impala in the lot and walked in. He was instantly greeted with what sounded like a jackhammer coming from the back of the building. The entire place vibrated from it. Ramona, Adele's assistant, poked her head out of the front office.

"What are you doing?" shouted Vega, cupping his ears. "Teaching a course on demolition?" In the front room, a gray-haired volunteer was scribbling an English lesson on a dry-erase board in front of a semicircle of day laborers. Vega wondered how the men could concentrate.

"A couple of clients are installing some bookshelves for Adele in the back room," shouted Ramona. "They have to drill through cement block to do it. She's back there if you want to talk to her."

"Thanks—I think."

Vega found Adele in the back room near the snack bar, directing three men on the installation of a six-foot-high bookshelf that would delineate an area in which children could do their homework after school. She was standing with her back to Vega, wearing a soft, cream-colored blouse over dark tan pants, her bob of silky black hair glistening under the strips of industrial lights. He tapped her on the shoulder. She turned and her face softened at the sight of him. He felt a momentary skip in his heart to know he could still do that to her. She said something. He shook his head. He couldn't hear her over the noise from the drilling.

"Can I talk to you for a moment?" He shouted. He motioned outside. At least they'd be able to hear each other there.

Adele mimed that she needed a jacket from her office. Vega waited, and they both walked into the parking lot. The sun was warm and felt good on their backs, but a stiff breeze fanned the trees on the hillside. Adele wrapped her jacket tightly around her shoulders. Vega nodded to the noise coming from inside.

"Make sure your guys installing those bookshelves don't put too much pressure on the drill bit when they sink those holes."

"But I want the screws to hold in concrete."

"Too much pressure will just pulverize the concrete and plug up the holes," Vega explained. "You'll end up breaking apart the very thing you wanted to hold together."

Adele tucked a strand of hair behind one ear and studied him for a long moment.

"What?" he asked. "I know construction, Adele. That's how it works with concrete."

"That's how it works with people too."

"Huh?"

She turned away. "Forget it." The sandwich truck across

the street was leaving. "You didn't come all the way over here today to tell me how to mount a bookcase."

"No." He could see she was cold. "Wanna sit in my car?"

"I was just about to grab lunch."

"From the truck?" Vega made a face.

"No. I was going to drive over to Claudia's. Her food is much better. Want to join me?"

Vega kept his gaze on the hillside. Yellow crime-scene tape still fluttered like ribbon in a girl's hair. Baby Mercy's death and all its implications rested like a giant minefield between them. He wasn't sure they'd ever be able to breach the divide.

Adele must have read his mind. "We're not going to solve our problems over lunch, Jimmy. I know that. But you came to talk to me about something and I'm hungry."

He nodded. "You're right. Hop in. I'll drive."

On the outside, Vega's unmarked Chevy Impala looked like a standard, forgettable medium-blue American sedan. Inside, it was equipped with scanners, a radio, and a laptop computer. He lowered the volume on his police radio and closed up his laptop. Nothing much was happening in the county at the moment. A few minor traffic accidents. A request for uniformed assistance on a couple of highways. He pulled a flyer from his envelope and handed it to Adele while he drove the six blocks through town to Claudia's.

"That dog? The one that belonged to the state trooper? This is the body it found in the woods yesterday."

"Oh my God," said Adele. "Was she a student?"

"Not that we can ascertain so far. She's Hispanic, between the ages of fifteen and seventeen. She's not on any missing persons' registries. Her prints don't show up in any federal databases, so she's never been arrested for a crime or illegal entry into the United States. Do you recognize her?"

Adele pulled her glasses from her purse and settled them on her face. She hated wearing them, Vega knew. But they didn't look bad. The black rims gave her a scholarly appearance, filled his head with fantasies of getting down and dirty between the stacks with the school librarian. A very voluptuous school librarian. He felt his cheeks go hot. Here they were, about to break up, and his thoughts still flowed in one direction. That was his curse.

Adele seemed oblivious. That was hers.

She frowned at the flyer. "The picture looks like a few teenagers I've seen come through La Casa. But it's hard to say. People look different when they're . . ." Adele's voice trailed off. She folded her glasses and put them away. "I'm confused how a dog that was supposed to track Joy ended up tracking this girl instead."

"The dog *did* track Joy. As it turns out, the hoodie the girl was wearing once belonged to Joy—"

"*What?*"

"According to Joy, she cleaned out her closet over the summer and Wendy gave her stuff to Goodwill. It's just a coincidence that the hoodie happened to be on this girl."

"Creepy coincidence," said Adele. "And serious, besides. Have you checked with Wendy?"

"I can't. It'd look like I was tampering with a witness. I have to let Teddy Dolan check it out. He's been assigned to the case."

"Are you worried?"

"That Joy is involved?" Vega blew out a long breath of air. "Right now, all I can do is hope we figure out who this girl is. Maybe then the rest will fall into place. When we get back to La Casa, can you take some flyers, show them around?"

"Sure."

Claudia's didn't have a parking lot. Vega parked across the street from the stucco two-story building with the red awning. He was glad to be here with Adele, even if he knew he was fooling himself. For an hour at least, he wanted to pretend.

"Do you think Claudia will let me put up a couple of flyers in her store?"

"She has a bulletin board by the register," said Adele. "I don't know. A dead girl can be sort of off-putting."

The sleigh bells on the back of the door announced their presence in the tiny store. Claudia was bustling behind the deli counter, slicing roast pork and various types of luncheon meat while three customers in dusty jeans and baseball caps grabbed sodas from the refrigerated case and slapped them on the scuffed counter. They cracked goofy jokes in Spanish and chatted up the pretty woman ringing up their order—a relative of Claudia's, no doubt—who pretended not to notice how hard the men were trying to flirt. Vega could see why. She had full, pouty lips and big astonished eyes that reminded Vega of those Beanie Baby stuffed animals Joy always favored when she was younger. Adele called her Inés. Vega got the sense she was Claudia's daughter.

Everyone said hello to Adele the moment they saw her: the workmen, Claudia, Inés. They called her Doña Adele, as a sign of respect. Vega wondered if anyone would call her Doña Adele if she moved to D.C.

The people in the store said hello to him too, but it was a guarded and formal greeting, and their eyes quickly shifted away. The gossip mill in town had no doubt spread the fact that Adele was dating him. But even so, his presence spooked them. Nobody in Adele's world ever looked at him and saw a man. They always saw a cop. The fact that he was Hispanic seemed beside the point.

The only person who said hello to him with unabashed gusto was a young man he hadn't noticed at first. He was short and round and dressed in the dark blue pants and blue-and-white-striped uniform shirt of the employees over at the Car Wash King. There was something glazed and off about his eyes.

"Hello, Mr. Police Officer! Can you put on the siren?"

Vega realized he'd seen the young man in the store before. He was Claudia's grandson or something. Claudia must have told the teenager that Vega was a cop.

"I'm not driving a patrol car," said Vega. "I don't have a siren."

"I love sirens!"

"Well, uh—next time I'm near a patrol car, I'll see if they can switch one on for you." Vega was never particularly good with people with cognitive disabilities. He always over- or underestimated their intellect, which left him feeling frustrated or embarrassed or both. He hung back and scanned the aisles until the other customers finished their orders.

Some of the items brought back memories of the bodegas and *mercados* of his youth in the South Bronx: the ubiquitous blue jars of Vicks VapoRub, the yellow-and-red cans of Café Bustelo, the bruised stalks of ripe plantains dangling from ropes on the ceiling. But the South Bronx of his childhood was poorer and the people much less sophisticated. There were so many things here that Vega never could have imagined at Manny's Bodega on East Tremont Avenue. Exotic fresh fruits. Colorful peppers. Vials of herbs whose names and purpose Vega could only guess at. The world, it seemed, had gotten much smaller.

Inés finished wrapping the men's sandwiches and rang them up. Vega gestured to the car-wash kid that he was next.

"No, no. My mami gives me a sandwich."

"In a minute, Neto," Inés answered. "First, I take care of Doña Adele and the señor."

Mami? Vega did a double take. No way could Inés be Neto's mother. The kid had to be at least eighteen or nineteen. Inés still had the sweet, firm face of a girl. She turned heads. Maybe she'd turned one too early. Vega could only imagine what a difficult life it must have been for her to be saddled with a child with special needs at such a young age. He wondered if there was a father around or if he'd picked up and left the moment he saw what he was in for.

Adele asked Vega what he wanted to order.

"I'll have ham and Swiss on a roll with lettuce, tomatoes, and hot peppers," said Vega.

Adele debated less than a minute before ordering the same on a wrap. Vega was so glad to finally be with a woman who didn't consider a lettuce leaf and a wedge of lemon to be lunch. Eating with his vegan, macrobiotic, gluten-free daughter and ex-wife felt less like a meal and more like a science experiment.

The men in baseball caps and jeans were putting their money away and gathering up their sandwiches. Vega wanted as many eyes on his flyer as possible, so he approached them at the counter. Their bodies stiffened the moment Vega made eye contact. Just being asked a question by a police officer seemed to fill them with dread.

"Relax, *muchachos*," he said softly in Spanish. "I just want to show you a picture, see if you recognize this girl."

They looked at the picture. They looked at each other. They shook their heads, no. Vega felt like he was a high school principal asking who broke the gym window. They were nervous, but it was the general nervousness of young men who likely had no papers and no wish to hang around an officer who might decide to ask for them.

"Let me see the picture," said Claudia, ever the snoop.

Vega passed a copy of the flyer to her and Inés.

"Do you recognize her?" Vega asked the women.

"The girl—she's dead?" asked Inés.

"Yes," said Vega. There was no way to disguise the obvious.

"I don't know her," said Inés. "How did she die?"

"That's still under investigation."

Claudia stared at the flyer. "Where did you find her?"

"She was discovered on the grounds of the community college campus," said Vega. "Maybe you've seen her around town?"

Claudia tucked a wiry strand of hair back into her bun. She shook her head. "I'm sorry. I can't help you."

"Can I put up a flyer on your bulletin board?" He nodded to the overflowing corkboard by the register that was filled with notices for English tutors and courier services. "Maybe someone in town will recognize her."

Claudia hesitated. She had the reaction Adele had predicted. But like many Latinos, she hated saying no, especially to an authority figure. Instead, she took the flyer and mumbled, "I'll see what I can do." Vega was already betting the flyer would get tossed in the trash as soon as he was out the door.

The men took Vega's conversation with Claudia and Inés as their cue to be excused. Vega heard the sleigh bells jingle as they slipped out of the store. Inés was leaning on her elbows, biting her pouty lips and staring at the flyer, when Neto came over again, asking for his sandwich.

"Oh, sorry," said Inés. She walked off to make it, leaving the flyer still resting on the counter. Neto pointed a stubby finger at the photograph.

"Mia's—sleeping?"

"*Mia?*" Vega felt his breath cinch in his chest. "You *know* her?"

Neto screwed up his face and bit down on his lip just like his mother. "That's Mia."

Claudia hustled over. "Neto! Don't make up stories!"

Vega ignored her and focused on Neto. "How do you know Mia?"

"I see her with her mami. At the car wash. She likes Chicha, my dog. She says hi to me. A lot of people don't say hi to me."

Vega pulled out a pen. "When did you see her last?"

"When?" Neto repeated.

"Today? Yesterday? Last week?"

Neto shook his head vigorously back and forth like he was trying to shake something loose.

"You see?" said Claudia to Vega. "He doesn't understand. You're wasting your time."

"Doña Claudia," said Vega, using his most respectful tone. Adele would have his head otherwise. "Please let me be the judge of that." He turned back to Neto and decided to try a different approach. "So Mia's mother is a customer of the car wash?"

Neto frowned. "Customer?"

Carajo! Vega hated to admit Claudia was probably right. "Mia's mother—she gets her car washed there?"

"Oh yes. Yes! She gives me a good tip!"

"So other people have seen Mia at the car wash?" Vega was hoping he could find another witness.

"I don't know," said Neto. "Mia goes away sometimes."

"Where does Mia live?"

"In a birdhouse."

"A birdhouse?" *Coño!*

"I told you," said Claudia. "Neto doesn't understand."

For the next fifteen minutes, Vega tried every which way to get something more out of the teenager—a description of the girl, a description of her mother—the name of another witness. Neto wanted to help, but he was so suggestible that in the end, Vega couldn't tell whether anything Neto readily agreed to had actually happened. After fifteen minutes, Neto seemed on the verge of tears, and Adele was glaring at Vega like he'd just water-boarded the kid. As soon as they got into his car with their sandwiches, she exploded.

"What the hell did you think you were doing in there?"

"I wasn't doing anything."

"You were riding Neto like he's a suspect. He's a disabled kid, Jimmy! His grandmother and I go back years."

"I asked him a few questions, that's all."

"And he answered them because he trusts you. *Claudia* trusts you. Because we're—we're—"

"—We're what? I don't even know myself anymore." Vega tossed his sandwich to one side. He suddenly didn't feel very hungry.

Adele blinked at his reflection in the window, then slumped in her seat. "You're not coming to Schulman's gala Saturday night, are you?"

"To watch you dump me publicly?"

"I never said we had to break things off. That was your idea."

"And how are we supposed to have a relationship with me here and you down in D.C.? I'm supposed to tuck my laptop between the sheets and pretend it's you in bed beside me?"

"That's all I am to you? A friend with benefits?"

"*Ay, puñeta!* Of course not!"

"Then why can't you support my desires and ambitions?"

"I do! I know you're smart—much smarter than I'll ever be. And I want what's best for you, Nena. It's just—why is it that what's best for you is not to be with me?"

They were both silent after that. Then Adele laid a hand tenderly on his thigh. "I want you, Jimmy. That part hasn't changed."

He pulled her toward him and cupped her face in his hands. He brushed a calloused thumb across her mouth, then leaned in and gave her a long, sensual kiss, his tongue softly caressing the contours of her lips until they parted and she welcomed him, the sandpaper thrust of his tongue, his hot breath on her neck, the stubble of his skin.

The temperature inside his Impala rose ten degrees. Already, he felt sweaty with desire. He brushed her hair back from her neck and ran his fingers playfully down to her collarbone before he remembered he was on duty in an unmarked police car. He pushed away and took a deep breath like some pimply-faced adolescent caught French-kissing behind the school.

"Sorry," he said when he'd regained his composure. "Losing my job's one way we can be together."

Their eyes met in the reflection of the front windshield.

"Maybe when you get off work tonight," said Adele, "we should talk—"

Her words were interrupted by Vega's cell phone. He pulled his phone out of his pocket and looked at the screen. He cursed under his breath. "It's Greco. I have to take it."

"Vega," he answered, the way he always did when on duty.

"Where's Joy?" Greco growled into the phone. An odd question.

"Dunno. Probably finishing up her classes. Why?"

"Can you get hold of her?"

"We already cleared up everything with Dolan this morning."

"From your mouth to God's ear, Vega. Joy's gonna need to come home ASAP. And you're gonna need to call a lawyer. Dolan's executing a search warrant at your ex's place as we speak."

"*What?*" Vega leaned forward, his muscles suddenly rigid. Adele must have sensed the change because she put a hand on his elbow and gave him a quizzical look. He shifted away. He didn't want any distractions at the moment.

"Your pal Dolan just finished paying a little visit to WastePro Management," said Greco. "Lake Holly has a contract with them for garbage pickup."

"So?"

"Seems Dolan got that lady state trooper to take her

dog to their sorting facility down in Port Carroll. And the word coming back ain't good. That mutt just picked up traces of the dead girl's blood on a quilt—"

"Which could have come from anywhere, Grec."

"Not when the quilt has your daughter's name on it in laundry marker."

Chapter 18

Vega dropped Adele back at La Casa with a thumbnail sketch of his conversation with Greco and a quick "I'll call you later." He managed to get hold of Joy by phone just as she was about to leave campus to meet with a student. He told her only that the police were at her house and she should cancel her afternoon tutoring sessions. He didn't want to alarm her more than he had to. Instead, he asked her to meet up with him in a commuter parking lot ten minutes south of town so he could explain things more fully. Thank God Greco had given him a heads-up. The man had broken every rule to do it—and Vega would be forever grateful.

As soon as Joy's white Volvo pulled into the parking lot, Vega nosed his blue Impala behind her, parked, and let himself into the Volvo's front passenger seat. He began speaking as soon as he shut the door. There was a good chance that his guys were on the lookout for her car, and he didn't want to get spotted before they'd had a chance to talk.

"That state police trooper on campus yesterday?" he said. "The one with the dog?"

"Daisy." There was a hint of wistfulness in her voice. She still saw that culturally confused German shepherd as some cute pet-shop puppy instead of the relentless police tool it had been trained to be. She jingled her keys, already bored by what she perceived would be some sort of parental lecture.

"Well, *Daisy,* as you say, is at your mother's house right now. With the trooper. And they're not giving demonstrations. This is for real, Joy. Detective Dolan obtained a warrant to search the property." Vega wanted to deck that Irish bastard with his smooth-as-Guinness charm for going behind Vega's back today. But he knew it wasn't personal. Dolan wouldn't be a good cop if he allowed himself to be blinded by their friendship. Taking that stupid dog to the dump was a clever bit of police work. It required no warrant, so no one would have been any the wiser if it had produced nothing. Of course, once that dog found Joy's quilt, all bets were off.

"You told me about the search warrant on the phone," said Joy impatiently. "I guess if they have to do it"—she shrugged—"I understand."

"You understand? You *understand?*" Vega felt his blood pressure rising, felt it pulsing up his neck and through the arteries to his brain until his whole head throbbed from it. "That dog you like so much uncovered a quilt in the dump today in Port Carroll with your name on it and this girl's blood."

"A quilt? I didn't throw away a quilt in Port Carroll. Why would I go all the way down to Port Carroll to do that?"

For a smart girl, she could be pretty thick sometimes, thought Vega. "The garbage company that picks up trash in Lake Holly has their sorting facility in Port Carroll. The quilt is yours, Joy. It has your name on it in laundry marker."

"But I don't know her!"

"I've got a witness who says her name might be Mia."

"The only Mia I know is Mia Soloff. We were on the same tennis team in high—"

"She's not Mia Soloff!"

"Okay, Dad. Chill."

"*Chill?* That girl was found in *your* hoodie, on *your* college campus, and now her blood is on *your* quilt."

"You think I'm lying?"

"Are you?"

"How could you even ask me that?"

Vega slumped in his seat and rubbed his eyes. "I want to believe you, Chispita. I do. But see . . ." He couldn't tell her about the link between the dead teenager and the abandoned baby. It could compromise the whole investigation. Yet he had to know what he was dealing with here. He just had to.

"The other day when we were at the hospital, you asked me what would happen to a girl who abandoned her baby—do you remember?" asked Vega.

"I remember."

Vega closed his eyes and chose his words carefully. "You—expressed a lot of sympathy for a woman in that situation."

"So?"

"If someone like that came to you—would you—would you maybe try to do something to help them?"

"Help them how?"

Vega leveled his gaze at her and spoke the words slowly. "Make the child go away."

"What? You mean like an abortion?"

Vega wanted to scream the facts to her: *A teenage girl died in a botched childbirth. Her blood was found on a quilt with your name on it. Her body was buried on your college campus. Wearing your hoodie. Her newborn was smothered by a female hand in the woods not far from where you live.* People were sent away for twenty-five to life on less evidence than this.

Instead, he stayed very still and said nothing.

"I didn't help anyone get an abortion, if that's what

you're asking me. Is it, Dad? Did this girl die from an abortion?"

"I can't comment." He sighed. "You'll need a lawyer." He dialed Wendy's cell and explained the situation as best he could. He had to repeat, "I don't know" and "I can't comment" so many times, Wendy finally hung up on him. Then he called Dolan and told him Joy was coming home and he would be following her in his unmarked.

Twelve minutes later, they were pulling up to Wendy's house, a massive whitewashed Georgian with columns down the front, a three-car garage, and a wide, Belgian-block-lined driveway that bisected a nearly treeless acre of lawn.

There were six police vehicles parked at the curb and along the driveway by the time Vega pulled behind Joy's Volvo. Cops in and out of uniform were traipsing through the double-height front entrance door, yammering on their radios, treating the whole event like a giant opportunity to milk some overtime. A lot of them knew Vega, so his presence had a chilling effect on the scene. They kept their heads down as soon as they caught sight of him or ducked back into the house to avoid an encounter. Cops defined the world as "us" and "them." They didn't have a clue how to handle a situation where "us" and "them" were one and the same.

Dolan hustled over as soon as Joy got out of her car. He kept his body language light and breezy, but there was no mistaking the forced good humor in the smile beneath his bushy blond mustache as he extended a hand. Joy must have felt it too. She looked pale and shaky when she shook it. Dolan held out his hand to Vega. Vega ignored it, gesturing instead to the gridlock of black-and-whites.

"Jesus Christ, Teddy! Did you have to turn this into a freakin' circus?" Behind the neighbors' expensive window treatments, they had to be taking notice.

"I can't change the rules just because she's your daughter, man. Serving a search warrant's a messy business. You know that. Believe me, I don't want this any more than you do."

"How long did you wait to search the dump after we met this morning? Ten minutes? Did you even take a piss first?"

"C'mon, Jimmy. In my shoes, you'd have done the same thing. I didn't expect to *find* anything. This"—Dolan gestured to the open front door and squawk of radios inside—"is as much of a surprise to me as I'm sure it is to you." Dolan turned to Joy. He kept that used-car salesman's smile on his face. "Joy? I'm gonna need to talk to you for a little bit."

Vega stepped in front of her. "My daughter talks through her lawyer. Same as any suspect with half a brain."

"That's the way you want to play it?" asked Dolan. "You want a formal arrest? Your daughter handcuffed in front of all your ex-wife's neighbors?"

"Daddy!" Joy started crying. It was finally dawning on her what she was up against. "I didn't do anything. I swear!"

"Shhh." Vega put his arms around her and pulled her close. The shushing wasn't just to calm her—it was to shut her up as well. For all Vega knew, Joy could be protecting someone else, someone whose full culpability Joy didn't even fully understand yet. A statement like, "I didn't do anything" was all prosecutors would need to convict her as an accessory down the line.

"Please don't let them arrest me, Daddy!"

Vega rubbed her back and stared over it at Dolan. "He's not gonna arrest you. If he were, he'd have done it already." They both knew that no cop gives a damn about neighbors if he's got enough evidence to slap on the cuffs. Dolan's threat was a bluff to get Joy to talk. She couldn't see it, but Vega could. His heart lifted slightly. If Dolan didn't think he had enough for probable cause, there was still a chance to set things right.

"Go inside," Vega instructed her. "Find your mother. And don't open your mouth to *anyone*. Not even to Mom. Do you understand me?"

"Yes, Dad." Her voice sounded swallowed and scared. Vega waited until she'd gone inside before he spoke again.

"Level with me, Teddy. What have you got?"

Dolan shook his head. "Enough to arrest her, despite your little show of bravado just now."

"Then why haven't you?"

"Because I'm a dad and a cop too, Jimmy. Andre and Keisha will be teenagers one day, and I don't want to take a fellow cop down that road if I can help it." Dolan held his gaze. "That's why the best thing for Joy right now is to talk to me."

"Yeah, right," Vega snorted. "Let her swim with the sharks."

"Sounds like you think she's guilty."

"She's not."

"Says every parent."

"No. I know by her dopey, glib answers that she's telling the truth. Plus, I've got information that may clear her."

"Yeah? What?" asked Dolan, not really listening.

"I just came from Claudia's bodega in town. Her teenage grandson ID'd the dead girl as someone named Mia who visits the car wash where he works. He mentioned her visiting with her mom."

Dolan pulled out his notebook. "Go on."

"That's—sort of it," said Vega. "The grandson's mentally retarded—"

"So in other words, you don't know if any of it's accurate."

"It bears checking out."

"And I will." Silence.

"See, the way this works," said Vega, "is that you offer me something now."

More silence.

"All right. I'll begin," said Vega. "As I understand it, you went to WastePro's dumping facility down in Port Carroll and the dog found a quilt with Joy's name on it and the girl's blood—"

"Who told you that?"

"The tooth fairy." Dolan probably knew where Vega got his information from, but it did neither cop any good to start pointing fingers. "Are you sure it isn't Joy's blood?" asked Vega.

"Positive," said Dolan. "I can't give you any details, but we're awaiting a DNA matchup, and I'm ninety-nine percent sure it's gonna be a match to the dead girl on campus."

"Okay. So you found her blood on Joy's quilt. A lot of it?"

Dolan hesitated. "I can't answer that one."

"You find it on anything besides the quilt?"

Dolan ran a hand across his shaved head and looked away. "Jesus, man. I shouldn't even be talking to you—"

Vega could feel Dolan disengaging. He plowed ahead. Joy's life depended on it. "If you'd found evidence of the dead girl in the house or any of the vehicles, Joy would be in custody now. So I'm guessing you haven't gotten another hit outside of that quilt at the dump."

"We haven't checked Joy's car yet. She had it with her."

"Which backs up my theory that you haven't found blood elsewhere or you wouldn't be all that concerned about checking her Volvo."

Dolan didn't argue. Vega knew he was right. "So we're back to the quilt at the dump. Did my ex-wife tell you whether she'd given it away like she did the hoodie?"

"She said she gave both items away over the summer. But she's got nothing to back up her claim. She didn't give it to a store. She says she put a couple of trash bags of donations together sometime in July or August and gave them to Rosa, her live-in housekeeper, to dump in the bins over by the shopping center."

"Doesn't mean that's not what happened."

"And what are the odds, Vega, that a dead girl is in possession of *two* items of your daughter's in separate locations and your daughter's *not* involved?"

"For all you know, maybe Rosa knows the dead girl. Maybe she helped out at the house and she cut herself at some point—"

"We interviewed Rosa. She says she never saw the girl before."

"Not for nothing, but my daughter's saying the same thing. Why take Rosa's word?"

"Because the girl wasn't found wearing Rosa's hoodie."

Vega tried a different tack. "Listen, Teddy—I want to do the right thing. If Joy's involved, I want her to own up to it. So convince me. I believe you that the dog found that teenager's blood on Joy's quilt. But what's that prove? Nothing, in my book."

"All of that trash the dog went through was picked up today in Lake Holly," said Dolan.

"It could have come from anywhere in Lake Holly. Can you say for sure that it came from Joy's garbage?"

"No. But you're focusing on the wrong part of the equation," said Dolan. "*Where* we found our evidence is the one thing keeping your daughter out of jail this minute. But you need to focus on *what* we found and why it's the whole case."

"Blood—I get it. From the girl."

Dolan held his gaze, and a slow dawning crept into Vega, curdling the remains of the ham and cheese sandwich he'd eaten earlier. *Blood.* From a teenager who'd just given birth. A girl whose body showed no external wounds when Vega saw her in the woods yesterday. This wasn't a cut or scrape. This was—

"Holy—" Vega kicked at the Belgian blocks lining the driveway and cursed. He felt queasy and light-headed. *"No."*

"That's why I'm saying it's not random, man. It doesn't matter whether we found it in Joy's trash. She'd be pretty stupid to stick it in her own trash anyway. We could have found it anywhere and it wouldn't change much about the case. Do you understand now?"

"You found the afterbirth."

Chapter 19

Vega barely slept that night and awoke Thursday morning just as the sky was turning from black to bruised. He was scheduled to work this upcoming weekend, so he had the day off. That meant a whole day ahead at his lakeside cabin to stew in his thoughts.

Not good. Not good at all. The only thing he could think about was clearing Joy. But he was powerless to do so. Citing conflict of interest, Captain Waring had taken him off the case entirely.

He made his coffee too strong just to feel the bite of it on his tongue, the sharp warmth as it traveled through his body. He felt lost in every other part of his being, hollowed out by doubts and recriminations. He had a long list of things that could keep him busy at home: a leaky faucet that needed replacing, guitar practice for a club gig with his band. His refrigerator was empty. His laundry hamper was full. He needed to make his monthly call to the homicide detectives in the Bronx—a useless exercise that always filled him with sadness and frustration. His mother's unsolved murder was a wound that never seemed to close. On an index card above the phone, the original squad number grew ever more faded as detectives' names were added and crossed out with each new officer assigned to the case.

He drained the last of his coffee and walked out to his deck. A fog obscured the view of the lake. The air smelled of wood smoke and damp leaves. When he bought this two-bedroom, vinyl-sided cape after his divorce, friends told him he was crazy. It was on a postage-stamp of weeds, almost an hour's commute from his office and a whole county north of his jurisdiction. A former summer cabin, it lacked insulation, decent wiring, or adequate plumbing. His first two winters here were the coldest he'd ever known.

The lake, however, made it all worthwhile. Vega never tired of it—its perfect stillness, the way it caught and held the moods of the sky. In the mornings, from his back deck, he loved to watch herons skate low across the water. There were toads in the spring and perch that broke the surface with a *whoosh* in summer. There were morning mists and evening crickets and red-tailed hawks that hovered like kites overhead in the plenty of time. Here, he could prop his feet on the railing of his deck, play his Gibson six-string, and pretend for just a moment that this was his real life, that he'd never traded the hardened callouses on his fingertips for a gun and a steady paycheck.

He threw a flannel shirt over his T-shirt and jeans and hiked down the steep slope to the edge of the lake. Matted leaves and twigs gathered along the shoreline, and a pearly softness floated like cotton candy in the feathery groupings of dark green hemlocks and eastern white pines that surrounded the water. Somewhere out in the fog, a fish splashed to the surface and a crow cawed overhead. Vega wanted to enjoy this rare moment off the clock, to drink it in, not cross it off like a con marking time. Yet he couldn't stop the meth-addict voice inside his head that played an endless loop of all his worries at warp speed.

Joy is going to be arrested . . . Adele is leaving forever . . .
Maybe he could have reversed everything if only he'd let

Adele go to La Casa Saturday night, if only they'd found that baby in time. *If, if, if . . .*

Vega kicked at the rocky mud beneath his work boots, listening for the pleasing crunch of gravel. His left calf where the dog bit him was healing at least. The skin wasn't quite so tender and the stitches itched less. He grabbed a flat piece of shale at the lake's edge and skipped it across the water. It nicked the surface four times before disappearing into the gray depths. Vega watched the concentric rings grow in the pebble's wake, each one blooming and spreading, seemingly of its own volition.

Vega found another stone and skipped it, marveling at how such a small object applied at just the right angle could create all this turbulence and motion. Everything leaves a mark, he supposed. He didn't want to think about the parallels to his own life, the way he'd carelessly cast things out only to realize the repercussions of his decisions when they were too late to call back. He had missed all the warning signs, all the clues.

Vega thought about the dead teenager. She'd carried her baby in her womb for nine months—given birth to her, if not in Lake Holly, then somewhere close by. How was it possible that no one but a mentally disabled car-wash attendant had ever noticed her?

Vega wiped his muddy hands on his jeans and straightened. He watched the morning sun poke through the clouds, dissipating the mist on the lake. And all of a sudden, everything came into focus. Vega saw tiny cabins like his that had lately started to get year-round owners. There were curtains on new dormered windows; stacks of fresh-cut wood for the winter, newly erected swing sets and flower boxes. He just couldn't see it before. But it was there all along, right beneath the fog.

Everything leaves a mark.

Someone had to have seen that pregnant teenager, just

as people saw Dominga Flores. They saw, but they didn't see. What was he missing?

He thought about Dominga in that huge, fortresslike house giving birth. Even she hadn't been entirely alone. She said a midwife—a Spanish woman—had helped.

Vega took a deep breath and felt a sharpness travel down his lungs as though the air were infused with peppermint. And all at once, he saw what he'd been missing. He ran back to the house, bounding up the steps of his deck like he was in a marathon. He opened the sliding glass door, grabbed his cell phone on the counter, and scrolled down his contacts list until he found the cell number of the Wickford detective who was in charge of Neil Davies's arrest. *Hammond. Detective Sergeant Mark Hammond.* Vega remembered him from Monday night. He had a square jaw and big white teeth that reminded Vega of the Kennedys.

Vega dialed Hammond's cell. It rang and rang. Just when Vega thought it was going to go to voice mail, Hammond picked up.

Vega reintroduced himself. He could hear voices in the background. Wherever Hammond was, he wasn't alone.

"Quick question on the Davies case: Did your guys ever track down the midwife or whatever she was who delivered Dominga Flores's baby?"

"Still looking," said Hammond. "Flores claims she doesn't know her. Davies claims Flores called her in. So far, we've had no luck finding her. I think Flores may be covering for her because the woman's probably unlicensed and illegal."

Vega's thoughts precisely. "Any chance I can swing by the station house and get a copy of what you've done so far?"

"What we've done is gone through the available lists of licensed midwives *thoroughly*—"

"I'm sure you have—"

"Then any further checking on your part would be unnecessary, Detective." Cops and turf. Vega wished just once everybody would cooperate.

"See—the thing is—it's for a different case." *Shit*. Vega didn't want to have to say that. If Captain Waring found out what he was trying to do, he'd get charges for sure.

"In that case," said Hammond, "I can probably pull something together for you tomorrow. Not today. Flores has gone back to living with the Reilly family if you want to contact her and ask her yourself. I'm in the field right now. Two hikers just called in a 10-47 in the woods off Route 170. That'll take up all our extra manpower for the day."

A dead body on the two-lane that connected Wickford to Lake Holly. Hammond didn't seem too broken up about it.

"Something you want help from our guys on?" asked Vega.

"Negative. It's not a homicide. Just a local homeless mutt who drank himself to death."

Vega gripped the phone tighter. "You get a description of the decedent?"

"Male. Hispanic. Approximately five-foot-three. One hundred and forty pounds. He was found lying facedown about two hundred feet from Route 170, a quarter mile from the border of Lake Holly."

Vega's mouth went dry. He didn't want it to be true. And yet some part of him already knew that it was. That mutt could barely stay sober long enough to find his way to Wickford. No way was he going to make it two thousand miles to Guatemala.

"Any ID on the guy?"

"Negative. But he was well known to the uniformed patrols. They recognized the body as soon as they saw his bowed legs."

"Zambo." It wasn't even a question.

"Yeah. That's him," said Hammond. "From what the uniforms tell me, he was a real pain in the ass. Kept our guys and Lake Holly's guys hopping with petty nonsense for years. Nobody's gonna be all that broken up that he's gone."

Vega just breathed on the line. Their only witness. The one person who might be able to exonerate Joy. Hammond was wrong when he said nobody was all that broken up that Zambo was gone.

He was.

Chapter 20

The Serrano family was scrubbed and dressed and in their best church clothes by five past nine that Thursday morning. Luna paced back and forth by the front window of their apartment, watching for Señora Gonzalez's black Escalade at the curb. Papi packed the last of the dishes in the kitchen before slipping on his lucky red tie. For once, Mateo and Dulce weren't fighting. They were both glued to their father's sides—so much so that when Papi went to dry his hands from the sink, he accidentally elbowed Dulce in the eye. She wailed uncontrollably, and Papi fell all over himself to make her stop.

They were all exhausted and wound tighter than a bunch of spinning tops. None of them slept last night. The *last* night. *La última noche.* None of them referred to it like that. To say it was to make it true. They'd spent it in Papi's bed, curled around him like newborn puppies. At one point in the night, Luna heard him get up to go to the bathroom. He didn't turn on any lights, but she heard his choked sobs through the door. When he came back, she closed her eyes tight and pretended to be asleep. She didn't want him to know she'd heard him. Her father was so strong. A meat slicer amputated part of his finger and he went back to work in two days. Meningitis took Mami and he became both father and mother. A fire burned out their apartment and he found a new place to live and made it home. She couldn't believe after all this that he could be broken by a piece of paper.

Her father had called their schools to say they couldn't come in today. Then he made them breakfast, but none of them could eat. And now they waited for the señora's car, surrounded by the contents of their apartment packed away in cardboard cartons—all except for Mami's pink begonia plant. It sat on top of the cartons in the terra-cotta flowerpot Luna had painted all those years ago.

Luna looked at her watch. "Señora Gonzalez is late." Papi gave her a sharp look, though she knew he was checking his watch too.

"You must remember to call her Doña Esme now, Luna. And the señor Don Charlie. They deserve those terms of honor."

Luna knew her father was right that she should be grateful and do as they'd asked. But it was awkward to suddenly pretend that this balding little man with the sweaty palms and his no-nonsense young wife were anything but strangers. Luna didn't know her father's cousins Alirio and Maria José very well, but at least they were family.

Besides, she didn't think Doña Esme liked her very much. The woman was okay with Mateo because he was a playmate for her sons. She responded to Dulce because she was young and needed a mother figure. But Luna? Doña Esme seemed to have no idea what to do with a teenage girl in her house. Luna got the sense that taking all of them in was the señor's idea. They were a burden she had to carry because it went against her husband's honor not to. Doña Esme had told her more than once that she was only two years older than Luna when she got married. Did she expect Luna to take a husband at seventeen? Not that Doña Esme would even be in Luna's life by then. Papi will be here. He has to be.

Dear God, he can't leave us like this!

Luna's stomach was tied in knots by the time Doña Esme drove up. She felt like she had to use the bathroom again, but there was no time. Papi wasn't driving to the courthouse. If the worst happened today, he couldn't drive back. Another adult had to be there to sign the guardianship papers and take custody. Otherwise Luna, Mateo, and Dulce would end up in foster care and could be separated.

They hustled out the door and put on their most hopeful faces for the drive to Broad Plains. None of them spoke in the car. The señor couldn't get out of work today, so it was just Doña Esme and them. Her father's lawyer, Mr. Katz, was supposed to meet them at the courthouse.

There was a lot of slow-moving traffic on the roads. Luna could tell her father was getting nervous that he'd be late and make the judge angry. Papi scanned the rearview mirror, looking for opportunities to change lanes and speed up the journey, but he knew he couldn't tell Doña Esme how to drive, so he just sat holding it in until they were off the highway. They passed the lawyer's building they visited last Sunday, and Luna saw and smelled the warm, cheesy pizza parlor where Papi had bought those slices. It seemed like an image already frozen in her memory. Luna would grow up. Papi would grow old. And they'd have only that day at the pizza parlor to hang onto. She could feel the tears coming on and she sucked them back. But she wasn't the only one holding everything in. As soon as Doña Esme parked the car in the courthouse garage, Mateo got out and vomited on the cement.

"Eeew, gross!" squealed Dulce.

Mateo started to cry. "I'm sorry, Papi! I'm sorry!"

Papi rubbed his back and murmured in Spanish: "It's okay. You're going to be okay." Doña Esme handed Luna a bottle of water and some tissues, and she helped her father clean her brother up. Fortunately, he'd vomited on the cement, not in the car or on his clothes. They were able to make him look presentable and wash most of the mess away from the cars.

"Are you okay now, Mijo?" asked Papi. Mateo nodded. He didn't trust himself to speak, but at least the color was returning to his face. Luna checked her watch. Papi's court date was for ten a.m. It was almost ten-thirty. She wondered if Mateo's throwing up had already sealed her father's fate.

They took an elevator to the lobby and walked outside and across a big cement plaza with a fountain and some statues and flags in the center. The fresh air seemed to do Mateo good. It was a bright sunny day and not too cold. People hustled past with shopping bags from Macy's and Nordstrom's. A teenager on a skateboard rolled along the sidewalk, the rap music from his earphones loud enough for all of them to hear.

They followed Doña Esme and their father into another office building, where they lined up to walk through a metal detector. From there, they took an elevator to the fifth floor, where they got off and looked for Papi's lawyer, Mr. Katz. He was nowhere to be found. Luna wondered if he'd grown tired of waiting for them and had left already. Or perhaps they were in the wrong place?

This didn't feel like a courthouse at all. Luna pictured polished brass and white marble with high ceilings and gleaming wooden benches where black-robed judges looked down from on high. The corridor they walked along had low ceilings and dingy white walls that were covered in scuff marks. The air smelled of sweat and coffee. There were people everywhere—black, brown, Asian—leaning up against grimy windows, sitting on hard wooden benches scattered along the wall. Some were talking on cell phones. Others were holding crying babies. Still others were sitting silently with their eyes closed and heads bent as if in prayer. There were even a few young children sitting with women who didn't look like their mothers. The children looked scared and anxious, and the women were checking their cell phones like the children weren't even there. Luna had thought they were the only ones going through this nightmare. But she saw now that they were just one family of many, not all of them even Spanish.

Papi excused himself to see if he could find Mr. Katz. Luna waited with Dulce, Mateo, and Doña Esme and watched the crowd swirling around them. She noticed that the other people waiting had no one who looked like a lawyer with them. Some of them were pregnant women. Some were families with young children.

"Are all these people Mr. Katz's clients too?" Luna asked Doña Esme.

"I should hope not!" Doña Esme sounded irritated by the question.

"It's just that"—Luna tried to explain herself—"I don't see any lawyers."

"You think everyone can afford a lawyer to help them through a deportation proceeding? Chica, you *are* naïve."

Doña Esme nodded to a fidgety Spanish-looking boy of about five years of age sitting with a white woman. The boy's sneaker shoelaces were undone. His shirt was inside out. The tag was poking out beneath his chin. He must have dressed himself. "Even little children like that boy must go before the judge without anyone to speak for them," she said. "That's the harsh truth of the world. Every day at the border, there are hundreds of children just like him crossing alone. You have no idea. Your Papi has sheltered you from it."

"But when people in the U.S. are charged with a crime," said Luna, "they're entitled to legal representation." Her words sounded condescending as they left her mouth. Luna wanted Doña Esme to know she wasn't stupid. But she was stupid enough, she supposed, to want to prove otherwise.

Doña Esme pulled out a mirrored compact and reapplied her bright pink lipstick. "This is immigration court, chica. Not criminal court. The law provides nothing. Most people with a prior deportation order like your father just get swept off the street and deported back to their home countries without any hearing at all."

She pressed her colored lips together and studied her reflection. When she was satisfied, she slipped the compact back into her bag. Her cool indifference made her words that much more chilling. Luna was angry, not just at what was happening to them but at the fact that no one else seemed to care.

"That's so unfair," said Luna.

Doña Esme shrugged. "That's life, chica. These four months you've had with your father while lawyers worked on his case? They were a gift—an *expensive* gift."

So Doña Esme thought she was haughty and ungrateful. Luna wondered if she could ever set things right between them.

Her father reappeared now with Mr. Katz in tow. The lawyer was dressed in a crisp gray suit and maroon tie. He didn't look angry at their lateness.

Papi took a deep breath, as if trying to gather all the parts of himself. He addressed them in stilted English.

"Mr. Katz says always immigration court has delay. So we did not miss." Mr. Katz smiled confidently at Luna and her siblings. He could afford to be confident. He was going home tonight. Still, as Doña Esme said, they were lucky to have him at all.

Mr. Katz pushed up the sleeve of his gray suit jacket and checked the time. "Our case is next, so the wait shouldn't be long now."

Papi gestured to the benches. "Luna—you and Dulce and Mateo will stay out here with Doña Esme. I will be in there."

Luna peeked into the room behind her father. There were some chairs and tables facing a raised wooden desk with flags on either side. The lighting had a sickly yellow tint. There were no windows or polished brass or white marble.

A white woman with frizzy gray hair and glasses on a chain around her neck sat behind the desk. She looked less like a judge and more like Luna's high school librarian, like she was going to fine her dad for overdue books. A young black woman with long beaded braids sat at a keyboard on one side of the desk. A Spanish-looking court officer with a shaved head leaned over the black woman's shoulder, muttering something. Luna could tell they liked each other by the way the woman kept trying not to smile.

At a table facing the judge, a blond woman in a dark blue suit opened her briefcase and thumbed through some papers. Across the aisle was another table with two empty seats. Luna guessed the woman in the blue suit was the prosecutor who wanted to deport her father back to Mexico and the two seats across the aisle were for her father and Mr. Katz to tell the judge why he should stay. The judge slipped on her glasses, perhaps to read something about Papi's case. Then Luna noticed that she wasn't looking at paperwork—she was texting on her cell phone. Luna wondered if at the end of the day, she'd even be able to recall her father's name.

Mr. Katz patted her father on the shoulder. "Let's take care of business, Manuel, shall we?"

Papi gave Luna, Dulce, and Mateo a quick nervous glance. "Will I"—he ran his thumb and forefinger down his mustache—"will I get to see my children after?"

"Yes," said Mr. Katz.

"Ahh—either way?"

"Yes."

Papi forced a smile and gave them a quick thumbs-up before disappearing with Mr. Katz through the courtroom doors. They closed behind him, and Luna and her siblings were left in a hallway with too few benches and too many people.

Esme staked out a corner of a bench, crossed her legs, and whipped out her cell phone to check her messages. She didn't say a word to any of them, not even to Dulce. Luna wasn't sure what she expected, but this wasn't it. Dulce reached for Luna's hand. Her grip was tight. Mateo stood close by her other side. Luna could feel their fear. She understood for the first time the responsibility that had been placed on her shoulders. Dulce and Mateo were all that could be left of her immediate family when this was over. Whatever else happened, she had to take care of them.

All the things that used to matter—classes, grades, the summer science program, the talent show—Luna couldn't imagine caring about any of that ever again. They were in a war here, her family and she, even if no one else could see the bullets whizzing by or feel their terror as they curled themselves tightly and searched out every crevice for protection. Her friends were on the other side of an uncrossable divide, consumed as they were with dates and gossip and midterms. Everything seemed petty and insignificant—everything except for her father, brother, and sister. Luna felt a sense of great purpose and great despair at the same time. She wanted to be up to this challenge. She feared she was not.

Luna put her arms around Mateo and Dulce and inched them all toward the windows. Doña Esme didn't look up. Luna pointed out the hot dog vendors in the street. Mateo, who loved cars, tried to guess the models of each one that drove by. They played I-spy with the people below. It kept them busy. It did nothing to ease the churning she felt inside or the great weight that pressed on her chest.

She expected the case to take at least an hour. This was her father's life they were talking about. *Their* lives. But it was over in twenty minutes. Mr. Katz came to the door. He searched for their faces in the crowd, but when he located them, he didn't meet Luna's gaze. And she knew. She thought she was prepared for this moment, but it hit her like a shot to the jaw.

"Papi can go now?" Dulce asked Mr. Katz hopefully. Her little hand squeezed Luna's so tight, Luna's fingers were starting to lose circulation.

"I'm sorry," said Mr. Katz. "They're allowing you five minutes in the courtroom to say good-bye."

Dulce began to wail. The noise came from so deep inside of her, she sounded like a flock of seagulls rather than a seven-year-old girl. Mateo, who was normally so stoic, sat on the floor and began rocking himself back and forth. Mr. Katz looked scared and shaken. He searched for Doña Esme, who was behind them now.

"I did everything I could do!" he shouted. He was angry, though Luna didn't know whom he was angry with.

"I'm sure you did," Doña Esme said calmly. "And Manuel is most grateful. Do I need to go inside and sign the paperwork?"

"Yes. Thank you. I'll be in touch." And then, just like that, he left. Without even a good-bye.

Doña Esme managed to get Mateo off the floor and stop Dulce from crying long enough to lead them inside. Papi was standing by the table where he'd been sitting before with Mr. Katz. The Spanish officer was next to him. The blond lady in the dark blue suit had already gone. Luna knew her father would be handcuffed as soon as they left, but for the moment, Papi had no restraints. His Adam's apple bobbed up and down along his windpipe. His eyes were red and watery. He held out his arms. Dulce and Mateo ran into them. Both of them were crying, and Luna tried very hard not to join in.

Papi stroked their hair. "This is not for always," he told them in Spanish. His voice broke on *siempre—always*—as if the word were too difficult to even think about. "This is just for a little while. Mr. Katz told me that he and Don Charlie will fight this. If Mr. Schulman gets elected, they will find a way to bring me back. In the meantime, we will talk to each other every day, yes? On the phone. Through Skype. And you can visit. See your uncles, your grandmother. Won't that be nice?"

Papi didn't look at Luna when he said this last part. Maybe Dulce and Mateo could visit their father if they came up with the money for plane fare. But Luna couldn't. Her immigration status was in limbo. If she left the United States, she wouldn't be allowed to return. *I want to leave,* she thought. *I want to be with Papi. I don't care where I am so long as we're together.* But Luna knew this wasn't what her father wanted. She had to stay, if only to give Dulce and Mateo the lives they deserved.

Papi reached across Mateo and Dulce and pulled Luna close. She drank in the warmth of his touch in the hope that it would make her feel less alone. He brushed back her hair and whispered in her ear in Spanish: "You must be strong, Mija," he said more forcefully than Luna would've expected. "If you let this stop you from getting a good education and making a good life here, everything Mami and I sacrificed will have been for nothing. *Nothing!* Do you understand?"

He cupped his hands firmly around each side of her face. His calloused palms pressed against her cheeks. His moist brown eyes looked directly into hers. "Take care of your brother and sister. Keep them on the path of God. And whatever else happens, don't let anything come between you and what you want to do in this life. I have faith in you, Luna. In you, most of all, I have faith."

Luna couldn't speak. She didn't want to break Papi's hold on her. But already the court officer was murmuring to her father to finish his good-byes. Dulce was clinging to his waist, and it was Luna's job to pull her away. Dulce tried to bite her when she did. Her sister had never done such a thing before. Luna searched for Doña Esme to help, but she was watching them all from a safe distance. Her arms were crossed. There was something sharp-edged—almost resentful—when her gaze settled on Luna. The room was warm and stuffy, but Luna felt a chill run down her spine.

Papi believed all these things he'd asked of Luna were within her power. He had no clue that she was as much a prisoner of her circumstances as he was of his.

Chapter 21

A dead body draws cops the same way it draws flies: First, you get one or two. Then before you know it, they're swarming and multiplying and making a general mess of things. It didn't seem to matter whether the cause was man or God, the spectacle and commotion and general stink were near enough the same.

Traffic slowed on the eastbound side of Route 170 as Vega drove past the WELCOME TO WICKFORD sign. Up ahead, he saw a black-and-white patrol car parked at an angle to the road, its light bar flashing, red and blue. Vega put his foot on the brake and turned up the volume on the police scanner in his pickup truck. There had been little in the way of radio communication since the original 10-47. Wickford had called for the medical examiner's van but not the crime-scene unit. If the radio traffic was correct, Zambo's death was being treated as the legal and emotional equivalent of an abandoned jalopy in need of a tow.

Greco had to be here. Zambo was too important to the Baby Mercy case not to be.

Route 170 wasn't the sort of road anyone would expect to discover a corpse on. It was a winding calendar-worthy stretch of two-lane dotted with horse farms, old stone walls, and sprawling white clapboard homes, some with bronze plaques that proclaimed their history dating all the way back to the Revolutionary War. In between were fields of brittle grass that trailed off into vine-covered woods. It was easy for a person to go unnoticed even just a few feet from the road. Why the cops always dumped Zambo here was anybody's guess. It was probably a punishment since there was absolutely nothing a drunk who subsisted on twenty-first-century castoffs could want from a road that hadn't changed much in three hundred years.

A uniformed patrol officer directed traffic around a set of orange cones. Vega flashed his badge and quickly maneuvered to the side of the road before the young cop had a chance to process anything beyond Vega's department and title.

He wasn't supposed to be here.

He parked his truck on the shoulder and studied the area from his rearview mirror. There was a field the color of hay cordoned off by yellow crime-scene tape. It was tamped down along a rough approximation of a path that trailed off into a copse of dense green hemlocks and maples. A crumbling stone wall meandered near the path, some of its boulders loosened and scattered like a child's set of blocks. Vega saw movement through the trees. Cops were like sheep: they never wandered by themselves. Even at the entrance to the cordoned-off area, Vega counted not one, but two uniformed officers—one from Lake Holly and one from Wickford. The Lake Holly cop was guffawing. Vega caught the last stanza of a familiar children's song that the Wickford cop had supplied with new lyrics:

"Z . . . A . . . M . . . B . . . O, *and Zambo was his name-o!*"

The two cops stopped the moment Louis Greco emerged from the woods. He had a way of walking—knees out, chest forward—that gave the impression he could knock you down without breaking stride. He shot one glance in the officers' direction and sliced a blue-gloved finger across his throat. The singing stopped immediately. He had that effect on people.

Vega hopped out of the cab as soon as Greco caught sight of his truck.

"What the *hell* do you think you're doing here, Vega? And which dipshit rookie let you in?"

"Our one freakin' witness is dead and you don't call me about it?"

"'Cause it's not your case anymore. Go home."

"I would if you were doing your job. How come nobody called in my crime-scene unit?"

"Because it ain't no crime scene." Greco peeled off his nonlatex gloves and shoved them in the pocket of his insulated jacket. "Zambo drank himself to death, plain and simple."

"Says who? Those Boy Scouts with guns?" Vega nodded across the field to the Wickford officer who had just given his "Bingo" rendition, no doubt replete with lots of politically incorrect stanzas.

"I just looked at Zambo's body," said Greco. "There are no knife or gunshot wounds. No bruises. No evidence of a struggle. He was a lifelong alcoholic. It was bound to happen. It just sucks that it happened now."

"I don't believe that."

"Because you don't want to." Greco squinted out at the roadway and cursed under his breath. "For chrissake, at least get in my car in case the brass drives by."

Vega followed Greco over to his unmarked Chevy. They got in and Greco pulled out a package of red licorice Twizzlers from his glove compartment. His addiction. He tore open the cellophane and offered one to Vega. Vega waved it away.

"How did you even find out about Zambo?" asked Greco between bites.

"From Mark Hammond. I called him this morning because I think maybe the same Spanish woman who delivered Dominga Flores's baby delivered Baby Mercy as well."

"And this is based on—?"

"It's a theory."

"Well, here's something that isn't a *theory*," said Greco. "Joy was the midwife. Your daughter. That's what the evidence says. The afterbirth on the quilt, Joy's hoodie on the victim, your daughter's medical familiarity with pregnant women—"

"Did you talk to Dolan yet about Claudia Aguilar's grandson?" asked Vega. "He claims he knew the girl."

"You mean Neto Forgeto?" Greco swallowed the rest of his Twizzler and licked his fingers. He never lost his appetite, not even at a crime scene. "Dolan talked to everybody at that car wash this morning. No one's seen the girl. No one knows anyone named Mia. Dolan took a DNA swab from Neto just in case there's a reason we're not seeing. Neto's dad's a landscaper in town."

"Neto has a father?"

"Yeah. Inés's ex. His name is—get this—*Romeo*. Aptly named. He's a favorite of the soccer moms in Lake Holly. And believe me, it ain't for his green thumb."

Vega shook his head. "My daughter didn't do anything, Grec."

"Give us time, maybe me and Dolan will believe the same thing. But you keep messing around where you don't belong, you're gonna force our hand. Don't be a jerk. Go home. Or better yet, find Adele and do what got you in trouble in the first place."

Something inside of Vega deflated. He stared at his hands. "She's leaving."

"Huh? Adele?"

"She's taking a job with Schulman in D.C. if he wins the election."

"Well, that sucks. For you, I mean," said Greco. "For our guys, it might be cause for a little fiesta. But either way, I suppose it was bound to happen."

"What do you mean?"

"C'mon, Vega, Adele's an Ivy League lawyer who was slumming for a while—in her career and uh . . ." Greco's voice dropped away.

"You're saying I wasn't good enough for her?"

"I'm not Dear Abby, okay? I'm just saying, you know—you're a local cop. A blue-collar working stiff. And you two—aren't exactly alike in a lotta ways."

"Yeah? Well, fuck you very much."

Two attendants from the medical examiner's office emerged from the woods now with a body bag on a stretcher.

"Look, I'm sorry about Adele. But I gotta go." Greco nodded to the attendants walking the body bag to their van. "Guess we won't be having any more Virgin Mary sightings." He put a hand on the car door and began to open it.

"Zambo didn't call her the Virgin Mary."

"Sure he did."

"Not this last time," said Vega. "He told Rafael he saw the Lady of Sorrows."

"Same thing. So?"

"Maybe this time, he really saw someone. Someone carrying a baby in those woods. Someone he associates with the Catholic church in town. And now he's dead."

"You're reaching." Greco hopped out of the car and walked over to the attendants. They laid the stretcher down for a moment and Greco unzipped the bag. It was a personal habit of his and one Vega respected him for. He always liked to take one last look at a corpse away from the place of death, to remind himself that the person was a person before they were a body.

Vega got out of the car and walked up behind Greco. He saw Zambo's unshaven face, the skin dark gray with underlying splotches of purple. From the smell and the skin color, it was clear Zambo had been dead a few days. Up close like this, the man lost all his cartoonish humor.

He was a human being, not a punch line to a joke. His mouth was crusted in bloody vomit; his cheeks had turned concave as if he were being eaten alive from the inside. But even in death, his eyes had a depth to them that Vega never would have expected, as if beneath the booze and the squalor, there was an intelligence that had tried to survive the onslaught. Vega noted his hair. It was still dark—naturally so. Not more than a few strands of gray. He wasn't nearly as old as everyone thought.

Greco zipped up the bag and nodded to the attendants to take him away. Then he began walking across the field toward the woods. Vega called out after him.

"You find any liquor bottles back there?"

"A ton of beer cans." Greco said over his shoulder. "Wickford's doing the paperwork to get them tested. And that's the last thing I'm gonna tell you."

"They're going to come up clean. They're not even going to have his DNA on them."

Greco turned. "You know his drinking preferences all of a sudden? Maybe *you* should be my suspect."

"Beer's too heavy to lug out here without a car. That's what the teenagers bring. The hardcore guys like Zambo want a lot of bang for their buck. Look for cheap plastic vodka bottles. Like we saw in the woods behind La Casa."

Greco held Vega's gaze for a moment. The radio on his hip squawked with a voice Vega recognized as Mark Hammond's. He could almost picture that Kennedy jawline.

Greco clicked on his radio. "You find any liquor bottles, Mark?"

"Negative. Just beer cans."

"Have you ever known Zambo to go somewhere and *not* drink?" asked Vega. Greco motioned for Vega to be quiet. Greco clicked on his radio again. "I'm coming out there. Ask your guys to do one more sweep for liquor bottles. Copy?"

A pause. *That territory thing again.* Finally, a voice over the radio: "Affirmative."

Vega nodded. "Let me know if you find any."

Greco feigned a salute but only his middle finger was extended. Vega got the hint.

"Get out of Dodge."

He didn't.

He was only a five-minute drive from Bob and Karen Reilly's house. It was easier to speak to Dominga directly than to wait for the Wickford police to get around to sending him their report. He walked up to the front door and rang the bell beside the ERIN GO BRAGH plaque.

Dominga answered. She had her infant son propped over her shoulder. She looked surprised to see him—and a little wary.

"Detective?" The dark shadows had faded beneath her eyes. Her color had returned. She had sneakers on her feet, not plastic sandals anymore. All good signs.

"Miss? I'm sorry to bother you," said Vega in Spanish. "I just had a few quick questions. May I come in and speak to you?"

"The Reillys aren't home."

Vega wondered if she was fearful of letting a man in the house while she was alone. He couldn't blame her after what she'd been through. The fact that he was a cop would offer very little in the way of assurance. Many immigrants, Vega knew, had bad associations with the police in their own countries.

"Would you prefer I speak to you out here by the door? I can do that."

She hesitated. "No. It's okay, I guess. But I'm watching the children."

"I understand."

Vega expected even more chaos in the house than before. But when he entered, there was a measure of calm he hadn't experienced the last time he was here. The five-year-old girl was in the living room, coloring. The two-and-a-half-year-old boy was near her, playing with his trucks. The eight-month-old was taking a nap on a pad on the floor. The living room toys were neatly stacked in piles. Vega could smell something cheesy and comforting simmering on the stove.

"I didn't think you'd move back in here," he said.

"I didn't either," Dominga admitted. "But they missed me. And I missed them. I don't want to live in a shelter. After everything that's happened . . ." Her voice trailed off. "The señora and I are trying to make it work."

Vega nodded. "Don't tell her I said this, but you're doing way better with four than she was with three."

Dominga smiled, the first smile he'd seen on her. She looked so much younger and prettier when she smiled. "I'm the oldest of eight. I've had practice."

She led him into the living room. They sat on the beanbag sofa and spoke over Nick Junior cartoons. Gradually Vega eased the conversation around to the woman who helped deliver Dominga's little boy.

"Do you remember her name?" he asked.

"No." She fussed with her son on her shoulder.

"No, you don't remember? Or no, you never knew it?"

Dominga shrugged. She did not meet his gaze.

"See, the thing is," said Vega slowly, leaning forward to catch her eye, "Neil Davies doesn't speak Spanish and doesn't live in an area with a lot of Latinos. I find it hard to believe he'd be able to hire a Spanish-speaking midwife for you. But you? I know from Karen Reilly that you helped her run her eBay business. Karen said you know all the nannies and housekeepers in town. Maybe one of them also delivers babies? Or knows someone who does?"

"I did nothing wrong."

"Of course you didn't," Vega assured her. "I just want her name as a witness. Against Davies. Don't you want that? Don't you want to make sure he goes to prison for a long, long time?" Not the whole truth, but then as a cop, Vega rarely dealt in whole truths.

"I don't see why I need a witness," she said. "The police already asked me if I could leave that house. And I told them what I told you: Where could I go? I could always walk away. But then where would I go with my baby?"

"Are you afraid you'll get this woman in trouble? With immigration? With the licensing boards?"

"Mr. Neil would have made me deliver by myself if I hadn't called her. He would never have let me go to the hospital."

Bingo. She did know the midwife. "If she was helping you," said Vega, "why didn't she tell the police your situation?"

"Mr. Neil is a rich and powerful man. What could she do?"

Vega had heard Adele speak with frustration at the passivity sometimes of her female clients. They accepted abuse and powerlessness as their lot in life. It was very hard to convince them they had a choice.

"This woman, she's a midwife? A *partera*?"

"And *curandera*," said Dominga.

A traditional healer. Vega suspected she was most likely unlicensed. "Has she delivered other women's babies?"

"Please, Detective. She's old. She started delivering babies years ago, beginning with her own family. She doesn't do it so much anymore. Mostly, she just mixes herbs for clients now. She was trying to help me."

The eight-month-old began to stir from his nap. Dominga put her own baby in an infant swing to free her hands for a diaper change. Vega could do without reliving those glory days. He hung back with the five-year-old girl.

"Want me to draw you a picture?" asked the girl.

"Um, okay," said Vega. The girl grabbed a sheet of purple paper and started making bold lines and big circles. "This is a puppy, see? And she's smelling a flower."

The child talked nonstop just like Joy had at that age. Vega oohed and aahed in all the appropriate places. She filled up most of the page and handed the paper to Vega. "It's a gift!"

"Wow. You're a good artist. Thank you." Vega turned the paper over and noticed printed words in Spanish on the other side: *Want to sell your things on eBay?*

"We ran out of scrap paper," said Dominga as she came back in the room with the eight-month-old and sat him down on the carpet to play.

Vega put the drawing down beside him. He gestured to the eBay ad on the back. "Your friend, the *curandera*—is she a client of your business?"

Dominga hesitated. "I have many clients."

Vega knew a hundred ways to push her for a name. But then he ran the risk of alienating her so much she might refuse to cooperate on the case against Neil Davies. That slimeball would walk free. No way could Vega stomach that, so he tried for a softer approach.

"How about you ask if I can call her? Or she can call me." He handed Dominga his card.

"Okay. I will ask."

She agreed because it would be impolite not to. Whether she would do it was another matter. Still, he had to try. Otherwise, everything came back to Joy. The hoodie. The quilt. What were the odds that both would end up with the same girl and Joy *not* be involved?

Zero. Unless . . .

Vega flipped the girl's drawing to the ad on back: *Want to sell your things on eBay?*

He thought about the fuzzy Pepto-Bismol-colored jacket that he saw downstairs the other day. It looked just like the one Joy used to wear. *Exactly* like it, to be precise.

Dolan would have checked, wouldn't he? Then again, what was there to check? Wendy had no receipt. His ex-wife would have bagged up the clothes and then assumed . . . Of course she would have assumed . . .

"The woman who helped deliver Emilio—she lives in Lake Holly?"

"Yes. But please, Detective—let me speak to her first. I'm sure she'll help you if she can."

Vega wasn't going to wait around to find out.

Chapter 22

Wendy's neighborhood looked nearly deserted on a Thursday at noon. Vega parked his truck in her driveway and walked up to her side door. It was a simple door, nothing like the double-height front entrance door with its raised, hand-crafted walnut panels and etched-glass windows running down either side. Vega had never stood at that door, never felt the cool grandeur of its welcome. Even when he picked up Joy for a father/daughter evening out, he never considered himself invited. He was an occasional inconvenience borne of necessity—similar in rank to the plumber and deserving of the same reception.

He rang the side doorbell and waited. Rosa opened the door.

"Señor," she said, surprised. She wore black glasses with narrow frames that sat low across the bridge of her nose, so she had to look over the tops to see him. "Joy is not here." She spoke to Vega in Spanish. They always conversed in Spanish.

"Yes, I know. Actually, I came to speak to you."

"Me?" She touched a hand to her chest. She had sturdy hands with long fingers that reminded Vega with a pang of his mother. For all the times he'd chatted with Rosa Soliz as he waited to pick up Joy, this was the first time he'd given her more than a passing glance.

"May I come in?"

A small frown wrinkled her lips and formed little pouches along her jaw below her prominent cheekbones. She ran a hand from her widow's peak of graying hair to the bun that held it tightly in back.

"The señora—she said it's okay?"

Of course not. Wendy would never say it's okay. Last night was probably the first time Vega had ever stepped into his ex-wife's house beyond the little mudroom off the kitchen, and Wendy was as jumpy as a nesting sparrow. Did Wendy really think that while they were sitting there with Joy in tears and their $300-an-hour lawyer explaining the case, Vega was going to be sizing up her furniture and who was leaving messages on her answering machine? (Okay, maybe a little.)

"I just have a couple of things I really need your help on. It won't take long." He hoped to bypass the issue of Wendy. He didn't want to lie. "I can stay in the kitchen if you'd like. I was in the kitchen last night when the lawyer was here," he reminded her.

Rosa pressed her lips together and considered the request. She nodded and opened the door wider.

"Okay." She said the word in English, the way Vega had seen her do when something wasn't "okay," but she just had to accept it. *Okay, I stay late tonight. Okay, I fix the twins dinner. Okay, I hem Joy's dress when the señora should really pay a tailor to do it.*

Vega often cringed from the mudroom when he witnessed these little interchanges between Rosa and his ex-wife or daughter. Growing up, he'd had friends whose mothers and grandmothers were housekeepers and nannies. They often came home with stories of having to smile and say yes to ridiculous requests or thoughtless behaviors. The employers were usually decent people—even generous people. But they were clueless about how spoiled and self-centered they came across to their tired, poor, and overwhelmed help.

Worse, the mothers and grandmothers of his friends developed a double standard. The same behavior they tolerated and even indulged in their employers' children made them furious in their own. His friend Henry Lopez once tracked dirt from a vacant lot where they'd been playing onto his mother's living-room sofa (one reason Vega's own mother covered hers in plastic). Señora Lopez, a housekeeper, beat Henry so hard with her rubber-soled *chancletas* that Vega saw the shoe outline on his friend's legs the next day. After what Vega saw as a child, he could never be comfortable with an employer/servant relationship. *Ever.*

"Would you like some coffee, señor? Something to eat?"

"No, thank you." He pulled a stool out from under the center island counter. "May I?"

Rosa nodded.

Vega straddled the stool and rested his elbows on the counter. Sunlight streamed in from skylights overhead and lit up a vase of white hydrangeas next to him. On the surrounding walls were framed photographs of the family on vacation. Seeing Wendy and Joy in those pictures filled Vega with a deep sense of loss. He wondered if he'd be staring at a photo of Adele in D.C. one day and wondering, as he did now, if he'd ever had the power to make it different.

"I'm very sorry about what is happening to Joy," said Rosa.

"We all are," said Vega. "I know you spoke to the police yesterday."

"I told them I don't know the girl. I'm sorry."

Vega folded his hands under his chin. "Detective

Dolan—can be very intimidating. Perhaps now that it's just you and me—"

"I would have told him if I knew the girl," Rosa insisted. "I don't."

Vega pulled the Reilly girl's drawing out of a pocket in his jacket. "But you know this." He flipped over the paper to the eBay ad and smoothed it out on the counter in front of Rosa.

"Dominga gave you this?" she asked.

"Yes." *Sort of.*

Rosa swallowed. Her eyes turned glassy. "I meant no harm."

"I need you to tell me what happened."

"The señora was going to throw it out."

"Huh?" Vega leaned forward. He couldn't believe what he was hearing.

"It seemed like such a waste. I didn't think anyone would find out."

"You didn't think anyone would find *out?*"

"Please don't tell Señora Wendy."

"Wait"—Vega's head was spinning—"are we talking about the same thing?"

"The clothes. That the señora gave me to put in the Goodwill bin. I gave them to Dominga to sell. That's what you're asking me, isn't it?"

"I'm asking you about Dominga's baby."

Rosa frowned. "I didn't give her any baby clothes. Did she deliver already?"

"Don't you know?"

"I haven't seen Dominga in months."

Vega massaged his forehead. He'd come in search of one piece of the puzzle and ended up with an entirely different piece. He folded Dominga's ad and stuffed it back into the pocket of his jacket, where it resided with the flyer on the dead teenager. He still had Baby Mercy's photo on his cell phone as well. He carried dead people with him every-where these days.

"So let me get this straight," he said to Rosa. "Wendy gave you several bags of Joy's old clothes to put in the Goodwill bin and you gave them to Dominga to sell on eBay instead?"

"I didn't steal," said Rosa. "I would never steal."

"Why didn't you just ask Wendy for the clothes? She'd have given them to you."

"Yes. To give to my children and grandchildren in El Salvador. To wear. But what they need is money, not clothes. How could I ask to profit from what belongs to her? It would be—*uncomfortable*—to ask such a thing."

"But not uncomfortable to sell them behind her back?"

"She never knew. It was harmless, señor. Please don't tell her—"

"Why didn't you tell Detective Dolan that you never put the clothes in the Goodwill bin?"

"Because he wanted to know only about Joy's hoodie and quilt. Dominga didn't take those things. So what was the point of telling?"

"What happened to them?"

"I gave everything she didn't want to charity."

"So wait—you tossed them in the Goodwill bin?" If that was the case, Vega was back to where he started.

"No," said Rosa, "I donated them to Our Lady of Sorrows. The big Catholic church in town. They have a program there for the homeless called Helping Hand."

Mano Amiga. Vega had heard of it.

"So you see?" said Rosa. "I didn't steal anything. You don't have to tell the señora, do you? She'll fire me."

"Wendy's not going to fire you." Vega took out his notepad. "So you dropped everything off at the church?"

"No. Around the corner."

"I'm not following."

"The head of Helping Hand lives here. In The Farms. I walked the things over to her. Your daughter tutors their son, so I thought no one would mind—"

"Wait—" said Vega. "So you gave those things to—"

"Esmeralda Gonzalez. Don Charlie's wife."

Chapter 23

Esme Gonzalez was young—much younger than her husband. Her jet-black hair was pulled into a high ponytail, her eyelashes were thick with mascara, and when she parted her pink lips, Vega noticed a mouth full of porcelain veneers. Yet for all her attention to American notions of beauty, there was something traditionally Mexican about her. Perhaps it was the coquettish tilt of her head as she hung back in the doorway, the hesitant timbre of her voice, the way she never met Vega's gaze head-on.

"Pardon, señora. I'm looking for my daughter, Joy. Is she here?" Vega already knew she was. That was his pretext for coming in the first place.

"She's in the kitchen tutoring my son. Would you like me to get her?"

"Do you know when she'll be finished?"

Esme looked at her watch. "She has another twenty minutes to go. But if you need her—?"

"No, please. I don't want to interrupt. Would you mind if I waited for her inside?"

Esme ran a manicured hand along the sweep of her ponytail. Her bright pink lips drew in on themselves. Vega could see that strangers made her uncomfortable, but she was too polite to turn him away.

"Of course, señor. Come in."

Vega stepped into the front hallway. The floor was tiled in green and white marble. A sweeping staircase billowed like silk beneath a crystal chandelier. To the right of the stairs stood a grouping of brightly colored vases in rainbow shades of hand-blown glass and painted terracotta. On the walls were large oil canvasses of rural hillsides and red tile-roofed houses. Vega was amazed that a home with young children in it could have such a museum-like feel.

"Would you like some coffee, señor?"

"Call me Jimmy. And no thanks, I'm good."

His voice must have carried because at that moment, Joy poked her head out of the kitchen.

"Dad? What are you—?"

"Just wanted to talk to you a moment when you're through. I'm happy to wait."

The longer, the better.

Two boys, both about nine, came through the kitchen to ask Esme for something to drink. She looked momentarily overwhelmed. Vega guessed one was her son and the other a friend or cousin. He noted from the kitchen window that there were several more Hispanic-looking children in the yard—two younger ones sliding down the play-gym slide and a teenage girl sitting off to one side, knees curled up to her chest. There was something guarded and a little sad about her. Vega thought of Joy. Girls could be sulky and hard to read once they reached adolescence. Not that they were any easier to read afterward, either.

"I'll make lemonade if you go outside and leave Christian to do his studies in peace," Esme told the boys.

They nodded and disappeared. Vega followed Esme into the kitchen.

"I've got you on a bad day," he said, switching to Spanish.

Esme gave a small nod of appreciation at the shift in tongues.

"Every day is like this," she replied, also in Spanish. Her voice carried a level of fatigue that was absent from her body. Her skin was smooth, her makeup flawless. She wasn't thin, but she carried her stockiness well, accentuating the curves and minimizing the excesses.

She pulled a glass pitcher out of a cupboard.

"You and your husband are very active in the community," said Vega. "You do a great deal for people, I know."

"We do what we can."

Esme put the pitcher on the granite counter next to a spray of delicate pink orchids and a birdcage with two parakeets fluttering about, one with a blue breast and one with a green. When Vega was a boy, his mom did their wash at a Laundromat in the Bronx run by a lady who kept parakeets. Vega used to spend hours watching them. Aside from the foul-mouthed parrot who lived upstairs in their building, those birds were the only pets he'd ever experienced in his childhood. None of their landlords allowed dogs or cats.

Esme began spooning pink powdered lemonade into the pitcher. Vega tried hard to ignore the dirty looks from his daughter on the other side of the kitchen. For once, he was thankful Joy's Spanish was limited. She wouldn't know enough to stop him from what he had to do.

"Please, can you reach those cookies up there?" asked Esme, pointing to a high shelf. "I like to keep them somewhere where the children don't get into them and eat too many."

"Of course." Vega pulled down a package of generic-looking chocolate-chip cookies. They didn't look especially tempting to begin with.

"You know Rosa Soliz, right?" he began.

"She's your wife's"—Esme corrected herself—"your ex-wife's—housekeeper, yes?"

"That's her," said Vega. "She tells me you run the homeless program at Our Lady of Sorrows."

"Yes." Esme measured out cold water from a dispenser on the door of her refrigerator. Vega waited for her to say more, but she didn't.

"That must be a lot of work—feeding and clothing people. You must have a lot of help."

"I have some," said Esme. "But I do a lot of it."

"You run the clothing drives? That's a big job in itself, I suspect. All the sorting and cleaning."

"We don't clean donated items."

"No?"

Esme poured the water into the pitcher of powdered lemonade. The water turned a pink not found in nature. "We assume people wash the clothes before they donate them, but we don't have the resources to do it if they don't. Goodwill and most thrift stores have the same policy."

"Ah," said Vega. "I didn't know." If nothing else, Esme's statement would back up Joy's assertions that she'd worn that hoodie, given it away, and her scent had remained for the state trooper's dog to find.

"Rosa tells me she donated some of Joy's things to your clothing drive maybe a month or two ago," said Vega. "A black zippered hoodie and a flowered quilt. You wouldn't happen to remember those items, would you?"

Esme stopped stirring the lemonade. "People donate things all the time. I can't be expected to remember everything they claim to have given me."

"I totally understand. I wouldn't ask if it weren't important, señora. Joy *has* told you I'm a police officer, I assume?"

From Esme's blank expression it was clear that Vega's

name never came up in conversation, much less his occupation. Vega sometimes felt like an asterisk in his daughter's life. He tried to brush back the hurt and plunge ahead while the moment was in his favor.

"A few days ago, a teenage girl was found dead wearing the hoodie I just described," Vega explained. "No one knows who she is, including Joy. I thought perhaps you might be able to identify her."

She frowned. "No. I don't know any girl."

Vega pulled a flyer of the girl out of a pocket of his jacket and began to unfold it across the counter. "Perhaps if you saw her—?"

"Please." She waved it away. "That's not necessary. Not here."

"Perhaps in the other room?"

"I told you, I don't know her."

"Maybe your husband does?"

"I'm sure he doesn't."

"Could you show it to him? The police have a witness who saw her at your husband's car wash here in Lake Holly. With her mother."

"Her *mother?*"

"Maybe she was a local girl who had some troubles?"

"Once they get with a boy, it's all troubles."

"Get with a boy?"

"You know, pregnant."

Vega stood very still with his hand resting on the crumpled flyer. "Do you have reason to believe she was pregnant?"

She turned away from him and wiped her hands on a towel. "I'm just saying with girls"—she sounded flustered—"that's always the problem, isn't it?"

"How about with this girl?"

"I don't know. Now, if you'll excuse me." She grabbed some plastic cups from a cabinet and put the cookies on a paper plate. She switched to English and spoke over her shoulder. "I think the lesson is over."

"We just have one more page to do," said Joy.

"It's over! Your money is on the counter, Joy. Thank you." She stuffed Vega's flyer in a drawer. "I need to take these things to the children. I'm sure you and your daughter can find your way out."

At the car, Joy could barely contain herself.

"What did you say to her, Dad?"

"Nothing."

"I may not speak Spanish well, but I heard her tone of voice. You upset her. And probably got me fired! What did you do?"

"Nothing—I just asked if she knew the dead girl."

"*What?* Why would you ask a thing like that?"

Vega hesitated. He couldn't tell Joy all he knew, so he settled on the little bit that Rosa was likely to confess to her and Wendy anyway. "Rosa gave that hoodie and quilt of yours to Esme for Mano Amiga's clothing drive."

"Goodwill—Mano Amiga—what difference does it make? You sounded like you were accusing her of something. And you were doing it while I was in the room. You embarrassed me, Dad!"

"I just want to help you—"

"No! What you want is to prove to yourself that I have nothing to do with this situation. I've already told you that, but you don't believe me."

Do I? Vega couldn't deny the nugget of truth to her words. She'd become a complex girl in her teenage years. He couldn't always read her correctly. He needed to be sure.

Joy clicked her remote, and the Volvo's doors all powered open. She opened the driver's side and tossed her backpack onto the front passenger seat. Then she turned to her father. "You know how you can help me?"

"Tell me and I'll do it."

"Back off." She got into her car, slammed the door, and pulled out of the driveway. A moment later, she was gone. Like her mother. Like Adele. Women always walked out on him, one way or another.

He couldn't head home—not yet. Not with everything running through his head. He pulled off at the next side street and dialed Greco.

"You better be calling me long distance from that lean-to in the woods you call home."

"I'm headed there now."

"I don't like the sound of that."

"Well, here's something else you might not like the sound of." Vega began telling Greco about his conversation with Esme Gonzalez. Greco erupted in an explosion of curses.

"What the—? Are you smoking something, Vega? You interrogated a respected member of the Lake Holly Hispanic community—in *my* backyard, on a case that you've been ordered to stay away from?"

"It wasn't an interrogation, Grec. It was a conversation while I was picking up my daughter from her tutoring gig. I have a right to pick up my daughter. And besides, I got a hunch Esme knows something."

"Well, you're wrong."

"Says you?"

"Says a DNA test from the county lab."

Vega turned off his engine. "What DNA?"

Silence.

"Not *Joy's* DNA?"

"Relax. It's not Joy's."

"Then whose?"

Greco sighed. "Let's just say your Neto lead wasn't a total waste."

"Don't tell me Neto's the baby's father?"

Greco laughed. "I don't even want to picture that one. But you're warm. The DNA came back a ninety-nine percent likelihood that Neto and Baby Mercy share the same father."

"You're kidding," said Vega. "So that means—?"

"That gardener, Romeo Rivera, really gets around."

Chapter 24

The rest of Thursday passed in a blur for Dulce, Mateo, and Luna. Doña Esme offered to take them to McDonald's after they left court, but none of them were hungry and Mateo was afraid he'd throw up again. So instead she took them back to their old apartment and told them to each pack one black garbage bag of clothes and personal items to take to her house.

"Only one bag?" asked Dulce. She had enough stuffed animals alone to fill a bag.

"I can't have all this stuff in my house," said Doña Esme. She dismissed their mementos and family pictures with a wave of her hand. "Your things will be safe. Don't worry. We'll put them in storage for you."

The Gonzalezes had such a big house and their place was so tiny, Luna thought they'd be able to bring all their personal stuff with them. Dulce's lips began to quiver. Luna knew she didn't want to part with her animals. Luna helped her pack her favorites: a duck with an orange beak and oversized feet she'd had since she was a baby, a pink and blue cow Mami used to sing to, a flowered pig Papi won for her at the county fair. Mateo took his Matchbox classic car set, his baseball bat and glove, and a picture of Papi and Mami at La Bella Vita. Luna chose a few of her favorite books, some family photos, and her mother's pot of pink begonias, which she rested on top of her garbage bag. She left her *Better Homes and Gardens* magazines behind. All they did was remind her of the things that could never be.

Until this day, Luna had thought of herself as an American girl—no different from any other girl at Lake Holly High. She watched TeenNick and listened to One Direction. She recited the Pledge of Allegiance every morning at school. She knew all the words to "The Star Spangled Banner" (unlike most of her friends). She even shared a birthday with her adopted country: July Fourth. When she was small, she thought all those fireworks were just for her.

Luna didn't have a country anymore. Or an allegiance. Her father was her allegiance. The hole in her heart was so big, she couldn't imagine filling it with anything except bitterness.

Don't let anything come between you and what you want to do in this life. Her father's last wish. Luna was too angry to want to follow it. She was even angry at Papi. How could he bring her to this place only to abandon her with two young siblings to care for? Maybe if they'd stayed in Mexico, Mami would still be alive. At the very least, they'd be together. She'd feel whole.

"I wanted to take all of my animals," Dulce whimpered.

"It's just for a little while," Luna whispered. She kept trying to tell herself the same thing.

Doña Esme put her hands on her hips and surveyed their apartment. She sighed. "We'll give the keys back to the landlord later today, and I'll see if someone at your church can buy your father's car. We'll have to let the school know to pick you all up at our house tomorrow."

Luna knew what she was saying was practical, but it felt painful right now to contemplate. She couldn't imagine going back to school. She couldn't imagine sitting in class with Mr. Murphy yammering on about Catherine the Great and the Russian serfs and believing that any of it mattered.

If Grace changed her mind and asked Luna to do the talent show now, she'd say no. Who cares about a dumb talent show? Who cares about anything?

Doña Esme ordered the three children to grab their garbage bags to leave. Luna tried to help Dulce with hers, but she was carrying too many things. The terra-cotta flower-pot slipped from Luna's hands and cracked in two on the bare floor. Dirt scattered everywhere. Mami's beautiful plant lay sideways in the clay shards.

"No! No!" Luna began to cry. Mateo and Dulce dropped their bags and tried to gather the pieces of pottery and dirt around the little plant.

"Just leave it," Doña Esme ordered. "The landlord will clean it up."

"But it's my mother's plant!" cried Luna. "I can't leave without it!"

Doña Esme sighed impatiently. "Find something to stick it in and let's get going."

Luna found an empty coffee can in the garbage. Mateo and Dulce helped her scrape the dirt off the floor and into the can. They did their best to tuck it around the plant roots. The little begonia looked sad and displaced—just like them.

In the car, Luna held the can on her lap. Dulce and Mateo were quiet.

"When do you think we'll be able to talk to Papi?" Luna asked Doña Esme.

Doña Esme seemed annoyed by the question. Or maybe she just sensed that no answer she gave was the one they wanted. "Mr. Katz told me you have to search the ICE database by your father's alien registration number." *Alien registration number.* It made him sound like he was from Mars.

"I don't know where that is." What if Luna couldn't find the number? Then what?

"It's on his order-of-removal forms," said Doña Esme.

"Mr. Katz said they only update it every eight hours or so and your father has to be processed first, so I don't think you'll know anything until tomorrow at the earliest."

"Will he call? He still has his cell phone."

"I don't think they let you hold onto your cell phone until you're released from custody. I don't know."

"Will he be here? In New York?"

Doña Esme shrugged. "I had a cousin deported years ago. They moved her all around the country—Pennsylvania, Kentucky, Texas—before they finally deported her across the border. They don't take you all the way back to where you're from, you know. Your father will end up in someplace like Nogales, just across the border. He'll have to make the long journey home himself—unless he decides to try to cross back right away. Then I guess he'll stay around Nogales."

"Do you think he'll try that?"

Doña Esme bit her lip and considered the question. "I hope not. It's very, very hard these days. Your father isn't in the right frame of mind. Everything is very different than it was when he crossed with you and your mother."

"Would they deport him again?"

"That is the lucky outcome."

Oh God. Luna wished she'd talked more to Papi about these things when he was here. She'd closed her ears and shut her eyes. She didn't want to believe this could happen. And now her mind was filled with what-ifs. What if he tried to cross right away in a blind panic to get back to them? What if he died of thirst in the desert and they never heard from him again? Or he got kidnapped by a gang? Or some *cholo* in Nogales blew him away for the price of a pack of cigarettes? Her father was a very openhearted man. He took everyone at face value. She was a bundle of nerves just thinking about where he might be and what might happen to him. She'd give anything to hear his voice on the other end of a telephone.

Ten minutes later, Doña Esme pulled up to their house. Its fake grandeur no longer excited Luna. It looked tacky and cheap, like a roadside motel. Even Dulce and Mateo, who had liked the place so much as visitors, were decidedly more subdued now that this was their new home. Doña Esme took them in through the side entrance again. Luna got the impression they'd never enter through the front door. Just to make sure the children understood this, Doña Esme gestured to the front foyer, with its crystal chandelier and huge, brightly colored glass and ceramic vases.

"You do not play in or near this area. Do you understand?"

Mateo and Dulce nodded silently. They both seemed a little overwhelmed and frightened by this first formal introduction to Doña Esme's house.

"Also, the living room," said Doña Esme, gesturing to a room on her right. "You do not play in there, either."

The living room was two stories tall with a white marble fireplace mantel, a black leather sofa, and a cream-colored rug that looked as if no one ever walked across it. A sound Luna wasn't expecting floated out of the room: chirping.

"Birds!" Dulce said excitedly. It was the first happy sound Luna had heard from her since they took Papi away.

By the living room window, Luna could see a parakeet with a sky-blue breast clinging to the outside of a large white birdcage. Another parakeet with a lime-green breast perched on the fireplace irons. Dulce began to walk in the direction of the birds.

"No," said Doña Esme, blocking the way. "The birds are mine. You are not to touch them."

The light went out in Dulce's eyes. She wouldn't have hurt the birds, thought Luna. They would have soothed her. But maybe the birds frightened easily. Luna didn't know birds, so she tried to give Doña Esme the benefit of the doubt. Still, she wished the woman had let Dulce pet or feed one, even with her supervision.

Doña Esme must have realized she was a little abrupt with Dulce because she added, "The blue-breasted one is the boy, Chavo. The green-breasted one is the girl, Flor. They are my babies."

Luna thought it was a strange thing to say given that Doña Esme had three healthy sons. And yet, looking around, she noted that there wasn't a single photograph of the children anywhere. Not on the mantel. Not on the bookshelf with its perfect groupings of pottery and glassware. Not in the front hallway. The whole house looked as if no one really lived here. What did it say about people when they could live in a place without showing a trace of their true selves?

The Gonzalez boys came home from school in the afternoon. They tried to be kind and respectful of Luna and her siblings' grief. They didn't ask a lot of questions or talk too animatedly about their day. After their homework, Alex and David took Mateo and Dulce outside to play. Luna sat with them while Christian got tutored in math. After the tutor left with her father, Luna asked Doña Esme for a container to repot Mami's begonia. Doña Esme found an old plastic pot, and Luna did her best to tuck the roots back into the dirt they'd managed to salvage off their floor. Doña Esme offered to keep the plant in the kitchen, but Luna opted instead to keep it in the bedroom she and Dulce would be sharing. That way, she could look at it all the time. She hoped there would be enough light on the windowsill there.

After she replanted the begonia, Luna offered to help Doña Esme prepare dinner. Doña Esme set out a cutting board and some vegetables to slice, but when Luna was finished, Doña Esme complained that the tomatoes weren't thin enough and the peppers still had seeds in them.

"Your mami didn't teach you how to cook?"

Her question sounded like a criticism of Luna's mother.

"Papi was such a good cook," said Luna. "He always did the cooking. I did other things."

"Hah. He spoiled you." Maybe it was because Doña Esme only had sons, but she seemed prickly with Luna and even Dulce in a way she wasn't with Mateo.

In the evening, the señor came home and softened the atmosphere a bit. Luna could tell he was happy they were here. He talked baseball with Mateo and promised both Dulce and Mateo that he would get them bikes, which brought a bit of light to their faces. He didn't promise Luna anything, and she was glad. She didn't want anything from anyone right now but to talk to Papi.

She barely touched her dinner—chicken enchiladas. They were soggy and under-spiced. Papi was a much better cook. But she was glad that Dulce and Mateo were eating a little better again.

After dinner, the señor checked the ICE website on his computer. It had been updated to show that Papi was in Pennsylvania, in a place called Lords Valley, at the Pike County Correctional Facility.

"Correctional facility," said Mateo, mouthing the words like they were coated in something rancid. "But Papi's not a criminal."

"Of course not!" said the señor. "But he won't be there for long. The government here is like Mexico in one way: they don't work so much on the weekends. Tomorrow is Friday, and there is too much paperwork to do for one day, so he will probably be there until Monday. I think by Tuesday he'll be back in Mexico."

Luna wondered if Papi knew he was in a place called Lords Valley, and if he could take any comfort from that. She suddenly realized that the three of them hadn't prayed since her father was taken away. She vowed to try with Dulce and Mateo tonight, if only because she suspected that Papi would also be praying, and maybe somewhere in heaven, God would hear the same prayer twice and remember. She knew what their prayer would be too: the 23rd Psalm:

Aunque ande en valle de sombra de muerte,
no temeré mal alguno,
porque Tú estarás conmigo . . .

If anyone was walking through the Valley of the Shadow of Death right now, it was their father.

At bedtime, the Gonzalezes set up a cot in Alex's bedroom for Mateo. *Maybe this will be good for Mateo,* thought Luna. He'd always wanted brothers. Maybe having Alex around would help keep his mind off Papi.

The Gonzalezes put Dulce and Luna in their guest bedroom. It had its own bathroom and a queen-size bed.

"I'm sorry you have to share the bed," said the señor. Luna didn't mind. Dulce would have probably ended up in her bed anyway. The Gonzalezes left them alone to settle in. Luna led them in prayer. Then they split up.

Dulce had Papi's gift: no matter what was going on in her life, she always fell asleep easily. Luna suspected Mateo—like her—had more trouble. She couldn't sleep at all. The house was so big and sterile-feeling. There was even a bleachlike scent to the place. Luna was used to the hiss of their old steam radiators, the footsteps of neighbors overhead, the slam of car doors in the parking lot. Here, there was nothing. The only sounds of life came from those parakeets. Doña Esme put them in the kitchen in the evenings. The kitchen was directly below the guest bedroom so she could hear their fluttering and chirping through the floorboards. It was the one sound that comforted her.

Just after midnight, Luna sat up in bed. She could hear footsteps headed in the direction of their bedroom. The footsteps stopped outside their closed door. Someone knocked softly.

"Luna?" It was Mateo.

"You can come in."

Luna figured her brother was scared and couldn't sleep, but from the look on his face in the pale shadow of moonlight, she knew it was something more. A strong ammonia scent filled the room. He began to cry. "I'm sorry! I'm sorry!"

His pajama bottoms were soaking wet and plastered to his legs.

"*Ay, Dios mío!* You wet the bed?" Mateo hadn't done something like that since he was three years old.

"I'm so sorry, Luna. Please! Please help me!"

"Is Alex awake?"

"I don't think so, no. The Gonzalezes—they will throw us out on the street!"

"No, they won't. Go in the bathroom, take your pajama bottoms off and get cleaned up. Then climb into our bed. I'll see how bad it is. Maybe I can get the sheets and your pajamas clean and dry and no one will ever know."

Mateo handed Luna his wet, smelly pajama bottoms with more apologies. She balled them up and left her brother to wash himself. Then she crept down the corridor to Alex's bedroom. She just hoped Alex didn't wake up to see her standing in his room. He might freak out and then they really might be shipped to Queens (though she wasn't sure she wouldn't be happier with Alirio and Maria José anyway).

Luna opened Alex's bedroom door, thankful that the door was so flimsy, it didn't squeak. There was just enough moonlight to navigate to Mateo's cot. The sheets and underpadding were wet, but the mattress and blankets seemed dry. If she could just put the wet stuff in the washer and dryer tonight, no one would be any the wiser tomorrow. Alex Gonzalez was turned to the wall, breathing heavily. If Luna was careful, she could do this without him waking.

Carefully, she removed the plaid quilt and pulled off the race car sheets that clearly used to belong to Alex and probably were used on his little brother David's bed these days. They reeked of urine. Luna hoped this was a one-time occurrence. She couldn't go to school and spend every night secretly washing her little brother's sheets. On the other hand, she knew he'd be humiliated if Alex found out.

She gathered the sheets in a pile and then realized she had no idea where the Gonzalezes' washer and dryer were located. In the basement? On the first floor? Her family didn't have a washer and dryer in their apartment. Mami used to take the clothes to a Laundromat down the street. After she died, that became Luna's responsibility. She'd hated it then, but now she was glad she knew how to do this for her brother's sake.

She bundled everything in her arms with the dry part against her nightgown and crept down the stairs and into the kitchen. She didn't see an obvious place for a washer or dryer, so she found the door that led to the basement.

She'd never been in the Gonzalezes' basement before. It looked warmer and friendlier than the rest of the house. The ceiling was the height of the ceilings in their apartment, not super high like in the rest of the house. There was a big playroom with shelves full of games. In one corner was a Ping-Pong table, in the other a giant flat-screen TV. The couch cushions looked lumpy but comfy. There was a quilt folded across one armrest. The rug had some reddish-brown juice stains across it.

Luna opened first one door and then another, searching for a washer and dryer. The wall at the back of the house had a set of heavy dark blue drapes pulled across what appeared to be a sliding glass door. There were no other windows in the space, just three doors off the main room, one of them with a thick slide bolt across it.

She opened the door beneath the stairs, but it turned out to be nothing more than a storage space for the Gonzalezes' oil tank and water heater. She skipped over the door with the slide bolt. It was probably an exit to the garage and was likely locked to keep anyone from breaking in. The third door turned out to be the door to the laundry area. A gleaming white washer and dryer sat next to a shelf full of clean towels and laundry supplies. When Luna was all grown up, the first luxury she wanted after a car was a washer and dryer of her own. There was nothing more humiliating than having to fold your underwear in a public place in front of dozens of strangers.

She tossed Mateo's bedding into the washing machine and added the liquid detergent. For a minute, she forgot herself and looked for a coin slot. Then she remembered and turned on the machine. Maybe she could take a nap on the couch down here while she waited for the sheets to get washed.

The sound of the water filling up the washing machine was comforting and familiar. The floral, powdery detergent scent reminded Luna of when she was little, trailing after her mother with her collection of plastic ponies when they first moved to Lake Holly and Mami cleaned people's houses. Luna wanted to be that little girl again. She wanted someone to take care of her. Already she was experiencing things Papi would never know about unless she told him. *If* she told him. How could she tell him about this? Mateo would be mortified. The moment would have passed. Already, her father was a ghost on the landscape of their lives just as they were a ghost on his.

She didn't close the lid on the washing machine but instead stood over it and watched the water gradually fill up the drum. She stuck her hand under the warm gush and tried to feel something that might get her through the emptiness and anger. The machine was loud. The cascade of water echoed through the small, windowless space.

"You're up so late, chica. "

She jumped and turned around. The señor was in the doorway of the laundry room, dressed only in a sleeveless white undershirt and plaid boxer shorts, his fat belly straining at the elastic waistband.

"I—I needed to do some laundry," Luna stammered, conscious suddenly that she was dressed only in her flannel nightgown. She hadn't packed a robe in her garbage bag, and she hadn't had time to change into sweats when she brought Mateo's bedding downstairs.

"Laundry? At this hour?" The señor took a step closer. Luna flattened herself against the washing machine. Her breath balled up in her chest. She tried to swallow, but her saliva was as thick as rubber cement.

"I—I couldn't sleep."

"Ah. Yes. I get that way too." The señor took another step toward her. His eyes traveled the length of her nightgown. It used to be Mami's. The gown buttoned to the neck, but Luna never buttoned it that high. The señor stared at her collarbone peeking through the open neckline and ran the back of one hand across his lips.

"Do I make you nervous, chica?" He frowned, and Luna wondered if she was being rude for no reason. The señor had been generous to her family, inviting all of them to stay in his home, helping her father with his immigration problems. She couldn't think of one harsh thing he'd said or done. What was wrong with her?

"No," she lied. "I'm just—tired. That's all."

"Of course. This situation is so hard for you." He took another step closer and reached out a fleshy hand. Luna thought he was going to touch her. She flinched.

He reached behind her and flipped down the lid of the washing machine.

"You need to close it for it to work."

She exhaled in relief. "Oh! Yes! Sorry."

He pulled his hand away, and the ridge of one of his knuckles rubbed up against the sleeve of her nightgown. It was a moment of contact, so brief that she couldn't say if it was accidental or not.

"You need to go to bed, chica. You have school tomorrow. I will put the wash in the dryer for you."

"Thank you."

"Things will work out here for you. You'll see." The señor smiled, but the curl of his lips never traveled to his eyes. "I'm looking forward to getting to know you better."

He stepped back, and she bolted from the room.

Chapter 25

Vega knew he was in trouble the moment he walked into the squad room at county police headquarters on Friday morning and Dolan greeted him by jamming his index finger against his own head and pretending to pull the trigger.

"The captain told me to fetch you the moment you came in." Word must have gotten out about Vega's little field trip to Wickford yesterday.

"I didn't go *near* Zambo's body, I swear," said Vega. "I stayed back behind the crime-scene tape."

"You mean there's more?"

"More what?" Vega tossed his keys on his desk and flung his jacket across the chair of his cubicle. It was a bright, sunny morning, but you'd never know it inside the building's beige cinderblock walls. With its acoustical tile ceilings, heavy metal doors, and narrow windows, the entire place had the look and feel of a cell block. The cubicles further diminished whatever natural light and ventilation attempted to penetrate the gloom. Vega got out as much as possible.

"All I did was suggest to Greco that the Wickford PD search for plastic liquor bottles," said Vega. "How is that a problem?"

Dolan dropped his voice to a near whisper. "Heads up,

Jimmy. This isn't about Zambo. It's about your little visit
to Charlie Gonzalez's wife. Waring is pissed."

"Greco ratted me out?"

"Greco has nothing to do with this. The captain got a
call from *Schulman*. You know? Our county supervisor?
The guy who authorizes our paychecks and is on his way
to becoming our next senator? Tell you one thing, man.
When you pick your targets, you aim high."

"Can I get some coffee first?"

"I'd make it quick if I were you."

Frank Waring's office was directly across from the
homicide squad room. Cops were so often in the field that
they never really took a lot of interest in their offices.
Waring, however, was the exception. The cornerstone of
his personality was his service as a Navy SEAL, and he hit
you over the head with it as you walked in the door. He
was only about five-eight and slightly built. But there was
a chiseled toughness to his lean features that suggested he
could not only go long periods without food, sleep, or
water—he might actually enjoy it.

All around the office there were framed photographs of
Waring in uniform and plaques with the Navy SEAL an-
chor and eagle insignia. There were inspiring quotes and
American flags and enough patriotic stuff to make it feel
like the Fourth of July every day.

What wasn't visible in Waring's office was a single stitch
of the life he'd led before he joined the navy and became a
SEAL. Vega had heard from other, more veteran detectives
that Waring had been orphaned young and raised by his
mother's unmarried sister, who was an Irish step dancer
and traveled a great deal. Apparently Waring showed talent as well, and as a teenager, he won trophies and scholarships for his dancing. The story was that he walked
away from a lucrative career at the age of twenty-three to
join the navy. Some detectives with a little too much time
on their hands found newspaper clips online complete

with pictures of a young Frank Waring in bright green vests and tight black pants doing a jig. These had been secretly shared around the office, along with such captions as: *Captain Twinkle-toes* and *They're after me Lucky Charms!* Waring didn't have a sense of humor, so none of this was ever said to his face.

Waring was at his desk and on the phone when Vega knocked, but he waved Vega inside and gestured for him to close the door and sit while he finished up his call. He was dressed as Vega was, in an open-collared knit shirt and khaki slacks, his sidearm in a holster at his waist, his badge hooked on his belt. His voice rarely rose above the soft tenor of a PBS children's television-show host. And yet there was something about being in Captain Waring's presence that made even his favored subordinates like Teddy Dolan uneasy. He had a habit of pausing before he answered questions as if you probably should have figured out the answer for yourself. Vega never quite exhaled when Waring was around. He certainly didn't exhale now.

Waring hung up the phone and slowly turned to face Vega. He folded both hands underneath his chin. When Vega was nervous, he had a tendency to focus on stupid things. Right now, he flashed to that picture of a young Frank Waring in a green vest and tight black pants doing a jig. That was all he needed to have a goofy smirk on his face when the captain addressed him. Waring already didn't care for Vega's sense of humor.

"I received a call from Steve Schulman this morning. Are you familiar with our county supervisor, Detective?"

"I've, uh—met him." Through Adele. But that was the last thing he'd bring up now.

"Yes, well. I don't know if he remembers the encounter, but he knows you now. Can you guess why?"

"Uh, no sir."

"It seems you took it upon yourself yesterday to question the wife of one of Mr. Schulman's chief campaign advisers regarding a case you've been removed from. Do you recall this conversation?"

"All I did was ask Esme—"

Waring raised a hand.

"So you're confirming that you made contact with Mrs. Gonzalez yesterday? Without any authorization from this department?"

"My daughter tutors her son in math. They live around the corner from her."

"I fail to see where that connection gives you the right to barge into her house, thrust a flyer of a dead teenager in her face, and start interrogating her."

"She said that?"

"To her husband. Who complained to Schulman. Who in turn accused this department of mounting a campaign to harass him and the Hispanic community. Charlie Gonzalez is like a god in Lake Holly. His wife is involved in all sorts of charity work. And her sole crime, as I understand it, was to run a clothing drive for the homeless to which your daughter might have donated some clothing."

"All I did was—"

"Detective, your daughter is a person of interest in the death of this teenager, is she not?"

"Yes, but—"

"And it has also come to my attention that you have a relationship with a woman who's involved with the Schulman campaign—a relationship that will be jeopardized if Schulman wins the election. Is this also correct?"

Vega straightened. "Sir? I believe that's nobody's business."

"Normally, I'd agree with you. But this is looking an awful lot like a witch hunt to me, spurred on by too much personal interest in this case. I'm ordering you to stay away from the Gonzalezes and anything to do with any part of this investigation. I don't want it said that the county police prejudiced the outcome of this election in any way. Have I made myself clear?"

"Yessir."

"You have plenty of other cases to keep you busy, Vega. If you want to stay on homicide, I suggest you make better use of your time."

Vega spent the rest of the morning typing up two witness statements on the case of Lil, Flaco, and Ruby, none of whom had yet reached age twenty. Now Lil never would. Flaco—aka William Rodriguez—would see thirty, maybe even forty, from the inside of a prison cell. And the next time Flaco saw Ruby, if ever, she'd be forty pounds heavier with a teenager in tow who might very likely go down the same path. Their hopes and dreams—whatever they may have been—were pocket change they'd squandered before they even realized they had it.

Vega knew something about squandered dreams himself. He looked up at the corkboard next to his computer. Tacked in a corner, away from all the time sheets and photographs and departmental memos was a faded photograph of him and three other men in their early twenties with baby faces and too much hair. It was the cover shot of the one CD Vega ever cut with his first band, Straight Money, the one he'd had to leave when Wendy got pregnant and he became a cop.

As tough-edged as they all looked in the photo, posed around the wreckage of an old Camaro, Vega could see in hindsight just how callow and naïve they were. None of them made it as professional musicians. The drummer joined the army and later moved to Texas and became a mechanic. The keyboardist became a high-school science teacher in New Jersey. The bass player, who shared lead vocals with Vega, was now a supervisor for Con Edison way upstate. Vega suspected they still played weekend gigs like he did, hired out for weddings and bar mitzvahs and *quinceañeras* where no one really paid attention to anything but the beat, and all the songs were covers because people just wanted to hear what they already knew.

By the afternoon, the medical examiner's office had completed Lil's autopsy, but the fax machine was jammed up, so Dr. Gupta's office suggested Vega take the short drive over and fetch the paperwork himself.

The autopsy results were waiting for Vega in a folder at the front reception desk. Vega took a moment to sift through the paperwork to make sure everything was in order and he had no questions. He was suddenly aware of a pair of bright orange and green athletic shoes standing in front of him. He lifted his gaze to take in a white lab coat over a skirt with orange and pink flowers on it. Dr. Gupta smiled at him.

"Detective Vega. I was just going to call and ask if you had any interest in getting a copy of the Garcia autopsy as well."

"Garcia—?" Lil's real name was Benito Diaz.

"Ah, yes. I forgot," said Gupta. "You probably didn't know him as Saturnio Garcia, but rather by his bowed legs."

Zambo. Vega blinked at her.

"You were looking for him, as I recall?"

"Uh, yeah."

"I assume you're aware that the Wickford police found his body?"

Clearly, no one had told Gupta that Vega had been taken off the Baby Mercy case. He felt just like a kid who'd been warned not to touch a hot stove, and yet here he was, reaching out for it with his bare hands. He couldn't lie. But so far, at least technically, he hadn't.

"I guess Zambo—that is, Mr. Garcia"—Vega corrected himself—"died of alcohol poisoning?"

"Do you have a moment? I think it would be better if I showed you."

Vega looked around as though he half expected Captain Waring to come charging out of some room equipped with a hidden camera and suspend him on the spot. But the only people in the brightly lit, plant-filled lobby were the receptionist and a couple of white-coated assistants on their way to lab rooms. No one was likely to know or care if Gupta told Vega about Zambo.

"Sure. Show me."

For the second time this week, Vega found himself standing beside a steel vault, staring down at a dead body. He did not grieve quite the same way for Zambo that he had for Baby Mercy or even for a teenager like Lil. He was able to judge this death with more clinical eyes. Still, it looked like a horrific way to go. Vega hadn't taken a good look at the body when Greco unzipped the bag. Now, he was able to see a chalky white residue around Zambo's mouth that looked like the powdery ash from a charred log. The man had the same white charring on his fingers too. Vega noticed that the fingers appeared to have shriveled up on themselves, as if the top part of each digit had simply melted away.

"The immediate cause of death was tracheal edema," said Gupta.

"Which means?"

"His windpipe swelled after he began vomiting massive amounts of blood."

"Hell of a way to die," said Vega. "Is it common in alcoholics?"

"I've seen it," said Gupta. "But right away what troubled me is the necrosis in his fingers. Quite literally, the digits have been liquefied. That's not from alcohol. Do you happen to know if Mr. Garcia was employed?"

Gupta's British inflections muted the horror of Zambo's last moments. Even her questions had an air of normalcy about them, almost as if she were conducting a job interview.

"He probably collected cans and stuff," said Vega. "Maybe he picked up a few bucks from La Casa once in a while for some grunt job." Adele was a soft touch. Vega was sure at some point she would have thrown a few dollars his way. "I doubt, however, that he was sober enough for regular work," Vega added. "Why?"

"Because his blood work showed extremely low levels of serum calcium. The toxicology screen confirmed my suspicions. Although his immediate cause of death was tracheal edema, the proximate cause was systemic hydrofluoric acid poisoning."

"He was poisoned?"

"Yes. But I can't say if the poisoning was accidental or not. That's why I'm asking if you knew whether he was employed. Hydrofluoric acid is an industrial solvent used in glass etching and metal polishing."

"Hydrofluoric acid—" Vega tried the words out on his tongue. "—I've never even heard of it before. Is it like sulfuric acid?"

"Worse," said Gupta. "Unlike sulfuric acid, hydrofluoric acid has a delayed effect on human tissue. Mr. Garcia might not have experienced any pain or obvious effects for an hour or more. By then, it would have already damaged his gastrointestinal tract enough to cause severe hemorrhaging. Vomiting would have brought the acid back up his windpipe and swelled it shut. I'm guessing he splashed some of the solvent on his fingers." Gupta pointed to the shriveled digits. "The tissue necrosis you're seeing here happened when the solvent leeched the calcium from the bones in his fingers and liquefied them."

"Holy—" Vega felt terrible for the guy. "—Where would he get something like this?"

"He ingested it, Detective. The question is 'from where?' I checked with the crime lab. The Wickford police tendered ten beer cans and two empty whiskey bottles, but I already know there was no HF in them."

"How come?"

"Because HF dissolves metal and glass. It needs to be stored in plastic. And I've never seen beer or wine in plastic."

Vega grinned. "That's 'cause you hang in better circles than I do. All the hard-core drunks drink bargain-basement vodkas. And they're all stored in plastic."

"Then where is the container Mr. Garcia drank from?"

In the woods still? Vega wondered. *No. Impossible.* Greco and Hammond would have found it. Unless . . .

Unless the bottle's not there, thought Vega. *Because the person who gave Zambo the solvent—in whatever form— took it with them to hide the evidence.* This was no accidental poisoning. This was planned and calculated.

This was murder.

"You said HF is an industrial solvent," said Vega. "I would imagine it's hard to get a hold of, especially in fatal concentrations."

"Not at all, Detective," said Gupta. "It's usually purchased in high concentrations and then watered down for various industrial uses. That's why I asked whether Mr. Garcia worked."

"What sort of work could a guy like Zambo"—Vega caught Gupta's frown and corrected himself—"Mr. Garcia do that would require something as exotic as hydrofluoric acid?"

"HF is a common ingredient in tire-rim cleaners," said Gupta. "I thought perhaps he worked at a car wash."

Chapter 26

It was Adele's turn to bring snacks to Sophia's Friday after-school soccer practice and act as parent chaperone. What did other mothers bring? Grapes? (Weren't they on the list of pesticide-laden fruits?) Oranges? (Too messy.) Pears? (They bruised too easily.)

Last week, Libby Reynolds's mom brought organic fruit kebabs, home-baked oatmeal-raisin cookies, and lemon-lime seltzer. Adele settled on a bag of McIntosh apples, a package of Oreos, and a gallon of no-name springwater with paper cups. She heard her daughter groan the moment she appeared with it on the sidelines.

Adele delivered the snacks and walked back to the other side of the field. The hills were a tapestry of orange and gold set off by mown fields of deep green, squared off with white lines, nets, and orange cones. The afternoon sun bathed the landscape in a butterscotch glow that looked warmer than it felt, so Adele had to alternate between watching the scrimmages from the sidelines and from the warmth of her car.

There were several teams practicing on the field today, some boys and some girls. Every last kid wore a navy blue uniform jersey with their names and numbers on their backs. You'd have thought they were all playing for the

World Cup. Sophia dribbled the ball down the field to her team and then ran over to the scrimmage line to laugh and joke with her friends. She was more social butterfly than soccer standout. Still, Adele's heart sank watching her confident nine-year-old doing some complicated hand slap with a teammate. Lake Holly was Sophia's whole world. She was born here. She expected to graduate high school here.

How can I even think of ripping her away from all of this? Her friends. Her school. Her team—her father?

I'll turn Schulman down. I'll stay at La Casa.

Definitely . . .

Probably . . .

Perhaps . . .

Why couldn't she make up her mind?

Adele ducked into her car to warm up and check her messages on her iPhone. She was looking for one message in particular. From Falls Church, Virginia. From the Honorable Judge Quentin Hallard of the U. S. Board of Immigration Appeals.

Ever since Charlie Gonzalez called her yesterday to tell her that Manuel Serrano had lost his bid to stay in the U.S., Adele had been trying to come up with some way to do what Adam Katz could not. It was sheer hubris on her part. Katz was an expert in these areas. Still, she couldn't sleep knowing that she hadn't tried every last thing to help Serrano. And so, for the past twenty-four hours, she'd called in favors from every contact she could think of: from Harvard, from her law firm days, from her immigration contacts. Through a chain of connections, she'd managed to come up with someone who knew someone who could put Serrano's case before Judge Hallard.

Whether Hallard would look at the case or answer her call was another matter. In all likelihood, Hallard would do the politically astute move: he'd wait to return Adele's call late on Monday or possibly Tuesday. By then, he could reasonably argue that it was too late to do anything for Manuel Serrano. The matter was out of his hands.

There was no message from Hallard. Adele put her phone away and stepped out of her car again so Sophia couldn't claim later that her mother had been too busy with work to watch the practice. A faded red Honda Civic nosed into the parking space beside her—perhaps a parent who'd decided to pick up their child early. They still had fifteen minutes of practice time left. Adele turned to say hi. But it wasn't a mother or father. It was Claudia Aguilar's daughter, Inés. Adele recalled that she had a couple of daughters as well as her son, Neto. But Adele remembered them being older than Sophia. Maybe they were on other teams.

Inés got out of her car. Adele rarely saw her without a counter between them. The woman had to be in her early to mid-thirties, but her round girlish face and tiny, childlike body made her look younger than her years. She could have almost fit in as a player on Sophia's team.

Inés wrapped a jacket tightly around her waist and sidled up to Adele. "I'm so sorry to bother you at your daughter's soccer practice, Doña Adele. Ramona at La Casa told me I could find you here."

So this wasn't a coincidence. "Is something the matter?" asked Adele.

"The police, they've got Romeo at the station."

"Your ex-husband? Why?" But Adele could already guess why. Romeo was a good-looking Salvadoran who seemed born to his name. When he and Inés were married, it was common knowledge that he cheated. Since their divorce, he'd apparently moved on to short flings with some of his American clients in his landscaping business. He'd never been picky about trampling marriage vows—his or anyone else's. It was only a matter of time, in Adele's opinion, before one of these gringas had second thoughts or was caught by her husband and cried "rape."

Adele couldn't say she felt bad for Romeo. He'd been a cheat with Inés and a possible abuser too, from some of the things Claudia had hinted at through the years. But Adele felt bad for Inés and her children. It had been hard enough having her first child so young and dealing with his disabilities without having to deal with all the stuff Romeo had thrown at her since.

"The police want to stick a Q-tip inside Romeo's mouth," Inés told Adele. "They told him they need to test his DNA. He's afraid to give it. He does not have—um—"

"Papers?"

Inés nodded. "He's afraid they'll do to him what they did to Manuel Serrano."

"Has Romeo ever been arrested before? Has he ever received an order of removal?"

"No. Nothing."

"Then he's not in the same situation as Manuel. Either way, he can refuse the DNA test until they get a court order."

"He can?"

"Do you want me to call down to the police station and find out what's going on?"

"Can you?"

Ay, Dios mío! It was always something. "Okay," said Adele. "But first, I need to know why they want to test Romeo's DNA." She didn't want to get embroiled in a rape case that he'd brought about through his own stupidity—or worse.

"The police told Romeo that the dead baby they found in the woods behind La Casa is his."

Adele raised an eyebrow. "Is it?"

"He says no. He lied all the time when we were married. Now? No. I believe he's telling the truth."

"Why would the police think the baby is his then?"

"They told Romeo they have Neto's DNA and it shows that my Neto is the baby's brother."

"You're kidding." Adele was floored. She had to repeat it to be sure. "Neto is the brother of the baby in the woods?"

"That's what the police are telling Romeo."

Inés's ex was up to his eyeballs in this one. Adele was already regretting her offer to speak to the police on his behalf. "I don't know what you want me to do here, Inés. DNA doesn't lie."

On the field, the coach blew a whistle. Practice was over. The girls were fetching their balls and getting their bottles of water. Sophia would be hungry. Adele didn't want to get mixed up in Romeo's sexual escapades and their inevitable fallout. She tried to explain to Inés why the police would likely get a court order to do the test, no matter how much Romeo protested and how it would probably prove exactly what they were claiming.

"If Neto is the baby's brother, then Romeo is the baby's father, Inés."

"But Romeo isn't Neto's father."

"He isn't? Who is?"

Inés shook her head. "I can't say."

"Why?"

"Please. That's not possible. If Romeo gives the police his DNA and it shows he's not the father, will they let him go?"

Sophia was headed across the field toward Adele's car.

"If that's all the reason they have to detain him, I don't see why not," said Adele. "But there's still a dead baby without a name, and the police deserve to know who her parents are and what happened. If you know who Neto's father is—"

"No! Please, Doña Adele! Please don't make me go through all that again!"

Inés started to cry. In the parking lot of the soccer field. Before all of Sophia's teammates. Before all of their parents. Anyone observing would think Adele had said or done something terrible to the woman. Adele saw Sophia hang back, her face red with a mixture of shame and fury. Maybe it wasn't such a bad idea that they might be leaving town after all.

"In your car," Adele ordered Inés under her breath. "Right now." Then she turned to the field and called to Sophia to get in their own car and wait for her.

Inside Inés's car, Inés opened her handbag and searched for tissues. Tears dripped down her face, smudging her mascara. "I'm so sorry, Doña Adele. I didn't mean to embarrass you in front of your daughter like that."

"It's okay," said Adele. What could she say? It was her own fault that there were no dividing lines between her personal and professional life. Some days it seemed, she failed in both. She didn't even have a tissue to hand Inés. All the other moms leaving the field probably had packages of tissues in their bags—in addition to hand wipes, safety pins, sunscreen, Life Savers, and bottles of water. All Adele had in her purse was a small container of hand sanitizer, and that wouldn't do anybody any good. Inés ended up palming the tears from her face, streaking her mascara until she looked like Adele had given her a black eye.

Adele patted Inés on the shoulder, trying to calm her down. She seemed so fragile right now, like a little porcelain doll Adele might break if she handled it too roughly.

"I'm just trying to understand," Adele said softly. "Were you with Romeo at the time you got pregnant by someone else?"

Inés shook her head, no. She stared into her lap. "I was barely fifteen. An innocent. I didn't even meet Romeo until I was seventeen, and then we married a year later when I got pregnant with Isabel."

"So Romeo knows who Neto's father is?"

"No. I can't say—ever."

Adele heard the rising panic in her voice again.

"Can you tell me why you can't say?"

Inés dabbed at her eyes. "I can't."

"Did the baby's father rape you?"

Inés looked at Adele darkly. "I had no choice. Do you understand?"

Unfortunately, she did.

"Was he a family member?" Adele's mind spun with possibilities. *Father? Stepfather? Uncle?*

"I can't say—not even to you."

"Does your mother know?"

Silence. *Claudia knows.* Which was one more person than Adele ever told.

"Inés," said Adele gently. She touched her hand. It was ice cold. She tried to get Inés to look at her, but she could see Inés was ashamed. Adele wished Inés could open up— wished they both could. But that was impossible. Twenty years ago, talking about sexual abuse was rare, even in North American culture. It was unheard of in the Latin world.

"Inés—listen to me. The man who did those things to you may have done them to the mother of that baby who died in the woods. He could be doing them to a girl right now. Don't you feel perhaps you should come forward?"

Inés closed her eyes. "No one will believe me."

"I believe you."

The air in the small Honda Civic turned warm and close. Through the windshield, Adele watched Sophia and her friends running after each other like puppies, all of them so comfortable in their bodies, so bold and fearless. Adele wished she could tell Inés she understood. But some things are buried so deep, you can't unearth them without destroying the entire structure that's been built on top.

Inés took a deep breath. She looked ready to speak.

Sophia ran up to the passenger-side window where Adele was sitting and thumped on the glass. "Mom! I'm hungry! Can we go home?"

"In a minute, Sophia!" barked Adele.

The spell was broken.

"I need to go," said Inés. "I have to be back at the store. Please tell the police that Romeo is not Neto's father. I hope that helps him. Please ask them not to tell Neto. He's very fond of Romeo and Romeo never told him . . ." Her voice trailed off and she shook her head.

"But the real father—"

"Men do what they want, Doña Adele. It does not matter what a woman says. Even you, surely, must know that."

More than you know.

Chapter 27

Detective Louis Greco was nothing if not a creature of habit. He always got his fringe of hair trimmed on Wednesdays when his favorite barber was working. He always bought his lunch—salami on a roll with roasted peppers—at the same little Italian deli every day around half past twelve. They had it packed and ready to go when he walked in. If he got called out on a case, they just refrigerated it and waited till he came in later.

And at four o'clock on Friday afternoons, he always went to the 7-Eleven next to the Car Wash King in town and bought ten Lotto tickets. Always ten. Always on Fridays at four. He was nothing if not superstitious.

When Greco came out of the store, Vega was leaning against Greco's car. It was a white Buick LaCrosse with a county police emblem on the rear window.

Greco stopped about ten paces in front of Vega and regarded him like he'd rolled in something nasty.

"Unless you're here to talk about that crappy Yankees pitch in the fourth inning last night, I've got nothing to say to you, Vega."

"You see the autopsy report on Zambo yet?"

"No. That's Wickford's case. Hammond will give me the highlights on Monday, I'm sure."

"I've seen it."

"I don't even want to *know* how that happened." Greco fished his keys out of his pocket and pushed the remote to unlock his car. Vega immediately helped himself to the front passenger seat.

Greco looked over at Vega and sighed. "See, the way this works is, I get in my car and head home, and you figure out a way not to get yourself fired—unless you're planning to skip the pension, buy some lottery tickets, and handle your financial planning the Puerto Rican way."

"You're the one buying the lottery tickets."

"'Cause I've had the unfortunate luck of knowing a Puerto Rican who's gonna get me fired."

"Zambo was poisoned, Grec."

Vega watched the shock resonate and then recalibrate itself to cop cynicism immediately. "This your theory?"

"Gupta thought I was still on the case, so she walked me through everything."

Greco put his fingers in his ears. "I didn't hear any of that. And I'll swear to it on a witness stand."

"Okay. Here's something else you didn't get from me: Adele just texted me and told me Romeo Rivera's not Neto's dad."

"Huh?"

"Adele says she just spoke to Inés. Inés won't say who Neto's father is, but apparently it's not Romeo. It's some guy who raped Inés when she was a teenager and, for all we know, raped that dead teenager too."

"Did Claudia or Inés report it?"

"I can't reach Adele to ask, but I get the impression they didn't. In any case, she says Romeo's not your boy."

"And my guys are always keen to hear suspects tell us why they aren't," said Greco dryly.

"Suit yourself. Do the DNA test. Just thought you

should know. Those are the film highlights. So—you want to stay for the whole show?"

"There's more?"

"I got some things you should look into."

Greco looked over to the other end of the blacktop where the car wash was located. Men in striped uniform shirts and rubber boots were hosing down vehicles before they went through the automated conveyor. Greco turned on his engine and began to back out of his parking space.

"Where are we going?" asked Vega. "My car's parked here."

Greco made a sharp right into the entrance for the Car Wash King. "I'm gonna talk to you, I want a dark tunnel where no one can see or hear us. You got three whole minutes to talk and I'll listen."

"I can't tell you everything in three minutes."

"People make babies in under three minutes, Vega. You can lay out your bullshit theories."

A rainbow-shaped sign welcomed them to THE CAR WASH KING. The cheapest basic car wash was eight dollars. Greco pulled between the orange cones and held his hand out to Vega. "I listen. You pay."

Vega dug a ten-dollar bill from his wallet. "That's what Joy's lawyer says."

"Yeah, but I come cheap. Eight bucks wouldn't buy you pissing time with a lawyer."

The attendant beckoned Greco's car forward until his wheels locked into the metal tracking. Greco shifted into neutral. He took his foot off the brake and his hands off the steering wheel. Then he popped open the glove compartment and offered Vega a Twizzler. Vega waved him away.

"Still looks like wire insulation to me."

"Better wire insulation than—what's that dish you Puerto

Ricans eat? The lumpy, mushy one that looks like someone cleaned out their garbage disposal on your plate?"

"You mean *mofongo?* Mashed green plantains, garlic, and pork crackling?"

"Yeah. That's the one."

"I love *mofongo,*" said Vega. "It's like Puerto Rican stuffing. My mom used to make it all the time when I was a kid." He wished his mom were still around to make it for him now.

"I'll stick to my Twizzlers, thank you." Greco pulled one out of the package and bit off an end. The attendant swabbed suds across the Buick's windshield, obscuring their vision.

"So talk," said Greco. "You've got three minutes."

The track began to pull the car forward into a maze of brushes and long, soft strips of yellow cloth that batted against the windows. Vega had a vivid memory of the first time he went through a car wash. He must have been about five. It was in the Bronx on one of those rare occasions his father came by to visit. Orlando Vega was a bass player in a Dominican merengue band, but to earn money, he did a variety of odd jobs from handyman to house-painter to limo driver.

His father must have been working as a chauffeur at the time because he had a big Lincoln Town Car with him. He offered to take Vega for a spin. Vega had only been in a car once or twice before that, and he thrilled, as all boys would, to the speed of the vehicle, the smell of the fine-tooled leather, the purr of the engine. Add to that the sheer showiness of his good-looking father in a sharp suit behind the wheel of this big flashy car cruising along Tremont Avenue. It was the sort of day Vega had always wished for, the sort of day he should have been able to recall with warmth and fondness.

Then his dad decided to take the vehicle through a car

wash. Looking back, it was probably part of the reason Orlando Vega was driving the car around in the first place. Still, the noise and darkness terrified Vega. It was probably all of three minutes, but he cried the entire time. His father yelled at him for smearing the windows with tears and snot. He called Vega a *miedoso*—a coward. By the time they were out the other side, Vega just wanted to go home.

When he thought back on that day, he wanted to remember the breeze on his skin through the open windows, the smell of new car leather, his dad's sharp suit and Brut aftershave. But what he really thought about was the dark, noisy car wash and that sense of failure when his dad called him a coward. He didn't see his father for a long time after that. By the time they moved to Lake Holly when he was eleven, he didn't see him at all.

Vega tried to shake those thoughts from his head. He knew he didn't have much time, so he told Greco about Gupta's findings that Zambo had ingested hydrofluoric acid.

"Where did it come from?"

"That's just it. None of the bottles or cans you and Hammond found match up. HF can only be stored in plastic. I think somebody gave Zambo a swig of something— maybe some cheap vodka in a plastic bottle—and then took it away."

"Whoa. Hold on," said Greco. "How do you get from Zambo being poisoned to Zambo being murdered? The guy was a homeless alcoholic. He'd drink paint thinner if he thought he could get off on it. You're talking about an industrial solvent that could have come from anywhere."

"Not anywhere. HF is an ingredient in wheel rim cleaners. You're driving through the very business that uses it all the time. And who owns every car wash in the area?"

Vega gestured through the windshield of the Buick. Great

vacuums were sucking up fat amoeba-shaped droplets of water from the glass. The noise sounded like a jet engine.

Miedoso . . . Miedoso . . .

Vega felt foolish for letting his five-year-old self come back to haunt him.

"You know how ridiculous you sound?" asked Greco. "Zambo would have sucked down lighter fluid if he thought he could get drunk on it. I'm not surprised he's dead. I'm surprised he didn't die sooner."

"You're not even the least bit curious why someone would poison him?"

"Because I'm not convinced it wasn't accidental! Look, Vega, I know what you're trying to do. But you make an accusation against people like the Gonzalezes—and by extension, Schulman—you better be sure you're right and have all the evidence to back it up. Not to mention the blessings of your own department. What do you have? Some vague ramblings from a drunk who easily could have been the source of his own demise? A mentally retarded teenager's sketchy ID? You have absolutely nothing. You go after the Gonzalezes with any of this, you're guaranteed to embarrass everyone: your department, *my* department, Adele. Hell, if I were her, *I'd* walk away from you after this."

As soon as the track let them off on the other side of the car wash, Vega hopped out of the car. He dug through his pockets and handed the guy drying down the car a $5 dollar tip.

"I can do that," said Greco.

"Yeah. Sure. You're great at giving tips."

Vega slammed the door and began walking back to his car at the 7-Eleven. No one wanted to listen to him. Then again, if roles were reversed, would he? He sounded like the panicky father he was, grasping at anything that might clear Joy once and for all of any involvement.

Nothing could ever clear him. He'd have the guilt of what he'd done to this baby on his conscience forever.

From the corner of Vega's eye, he noticed a round figure huffing toward him. It was Neto Rivera. He was in his car-wash uniform with a rag in his hand. His little dachshund was trailing behind him. Vega figured he just wanted to ask about the police siren again. Then he saw the young man's face. Neto was crying.

"Mr. Detective! Mr. Detective! I just heard that the police—they arrested my papi!"

"I'm not involved in the case, Neto. You need to speak to—" Vega searched the lot, but Greco had just turned onto the roadway, headed for home. *Puñeta!* Greco had just said to back off. And here he was, drawn right back in. "—I think it's best if you talk to your mother and grandmother about this."

"I called Mami and Abuelita. They didn't answer. Papi is a good man. Not bad. Why the police put him in jail?"

A dumpy little Spanish guy came out of the office in front of the wash tunnel and yelled at Neto in Spanish to get back to work. Neto tucked his rag in his back pocket and palmed his eyes. Vega felt bad for the kid. The dog seemed to sense it too. He danced around Neto's feet.

"Look, Neto, why don't we go talk to your boss and see if he can give you some time off to speak to your family? I can give you and your dog a lift to your grandmother's market, okay?"

Neto agreed, and Vega walked the teenager over. The little dachshund trailed behind them. Vega was surprised the dog had never gotten run over with so many cars going through this place. At the sight of Vega, the supervisor immediately disappeared into the office. He was on the phone when Vega entered. Clearly, he didn't want to get between Neto and a cop.

"Why the police want Papi?" asked Neto. "Why?"

"The police just want to ask him some questions."

"Then Papi can go?"

Vega didn't know how to answer that, so he drummed his fingers on the countertop, hoping the supervisor would finish his call so Vega could get out of there.

The car-wash office was like the counter of a rental car agency: clean, sparse, and cheap. There was a cash register, a placard that said "Ask about our monthly maintenance program," plaques testifying to membership in the chamber of commerce, and posters in support of various local sports teams.

In the middle of all of this was a framed color photograph of a stocky young Hispanic man in a car-wash attendant's uniform. The picture had that blurry, yellowish tint of older photographs before everything was digitalized. The man was wearing a baseball cap, possibly to hide the first traces of a thinning hairline. He had a broad, hopeful smile. Who could have guessed that Charlie Gonzalez would go from that to all of this? Vega supposed it was both an inspiration and a source of frustration to his employees that Gonzalez had done what they could only dream of doing. Maybe that's why people call it the American Dream. For most, it will always be just that.

Neto was mouth-breathing loudly next to Vega. The supervisor was still on the phone.

"Why the police arrest Papi? Why?" The teenager was becoming a broken record. Vega tried to be patient.

"I don't think they've arrested him yet, Neto. They just want to ask him some questions."

"Like you asked me? About Mia?"

Vega blinked at the teenager. He had no idea how close he'd come to the truth.

"I don't know."

"Papi doesn't know Mia."

Maybe yes. Maybe no, thought Vega. That's what the

DNA was going to find out. Vega cleared his throat, trying to catch the supervisor's attention.

"Papi doesn't *know* Mia!" he said more forcefully. Vega was losing his patience.

"Look, Neto, at this point *nobody* knows Mia. Except you."

Neto pointed to the photograph above the cash register. "He does. Mia lives with him. In the birdhouse."

Chapter 28

Steve Schulman's campaign headquarters was in a former car dealership a short walk from his law offices in Broad Plains. The building—a large one-story showroom with floor-to-ceiling plate-glass windows—offered the unusual advantage of being both a command center for the campaign and a walking billboard. All the windows were filled with posters of Schulman looking robust and commanding. He was ten years older than his opponent, John Sawyer, and his habit of hunching his shoulders made him sometimes appear scholarly and disengaged—like more of an observer than a doer, though that really wasn't the case.

Schulman wasn't expecting Adele, but she knew he'd be here this evening, running through his speeches for tomorrow night's gala. She knew Charlie Gonzalez would be here too, working the phones and conferring with Schulman's biggest supporters in the Hispanic community. She could have called to talk to Schulman, but then she'd have had to run the gauntlet of assistants and college interns. This request was too important not to deliver in person. So she'd asked the mom of Sophia's good friend and soccer teammate to take the girls for pizza after practice. Sophia grumbled that she wanted to go home instead. But a man's life was on the line. Sophia couldn't understand why that trumped her needs. Adele hoped one day she would.

A perky young college intern met Adele at the front door of the campaign headquarters and thrust a flyer and button into Adele's hand. It took Adele ten minutes to convince the intern that she really, really needed to see Schulman and nobody else would do. It took another ten minutes and five more people before Schulman finally appeared, saw that it was Adele, and ushered her into his temporary office.

He had a big hopeful smile on his face. "You came all the way over here tonight to give me your answer?"

"Um, no." She had no excuse—no excuse at all. But she tried for one anyway. "I'm sorry, Steve. I can't yet. This whole situation with Manuel Serrano has been occupying my mind nonstop. I'll be able to think much more clearly when it's resolved."

"I thought it was," said Schulman. "Not to our satisfaction, mind you. But . . ." He spread his hands.

"I thought so too. But I have good news."

Schulman walked over to the door of his office. "Mind if I bring Charlie in? He'll want to hear this."

"Absolutely. He can share it with Manuel's children."

Schulman leaned out his door and collared another perky intern. A different one, Adele thought. But she couldn't tell. They all looked like fresh-faced Mormons at their first missionary event. There was something Adele could only describe as religious fervor in their eyes.

A few minutes later, Gonzalez appeared in the doorway.

"Doña Adele! What a pleasant surprise." He shot a quick glance at Schulman, who gave the slightest shake of his head. Adele read their unspoken exchange. Clearly Gonzalez too had thought she'd stopped by to accept the position.

Gonzalez closed the office door. He and Adele took seats while Schulman sat behind his desk, stretching a rubber band between his fingers. Adele realized she was taking up valuable campaign time. She'd try to make it brief.

"I've spent the better part of the last two days working through friends and former colleagues to secure a personal contact at the Board of Immigration Appeals," said Adele. "About an hour ago, I finally got a call back from Judge Quentin Hallard." She read a look of concern pass between Schulman and Gonzalez. "Don't worry. I didn't involve Steve's candidacy in any stage of the process."

"That's good," said Gonzalez.

"But see, the thing is"—Adele addressed Schulman with her words—"Judge Hallard has Manuel's case on his desk. He's willing to read the whole thing and render an opinion right away. But he says he wants to speak to Steve first—"

"Adele, no," Gonzalez interrupted. "Steve can't do that—"

"Off the record." Adele felt as if the room were filling with fire, as if she had just seconds to break the glass and vent the smoke or she'd be consumed. She ignored Gonzalez and focused entirely on Schulman—her mentor, her support in those early years when she'd needed it most. "Judge Hallard promises confidentiality. He just wants reassurance from Steve that John Sawyer won't get into office and find a way to punish him. He's not even promising he'll intercede on Manuel's behalf. But he's willing to look at the case. It's Manuel's only chance. Once he goes back to Mexico, who knows what anyone can do? Even Steve. Even from the position of an elected senator. Manuel's still on U.S. soil. All Steve has to do is make the call."

Schulman removed his glasses and massaged the bridge of his nose. "It's past six p.m., Adele. On a Friday night. By Monday, Serrano could already be in the process of being deported across the border."

"Judge Hallard realizes that. So he gave me his cell number. He's leaving the country Saturday night on a two-week trip to China. He told me if you can call him by nine tomorrow evening, he could probably get one of his assistants to put together the paperwork Sunday and rush it over to the jail in Pike County first thing Monday morning. The sooner you call the better, since Judge Hallard has to look over the case and make phone calls, and he can't very well do that from the plane."

Schulman looked up from his hands and sighed. "Adele—maybe this is one we have to let go—"

"No!"

"But why Serrano? Why him?"

"Because . . ."

Because of Luna. When Adele looked at Luna, she saw herself, the girl she had once been, the daughter of undocumented immigrants who placed all their hopes and dreams on their oldest and most serious child. Luna read voraciously, just as Adele always had. She got straight As in school. She dreamed big. She worked hard. She gave her heart to her family. She kept her feelings to herself. If ever there was a girl who brought back every hope and fear of Adele's adolescence, it was Luna Serrano.

But there was something else, too. Something more basic. No matter how well intended everyone tried to be, the simple fact was, children need their parents. Where would Adele be today if her parents hadn't been there to guide and support her?

"Those children need their father, Steve. He's all they've got left. You talk in your campaign about the importance of family. Well, here's a family. They need your help. *I* need your help."

Adele waited. Schulman twirled a rubber band between his fingers. He and Gonzalez exchanged glances. Outside the office, phones rang, copiers churned, and televisions blared with campaign commercials. Schulman shot the rubber band into the garbage like a little kid scoring a three-point basket. He nodded to himself as if there were two people inside of him having an argument. Then he held out a hand.

"You have Hallard's cell?"

Adele was so excited; she walked around the desk and

hugged him. She probably would have agreed to the job in
D.C. right then and there if he'd asked. But he didn't, and
for that, she was grateful. She handed him the slip of paper
with all the contact information neatly typed out.

"Thank you, Steve. I owe you." She turned to Gonzalez
and swept him up in her gaze. "I owe you both."

She started for the door. "Adele?"

She turned. Gonzalez grabbed a campaign envelope and
a sheaf of papers on Schulman's desk. "Can you do us a
favor?"

"Anything."

Gonzalez folded the papers, inserted them into the envelope, and licked the envelope shut. Then he handed it to
her. "This is the section of Steve's speech for tomorrow
night that deals with his position on immigration. Can you
look over the wording and see what you think?"

Adele tucked the envelope in her bag. "Of course. I'd be
delighted. I'll read it over tonight."

"Good. Thank you."

Gonzalez watched Adele practically skip through the
maze of phone banks and computers. Then he closed the
office door and stared at the piece of paper on Schulman's
desk with all of Judge Hallard's contact information.
Schulman tented his fingers in front of him and said nothing for a long spell. When he did speak, it was one word:

"Well?"

Gonzalez and Schulman went back years together politically. One word was all that was needed.

Gonzalez sat back in his chair, his belly like a small pillow in front of him. He studied his fingernails. He kept
them clean now. Scrupulously clean. He hadn't always had
that luxury.

"Adele is very—enthusiastic at times, yes?" asked Gonzalez slowly.

"And this is bad?"

Gonzalez gave Schulman a painful look. "She does not always understand the situation."

"Speaking of situations, I didn't like making that call to the county police yesterday. I don't like to play bully."

"I understand, Steve. I don't think it will be a problem again. That's why we need to deal with this the right way. We need to understand that there are *issues* involved." Gonzalez held Schulman's gaze.

"And by issues, you mean personal issues?" asked Schulman.

"Yes. Personal issues."

Silence.

"These personal issues," said Schulman. "Is it too late to, um—deal with them another way?"

"In the time frame we're talking about? Yes. I would say so."

Schulman reached across the desk and crumpled the piece of paper with Judge Quentin Hallard's cell phone neatly typed out. He tossed it in his trash.

"These issues will remain personal this time, I trust?"

"You have my word."

Chapter 29

A soft rain dripped off the leaves and glistened under the streetlights as Vega made the familiar rights and lefts that had come to feel second nature to him now. He wondered if this would be the last time he'd pull up in front of Adele's little blue Victorian on Pine Road. Last summer, he'd replaced the floorboards on her front porch and re-hung a couple of doors. A few weeks ago, he repaired some of the shingles on her garage roof. It wasn't even his house and he felt so much nostalgia for it. He was happy here. He was happy with Adele. He couldn't imagine being happy without her ever again.

Adele's porch lights were on, but her house was dark. Vega found a parking spot four doors down and decided to wait a while to see if she'd come home. He sat in his car—watching the street, watching her driveway—and brooded about the case. None of it made any sense. He had a teenage mother dressed in Joy's hoodie who had died in childbirth, and the only person who could identify her was another teenager with the IQ of a five-year-old. He had her baby, abandoned to die in the woods, and the only witness was a delusional alcoholic who was now dead himself from poison that no one could find. And he had one of the most politically powerful Hispanic couples in the county linked in very tenuous ways to all of it. By a disabled teenager, a drunk, and his ex-wife's maid. What was he missing?

Everything leaves a mark.

Vega was positive that Esme knew the girl and knew she was pregnant. The fact that Esme hadn't come forward suggested she was covering up for someone. The baby's father? A few days ago, Vega would've thought that it was some love-struck, pimply-faced nephew of Esme's who'd panicked that his girlfriend was about to give birth. But that was before the DNA came back on Neto. Now Vega knew he was looking for a man who had to be pushing forty, at least, to have fathered both children. So he was looking for a forty-something-year-old man who had fathered a child with a fifteen- to seventeen-year-old girl. In New York State, that was a felony—reason enough for Esme to want to cover it up.

Mia lives with him.

It had to be Charlie Gonzalez.

Still, like Greco said, Vega needed more than the word of a mentally disabled teenager. He needed something to prove that this might have happened before. He clicked on his dashboard computer and typed "Carlos Gonzalez" into the Department of Motor Vehicles database. Hundreds of Carlos Gonzalezes appeared on the screen. Vega typed Gonzalez's address into the system and eliminated all but one. The file before him contained Gonzalez's date of birth and the Social Security number that had been issued to him after he became a U.S. citizen. Vega copied those and fed them into a national crime database. He expected to find nothing. Gonzalez had a reputation for being squeaky clean. He wasn't even much of a drinker.

One arrest did come up, however. It took place nineteen and a half years ago, when Gonzalez was twenty-seven, before he became a citizen. The charge? Sexual assault of a minor. The alleged victim was a girl of fifteen.

Inés? The age corresponded to Neto, but there was no way to tell. Police work was an entirely different game two decades ago, much less about science and much more about witnesses. The victim's name had been expunged from the record because of her age. There was no DNA, and apparently by the time the charges were brought, no physical evidence either. The victim eventually dropped the charges. It would have been a hard case to prove without physical evidence anyway. In all likelihood, if Gonzalez had gone to trial, he would have been acquitted—

Unless Neto was the product of that rape. Neto's paternity could have been tested. Neto's birth would have made the case stick. And since Gonzalez only had a green card at the time—not citizenship—a conviction would not only have meant jail time, it likely would have resulted in deportation. Clearly, Charlie Gonzalez had a lot to lose.

So what happened? How had the two families managed to coexist and even thrive in the same town under such a shameful secret? They didn't avoid each other, that was for sure. Esme shopped at Claudia's store. Neto worked at Charlie's car wash. How was this possible if Gonzalez had done this terrible thing?

Vega had an idea how. He typed Claudia Aguilar's name into the database. No arrests came up, but ICE records showed that the person who sponsored Claudia and Inés for green cards was Carlos Gonzalez—who had obtained his own citizenship less than a year after his unnamed victim dropped her assault charges. Vega dug a little deeper and found real estate records that showed that Gonzalez bought the building Claudia's store was housed in within a year after the dropped charges. Gonzalez also cosigned a loan to help finance the opening of the store.

Vega sat back from the glow of his screen and felt a vague queasiness come over him. Up until this moment, he'd always loved walking into Claudia's bodega. He loved the lemony scent of ripe guavas, the rows of prayer candles, the exotic foods and spices that served as poignant reminders of a motherland that for him, at least, was as imagined as it was real. But he felt something dark and unsettling now when he thought of those rough-hewn plank floors and ropes of yellow and green plantains hanging from the ceiling. Beneath the homespun comfort there was something rancid. Something that smelled to him an awful lot like blood money.

Up ahead, he saw two headlights pull into Adele's driveway. He got out of his car and jogged over, pulling his collar up against the rain. Sophia jumped out of the car and ran under the eaves of the porch.

"Hey there, Sophia."

The girl smiled back shyly. She was all stick limbs and big teeth, just like Joy at that age. Vega had a sense the child liked him but was afraid to show it too much out of loyalty to her dad. Vega never pushed. He didn't want to become Wendy's Alan in some other divorced father's life.

He noticed that Sophia was still wearing her soccer uniform and cleats. "Little late for practice, isn't it?"

"I had dinner afterward with my friend Katie. Mommy had to work—*again*."

Vega noticed Sophia didn't mention D.C. He wondered if he wasn't the only one who'd been left in the dark. He found himself getting annoyed with Adele that she hadn't told her own daughter yet. It didn't seem fair to spring it on her all of a sudden. Not his business, he supposed. But still.

Adele got out of her car and walked up the front steps carrying a bulging briefcase. She didn't look happy to see him.

"I can't talk tonight, Jimmy. I haven't eaten. Sophia needs a shower before bed, and I've got part of Steve's speech for tomorrow night to look over."

"I'm happy to spring for pizza or Chinese for the two of us while Sophia takes a shower."

"I don't think that's a good idea." Adele didn't like doing "dates" when Sophia was in the house. Vega knew that. But this was important.

"I really think we need to talk."

Rain hammered the porch roof. Adele remained rooted in place.

"Guess what?" Sophia blurted into the silence. "I'm taking guitar lessons!"

One more thing Adele hadn't told him.

"She's only had one lesson so far," said Adele, as if to excuse the omission.

"Can you show me how to play chords?" Sophia asked Vega.

"Uh—" Vega looked at Adele. "—If your mom says it's okay."

He was playing good cop to Adele's bad, just as he used to do with Wendy over Joy. Old habits die hard.

Adele sighed. "You can stay for pizza. And then I have to work."

In the house, Adele seemed preoccupied and tense. Vega tried to stay out of her way.

"The teacher wants me to strum 'Kumbaya,' " said Sophia, leading Vega into the living room and handing him her nylon-stringed guitar. "That's so boring."

The guitar was out of tune. Nylon strings always went out of tune quickly. Vega preferred steel. He tuned it up. "What do you *want* to play?"

Sophia named a song Vega didn't know by an artist who was probably the current bubblegum favorite.

"Can you sing it?" he asked.

She did—better than her mother, though Vega would never tell Adele that. He quickly picked out the melody and figured out the chords. He had a good ear and could usually replicate a pop song on the guitar note for note in under ten minutes. He handed the guitar back to Sophia and began to show her the fingerings. She tried to do a bar chord, holding her entire finger horizontally across the strings, but they just buzzed. She looked disappointed.

"Don't worry. You'll get it in time," said Vega.

Adele called out from the kitchen. "Time to take a shower, Sophia."

"But Mom—"

"Now."

"Just five more minutes?"

"I said now!"

Sophia returned her guitar to its case and stomped upstairs to the bathroom. She slammed the door. When Vega was sure the child was out of earshot, he walked over to the kitchen and leaned in the doorway. Adele was standing at the counter with her glasses on, reading what appeared to be Schulman's speech and scribbling in the margins. She didn't lift her head to look at him. Vega could see the soft swells of her breasts pushing against the buttons of her pale pink blouse. He felt the same tug he always felt—in his loins, his lips, his arms, but most of all, his heart.

"She was having fun," said Vega softly. "You could have let her continue a little longer."

Adele put her pen down and flipped her glasses on top of her head. "Sophia's beginning to get attached to you— in case you haven't noticed. Why are you making what I have to do even harder? Or is that your plan?"

"My *plan?*"

"Coming over here tonight unannounced. Charming Sophia. Trying to stir up dirt on the Gonzalezes yesterday."

"You think this is some sort of *plan?* To get you to stay?" Vega clenched his jaw and tried to control his anger. "I came here tonight to warn you, Nena. You need to be careful."

"In other words, I need to turn down the job in D.C." Adele crumpled up an envelope sitting next to her paperwork and threw it in the garbage.

"You're not even listening to me."

"I am. And what I'm hearing is that you don't think we can put a few hundred miles between us and keep a relationship going."

"That's not it." He paced the kitchen. "Okay, maybe it was before." He ran a hand through his hair. "But not now. Now, it's something real. Something you need to know."

He finally had her attention, and he wasn't sure how to start. He took a deep breath. "You texted me this afternoon that Inés told you she was raped at fifteen, yes? And the man who raped her is Neto's father."

"That's what I gather."

"I'm pretty sure I know who the rapist is."

"Who?"

"Charlie Gonzalez."

"*What?* You're crazy."

"Gonzalez was arrested nineteen years ago in Lake Holly for the sexual assault of a minor. The victim eventually dropped the charges, and less than a year later, Gonzalez not only sponsored Claudia and Inés Aguilar for green cards, he bought Claudia's building and cosigned a loan so she could start her grocery store."

"He's a very generous man."

"You know any other businesses he's done that with?"

"I haven't asked," she said coolly.

"Adele, the police have DNA that says Neto Rivera and

Baby Mercy were fathered by the same man. So Baby Mercy's father is at least around forty—"

"For all you know, Baby Mercy's mother is near forty too, so whatever the relationship was, it was completely consensual."

"It couldn't be. Not in the eyes of the law." Vega held her gaze.

Adele saw the truth without him saying. She gripped the edge of the counter. "Oh God, Jimmy." She looked pale and shaky. "That teenage girl on Joy's campus. You're not saying she's—"

"I'm not saying anything, Nena. As a police officer, I can't. Do you understand?"

She closed her eyes and tented her fingers to her lips as if in prayer. "That's two young teenage girls over the space of two decades," she whispered. "If what you're saying is true, they can't be the only ones."

"I suspect not."

"I trusted him."

"That's what molesters do. They get people to trust them."

The pizza deliveryman rang the doorbell. Sophia opened the bathroom door and called down the stairs that her shower was over and she was ready to say good night. Adele looked suddenly overwhelmed. She sank down in a chair and put her head in her hands. "Oh God," she mumbled. "Oh God."

"How 'bout you say good night to Sophia while I pay the pizza guy, okay?"

Adele nodded and went upstairs. Vega paid for the pizza and moved Adele's papers to one side on the kitchen counter to make room for the box. On top of the first page he noticed some handwriting: *Adele—can you look this over for Steve? Thanks, Charlie.* Vega stared at the handwriting then stared at the torn envelope in the trash. He felt something percolating in his gut—part hope, part fear. It would answer all their questions. It would generate a hundred more.

When Adele returned to the kitchen, Vega pointed to the envelope in the garbage.

"Did Gonzalez give that to you?"

"Yeah. It contained Steve's speech."

"Did he lick it?"

"I think so. I don't remember." And then it dawned on her. She was still enough of an attorney to realize what he was asking. "Oh no, Jimmy. No! You don't mean—"

"If his saliva's on the envelope, we'll know once and for all." Vega grabbed a set of dishwashing gloves by the sink. "Get me a clean Ziploc bag, will you?"

Adele opened a drawer and held a bag out to him. Vega fished the envelope out of the garbage, stuffed it into the bag, and sealed it. "I'll get this tested at the lab tomorrow."

"How fast will you know?"

"Probably within a couple of hours. Why?"

"The cook who's being deported? Manuel Serrano? I encouraged him to let the Gonzalezes take custody of his children."

Vega went very still. "How old are they?"

"Seven, nine—and fifteen."

"And the fifteen-year-old—?"

"Is that girl I like, Luna. You've heard me mention Luna." Adele smacked her palm to her forehead. "Oh God, Jimmy. What have I done?"

Vega walked over to Adele and wrapped his arms around her. "You couldn't have known."

"But—I should've. I, of all people."

Vega chucked a fist under her chin and brought her eyes up to meet his.

"Why 'you' of all people?"

A terrible darkness flashed in her eyes. And in that moment, he knew.

"Nena," he asked softly, rubbing her shoulders, "when you were young, were you—?"

She pushed out of his embrace. "If you're right about Charlie, I will never forgive myself, Jimmy. Ever."

Chapter 30

Papi called! Luna was so excited, she babbled like a preschooler when Doña Esme picked up the phone on Friday evening and the operator asked if she'd accept the charges. Her father being her father, he spent the first two minutes of the call apologizing profusely to Doña Esme for asking her to pay for it.

Dulce and Mateo hogged the phone. Dulce seemed to forget where Papi was. She told him about the upcoming Halloween parade at school and how her friend Caroline was going as a princess and Dulce could only go as a ghost. Luna wanted to strangle her sister. She sounded so petty and self-absorbed. But judging from Papi's voice on the Gonzalezes' speakerphone, he didn't seem to mind. There was a lot of noise in the background where he was: voices, bells, metal doors slamming shut. It sounded like the locker room at school. Luna suspected he was having a hard time hearing all of them anyway, and Dulce's banter was probably about as much as he could concentrate on at the moment.

There was no privacy. Not on his end. Not on theirs. His answers were short. His pauses were long, as if he could only catch some of their words over the noise. Mateo told Papi he'd had a math test today at school that he didn't do well on. Papi told him to study harder, but they all knew how impossible that was right now, so Papi ended up reassuring Mateo he'd do better next time.

Mateo and Dulce managed pretty well talking to Papi over the speakerphone. Luna supposed that to them, it felt more like their father was in the room. But for her, the public nature of their conversation turned her shy and awkward. She could count on one hand the number of times she'd had a real conversation with her father over a phone. Papi was always "just there" in her life. His voice didn't even sound the same over a phone.

"How are you doing, Mija?" he asked when it was finally her turn with him.

"*Estoy bien.*" *I'm fine.* Her first real lie to her father. The first of many, she suspected.

Luna wished she could tell him that all day at school, she felt like she was walking around in a bubble. She sat at lunch with her friends and listened to their chatter like it was a foreign language. She watched her teachers write on their smart boards and read from their lesson plans, and she couldn't imagine why any of it mattered. She didn't take notes. She doodled pictures in the margins: monsters with big noses, long claws, and bushy eyebrows. Fences made of barbed wire. People bleeding from their eyes. She had two hours of homework ahead of her tonight. She had to study for a major biology test Mr. Ulrich was giving on Monday. She hadn't even taken home the study guides. She wanted to tell her father that Mateo wasn't the only one who didn't care about school anymore. But all she said was, "We're doing fine."

Papi told them what they already knew, that he was in Pennsylvania. He didn't say he was in a prison, and they didn't either. He told them he thought he'd be there until Monday, and then they'd put him on a bus. He promised to call every day if they let him and also to call from Mexico as soon as he arrived.

A man barked at Papi in toneless English. He had to hang up. Until that moment, Dulce had willfully forgotten where he was. But Papi's good-byes started her crying again. Luna clasped a hand over her mouth and hissed: "You can't do that to him! Not now!"

Dulce pinched Luna's arm hard. The little girl's eyes were dead cold with hatred. She had no one else to take her anger out on.

The evening felt sad after Papi hung up. The señor was out at meetings. It was just the six kids and Doña Esme. Luna offered to do the dinner dishes, and Doña Esme quickly accepted. By the time she was done, she was too tired to do any homework. She put Dulce to bed and stayed in their room reading next to her. She hoped Mateo didn't pee his bed tonight. He'd promised her he'd empty his bladder before he fell asleep.

She heard the television for a while in a room down the hall. And then all she heard were the parakeets beneath them in the kitchen.

She woke up shivering in the dark, unsure of the time. The air was so cold, the tip of her nose felt frozen to the touch. Dulce was curled tight beside her on the bed. Their apartment was always overheated, so they slept in light blankets. But here, in this house, the air had a bite to it. Luna cuddled up next to Dulce for warmth, but then her back was cold. She pushed her back against her sister, but that didn't help either. They needed another blanket.

She tiptoed over to a dresser. No blankets. There were none in the closet either. She remembered seeing some blankets downstairs in the basement last night when she was laundering Mateo's sheets. She saw no option but to fetch one.

The hallway was lit by a single night-light. It formed a small puddle the color of apple juice on the gleaming wood floor. Luna took a moment to let her eyes adjust. The bedroom doors were all closed. There were no lights beneath their sashes. The señor must have come home—or not—while she slept.

She crept down the stairs. She was colder now than when she'd been in bed. If she couldn't find a blanket soon, she'd have to fetch their jackets. Without Luna's body heat, Dulce would likely wake up herself.

Luna followed the sound of the parakeets to the kitchen. The digital blue numbers floated on the microwave above the stove: 2:15 a.m. On the windowsill sat a pumpkin Doña Esme had carved with her boys. The triangle eyes stared back at Luna vacantly. The uneven zigzag smile carried a hint of menace to it. She shivered—from cold or nervousness she couldn't tell.

She opened the basement door and flipped on a light switch. The bright fluorescent ceiling lights made Luna's eyes water. She padded down the steps. The quilt that had been on the armrest of the couch yesterday was gone. Luna searched under the couch cushions and along the floor, but she couldn't find it anywhere. She opened the door to the laundry room again, hoping it was in there, but it wasn't. She was becoming desperate for warmth. Maybe there was a blanket in the room behind the third door. Luna slid the bolt and opened it.

It was a bedroom. The walls were painted in a cold and institutional shade of blue. There were no windows. A faint odor of bleach wafted out of the room along with something else. Something vaguely metallic.

Luna flipped another switch on the wall. A pale overhead light blinked to life, revealing a steel-framed twin bed along the far wall with a mattress on top. The mattress was bare except for a white plastic protection sheet. Luna wondered whether she should take the plastic sheet upstairs to put on Mateo's cot. Not that she wanted to embarrass her brother, but it would save a lot of headaches.

Directly across from the bed was a chest of drawers with three votive candleholders on top. All three votives had a picture of the Virgin of Guadalupe printed across them. A crucifix hung above the candleholders. Whose room was this? A live-in housekeeper's? If it was, she didn't live here anymore. Not that Luna could blame her. She wouldn't want to live in this room, either.

Still, maybe there was an extra blanket. Luna opened the drawers, hoping to find one. The top drawer contained a few women's sweatshirts and sweatpants, but the second drawer had two thin cotton blankets inside. She pulled them out to take upstairs. And as she did, something between the blankets tumbled out. An envelope full of photos. They spilled across the floor. Luna bent down to collect them and stuff them back into the drawer. Her hand hovered above the images. They were photos of a girl—the same girl whose picture Luna had seen in the garage. Only in these photos, she wasn't wearing shorts. In these, she was naked. Behind her was a blue wall—just like the wall in this room.

Luna's hands shook as she shoved the pictures back into the envelope and threw the envelope in the second drawer. She bundled the blankets in her arms and decided to take the mattress protector too—just in case. She had no wish to return to this room for any reason.

She began to pull the protector off the bed. She gasped at what was beneath: a large, reddish-brown stain the size of a bicycle tire. Blood. Dried blood. In the middle of the mattress. She let go of the protector. It curled back on itself like a roll of wrapping paper, as if it could no longer cover over the raw evidence of something ugly beneath. Luna felt faint and woozy.

"Chica?"

The señor was behind her, standing in the doorway in his underwear again. For a heavy man, his footsteps were whisper soft. Luna turned. The thin strands of his remaining hair were tangled like spaghetti on top of his head. His skin looked sallow and drained under the harsh light.

"I was—I was looking for an extra blanket," Luna stammered. "To put on our bed. Dulce is cold." Luna lifted the blankets as evidence.

The señor's eyes traveled to the bloodstains on the exposed mattress. He saw the dresser drawers partially opened. He seemed to guess at what she'd already seen inside them. "Oh, chica, you shouldn't be in this room. This is no place for you."

"I'm sorry. I didn't mean to . . ." Luna held the blankets to her chest. She left the mattress protector curled on the bed. She didn't want it anymore. Not after seeing what was beneath it.

"This," he gestured to the blood on the mattress, "this was—an accident, yes? It does not concern you. Therefore, you should not discuss it. You understand this, chica, right?"

"Yes," Luna mumbled. She went to scoot by the señor. She could feel his eyes watching her, slowly traveling the length of her body. He didn't move. There was no way she could get past his girth without touching him, and she didn't want to touch him.

The señor wiped the back of his hand across his lips. The muscles in his face tightened, and a dark glint came into his eyes. He stepped closer. His chest heaved in and out as if he'd been running hard, and a layer of sweat gathered on his skin. Luna clutched the blankets tightly to her chest and inhaled, trying to make herself as small and slight as possible. The señor reached out a hand. She flinched as he touched her hair.

"Such pretty hair, chica. You know, one day soon, you'll become a man's wife. That's an important responsibility, yes? You need to learn how to handle that sort of responsibility."

Her head throbbed. Her legs tingled from pins and needles. She smelled bleach and blood and the sweat of a man who was older than her father. He was panting heavily now. His fat fingers traced a strand of Luna's hair from her ear to where it ended on her shoulder.

"I can teach you, chica. You'll like it, too. I know how to make a girl feel like a woman. It will be so good for you, yes?"

"I don't—"

"We can be good to each other. Very, very good."

"No, please."

The señor licked his lips. "Your papi—I know how much he wants to come back. You can make that happen. It's up to you. If you're quiet. If you're respectful—to this family, to me—you can bring your papi back. You can make your family happy. Or you can be selfish. And stupid. I don't think you're a selfish, stupid girl."

His cold sweaty hand began to travel across her shoulder to her breasts. Luna couldn't breathe. Her skin broke out in goose bumps.

"I believe you have many, many talents, chica. I'm very excited to have you share them with me. Very excited."

Something shriveled and died inside of her. In its wake, she felt only the cold, dead blankness of existence. The weight of it pressed on her chest and constricted her lungs. Nothing would ever feel whole or right again. *Dear God, what do I do?* If she refused him, he wouldn't help Papi. If she gave in . . . *Oh no, oh no, oh no!*

"Luna?" a little voice called down the stairs. "I'm cold!"

The señor's hand instantly pulled away. He stepped back. Never had Luna felt so relieved to hear her little sister's voice.

"I'm in the basement, Dulce!" she shouted, more forcefully than she needed to. "I'll be right up!" Her voice was hoarse as if she'd been screaming. Luna supposed that on the inside, she was.

Dulce stood on the stairs and peered into the room where the señor and her sister were standing. She frowned at Luna. She frowned at the señor. Luna could tell by her face that even though she knew nothing of what had just transpired—even though she was a complete innocent in those areas—she felt something strange and uncomfortable in the air between them. The señor ushered Luna out of the room and slid the bolt across the door again before Dulce could see the blood. Luna was glad. Dulce would have had nightmares forever otherwise. Luna knew that she'd never sleep soundly in this house again.

"You need to come to bed," said Dulce.

"Yes!" Luna replied, almost hysterical with the thought. "We'll go together!" She led Dulce up the stairs. She was shaking uncontrollably by the time they got back to their bedroom.

"Wow," said Dulce as Luna spread the blankets across the bed and climbed in beside her. "You're colder than I am."

And then Dulce did something wholly unexpected. She wrapped her arms around Luna and started rubbing her arms and legs to try to warm her up and stop her from shaking. Dulce's touch soothed. But it couldn't erase the images in Luna's head of the blood on that bed, the way the señor had put his hands on her, the things he'd said. It made her want to stand under a hot shower and never come out. Where did that blood come from? What happened in that room?

"I'll get you warm," Dulce whispered. But she couldn't. Luna wasn't sure she'd ever be warm again.

Chapter 31

Adele kicked Jimmy out of her house just after eleven on Friday night. She would never have allowed him to stay over—not with Sophia there. Besides, her mind was racing with so many worries and unanswered questions, she couldn't delight in his touch the way she normally did. She felt ashamed and embarrassed that when she closed her eyes, she didn't see Jimmy. She saw Señor Trejo. The way his gut rested like a bowling ball on a hammock between his hips. Those sweaty, grease-stained hands. The flaccid underside of his chin.

Certain scents brought back those years the Trejos watched her and her younger sister while her parents worked long hours. Diesel fumes. Spearmint gum. Glade air freshener. Señor Trejo was a bus mechanic. Everyone in Adele's family thought the smell of fuel made Adele nauseous.

It wasn't the fuel.

She supposed she was lucky in a way. Her own parents were kind and loving. Señor Trejo targeted only her, not her younger sister, and only when Señora Trejo wasn't around, which wasn't often. The abuse never went all the way, and by the time Adele was twelve, she was old enough to watch her sister and help out at her parents' business, so they didn't need a babysitter anymore. Adele never told her parents what Señor Trejo did to her; she assumed his wife didn't know either. But the older she got, the more she began to wonder: Was Señora Trejo really as innocent as she seemed? If what Jimmy had said tonight was true, Adele had to wonder the same about Esme. Did she know?

Peter was taking Sophia to his parents' house in Connecticut for the weekend. Adele spent the early part of the morning getting her daughter packed and giving her a good breakfast. But her mind was elsewhere—on the job offer in D.C., on whether Schulman would reach Judge Hallard in time to reverse Manuel's deportation. But most of all on Luna. When Sophia complained that Adele had failed to completely cut the crust off her toast, Adele exploded.

"This is your big problem in life, Mija? You have no idea what real problems are!"

Before Adele knew it, they were both in tears—Sophia because Adele had yelled at her and Adele? She couldn't even say anymore. There was so much, stretching all the way back to a man with sweaty hands who stank of diesel fuel. The house became filled with slamming doors and raised voices, and the dispute culminated in Adele's guilt-ridden apology. By the time she dropped Sophia off at her father's, she felt like the worst mother in the world. Not a good way to slide into what she had to do next.

The Serrano children often spent Saturday mornings at La Casa—Dulce and Mateo getting tutoring, Luna helping the other volunteers mentor the younger children. But they hadn't shown up this morning, according to Kay, the weekend volunteer coordinator. Adele wasn't really surprised. The children had been through so much, tutoring wasn't a priority right now. Still, after Jimmy's conversation last night, Adele felt she needed to check up on them, if not at La Casa, then at the Gonzalez house. She had the perfect excuse for dropping by: her staff had collected $150 for the children to help pay for any incidentals they might need. Plus Adele had come across a copy of one of Luna's favorite childhood books that she'd lost when the family's apartment was destroyed in a fire. She thought it might give the teenager some comfort right now.

Adele rarely drove into The Farms, where the Gonzalezes lived. The development was on the eastern side of town near the lake that gave Lake Holly its name. Jimmy's ex lived out this way. So did many of La Casa's biggest patrons. It was meant to look like a neighborhood, but Adele never got a neighborhood feel driving around the manicured streets. The houses were too big, the driveways too long. The grass never looked like children trampled it. Even now, in late October, flowers bloomed in perfect, well-tended arrangements like they'd just popped out of a Disney movie.

Adele pulled into the Gonzalezes' driveway and got out of her car. She was pleased to hear children's voices in the backyard. Maybe the Serrano kids had lost themselves in play. If so, that was certainly good news.

She rang the front doorbell. Esme answered. She had her coat on and a bag slung over one shoulder like she was just about to go out. She did not look happy to see Adele.

"I'm so sorry to bother you, Doña Esme. I just wanted to see how the Serrano children were making out. I have a little something from La Casa to give to them."

"Oh." Esme did not invite Adele in. Then again, if someone had dropped by Adele's house this morning unannounced, they'd have found Sophia crying about crusts on her bread and Adele screaming at her, so she certainly wasn't one to point fingers.

"It won't take long," Adele promised. "The children—they aren't coming with you?"

"Christian and Alex are at soccer. David is at karate. I'm going to pick up my boys now. I think Luna is old enough to watch her own brother and sister."

"Yes, of course," said Adele. "I'd be happy to visit with them a little if you need to leave."

Esme hesitated. "I suppose I can stick around for a few minutes. Mateo and Dulce are playing in back. Why don't you go out there and I will bring Luna?"

Mateo and Dulce were kicking a soccer ball back and forth without enthusiasm. They both came running over as soon as they saw Adele. They thought she had news. She felt bad to disappoint them.

"We're still working on some things," Adele told the children. She would've loved to mention Judge Hallard, but she didn't want to get their hopes up for nothing. "Have you spoken to your father yet?" she asked them.

"Last night," said Mateo. "He promised to call again."

The sliding glass door by the patio opened and out stepped Luna and Esme. Luna's hair looked stringy and un-washed. Her eyes were downcast, her gait hesitant. Esme put her arm around Luna's shoulder and combed her hair from her face.

"Poor Luna," said Esme. "She's very sad right now. We're trying hard to cheer her up."

"Look, Luna, I can almost do a cartwheel," said Dulce. The seven-year-old raised her hands high above her head and spun head over heel, leaving off the last part of the maneuver with two feet thudding to the earth. It was a good first effort. Adele applauded. Luna's smile looked like the corners of her lips each weighed a hundred pounds. Was this sadness over her father? Or something more? Adele tried to remember how she had behaved after Señor Trejo's advances. Whatever she'd felt, she must have been good at hiding it, the same way she could hide things now. To their dying days, her parents never suspected a thing.

"We're working on getting your father back," Adele told Luna, hoping that was the cause of her sadness. "You mustn't lose hope."

Esme stroked the top of Luna's head. "You see, mami?" she said, using the term affectionately the way some Spanish mothers do to their children. "Everyone is worried about you. You don't want to make them sad or make your papi sad, do you?"

"I brought something for you," said Adele. She pulled out the book, a paperback called *Esperanza Rising*. "Remember this? You said your copy was destroyed in the fire. I found this copy at a garage sale. I know how much you always loved it."

Adele placed the paperback in Luna's hands. On the sky-blue cover was a drawing of a windswept girl in a flowing, mustard-colored dress, her bare feet above the green croplands and twilight-colored hillsides of California. Like Luna, the title character was a teenage Mexican girl struggling with a parent's death, family separations, and hardship as an immigrant in the United States. The book was set in the 1930s, but for a girl like Luna, the story was as relevant now as it was in the character's day.

Luna stared at the cover. Adele felt a sudden panic that the fictional character's circumstances might be the last thing the teenager wanted to be reminded of right now.

"Say thank you to Doña Adele," Esme scolded. Luna mumbled a thank you, but that only made Adele feel more embarrassed that she'd done the wrong thing.

"I also brought this," Adele added quickly, pulling the envelope with the collection money out of her purse. She handed it to Luna. "Everyone at La Casa pitched in some cash for you and Mateo and Dulce to be able to buy things you might need. We raised a hundred and fifty dollars."

"Wow," said Dulce. "Can I have a phone?"

Adele grinned. That girl would survive a nuclear war.

"Please thank everyone there for their generosity," Luna mumbled woodenly. She inserted the envelope inside the cover of the book. There was no spark to her. Nothing.

Adele had always been able to read her before. Now she had no idea what the teenager was thinking.

"My cousin Yolanda is coming to visit this afternoon," said Esme. "Maybe that will cheer Luna up. I'm hoping. Right, mami?" Esme turned to Adele. "Let me walk you out."

Adele looked over at Luna. There was a fraction of a second when the teenager lifted her gaze and Adele saw something push through the fog. Panic? Anger? *Fear?* Dulce and Mateo seemed fine—well, as fine as any child could be who had just watched the government wrench their father away from them.

But Luna? Esme seemed so kind and loving. And yet—
So had Señora Trejo.

Adele grabbed Luna's hand. She squeezed it hard enough for the sensation to register. She waited for Luna to look up at her. "You know La Casa's number, right?"

Luna nodded. Adele took out a business card and scribbled her cell on the back. She shoved it inside the book.

"You need to talk, call me at La Casa or on my cell anytime. Day or night. I'll call you back right away. You understand?"

"You worry too much, Doña Adele," said Esme. "Luna will be just fine."

Luna's demeanor made Adele more anxious than ever to get Manuel returned to Lake Holly. As soon as she got back to her house, she dialed Judge Hallard's cell phone herself. Hallard picked up on the third ring. He sounded out of breath.

"Oh my goodness, Judge. Thank you so much for answering."

"I'm at the gym, Miss Figueroa. But if this is when Schulman wants to talk, okay."

"He hasn't called you yet?"

"No."

"There must be some mistake. He told me he was going to call you."

"I've had my cell phone on since I spoke to you yesterday, young lady. There are no missed calls from Schulman on it."

"Perhaps he dialed wrong. Can you call *him?*"

Silence. *Damn.* She'd overstepped her bounds. She heard him take a long pull of water.

"Look, Miss Figueroa," he exhaled. "Don't take this the wrong way, but a man eyeing a seat in the U.S. Senate will promise a lot of things he has no intention of delivering on. I have no idea whether that's the case here or not. But I can't stick this Serrano guy at the front of the line without a say-so from Schulman. That hasn't happened."

"But he promised," said Adele, well aware of how much she sounded like her nine-year-old daughter at the moment.

"In my long experience in Washington, I can tell you that the words 'I promise' have about as much weight as a college freshman's sobriety pledge. Maybe he's sincere; maybe he's just dodging a bullet. The only way for me to know is if he calls. I'm sorry I can't be more helpful than that, but if Schulman doesn't want to stick his neck out for this Serrano, I most certainly cannot."

Chapter 32

Doña Esme set Luna to work making lunch for the younger children before she left to fetch her boys from their sports activities. She ordered Luna to make grilled cheese sandwiches, but then complained that her tomato slices were too thick.

"You think if you do a bad job, you won't have to do it again—is that it?" asked Doña Esme.

"No," Luna insisted. Already this morning before Doña Adele came, Luna had done two loads of laundry, mopped the upstairs, and wiped down the toilets. "I'm trying my best," she said.

"This is your best?" Doña Esme held up a lumpy slice of tomato and flung it back at her. "This is not a free ride here, chica. You're a woman. Not a child. You stay, you help." She folded her arms across her chest and regarded Luna with narrowed eyes like she'd stolen something. "You certainly seem to be helping yourself in every other way."

Luna wasn't sure what she meant. All she knew was that she barely slept last night. She awoke cotton-mouthed, a metallic taste lingering at the back of her palate. Her hair had turned stringy here. She hadn't had a chance to wash it, but that wasn't the reason. Her whole body felt like it was carrying the scent of something decayed. Fear. That's what this was. She couldn't make her mind forget last night, the blood-soaked mattress, the raw evidence of something indecent and secretive in that basement. She knew, too, that if she didn't do everything Doña Esme and the señor told her to do, she'd never see Papi again. And so she kept her head down and tried to slice the tomato more evenly.

Mateo and Dulce came inside and helped her make lunch the moment Doña Esme went to pick up her sons. They took the plastic off the American cheese slices. They poured milk into glasses. They didn't fight like they usually did. They didn't say anything at all. Luna tried to pretend they were just making a normal lunch together, but even they knew something was wrong.

"We should call Alirio and Maria José," Mateo suggested softly. Luna shook her head, no.

"Papi is still in Pennsylvania," she reminded Mateo. "Mr. Schulman is the only one with the power to help him. The Gonzalezes are the only ones with the power to convince Mr. Schulman. If we leave, Papi will lose his chance."

"But Doña Esme isn't very nice to you," said Mateo. Dulce nodded in agreement.

"Maybe things will get better," Luna said. She wasn't sure even they believed that.

The atmosphere improved a bit in the afternoon. Christian, Alex, and David came home. After lunch, they kicked a ball around with Mateo. Doña Esme let Dulce pet one of her parakeets. After Luna stacked the dishwasher, she was allowed to go up to her room to do some homework.

She stared at her biology textbook, but her mind was a blank. Her mother's begonia sat on the windowsill. A few of the pink petals had dropped to the dirt. The leaves were yellow in the center and starting to brown and crinkle at the edges. Mami's begonia didn't like its new home. Luna understood.

She couldn't get herself to concentrate, so she took out *Esperanza Rising* and tried to read the opening paragraphs about Mexico that she had liked so much when she first read them in sixth grade. But all it did was fill her with sadness, thinking about Papi going to this place she didn't remember, this place he couldn't leave. She forced herself to answer some biology questions in preparation for her test Monday, but most of the review material she needed was on Mr. Ulrich's webpage. To access it, she needed a computer. Luna and her siblings used to use the computer at La Casa since they didn't have one of their own. Luna didn't know if the Gonzalezes would let her use one of theirs.

Before she could get up the nerve to ask them, exhaustion overtook her and she fell asleep. When she woke up, the house was quiet. There was a note shoved under the door in big, bold print that she recognized as Mateo's: *Doña Esme's cousin Yolanda took us all to the movies. See you later—Love, Mateo and Dulce.*

Luna walked downstairs. The house was empty and quiet save for the parakeets. She figured no one would mind if she used one of the computers to access her science teacher's webpage. There was a laptop on a small table in the corner of the kitchen. A Mac—much nicer than the boxy old desktop she used at La Casa. Luna turned it on. The screen lit up instantly with some kind of purplish space galaxy in the background and a row of icons below.

Luna knew she was supposed to be accessing Lake Holly High's website, but she ended up typing *Lords Valley PA* into Google just to see what the area looked like that Papi was in. It was silly, she knew, since Papi would never see any of it. Still, it comforted her in an odd way to see that it was an area in the Pocono Mountains full of wooded hills and streams. She wondered if perhaps he got to take a walk outside in some fenced area. Maybe he could see the trees. He'd always loved nature.

She closed out of the images and typed in her school's website, then clicked on Mr. Ulrich's webpage. Some of the study materials needed to be printed out. Luna didn't see a printer, but the information was simple enough that she could copy it by hand. She searched the kitchen drawers for a pen and scrap paper. Doña Esme was so fanatically neat that even scrap paper and pens were hard to find.

She finally located a few pens in one drawer, along with one crumpled piece of paper. One side was blank. The other side was a flyer of some sort with several photographs of a girl. A dead girl.

Luna stared at the pictures. She couldn't breathe. She couldn't tear herself away. On the bottom of the flyer, the police listed a phone number to call if anyone knew the girl or had information on her.

She had information.

She wished she didn't.

She wished she'd never seen the blue room in the basement with the slide bolt on the door and the bloodstains on the mattress.

The overhead kitchen light flicked on behind her. Doña Esme stood in the doorway, staring at Luna, staring at the flyer in her hands.

Chapter 33

The envelope that Charlie Gonzalez had given Adele would be easy to test for DNA.

The problem wasn't the test. The problem was the paperwork.

"I'm sorry, Detective. I need an authorized signature and case number before I can test this envelope," said Dr. Chang when Vega walked into the medical examiner's office on Saturday morning. Dr. Chang was a tiny Chinese woman with flawless skin and the iron disposition of a tank commander at Tiananmen Square. She refused to budge without the required signature.

Dr. Gupta would have. She knew Vega and bent the rules for him occasionally. But Gupta was in Virginia at her son's college for the weekend. Vega tried Dolan, who was off this weekend and visiting his in-laws at the Jersey Shore. Dolan agreed to give Vega the authorization over the phone. ("This better be good, Jimmy. No way am I putting my head on the chopping block over this.") But when Vega waved his cell in front of Dr. Chang with the good news that Dolan was on the line and would give the authorization, Dr. Chang just shook her head.

"I'm sorry, Detective. I need an original signature on the forms submitted by the investigating detective."

"*Ay, puñeta!* That's ridiculous!"

"Rules are rules," said Dr. Chang. "Surely, the DNA test can wait a day or two until an investigating detective can submit the request?"

But it couldn't. Vega already knew it couldn't. He had only to think of Adele last night, the way she shrank from his touch at the memory of something so dark and deep she wouldn't talk about it, not even to him. And he knew that the damage was too great, too permanent, to chance it on another girl.

He left the ME's office and went back to his own. He needed a warm body to sign the authorization, but it was hard to find one on a weekend. Captain Waring was at a police conference in Albany. Vega tried to hunt him down without luck. Greco's home and cell phones went straight to voice mail. Vega left vague but insistent messages on each (he couldn't commit anything confidential to a recording). He could already picture Greco cursing yet another false lead—on his free time, no less. Vega wasn't surprised when Greco didn't return the call.

He couldn't spend his whole workday chasing after people. He had reports to finish, emergencies to field. A husband had shot his wife in a domestic dispute last night when Vega was off-duty. She was clinging to life, but it was anybody's guess whether the attempted murder charge would turn to murder. Vega needed to read through the arresting officer's report and witness statements. He had to hunt down the neighbor who'd made the 911 call and reinterview her on a few key points.

By early afternoon, he'd made little progress on any front. Waring and Greco hadn't called him back, and the neighbor/witness on this new case was now backtracking, saying she hadn't seen everything she'd claimed the night before.

Vega was at his desk, picking at a soggy sandwich, when his cell phone rang. The caller ID said it was Joy. That surprised him. He hadn't spoken to her since Thursday afternoon on the Gonzalezes' driveway. He'd wanted to call since their argument, but he was afraid that anything he said right now could jeopardize the fragile house of cards he was trying to assemble around Charlie and Esme. If she needed him, however, that trumped all other considerations. He picked up.

"You haven't called," she blurted into the phone. She sounded hurt. It felt like a punch to the gut to think he was the source.

"I've been up to my eyeballs in work, Chispita. I'm at work now." He wanted to remind her that she was the one who told him to "back off," but he didn't think this was the time to bring it up.

"You could have called to apologize."

Vega sighed. "I'm sorry if you feel I was rough on you. But everything I did was to protect you. And I succeeded. You're not a suspect anymore—"

"That's not an apology, Dad. That's a rationalization. Don't you see the difference?"

"You're in the clear. That's what counts."

"Because you've arrested someone else, I'm guessing. Not because you finally believe me."

"I do believe you."

"Huh. *Now.*"

"No. *Always.* But I needed to protect you. That's what a father does."

Except when he can't, thought Vega. Who was protecting Luna Serrano now that her father couldn't?

Me. I have to. There is no one else.

"Listen, Joy, I've got to go. There's something important I have to do. Maybe we can grab dinner sometime this week? My treat?"

"No pizza. I can't eat gluten. Or meat. Or—"

"I'll rustle up a place that only serves free-range broccoli—"

"Daaad—"

"Okay, okay. Deal."

Vega hung up and dialed Greco's phones again. His cell phone still went to voice mail, but a woman picked up his home phone. Vega wracked his brains to remember Greco's wife's name: *Joan? Joanna? Joelle?* Greco always just referred to her as "the wife." Vega identified himself and explained that he needed to speak to Greco right away and that he wasn't picking up his cell.

"He went fishing," she said. "He always turns his phone off when he goes fishing. That's half the reason I think he goes out there."

"And where does he go?"

"He keeps a rowboat at the Eastlake Reservoir. If you're willing to drive over there, I'll bet you can find him."

The Eastlake Reservoir was about forty minutes away by car. It was almost three in the afternoon by the time Vega parked on the shoulder of the road next to the reservoir. Already the sun was eking out its final blast of warmth for the day.

Vega scanned the parked cars until he picked out Greco's big white Buick. Good. He was here at least. He trudged down a path of loose gravel until he came to what looked like a graveyard of steel-gray boats all turned over like turtles retracted in their shells. This was a reservoir, so only metal rowboats were allowed. Vega cupped a hand across his brow to block the glare and skimmed a glance across the water. There were several boats bobbing in the distance, all of them parked far away from one another like shy kids at a dance. Greco was easy to spot. He had a little beige fishing cap on his head with a couple of feather lures pinned to it and a red stick in his mouth that even at this distance Vega recognized as a Twizzler. Vega called out from the shore and waved his arms furiously.

"Grec! Turn on your phone!"

Greco ignored him at first, then squinted, then threw

the licorice out of his mouth and gave Vega the finger. But he picked up his phone at least, and for that, Vega was grateful.

"What did you do?" Greco demanded. "Plant a GPS up my ass? I swear, Vega, there are venereal diseases that are easier to get rid of than you."

"I need one favor. Just one," said Vega. "I need you to come with me to the medical examiner's office to sign a form to test Charlie Gonzalez's DNA. One signature. And then you can go."

"How the hell did you get Gonzalez's—? No, scratch that. I don't want to know. Either way, you're off the case."

"That's why you're signing the form."

"It can't wait till Monday?"

"No." Vega told him about Luna.

"And what if you're wrong?"

"We test the envelope and Gonzalez's DNA doesn't match the father profile on Baby Mercy, I won't bother you anymore."

"That's almost worth losing a day of fishing for."

It took nearly forty-five minutes for Louis Greco to row his boat to shore, lock it up, and follow Vega in his car to the ME's office. It took less than two minutes for Greco to sign the authorization form.

"How quickly can you do the test?" Vega asked Dr. Chang.

"I can run a full test in under ninety minutes. I can tell you whether it's a likely match in about thirty."

Vega looked at his watch. It was almost four p.m.

"You want me to call you with the results?" she offered.

"Please. As soon as you can."

He walked Greco back to his car. The sky was bright but the land was already fuzzy and pockmarked with shadows. Vega felt the chill in his fingers and across his back.

"Thanks for coming in for this," he said to Greco.

"Good thing I caught nothing worth keeping or I'd really be sore." Greco zipped up his goose-down fishing vest over his flannel shirt. He looked like a Mafia hit man on vacation. "You *do* realize, Vega, that even if the DNA comes back a match, we still gotta build a case against the Gonzalezes. These are powerful people. Politically protected people."

"I realize that."

"We go in on just the DNA, Gonzalez could claim he had a quick fling with a prostitute and didn't even know she was underage or carrying his child. See what I'm saying?"

Vega nodded.

"What we really need," said Greco, "is that old-fashioned, pre-science thing that won more cases for me than DNA ever could."

"What's that?"

"A witness," said Greco. "Somebody who could say they actually saw this dead teenager with Gonzalez or knew what he was doing—and don't talk to me about Neto, Vega. That kid's testimony would never hold up on a witness stand."

Everything leaves a mark. "The birth," Vega murmured.

"Huh?"

"She was just a girl," said Vega. "No way do I buy that she delivered her baby alone."

"Esme probably helped her."

Vega made a face. "Would *you* want to deliver the souvenir of your husband's infidelity?"

"I use the word 'help' loosely here, Vega. The mom died, so if Esme was the midwife, she did a crappy job."

"I think there was somebody else involved. Not Charlie. I get the impression he's through with these girls once he deflowers them."

"Then who?" asked Greco.

Someone who could be trusted to keep her mouth shut. Someone who'd been paid to keep it shut for decades al-

ready. Vega thought back to what Dominga had said about the midwife who'd delivered Emilio: *She's old. She started delivering babies years ago, beginning with her own family. Mostly, she just mixes herbs for clients now.*

"Dominga Flores's baby was delivered by an unlicensed Spanish midwife," said Vega. "I have a hunch the same woman was involved in the delivery of Baby Mercy as well."

"Did Dominga give you her name?"

"No. But I have a hunch it was Claudia Aguilar."

"Claudia? The fruit and vegetable lady?"

Vega's cell phone buzzed with a text message from Dr. Chang: *All markers are showing an exact match for paternity of Baby Mercy and DNA found on envelope. Full test likely to indicate same. Will send complete lab results later—Veronica Chang.*

Vega showed the text to Greco. "Are you up for a little grocery shopping?"

Chapter 34

"What are you doing going through my drawers and using my laptop?"

Doña Esme's voice was sharp and accusing. Luna tried to explain that she had to review for a science test and needed a computer and some scrap paper. Doña Esme ripped the flyer out of her hand.

"From now on, when you want something, you ask, chica." She crumpled up the flyer and tossed it into the kitchen garbage. "This is nothing."

Luna gripped the counter to keep her hands from trembling. She couldn't stop thinking about the photographs she saw last night of this same girl in that blue room downstairs. And now she was dead. Who was she? What went on in this house?

"I'm sorry," Luna managed to croak out. "I didn't know anyone was home."

"Yolanda took the children to the movies. I took a nap." Doña Esme closed her laptop and turned to face Luna. Her mood had shifted once again. She smiled, for once not trying to camouflage that perfect row of white fence-post teeth. Their fakeness frightened Luna on a primal level. She lowered her gaze.

"I have a wonderful surprise for you, Luna. We're going to Pennsylvania to visit your papi."

Luna felt something like helium in her heart. She tried to tug it back to earth and remind herself that this was Doña Esme talking. Nothing was for certain. "When?"

"Now, of course."

"But Dulce and Mateo are at the movies."

"Oh, mami," said Doña Esme. "The jail won't let little children in. They're too young. It would only make them sad to travel such a long distance and have to wait outside. That's why we're going now. We can get there before visiting hours are over today, and I'll have you back later this evening. You can tell Dulce and Mateo all about it then."

"Does Papi know?"

"It will be a surprise."

Luna hesitated. Doña Esme regarded her with impatience. "Don't you want to see your papi?"

"Yes, of course!"

"Then we have to go right now or we'll miss visiting hours."

"Can we call your cousin?" asked Luna.

"Why?"

"Well, shouldn't Dulce and Mateo know I'm going to see Papi?"

"Don't be silly. They're in the movie theater. Yolanda can't answer her phone. And besides, it will only make them sad to know they can't go too. Better to tell them nothing for now and leave it for when you're back."

"But—"

Doña Esme folded her arms across her chest and frowned. "Luna." She finally addressed her by name. "I have no idea what tomorrow holds for your father. He could be halfway to Mexico by then. He's in Pennsylvania right now. Less than two hours away by car. It's after four p.m. Visiting hours at the facility are until seven. If you want to go, we need to go right now. This is your last chance."

Luna closed her eyes. It scared her that Papi's face was beginning to lose its three-dimensionality. How far did his mustache extend past his upper lip? What color were his eyes in bright sunlight? Suddenly it was harder to picture him in their kitchen dicing onions or locate the pitch of his voice in her ears. He'd been gone only two days, and already it felt like a lifetime of separate experiences had passed between them. She knew that seeing him in that jail would fill them both with sadness. But what would *not* seeing him do? And besides, she needed his advice. She couldn't tell him what was happening here. But perhaps she could ask, in a roundabout way, how they might go about moving to Alirio and Maria José's apartment in Queens.

"Okay," she said to Doña Esme. "I just have to go to the bathroom, and then we can go."

Luna hid the pen she'd been using for her homework in the pocket of her jeans. On the way to the bathroom, she grabbed the book Doña Adele had given her. She scribbled a message to Dulce and Mateo inside the front cover: *Going with Doña Esme to see Papi. Back tonight. Love you, XXX Luna.* They didn't need any other surprise exits in their young lives.

Chapter 35

Vega and Greco left Greco's car in the parking lot of the ME's office and drove north to Lake Holly. It was just after four thirty p.m. Claudia's bodega normally closed around five on Saturdays. Vega wanted to catch her while she was still at the store. The sun had set, and the sky went from bleached to the color of faded denim. Already the hillsides had gone inky as if blotting up the night and holding it in abeyance until the heavens could gather the will to do the same.

"Assuming Schulman's Teflon," said Greco, "which I think he is—is Adele gonna follow him to D.C.?"

"Looks like it," said Vega, keeping his eyes on the road.

"You can still see her though, right?"

Vega shrugged. "It's like you said—she's been slumming. She'll have better pickings down there."

"She say that?"

"No—"

"So why the hell are you listening to me?"

" 'Cause I don't want to end up as collateral damage."

Greco shook his head. "Pride fucks every man better than any woman ever could."

Vega didn't answer. Greco stared out a side window and chuckled.

"What?"

"I never told anybody this, okay?" said Greco. "But when I was a teenager, I really liked this girl: Angelica Mariano. Spent my whole teens mooning over her. But I never asked her out. You wanna know why?"

"Okay."

"Because I figured she was too good for me. So I moved on with my life, met my wife. And—I'm not saying anything against Joanna; we've had a pretty good run, all in all—but I never stopped thinking about Angelica. So anyways, I go back to my thirtieth high school reunion a few years ago. Angelica's happily married with some grown kids, same as me. But guess what? She tells me she was *waiting* for me all those years ago to ask her out. I lost my chance with the girl of my dreams because I was afraid of getting rejected. I picked the *worst* outcome and turned it into the *only* outcome when all I had to do was let things happen."

"So you're saying I should just see what happens?"

"Why not? Look, Adele and I haven't seen eye to eye on a lot of things over the years. But I get that she's a really smart, attractive, and ambitious woman. She's not some little parakeet you can lock in a cage. She's like a peregrine falcon. She's gotta fly at her own altitude. Doesn't mean she won't fly back to you. Stop making this so difficult. If I'd listened to my own advice, who knows what would have happened between me and Angelica Mariano?"

They pulled up across the street from Claudia's. The lights were on. It was still open.

"Thanks, Grec."

"Do me a favor? Next time you plan some hot and heavy night with Adele? Do it in D.C. Any crap that happens will be the D.C. cops' problem then, not mine."

When they walked into Claudia's, there were a couple of men in mud-stained jeans and baseball caps buying small handfuls of items for dinner. A woman in a black felt coat was pinching every guava for the ripest one. Claudia was behind the counter, her white apron spotted with bits of grease, her bun of wire-brush hair coming loose at the edges. Inés was washing down the deli case and wrapping the luncheon meats to put in the refrigerator for the night. When she saw Vega and Greco, she stopped in her tracks and focused her attention on Greco.

"Romeo's been released?"

"He's out. We've got no beef with him." Greco spread his hands in a way that made it seem like he'd personally worked an all-nighter to free the man. "Me and Detective Vega here just want to ask you and your mom some questions when you get a chance."

"About Romeo?"

Greco shrugged. "And other things."

Vega and Greco wandered the aisles until all the customers were gone and Claudia could officially close up the store for the evening. Inés flipped the sign across the glass panel on the front door. The streetlights beyond gave the darkness a sickly glow. Vega had already decided that their strategy would be to divide and conquer. Greco gave the excuse that he wanted to talk to Inés privately in back when in reality it was Vega who wanted to talk to Claudia alone.

Vega waited until Greco and Inés had gone into the stockroom. Then he casually walked over to a shelf of herbs and squinted at some of their labels. He picked up a brown glass vial with an eyedropper on its lid and held it up to the light.

"I'm curious," said Vega, speaking to Claudia in Spanish. "What do people use"—he read the label—"chaparral for?"

"It's a kind of cactus," said Claudia. "It's used to make a poultice for arthritis pain. It can also be stirred into tea for cramps."

"You know a lot about herbs, Doña Claudia." He called her doña, not señora, to keep the conversation as personal as possible.

Claudia shrugged. "I know some things."

Vega returned the vial to the shelf. "So you're a *curandera?*"

Claudia nodded. "I come from a long line of traditional healers. I like to help people."

"I can see that." Vega looked at her squarely. He wasn't used to standing next to her without a counter between them. Her skin was creased like old waxed paper. The harsh fluorescents picked up every ridge and valley.

"And those people—do they include mothers in labor?"

Claudia's eyes grew dark as crude oil. "I don't know what you mean, Detective."

"I'm asking, Doña Claudia, if they include people like Dominga Flores?"

Claudia grabbed a rag from a pocket in her grease-stained apron and began wiping down a shelf. She kept her back to Vega. "The boy came out fine and healthy. I could not help her situation beyond that."

Claudia obviously thought Vega just wanted to question why she hadn't reported Dominga's abusive employer to the police. Good. He'd play on that.

"I understand completely, Doña Claudia. Sometimes, there is nothing you can do when you're at the mercy of a rich and powerful man."

Claudia wiped down the shelves in silence. Vega heard only the scrape of cans and jars punctuated by the intermittent hum of the refrigerated ice-cream chest. During the day, the place was so busy, Vega never heard any of these noises.

"Neto's delivery," he said softly. "That must have been very hard on you." Dominga had mentioned that her midwife delivered babies in her own family. Vega was gambling that Neto was one of them.

Claudia's hand paused on her rag. The silence grew like a stretched rubber band between them. Vega pushed a little harder.

"I understand that Inés was only fifteen."

"Why does that matter?" the old woman asked sharply.

"I know you've had a hard life, Doña Claudia. I know you've had to make some hard choices. Really, what could you do?" Vega was making it up as he went along, hoping that each silence would confirm he was on the right track. "How could you know that Neto would have complications?"

The old woman dabbed a corner of her apron to her eyes. "Every day I ask God to forgive me for not taking Inés to the hospital." Her voice was thick and nasal. "They could have performed a cesarean. They could have unwrapped the umbilical cord from around Neto's neck, But then they would have asked about her age. They would have asked about the baby's father. Who would have believed us against the word of—of—"

"Of Charlie Gonzalez." Vega watched Gonzalez's name work its way across the muscles of Claudia's face. Her jaw shrank inward. Her lips grew pinched and tight. "So you made a deal with him in return for keeping his secret."

"You think I could have gotten justice?" Claudia snapped. "This store—" Claudia lifted her hands and gestured to the roof above where plantains on ropes shared space with flypaper strips. "—This is my justice. It's not perfect. But it's the best justice a poor woman like me was ever going to get."

"And how about the dead girl I showed you a picture of the other day?" asked Vega. "Where's *her* justice?"

"No." Claudia shook her head. "I can't go there. I can't."

"Who was she, Doña Claudia?"

Silence.

"Neto said her name was Mia."

"I don't know how Neto knew that," said Claudia. "Maybe Don Charlie took the girl to the car-wash office and

Ncto saw them. I don't know. In any case, I never asked the girl's name, and Esme never said."

"You delivered her baby—"

"No! The girl was already in labor when Esme called me in a panic and said she was bleeding a lot. When I got there, I knew right away I couldn't help her. I told Esme to call 911. She wouldn't listen. She threw me out."

"Why didn't *you* call 911?"

"Esme told me if I ever said a word, the señor would cut me off financially. My business would go under. That girl? She was nobody, Detective. I have my own family to worry about!"

In one breath, Claudia Aguilar had gone from innocent to witness to accomplice. Claudia seemed to realize it too.

"I want a lawyer," she told Vega.

The backroom door opened, and Inés and Greco came out. Inés's eyes were swollen. Greco must have been trying to corroborate their theory. She looked at her mother. "Did you know, Mami?"

Claudia stiffened. She looked from her daughter to Vega. "Inés has nothing to do with any of this."

"Mrs. Aguilar?" said Greco. "We'd like you to come down to the station for a statement."

"Am I under arrest?"

"We'd prefer you come down voluntarily." Greco and Vega had already decided that Claudia's prime value might be as a witness. Arresting her too early might shut her up. The longer they held off charging her, the more bargaining power they'd have to induce her to testify against the Gonzalezes.

"And if I refuse?" asked Claudia.

"Doña Claudia," said Vega. "The Serrano children are still in that house. We're concerned about their welfare, particularly fifteen-year-old Luna. We know they go to your church and you care about them too. If you stop talking to us except through a lawyer, that girl remains at risk."

Claudia's shoulders sagged. All the fight left her. "I tried to tell Manuel that his children might be better off with his cousins. But he thought Luna would have more opportunities if she stayed in Lake Holly. He wanted her to go to college. I thought perhaps—there were three of them. Safety in numbers, yes? I thought—maybe things would be different with Luna."

"But Mami," said Inés, "don't you see? No girl is safe with him. It's only a matter of time before he does this to Luna. We have to come forward. This has to stop!"

Claudia sighed. "I understand."

Vega turned to Greco. "Call in one of your patrol cars to take you and Mrs. Aguilar to the station and get her statement. Start drawing up search warrants and arrest warrants." Vega headed for the door. "I'll be there as soon as I can."

"Where are you going?"

"To the Gonzalez house."

"We can get child services to go up there," said Greco.

"After five p.m.? On a Saturday? Nothing doing," said Vega. "I want those kids now. Not an hour from now. *Now.*"

Chapter 36

Doña Esme didn't talk in the car. She looked grim-faced and determined as she gripped the steering wheel. Luna heard the steady rhythm of the highway seams hitting their tires. She watched the sky ahead of them turn pink and the hilly landscape turn flat and black. Oncoming headlamps flashed at intervals across Doña Esme's face. Light and dark, light and dark. That's what Luna's life felt like right now. There were periods when everything seemed almost normal. And then suddenly, it didn't.

It was a straight ride west from Lake Holly, New York, to Lords Valley, Pennsylvania. They were traveling toward the Newburgh Beacon Bridge that spanned the Hudson River. From there, they would drive a little longer in New York, then head into Pennsylvania and the Pocono Mountains. There wasn't much traffic. Luna thought they'd make it in under two hours.

They were only in the car about fifteen minutes, not even over the bridge yet, when Doña Esme took a turnoff and began heading north.

"I need to stop at one of our car washes," she said. "I need some cash."

It was four-thirty p.m. and already dark on the side roads. She turned again and again until Luna had no idea what direction they were headed in. The land was mostly wooded. It looked rural, but not in the pleasing way of Wickford. This area was decidedly shabbier. Most of the houses along this stretch had been turned into businesses. A hairdresser. A mechanic's garage. A day-care center. They passed a billboard advertising a bail bond agency and another for credit counseling. They passed a gas station selling no-name-brand gas.

Luna looked in the rearview mirror. Behind her, the light had slipped from the sky. The darkness hemmed in the landscape, narrowed that sense of possibility. Her fate had felt like her own when they'd started this journey. Now, she wasn't so sure.

Doña Esme's voice pricked the silence between them. "You love your papi, yes?"

"Yes," said Luna softly.

"You're lucky. My father was a terrible man." Doña Esme kept her eyes on the road. "My mother died when I was twelve, and as soon as she passed, my father started raping me. He said her duties had to fall to me."

"I'm sorry." Luna was shocked by her confession. She didn't know what to say.

"My other relatives—they knew what he was doing. They didn't care—until I got pregnant at fourteen. *Then* they cared. They took my baby daughter away from me and sent me to a Catholic convent where the nuns beat me every day. I vowed that if I could escape that life, I would do anything it took not to have to live like that again."

Luna's saliva felt like glue. She couldn't swallow. It was cold in the car, but she started to sweat. Doña Esme didn't seem to notice. She was lost in her own life story.

"When I was seventeen," she continued, "the señor came to my town in Chiapas—the same town he'd left sixteen years before. He was thirty-two. An ugly little man.

But rich. And American. A citizen by then. He wanted a young virgin. I made him believe I was. And he married me. I knew about his obsession with virgins, Luna. I knew. But he treated me okay, so I accepted things the way they were."

A strand of hair fell out of Doña Esme's ponytail. It cut like a slash of charcoal pencil across her face. She tucked it behind one ear as she caught Luna's eye in the windshield. Was Doña Esme trying to tell Luna that she'd protect her?

"Men are wild animals," she continued. "You can corral a wild animal, but you cannot tame it. There were young girls before I knew him. There were young girls after. But nobody got hurt. *Nobody*."

Luna wondered what Doña Esme meant by "hurt." If the señor was forcing himself on young girls, wouldn't that qualify as "hurt?" But maybe to a girl who had known such brutality from her own father, it didn't.

"And then . . ." Doña Esme's voice drifted. It had been soft and trancelike until now, but there was a sudden sharpness when she shot Luna a sideways glance.

"Let's not pretend you don't know about the girl in the flyer, chica," she hissed at Luna.

Luna studied her hands. She folded them together to keep them from shaking.

"It was a terrible mistake." Doña Esme's voice was soft and pleading again. "I told my relatives to keep her in Mexico. I knew what he'd do to her. She'd just be another *campesina* to him, some farm girl of no consequence. I tried to stop it. But how could I, without confessing the lie that made him marry me in the first place?"

Her words swam across Luna's brain. Luna was afraid to understand their meaning.

"I tried to get her out," said Doña Esme. "And then she got pregnant. In a way, it was a blessing. He never touches a girl once she's pregnant. I figured I would hide her until she had the baby and then send them both back home. She would get money to stay quiet. Lots of money. He would pay. He always paid. But the birth—it was terrible. Things went wrong. Doña Claudia wanted to call 911, but how could I? I would have had to tell them the truth. They would have arrested the señor—arrested *me*. Can you imagine the gossip at Our Lady of Sorrows? At La Casa? At Claudia's? Everything would have been ruined. Everything."

Why is she telling me this? Panic rose in Luna's chest like a soda she'd gulped down too fast. Doña Esme made a right onto another winding two-lane, and Luna started to realize for the first time that this was not some motherly advice designed to guide or comfort her. This was a confession. And whom do you confess to? A priest. Someone who could never tell anyone what you've uttered. Ever.

Luna was not a priest.

What if she just opened the door and jumped out? True, they were traveling at easily thirty miles per hour. But she'd probably survive. She could run into the woods perhaps. *And then what?* Dulce and Mateo were still in that house. Her father was still in that jail and likely to be sent back to Mexico on Monday. His future rested in the señor's hands. Anything she did put her entire family at risk.

Doña Esme plunged ahead. Luna wasn't sure she even realized the effect her words were having. "I wanted this to be different," she choked out. At first Luna thought Doña Esme was referring to their relationship. But then she realized she was talking about the dead girl.

"I wanted to get back all those years." Her voice was thick and nasal. She palmed her eyes. "I couldn't tell Mia that, mind you. She could never know. No one could. But I think she knew there was some sort of connection."

Doña Esme turned to Luna and blinked back tears. "Do

you understand what I'm telling you, chica? Do you understand who she was?"

"I think so." Luna could barely get the words out because of the question that kept buzzing inside of her brain: *If she could do that to her daughter, what will she do to me?*

Chapter 37

The Gonzalezes weren't home when Vega went to their door. Esme's cousin Yolanda answered. She was a chunky girl in her twenties with skin-tight jeans and fake bright orange nails with black tiger stripes across them. She said she was babysitting for the Gonzalezes and had just gotten back from the movies with the kids.

"Charlie and Esme are probably at that political dinner already," she told Vega. She was an American-born Mexican, clearly. None of the Latinos in town would dream of referring to Charlie and Esme by their first names only.

The Wickford police had already told Vega that the Gonzalezes hadn't shown up to the country club where Schulman's fund-raiser was being held. Unless they were on their way, something was wrong. And that something was the next topic of Vega's concern. He peeked into the kitchen and counted five children with Yolanda: the three Gonzalez boys and Serrano's two younger ones: Dulce and Mateo.

"Where's Luna?"

"She didn't come to the movies with us," said Yolanda. "I don't know where she went."

"She didn't leave a note?"

Yolanda shook her head.

"How about Dulce and Mateo? Maybe she told them?"

"Maybe. I'll ask." She was the least curious person Vega had ever met. Perhaps that's why the Gonzalezes liked having her around.

Yolanda went into the kitchen and asked the Serrano kids to come into the foyer. Both children took in the badge on Vega's belt and the gun in his holster. They turned quiet and shy. The law was not their friend. Vega squatted down to make himself less threatening.

"Hey there," he said softly. "I'm a friend of Señora Figueroa's." He suspected the connection might help ease their fears. "I'm trying to find your sister Luna. Not for anything bad. I just need to speak to her. Does she have a special friend? Someplace she likes to go?"

It was the boy who studied him most carefully, whose eyes seemed to be measuring every twitch in Vega's face. He didn't trust adults anymore. Not that Vega could blame him.

"What do you want to speak to her about?" he asked Vega.

"A couple of things. But mostly, I need to make sure she's okay."

Vega saw the boy weighing his words. Their father had been gone only a few days, and already it seemed he and his sister had aged out of childhood.

"Get the book," Mateo told his sister. Dulce went upstairs and emerged a few minutes later with a children's paperback. She handed it to Vega. He flipped to the inside page to see the loopy scrawl of a teenage girl:

Going with Doña Esme to see Papi. Back tonight. Love you, XXX Luna.

"Where's your papi?" Vega asked the children.

The children exchanged wary glances. Vega realized they were embarrassed to tell him.

"I already know he's in a detention facility. I just want to know where."

"Pennsylvania!" Dulce blurted out. Mateo frowned at her. He wasn't ready to trust Vega with so much information.

"Do you know where in Pennsylvania?"

They didn't.

"Do you know if Señor Gonzalez went with them?"

The children shook their heads, no. Dulce studied her feet. "I saw the señor with my sister last night," she muttered.

"You saw him—where?"

"In a room in the basement. The one with the bolt on the door. He had his hand on her hair."

Vega exhaled like he'd been punched. There was no time to lose. "Okay. Wait here," he told the children. He walked outside, pulled out his phone and dialed Adele.

"Luna's gone." He breathed it into the receiver like he'd just run a mile. His whole body felt like he was trying to outrace a forest fire that was gaining on him. He was too slow. Too slow.

"*What?*"

"Luna left her brother and sister a note that she went to visit her father. With Esme. Where is Serrano being detained?"

"In Pennsylvania. At the Pike County Correctional Facility," said Adele. "But Esme and Charlie are supposed to be at the gala tonight."

"Have you heard from either of them? Do you know where they are?"

"No." Adele paused as it sank in. "Oh my God, Jimmy. Did the DNA—?"

Vega cut her off. He couldn't divulge the specifics, not even to her. "If you hear from any of them, will you let me know right away?"

"Luna will be all right, won't she?"

Vega hesitated. "Just focus on tonight, okay, Nena? It's a big night for you. I can't be there, but—whatever you do is fine with me. I mean it."

He hung up and asked Yolanda to gather the kids in the kitchen and keep them there pending the search warrant for the house. It finally started to dawn on Yolanda that something was wrong.

"Charlie and Esme would never deal drugs!"

"No one said they did."

"Then what is this about?"

"I can't comment. I would just like to ask for your co-operation."

Vega questioned Dulce a little more about Luna and Gonzalez, but the child knew very little. Whatever had gone on in that basement Luna had managed to shield fairly well from her siblings. Still, the child's account confirmed to Vega that Gonzalez had already started making moves on the teenager.

Vega conferred by phone and email with Greco, Dolan, and Captain Waring, who was on his way back from the Albany police conference. They issued arrest warrants for both of the Gonzalezes. They put out an Amber Alert on Luna. Vega still held out hope that the girl would turn up at the jail in Pennsylvania.

Within half an hour, Greco showed up with the search warrant and a squad of cops. Vega and Greco quickly found the room in the basement with the bolt on the door that Dulce had mentioned. They took pictures of the bloody mattress. They found the drawer of photos of the dead girl. And they knew:

Luna would never make it to see her father this evening.

"Charlie Gonzalez is well-known in these parts," Greco assured Vega. "He's not likely to get far." All around them, cops were traipsing in and out of the house, testing for blood and bagging every piece of evidence that looked the least bit valuable to the case. None of it gave Vega any solace.

"It's not Charlie I'm worried about so much as Esme," said Vega. "Luna was in that room. She knows what they did. She's a witness. That's reason enough for Esme to kill her. I think Esme's plan was to whisk Luna away and make everyone believe she'd run off because she was distraught over her father. If she disappeared after that, no one would pin it on the Gonzalezes. They'd just say the girl was grief-stricken and she ended up in the wrong place at the wrong time."

"There's a lotta road between here and that jail in Pennsylvania," said Greco. "We've got a cell tower search on the Gonzalezes' phones, but nothing's coming up. I think they're turned off. They haven't used a credit card or been picked up on a security camera. Unless a trooper calls in a license plate, we're going to have to sit back and wait."

"Maybe not." Vega pulled out his cell phone and typed *Car Wash King car washes* on Google. A couple dozen came up. He zeroed in on the ones situated between here and Lords Valley, Pennsylvania. He counted four between Lake Holly and the Newburgh Beacon Bridge and another three on the other side of the Hudson River before they hit the New York-Pennsylvania border.

"Those car washes wouldn't even be open after five on a Saturday evening in October," said Greco.

"I know," said Vega. "That's what makes them a perfect spot for Esme or Charlie to go to. They'd have access to cash from the register and could disable the video cameras. They'd have the equipment to hose down any surface covered in blood or other trace elements. In the locations where they do detailing, they'd even have access to customers' cars so they wouldn't have to travel in their own."

"We can ask the state troopers to swing by each and

check them out," said Greco. "But you're still talking seven locations spread over a hundred-mile vicinity. It's gonna take most of the night to hunt this down."

Vega watched two techs maneuver the bloody mattress—now bagged—out of the house.

"I'm not sure we have most of the night."

Chapter 38

Doña Esme drove until they came to a small shopping center with a McDonalds, a Dunkin' Donuts, a Payless shoe store, and a JC Penny. In the far corner of the mall, Luna saw a Car Wash King. It looked just like the one the Gonzalezes owned in Lake Holly—like a drive-through bank. No one was there. It was closed for the evening.

Doña Esme pulled her big black Escalade behind the car wash. Then she reached across Luna and opened the glove compartment. She removed a knit hat, a pair of gloves, a flashlight, and a ring of keys. She slipped into the hat and gloves. It was getting colder. Luna wished she had a hat and gloves herself.

"Stay in the car," Esme ordered. She unlocked the car wash and walked in. She didn't turn on any lights. She only flicked on her flashlight. Luna watched the pale beam zigzag across the walls. Her thoughts flew in every direction. It would be easy to get out of the car and run. She'd have to run to the other side of the shopping center to find people. But even so, they were in a well-lit public place. She could do it. But what would she say to them? She was a girl—let's face it—an undocumented girl. The police would never take her rambling accusations over Doña

Esme's. And still, the biggest question remained: What would happen to Dulce and Mateo and Papi?

So she sat cursing her indecision while she watched Doña Esme walk out of the office with a small zippered case in her hands and a set of car keys. She frowned like she was concentrating hard on something as she unlocked another garage behind the car wash. Then she walked back to the Escalade and barked at Luna to get out of the car and help her roll the garage door up. The garage door was probably operated by a remote that Doña Esme didn't have. It was hard work to get the thing up manually, but they did it. It growled as it rolled into place.

There were seven cars in the garage: three SUVs and four sedans. Doña Esme squinted at the set of keys she took from the car wash and clicked them at a dark blue Honda CRV with permit parking stickers for a town Luna didn't recognize and a Dave Matthews Band sticker on the rear window. She was pretty sure this car was here to be cleaned and didn't belong to Doña Esme. The door locks popped open.

Doña Esme threw the zippered bag in the glove compartment of the CRV and slammed it shut. "Get in," she ordered.

Luna hesitated. Her insides felt like she'd swallowed glass.

"Mami," Doña Esme said in a soothing tone. "The señor is a bad man. We both know that. He tried to hurt you. He's trying to hurt me too. He'll be looking for my Escalade. If he finds us in it, we're both in trouble. I want to take you to see your father, but I need to do it in a different car so he can't find us. Do you understand?"

Luna nodded slowly. Did she trust her? *Oh God, oh God.* She closed her eyes and offered a silent prayer. All her years in church hadn't prepared her for this moment. She was so lost and confused. But she wanted more than anything to go to Lords Valley and see her father, so she climbed in.

Doña Esme pulled the Honda out of the garage and parked her Escalade in its place. Then she locked everything up again, and they drove off.

"That wasn't so hard, was it?" She smiled her fake white smile. Luna took no comfort from it.

They headed west again. Luna could tell this because the sky was a little less dark in this direction. Her confidence returned a little. Up until now, it had felt like they were traveling in circles.

The weather got colder. Doña Esme kept her hat and gloves on all the time in the new car. Luna sat on her hands to try to keep them warm.

"Go into the glove compartment," Doña Esme instructed her. "There's a small bag in there. I want you to zip it open and see what's inside."

Luna hoped it was food. Her stomach was growling. The bag was heavy, the contents wrapped in thick cloth. She pushed the cloth aside and touched something cold and smooth and mechanical feeling. A small gasp escaped her lips. Doña Esme laughed.

"It's not loaded or anything, chica. I have the cartridge separately. Go ahead. Take it out."

"No." It made Luna nervous. She put it back in the glove compartment without even zippering up the bag.

"We need to protect ourselves, mami."

The gun felt like a wild animal sitting in a cage just inches from her body. Luna shook all over. Doña Esme didn't seem to notice. They were traveling on yet another wooded two-lane. Luna kept waiting for her to get onto a main highway and cross the bridge. They were eating up precious time. If they didn't make headway soon, the jail's visiting hours would be over before they arrived.

They came upon another shopping center, this one much smaller. Doña Esme turned in.

"Where are we going now?" Luna couldn't hide her frustration. It seemed to overshadow even her fear.

"It won't take long."

This shopping center was just a concrete block of stores, all one-story, all joined together. An insurance broker's office. A breakfast diner. A computer repair shop and a second-hand clothing store. There were no cars in the lot. All the businesses were closed for the evening—maybe for the whole weekend. The entire center was surrounded by woods. The lighting was half the wattage of the other shopping center.

In the far corner was a car wash with a FOR SALE sign over the windows. The drive-through area was shuttered with big roll-down metal gates. The little front office was locked up tight. There were planters by the office, but they were overgrown with weeds. The rainbow sign with the crown on top that Luna saw at the Lake Holly Car Wash King was missing here.

"Charlie's worst investment," Doña Esme muttered. "That was all I had to tell him and he knew where to come."

Where to come?

Doña Esme parked the CRV behind the car wash. Then she reached across Luna to the glove compartment and pulled out the zippered bag.

"Come on, get out," she said.

"I want to go see my father."

Doña Esme slapped Luna hard across the face. Her skin felt like it was on fire. Her jaw tingled.

"Well, I wanted a lot of things, chica. And they didn't happen. Life is tough. Maybe if your mami and papi hadn't protected you so much, you'd know that. Now get out."

"Where are we going?"

"Shut up and you won't get hurt."

The full measure of Luna's predicament hit her all at once. She started to run, but Doña Esme grabbed her by her hair and pushed her down onto the pavement. Something hard smacked her skull. The world went dark and silent.

Luna's last terrible thought was that her family would think she'd abandoned them.

Chapter 39

Colored floodlights lit up the long driveway beyond the wrought-iron gates of the Wickford Country Club. Adele had never driven inside before. She'd seen some of the grounds from a distance—the lush green of the 120-acre golf course, the bright blue of the swimming pools, the striped mustard-colored awnings over the windows of the sprawling white turn-of-the-century clubhouse. But this was the first time she'd pulled around the front oval, handed the keys of her Prius to a parking attendant, and stepped inside.

She hadn't been this nervous and unsure of herself since her first year at Harvard, when she felt like she was walking around with a sign on her forehead that read: *I don't belong here. Somebody made a mistake.* She grew into Harvard. She grew into being a lawyer and then starting La Casa. Could she grow into being the Hispanic affairs adviser to a U.S. senator?

More importantly, did she want to?

She stepped inside the front entrance, a massive hallway with two flowing staircases and a large chandelier in the middle. A man in a tuxedo directed her to a room on the right with French doors, more chandeliers, and a parquet floor the color of maple syrup. Waiters walked through the crowd with trays of hors d'oeuvres and fluted glasses of champagne. All the men wore tuxedos. All the women wore full-length evening gowns, most of them black and glittery. Adele's knee-length, teal-green fitted satin dress made her feel like a bridesmaid who'd stumbled into the wrong event. She had plenty of black dresses, some of them long enough to qualify as full-length. Was she, on some level, sabotaging herself?

She had dressed in a fog, her thoughts buzzing around in her head like a fly that never seemed to land. Jimmy's call had unsettled her. Where was Luna? Why hadn't she called if she was in trouble? Adele had the awful sense that being here tonight amounted to fiddling while Rome burned.

She felt a hand on her shoulder and turned. Steve Schulman held out a glass of champagne to her. He wasn't the sort of man who wore a tux well. The shirt pinched his neck and made it sag like a turkey's. His skin looked sallow in black and white. The padding on the jacket shoulders for some reason made him look even more hunched than usual.

"What did you think of the speech I'm going to give?"

Adele took the glass from him. "Good. I think it's good." Could she even speak in full sentences tonight?

"Well?" He opened his arms. There was no mistaking the context of the question. This was her moment.

"Did you speak to Judge Hallard? About Manuel?"

Schulman's face darkened. "This is not the time or place, Adele."

"Is that a no?"

"I couldn't reach him."

"Bullshit, Steve! He's been by his phone all weekend. You never even tried to call!"

Several conversations around them faltered. A waiter set to approach them with rolls of sushi ducked away. Schulman forced a chuckle like Adele had just told a good joke. He kept a broad smile on his face, but he spoke through clenched teeth.

"If you're going to screw me over, at least have the decency to do it behind closed doors."

"Got a door you care to close?"

He kept the fake smile on his face and glad-handed his way through the crowd with Adele in tow. They found a small mahogany-paneled library on the second floor stacked with gold-bound classics no one ever read. The Queen Anne wing chairs, brass lamps, and dark furniture looked as if they'd been there since the house was built. Schulman escorted her into the room and closed the door. Neither of them sat.

"You are so goddamned myopic, Adele!" Schulman smacked the back of one of the Queen Anne chairs for emphasis. Adele had never seen him so mad. "Do you realize that in Washington, you could help a hundred Manuel Serranos?"

"I don't *know* a hundred Manuel Serranos. I know one. His children need him, Steve. Especially his oldest, Luna. If ever there was a girl who needed her father's protection right now, it's her."

Schulman sighed. "I've heard the rumors flying around this evening about the Gonzalezes. I want you to know that I knew nothing about Charlie's private life."

"Where are they?"

"The Gonzalezes?" He shrugged. "I don't know. Charlie was with me at the campaign headquarters when he got a call and left. I haven't seen either of them since."

"You know what he's been accused of?"

Schulman held her gaze. "Yes. He's off my campaign, needless to say. But we'll regroup and survive."

Adele pulled her cell phone from her bag and held it out to Schulman. "It's seven p.m., Steve. Judge Hallard will accept a call until nine tonight. Give these children back their father. *Please.* As a favor to me."

"Why is this so important?"

"I encouraged Manuel to put his children with the Gonzalezes. And now it's my responsibility to make things right."

Schulman sighed. "I'm sorry, Adele. Really, I am. But I can't."

"Why?"

Schulman pulled out one of the gold-bound books and absent-mindedly thumbed the pages. The title on the spine was *Huckleberry Finn*. Injustice, Adele had to remind herself, was not a new thing.

"As I understand it, no one knows where his teenage daughter is at the moment," said Schulman.

"I think that's true."

"So—we have my chief campaign adviser missing and possibly guilty of sexual crimes against a number of teenage girls. And we have a teenage girl in his care missing. Do you see what I'm driving at, Adele?"

"No."

"I bring Manuel Serrano back, *I* get implicated in this whole mess."

"But you're helping the family!"

"It looks like I'm helping myself out of guilt."

"No one would claim that."

"John Sawyer's people would. That's how politics works, dear lady." Schulman slammed the book shut and returned it to the shelf. "And if you don't get that, then maybe you don't belong in D.C."

"Maybe I don't." She put her hand on the doorknob.

"Think long and hard about what you're doing, Adele. This is not a decision you should make in the heat of anger."

"The problem isn't that I'm angry, Steve. The problem is that I wasn't angry sooner."

She walked out of the library and slammed the door. She was shaking as she stumbled down the hallway and back out into the cool dark of the evening. She was conscious of people watching her from the banquet room, conscious of Schulman's voice greeting supporters as if nothing had just transpired.

She'd just blown her career. But that wasn't what brought her to tears as she drove away from the Wickford Country Club.

What really made her cry was the thought that she'd just blown the Serrano children's chances of ever seeing their father again.

Chapter 40

Luna woke up shivering on a concrete floor. Her head throbbed. It was so dark, she couldn't see anything. The first sensation that returned to her was smell. She was in a place that was cold and damp and musty. Her mouth was bound with duct tape. Her wrists were bound behind her back. Yet another length of tape was wrapped around her legs and tethered to what felt like a pipe on the wall.

Gradually her eyes adjusted. Luna was inside the car wash. She made out a puddle by the closed garage door. The edges glistened like oil, but the center reflected back the filmy light from a street lamp beyond the door. She tried to maneuver her hands behind her to claw at the tape but without a knife or scissors, she couldn't unravel even a tiny bit.

Far off, she could hear the occasional *whoosh* of a car on a roadway and the white noise of a plane traveling through the sky. Her head felt like it was being held together by rubber bands. Her tongue tasted metallic. She tried to scrape her mouth against the concrete floor to rip off the duct tape, but it wouldn't budge.

She managed to get up on her knees, but her ankles were bound so tightly she couldn't rise to her feet. And besides, she was dizzy. So she sank back onto the concrete and curled herself into a ball to try to stay warm and figure a way out of her situation. To the right of her were the grooved metal tracks of the car wash. Behind her, her hand rubbed against strips of spongy cloth on some kind of spinning brush.

At first Luna thought she'd been abandoned here, but then she heard Spanish somewhere in the parking lot. Two voices—a man's and a woman's. The woman was Esme—Luna could never think of her as "Doña Esme" again. Her voice sounded angry and accusing. The man murmured, his voice as thin as cheap socks. He was no match for Esme's rage.

"She was my daughter, Carlos! My only daughter!"

There were two quick pops. Like firecrackers exploding. The sound felt so huge and final, it seemed to suck every other sound from the landscape. Luna no longer heard the distant *whoosh* of cars or the rumble of the plane. She heard only the pounding of her heart. Esme had shot the señor. Luna was sure she was coming next for her.

Yolanda took the Gonzalez boys to relatives for the night. Manuel Serrano's cousin Alirio drove up from Queens to take Mateo and Dulce and their black garbage bags of belongings to his family's apartment. Vega's heart broke to look at the two Serrano kids. They'd lost their father and now Luna in the space of forty-eight hours. No one would ever be able to put the "child" back in their childhoods.

The evidence had been bagged and carted out of the house. A uniformed Lake Holly officer would remain stationed at the residence to protect the site and alert the police if the Gonzalezes returned. There was nothing either Vega or Greco could do but wait and hope that a state trooper somewhere would spot Gonzalez's silver Mercedes sedan or Esme's black Escalade.

Greco, still in his flannel shirt and fishing boots, got a lift to the ME's office to fetch his Buick and drive home. Vega was sitting in his unmarked, typing some final paperwork into his computer when he noticed a pale green Prius approaching the Gonzalez house. *Adele*. He thought she'd be at the Wickford Country Club all evening discussing her future with Schulman and his coterie of admirers.

Vega got out of his car and put a hand up to stop her. She pulled next to him and powered down her passenger-side window.

"What are you doing here?" He leaned in. "You're supposed to be—"

He stopped when he saw her smeared mascara and bloodshot eyes.

"Whoa. What happened?"

"Did you find Luna?" She sounded as desperate as he felt.

"Not yet. I thought you'd be at the gala all evening, making plans with Schulman."

"I thought so too." She shook her head, but the words wouldn't come.

"Park your car and come sit with me," said Vega. He didn't want to be out of radio contact in case something broke.

Vega's police radio was on when Adele slid into his car. They were both quiet for a moment, listening to the chatter over the department radio. She caught him eyeing her teal-green dress beneath her coat.

"You look really pretty, Nena," he said softly. "So what happened?"

Adele told him about her conversation with Schulman, the way he dismissed Serrano as collateral damage in the campaign. "Judge Hallard said if Steve didn't call by nine tonight, he wouldn't intercede."

"Can't *you* call?"

"Hallard already told me it had to come from Steve. It's going on eight, Jimmy. I don't have a prayer of helping Manuel now." Adele stared across the Gonzalezes' lawn to the house—dark except for security lights. There was something already spent about it, like a tent being taken down after a party. Whatever had once been there—good or bad—would soon be reduced to memory. "I came to check on Dulce and Mateo. I felt I owed them that."

"They're gone already. Their father's cousin drove them to Queens."

"You have no idea where Luna is?"

"We've got an Amber Alert on her. We've got troopers checking every road and rest stop between here and Lords Valley. I've even requested a patrol at all of the Gonzalezes' car washes. So far, nothing's turned up."

"Do you know which franchises the cops checked?"

Vega shrugged. "All the ones listed. Why?"

"Back in the summer, Steve had a campaign stop at a breakfast place off I-84 about twenty-five minutes' north of here. It was in a little shopping center with a car wash Charlie was trying to sell. I don't think he sold it. It's not in operation anymore, so it probably wouldn't show up on a list of his businesses."

Vega opened his car's laptop search engine. "Do you remember the name of the breakfast place? I could drive up and check that car wash out myself."

"I want to come with you."

"Absolutely not."

"Jimmy, listen to me. The only way I can get Schulman to make that call to stop Serrano's deportation is if I can find Luna."

"Why would that change anything?"

"The last thing Steve Schulman needs is for a fifteen-year-old girl to tell voters what she's endured at the hands of his chief campaign adviser. He'd do anything to keep that from happening."

Vega stared at his laptop. "I need a name of the breakfast place, Nena. Without a name, I've got nothing."

Adele massaged her forehead. "I'm drawing a blank."

"Were there any other businesses there you can remember?"

"Yeah. A clothing store. For kids. A secondhand place, I believe. I remember because I saw a really nice robe in the window that I thought Sophia would have liked, but the store was closed. And anyway, I couldn't exactly go in when we were supposed to be chatting up voters."

Vega typed *secondhand children's clothing* into his computer. He came up with only two stores in the county. He typed the first address into Google Maps Street View to show Adele. It was in a storefront attached to a Victorian house.

"No. That's not it."

Vega typed the second address into Google Maps Street View. The image showed a strip of single-story poured-concrete stores all joined together in front of a small parking lot. In the middle was a plate-glass window with the words ONCE AGAIN KIDS spelled out overhead.

"That's it," said Adele. In the same bank of stores was a plate-glass window with the words SUNRISE CAFÉ above it. "And that's the diner. I'm sure of it."

Vega typed the address of Once Again Kids into his GPS. "They're both in the Crossroads Shopping Center about ten minutes' north of I-84. But the Google view isn't showing a car wash."

"Because it's off to the side and away from the road," said Adele. "Plus, it looks like the image was shot in the summer when all the trees were leafed out, so it's harder to see. But that car wash is definitely there. I know it is."

Chapter 41

A door behind Luna opened, cutting a shaft of bluish light onto the cold, damp garage floor. Luna craned her neck to see a shadow filling the doorway. She made out the outline of a ponytail, the glow of those unnaturally white teeth. Luna was still tethered to the pipe, so she couldn't run. She couldn't even stand. Instead, she curled herself more tightly and tucked her head between her knees. Esme had killed the señor. Luna had no expectations that she would be spared. She just didn't want to see the bullet when it came.

Esme's shoes clicked across the concrete floor. She tripped on the grooves of the tracking but caught herself in time. She stood before Luna and huffed out a laugh.

"I'm not going to shoot you, mami. You are such a foolish girl."

Slowly Luna lifted her head. Esme was standing in front of her, the gun in her gloved hand, her breath forming white clouds in the space between them. "The señor raped my baby. He shamed me. Over and over again. He deserved to die. The only possible way to preserve my honor was to become a widow, do you understand?"

She squatted down next to Luna, grabbed hold of the duct tape on her mouth, and ripped it off. Luna cried out in pain.

"He's lying in his car," said Esme.

The skin around Luna's lips was throbbing. She tried to suck back the pain and focus on Esme's words.

"At some point the police will find him. I'll leave the gun with his body, or you can take it with you."

"I—don't want to take it," Luna stammered out.

Esme shrugged. "Suit yourself. The police will be looking for you. Probably it's better to travel without it."

"I don't understand."

"The señor has been shot dead with his own gun. Your prints are on it."

"But you shot him."

"And who will believe you, chica? My car was never here. There's no evidence we were together this afternoon. I'm taking the CRV back to the other car wash now. Don't worry. The police will understand. You're fifteen. A minor. The crime was self-defense. The señor brought you here to rape you, and you grabbed his gun and shot him. Everyone will understand."

"But I didn't—"

"Look, I'm running out of time. Either I cut you loose and you run or I leave you like this and you starve or die of exposure. What's it going to be?"

"Cut me loose."

"Let me get a scissors from the office."

Esme walked back through the door. Luna heard the harsh metal clang of her life as she knew it ending. This was not the future her father had planned for her. She couldn't believe how fast it had all unraveled.

She waited for the scissors, but Esme never returned. She called out and suddenly, in the puddle by the garage door, Luna saw alternating flashes of red and blue like the color of snow cones.

She wondered if her life was about to unravel even more.

*   *   *

Vega's car beams picked up a dark blue CRV in the parking lot by the Sunrise Café. He didn't pull into the lot. Instead, he parked the car on the gravel shoulder just south of the shopping center.

"Aren't we going in there?" asked Adele.

"I am. You're not. You'll stay locked in my car out here on the shoulder. I'm calling for backup and heading in on foot."

Vega radioed his location to dispatch. He reported the suspicious CRV in the lot. Then he flicked on his light bar. The bare branches on either side of the road came alive with splotches of red and blue. "This way, the cops who come will know you're not one of the bad guys."

"Do cops really say bad guys?"

"Nah." He winked at her. "We usually say lawfully disadvantaged."

"Smartass."

Vega pulled on his jacket and a pair of gloves and did a quick inventory of his gear. He had his gun in his duty holster along with a flashlight and a radio. From his glove compartment, he pulled out a set of handcuffs. In one back pocket he felt for his Swiss Army knife. In the other were his wallet and cell phone.

"If I find Luna, I'll call you and bring her to you, okay? Promise me you'll stay back where it's safe."

"But we haven't got much time—"

"Promise me, Nena."

"Okay," Adele sighed, "I promise."

He left her in the car and hiked back to the shopping center. He kept to the shadows around the perimeter while he surveyed the parking lot. The CRV appeared to be empty. There was another car parked in the lot as well. Near the car wash. Vega hadn't noticed it before, but he could see the front of it now: that silver hood ornament that identified it as a Mercedes. He couldn't see the license plate, but he was betting the car belonged to Charlie Gonzalez. He didn't see Esme's black Cadillac Escalade. Perhaps only Gonzalez was here.

Vega unholstered his Glock nine millimeter and kept it down by his side. He stepped gingerly into the open to get a better look at the CRV. It was locked and definitely unoccupied. He moved to the Mercedes. It was a silver-colored sedan just like Gonzalez's. Vega saw someone sprawled across the front seat. He took out his flashlight and shined it inside. Even in the half-light, he could see the big nose and balding head of Charlie Gonzalez. The beam picked up a dark, slick, dinner-plate-size stain on his shirt and another at his crotch. Vega wondered whether the shot to his heart or to his crotch came first. He could think of a lot of women who would probably have aimed low and worked their way up.

He opened the driver's-side door. Then he removed one of his gloves and felt Gonzalez's neck for a pulse. There was none. He put his glove back on, closed the door quietly, and backed away from the sedan. He scanned the shopping center and the woods surrounding it.

Somebody shot and killed Charlie Gonzalez. In all likelihood, they drove here in that CRV. Where were they now?

A muffled female voice called out behind him. Vega turned. It was coming from inside the drive-through car wash.

"Luna? Is that you?" Vega leaned up against the door of the car wash. It was constructed of heavy-duty steel and locked in the rolled-down position.

"Help me, please," the girl's voice cried out. "I'm trapped. Esme Gonzalez tied me up and shot the señor."

"Where is she?" asked Vega. He cupped his eyes and squinted past the harsh glare of the center's security lights. Nothing moved.

"I don't know," said Luna.

"Hang on. I'll get you out."

The roll-down door would be impossible to break into without a locksmith or a hydraulic saw. But the office was unlocked. Vega went in and found a door that joined the office to the garage. He pushed it open and scanned the space with his flashlight. It took his eyes a moment to adjust to the darkness, but then he saw her. She was curled up in a ball on the cement floor, her hands and feet bound in duct tape, her ankles joined by a long strand of tape to a pipe on the wall. Her face and arms were filthy and scraped. She blinked in the harsh glare of the beam. She was shivering.

Vega took off his jacket and wrapped it around her.

"I'm a police officer, Luna. A friend of Adele Figueroa's. She's in my car. You're safe—okay, Mija?" Vega took out his radio and called in a request for an ambulance. He was relaying the information when a loud slam echoed through the cavernous interior. The world went from shadowy to pitch black, save for the beam of Vega's flashlight.

"The door!" cried Luna.

"It's okay," said Vega. "I'm right here." Though he had no idea where "here" was anymore. He couldn't see his hand in front of his face. He couldn't tell where Luna was except by the sound of her panicked, rapid-fire breathing behind him. Vega retraced his steps, feeling his way along the metal tracking and across a set of pipes mounted on the wall. His flashlight beam picked up the door. It sat between two large spinning brushes. He tried the handle. It wouldn't budge.

Then Vega heard a gurgle and hiss that made his heart stop in his chest, made him feel five years old again, sitting next to his father all those years ago.

Someone had started up the car wash.

Chapter 42

Gears groaned as they shifted into position. Water percolated through the pipes. Vega heard the clanking of heavy machinery and the whir of brushes, some of which he couldn't see, not even with his flashlight. He ducked a boom that swung across his field of vision and stepped back from something spinning behind him. Strips of cloth thrashed his arms and legs, snagging on his trousers and dragging him closer to their whirling tentacles. He stumbled as he fought to free himself. A hiss of water circulated above him. Vega felt the ice-cold sting as it rained down.

"Help me!" Luna cried.

"I'm coming!"

Vega took a step forward, but a blast of water shot out from a pipe on the wall, drenching him and knocking the flashlight from his hand. It skittered off into the darkness. He took a step forward, tripped on the metal track, and landed hard on the concrete floor. He tried to get back on his feet, but a slick coating of soapsuds now covered the floor. It stung his eyes. He couldn't see. His gun, radio, and phone were waterlogged and useless. His flashlight gave off a faint blur in the distance. Huge brushes and buffers spun around him. Already Vega had seen how easy it would be for one of these spinning monsters to attach itself to his arm or his leg and reel him in like a fish. When there was no more reel, it would cinch him tight enough to sever a limb or fling him headfirst against a cement wall.

Miedoso, miedoso. His father's taunt of "coward" echoed in his brain. The old man was right. He was terrified of this dark, wet, slippery tomb with its giant machines that could kill him with one wrong move. But he was more scared of something else at the moment. He couldn't hear Luna.

"Luna!" he screamed through the churning suds. He heard something like a choked cry. He felt his way forward through the icy pounding water, trying to navigate away from the machines by touch and sound. His foot stumbled over a sneaker. She was gasping.

He groped around in the dark. His fingers were so cold he could barely move them. He felt the rubber soles of her sneakers and traced his hands along the duct-tape rope that was attached to her ankles like an umbilical cord. The rope stopped in a cinch around her neck. One of the spinning brushes was grabbing it, pulling it tighter with each rotation.

There had to be an emergency shutoff button inside the car wash, but it wasn't illuminated, and it was too dark to see it. By the time Vega found such a button, Luna could be dead. He had to get that duct tape off her neck right away, or she'd choke to death.

My Swiss Army knife. Vega dug into his back pocket. Cutting through the tape was the only way he could save Luna. But his fingers were numb and the knife sharp. He couldn't see, blinded as he was by the water, suds, and darkness. If he slipped, he could slit her throat. If he waited, the spinning brush would kill her anyway.

He opened his knife and tried to snake a finger between the soft cartilage of her neck and the rolled thickness of the duct tape. He was choking her, but he didn't have a choice. Better he cut his own finger than slice her jugular.

"Hold on, Luna!" he begged over the roar of the machines and the rumble of the spinning brushes. Every second that ticked by cinched the cord tighter. He pulled it as far away from her neck as he could and shoved the knife blade under. Then he yanked the knife toward him. He felt the duct tape bend and kink, but he couldn't get it to tear. He tried again, but the blade was no match against the sticky fibrous layers. He had stretched the tape enough to buy her time, but he hadn't freed her. With each rotation of the brushes, it would cinch a little tighter no matter what he did.

I have to find the emergency shut-off button. I have to stop the machines. It's the only way to save her life.

Vega spotted his flashlight glowing beneath the gears of one of the undercarriage washers. He dove beneath the spray to retrieve it, shivering from the blasts of water that assaulted him. He closed his eyes against the stinging soap and strained until his numb fingers were able to wrap themselves around the flashlight. He pulled it toward him and cradled it to his chest so it didn't skitter out of his hands again. Then he ran the beam of light along the walls. There had to be a way to cut the power. There just had to be.

Luna wasn't crying. She wasn't gasping. Was he already too late? Vega scanned the walls. And then he saw it—a glowing red button. It was on the other side of a boom that moved up and down, probably to spray water over the hood of a car. If he tried to cross under it at the wrong time, the whole boom would come down like a guillotine and crack his skull or break his back. It was like a deadly game of double Dutch. The girls in his old Bronx neighborhood could jump those ropes with their eyes closed. Vega had to hope that his timing as a musician gave him at least some of their precision and dexterity. Luna's life depended on it.

One . . . two . . .

. . . *Miedoso* . . .

Three. He slid under, skidding through the soap, his

eyes burning as he held on tightly to his flashlight. His feet hit the cement wall. His body barely missed the boom. He stood, made a fist, and pounded the button.

Instantly, everything stopped. The spinning brushes. The gears. The jet streams spurting from pipes. The only sound Vega heard was the feathery pitter-patter from the cloth strips overhead.

There were no other sounds.

"Luna!" he screamed, his voice rubbed raw from the chemicals and the cold.

She didn't answer. Vega scanned the darkness with his flashlight until the beam picked her up. She was lying on the floor of the car wash still covered in his jacket, not moving. Her skin looked pale. Was he already too late? He still couldn't cut the tape, but without the spinning brush yanking on the cord, he was able to unwind it from the rotors and ease it off her neck. He saw the red welt where it had been. Her pulse was weak. She wasn't breathing. He tilted her head and began CPR.

"Hang on, Luna. Your family needs you," he grunted to her between chest compressions. "Dulce and Mateo are waiting. You can't let them down. You can't let your father down."

He heard sirens in the distance. The ambulance was on its way. It felt like too little, too late.

Chapter 43

A state police trooper unlatched the bolt across the door that separated the car wash from the office.

"What the—?"

Vega pushed past him with Luna in his arms, both of them trailing puddles of water and white foam. She was breathing on her own at least now—a good sign. Still, her pulse was erratic and she was shaking uncontrollably. Vega laid Luna across a bench in the office and scanned the parking lot. He expected Esme to have taken the CRV and left. But the CRV was still parked in the exact same spot.

"Sir?" said the trooper. "I'm going to need to ask you—"

Vega cut him off. There was no time to spare. He fished a soggy wallet out of his wet pants and opened it to his badge and ID. "I'm a detective with the county police. I'm the cop who called in the shooting." Vega didn't want the trooper to mistake him for the suspect. "The assailant is a thirty-one-year-old Hispanic female by the name of Esmeralda Gonzalez. She's armed. Have you apprehended her yet?"

"I just pulled in and saw your car parked down the road a little ways and the victim in that Mercedes. I haven't seen anyone else."

Vega flashed on his last words to Adele: *Promise me you'll stay back where it's safe.*

Coño! For once, she'd listened.

He fished his cell phone out of his pocket. He couldn't get it to turn on. There were watermarks beneath the screen. He cursed.

"You need a phone?" asked the trooper, handing Vega his.

"Thanks. Do you have an emergency blanket in your car for the girl?"

"Affirmative. I'll get it now." Vega dialed Adele. Her phone rang, then went to voice mail.

Pick up. Pick up . . .

The trooper hustled back through the doors with a thermal blanket that looked like a roll's worth of aluminum foil. Vega spoke quickly. There was no time to spare.

"I need you to wrap the girl and stay with her until the ambulance arrives," said Vega. He bent down so Luna could see him. "I'll be right back, Mija. My vehicle's parked just down the road. I need to check on something." No way did he want to advertise that he'd brought a civilian to a crime scene. No way did he want Adele out there by herself.

His black leather lace-ups squished as he ran across the asphalt parking lot. Adrenaline was keeping him warm, pumping him up with anxiety and dread. She should have been at that gala for Schulman tonight. She should have been accepting a political post in Washington, D.C.—not out here on this dark, forsaken two-lane with a small-time cop who couldn't rescue a kid without nearly getting her killed. A lot of good he could do anybody now anyway. His phone was toast. It was possible his radio and gun were too. About the only thing that still worked was his cheap Timex watch. It showed eight thirty on the dial. The whole reason Adele had come out here was to try to free Manuel Serrano, and already, it seemed too late.

He turned onto the road and was momentarily reassured to see Adele standing behind the open front-passenger door of his car. Beneath her black coat, her green dress shimmered in the staccato pulse of red and blue police lights. But something in her face stopped Vega. Even in the hazy glow of police lights, he could see fear in the set of her jaw, the startled deer expression in her eyes. And then he realized why: Esme was standing behind Adele. He didn't need to see the gun to know it was there and that she'd willingly use it. She'd already killed the father of her three sons. She'd have no compunction about shooting Adele.

"Whoa, Esme." Vega skidded to a stop. "You don't want to do that." He spoke to her in Spanish, hoping the familiar sound might soothe her. He held his hands in the air. His body heat was wearing off, and his clothes had gone cold and clammy on his skin. Every movement felt like he was being jabbed with an icicle.

"Then give me the keys to the car and back off," said Esme in Spanish. "I'll drop Adele off when I'm away from here."

No way could he let her leave with Adele.

"Calm down, okay? I'll give you the keys," Vega lied. "Just put down the gun. Nobody needs to get hurt. You've got no argument with Adele."

"Give me the keys!"

"They're in my pocket, all right?" he said calmly. He took a step closer.

"Stay where you are."

"I'm just trying to get them out. My fingers are cold. My clothes are wet." He was shivering badly. He didn't want the tremors in his body to show up in his voice. She'd mistake it for fear. That was one thing he couldn't show, no matter how much he felt it. He pretended to dig in his pocket.

"Hurry up," she demanded.

"My clothes are stuck to my skin. This isn't easy."

He was playing for time. For what purpose? Even if ten police cars showed up right now, it wouldn't change the fact that Adele was Esme's hostage. He couldn't even get the jump on her with his gun. Hers probably worked. His probably didn't.

He dug into his pocket while he sized up the situation. He had Esme and Adele standing behind the passenger door of his county unmarked. He was standing a few feet in front.

"I'm getting the keys. Hold on." He started to tug a set of car keys from his pocket. The wrong keys—the ones to his Ford truck. His next step depended on Adele—on her reading him and him reading her. Could they still do that? After all that had happened? Vega had to chance it.

He shot Adele a look as he pulled the keys from his pocket and pretended to fumble them. They landed in the gravel and dirt by his feet. Esme's eyes followed. *Now,* Vega's eyes screamed to Adele. She seemed to get his drift. Instantly, she took a small step sideways from the open car door. It was the break Vega needed. He leapt forward and pushed the passenger door into Esme, catching her body in the middle like a vise. He felt the spongy give of pinched flesh and muscle, the thud as her head hit the top of the door frame. Esme screamed and dropped the gun. Vega kicked it to the side.

"Shoot me!" Esme yelled at Vega as he maneuvered to the other side of the car door and grabbed her by the shoulder. He pushed her to the ground, thankful that wet handcuffs worked as well as dry ones. He snapped a cuff on one wrist. He had to sit on her to snap the other, she was fighting so hard.

Uniformed troopers and local cops began running along the side of the road to assist. Vega just hoped they didn't trample his truck keys. He didn't want to spend half the night searching through the bushes for them. He pulled Esme to her feet.

"I told you to kill me!" she screamed again in Spanish. She tried to head-butt him in a vain attempt to force his hand.

Vega pushed her hard against the car, then patted her down. "That would be your choice, wouldn't it?" he said between breaths. "You wouldn't have to live with what you've done. The humiliation. The guilt. But you're going to."

"How about what *he* did? That girl was my daughter! That baby was my granddaughter!"

Vega stood very still as the full measure of the crime washed over him.

Esme hung her head and began to cry. "Do you see what he took from me?" she sobbed. "Do you understand *now?* Men make the rules. And women suffer. It has always been. It will always be."

A uniformed state trooper walked up to Vega and pushed a heat-reflective blanket onto his shoulders. He must have been shivering more than he realized. He couldn't have processed Esme's booking if he tried. They would sort jurisdiction out later.

Adele was shivering almost as much as Vega. He wanted to wrap her in his arms and comfort her. But he was too wet and grimy for that, and he didn't want any of the other cops to start asking questions about what she was doing here. They both got into the car and turned on the heater.

"Are you all right?" he asked her.

"I don't know what 'all right' is anymore." She took a deep breath. "Is Luna . . . okay?"

"I think she will be—in time."

"Esme shot her?"

"No, thank goodness." Before he could say more, they heard the siren and saw an ambulance turning into the shopping center. Vega glanced at his battered watch. Eight thirty-five p.m. "I guess you lost your chance to spring

Luna's dad. Maybe Esme has a point about men making all the rules. The powerful ones, anyway."

Adele sat up very straight all of a sudden. She began rummaging through her handbag. "Not this time." She pulled out her phone.

"What are you going to do?"

"Something I should have done a long time ago." She hit a speed-dial number on her phone.

"Y'ello," said a male voice as he picked up.

"Steve? Can you hear me?" Adele hit her speakerphone button so Vega could hear. There was congratulatory cheering in the background.

"I'm not talking about this Serrano situation anymore tonight. You hear me, Adele? I'm through."

"Oh no, you're not. You're dialing Judge Hallard right now and promising him any goddamn thing you need to to bring Manuel Serrano back to his kids. And I'm calling him afterward to verify it's been done."

"We already went through this—"

"Well, maybe you'd better go through it again. I'm at the police scene now. You don't even want to *know* about the shit that's gonna hit the fan tomorrow on this. If you don't get Serrano signed, sealed, and delivered back to New York by Monday and work to get him and Luna legal residency, when this storm hits I will see to it that every Hispanic organization in the northeast knows about your cozy little relationship with a longtime rapist and his murderous wife. By the time I'm through, you won't be able to run for a spot on the Lake Holly Garden Committee without exciting a media protest."

Schulman's voice got soft and steely. "You've just put the nail in your political future. I hope you know that, Adele."

"I'm calling Hallard in ten minutes. Come through or I start calling all my contacts."

She disconnected the call and sank back in her seat, covering her face with her hands to blot out the spectacle of police cruisers and cops before her. Vega put a hand on her thigh.

"Oh God, Nena," he said in a husky voice. "I'm so sorry."

"I thought you wanted me to stay."

"But not like this! Not stuck here because you burned all your bridges. It's like Greco said. You're a peregrine falcon. You need to fly at your own altitude."

She took her hands away from her face and looked at him. "*Louis* Greco said that?"

"Yeah."

Adele grinned. "And I thought his charms didn't extend beyond four letters."

"But he's right." Vega ran a hand through his wet hair. "I want you to do what makes you happy. Here or D.C. or—wherever."

Adele's phone rang. She looked at the caller ID. "Judge Hallard."

Vega watched her take the call. "Yes, eleventh-hour deal making. I quite agree. Yes, thank you, Judge." She caught Vega's eye and gave him a thumbs-up. "You have a great trip to China." She clicked off the call.

"So," said Vega. "Serrano's order of removal will be rescinded?"

Adele nodded. "Hallard already looked at the case. He was waiting for the go-ahead. I want to tell Luna before they take her to the hospital."

Vega laced his hand in hers. "You gave up a lot tonight."

"Yeah. I guess." She squeezed his hand. "Then again, maybe I held on to what counts."

Chapter 44

The commuter plane touched down on the runway. Vega watched it through the windows of the waiting area. The county airport was a small facility, used mostly for corporate jets and a few discount carriers that took passengers to Florida in the winter. But it did a regular route to Washington, D.C.

Vega clutched a bouquet of peach roses—Adele's favorite—as he searched the crowd of passengers pouring into the baggage-claim area. He saw families with strollers, businesspeople with laptops and briefcases. And then he saw Adele. She was dressed in a navy-blue jacket and skirt and wheeling a carry-on suitcase. Her black-rimmed reading glasses were perched atop her head and brought to mind the high-powered lawyer she'd once been, as if her time at La Casa had just been a quiet interlude before she set off again for bigger horizons. Vega wondered if he should have worn something better for the occasion than faded jeans, a flannel shirt, and a Yankees baseball cap. Joy had urged him to dress up when she called to wish him good luck this morning. He should have listened. If there was one thing Joy knew about, it was clothes.

He rocked back and forth on the heels of his lace-up boots, the way he always did when he was nervous. His mouth was dry. It was late November and cold in the terminal, but already he was sweating. She hadn't spotted him yet. The wheels of her suitcase had gotten snagged on an upturned part of the walkway rug, and she was trying to lift the case over the hump. He wished she'd see him so he could read the verdict in her eyes. Her face at a distance told him nothing.

The last few weeks had been a roller coaster for both of them. Schulman easily defeated John Sawyer to win a seat in the U.S. Senate. Adele, however, was no longer part of that victory. In return for Schulman's grudging cooperation in getting Manuel Serrano's order of removal rescinded, Adele said nothing publicly on the Gonzalez scandal. In private, she told Vega she felt certain Schulman knew more about Gonzalez's proclivities than he let on. Regardless of whether that was true or not, the situation had soured both Adele and Schulman on any sort of partnership.

Vega kept reminding Adele that she'd made the right choice. She could never have worked for him after what had transpired. But in the days and weeks after the election, Vega began to understand the deeper dilemma Adele was facing. Up until that moment, her life as executive director and founder of La Casa had been a choice. Now, it seemed like a sentence. A door had been shut, and Adele grieved the loss. Her political passions and ambitions weren't separate from who she was; they were part of her. She could no more live without them than he could live without his music. And so, in late November, when Adele received a call from Judge Hallard to tell her he'd been impressed by her drive and had recommended her for a policy position at a think tank in Washington, D.C., Vega encouraged her to interview for it. And now here he was, standing at the airport, telling himself that whatever choice she made, he'd learn to live with.

If the past few weeks had taught Vega anything, it was that you could do a lot of damage pretending that people were other than what they were. Esme Gonzalez had been so consumed with her family's reputation in the Hispanic community that she'd covered up her husband's crimes for years. After Gonzalez's death, several more women came forward with allegations that they'd been raped by Gonzalez when they were teenagers. Most had been too embarrassed at the time to tell their families, much less the police. The community's silence had kept a predator in their midst for decades.

Esme now faced a spate of charges in the murder of her husband, Zambo, and Baby Mercy and the kidnapping and assault on Luna Serrano. She was not the only respected figure facing jail. Claudia Aguilar too was facing charges for accessory to manslaughter. The DA was talking about cutting a deal with Claudia, offering her probation in return for testifying against Esme. Just as with Schulman, Vega had a suspicion that the true level of Claudia's culpability might never come out. There were layers of denial running through this case, some of which Vega wasn't sure he'd ever unravel. The search warrant on the Gonzalez household had yet to turn up the source of the hydrofluoric acid Zambo had consumed—yet another part of the puzzle. Vega was betting it came from the car wash and was mixed in with cheap vodka, and that the bottle was long ago discarded by Esme. But Vega would keep looking. Even if it took months, he was going to try to trace every part of this case, if only because he owed it to that little baby.

Mercy.

Vega would forever grieve that he had failed to save her. Her mother at least had a name now: Mia Tavares. Vega located relatives of Esme's in Chiapas who provided records to confirm the girl's identity and agreed to take her and the baby back to Mexico for burial. DNA tests confirmed that Mia and the baby were indeed Esme's biological daughter and granddaughter. There were also indicators to suggest that Mia's father was a blood relation of Esme's, but Esme refused to discuss the matter and it had no legal bearing on the case, so Vega didn't press. There were some humiliations even Esme was entitled to bury with the dead.

At the door to baggage claim, Adele lifted her gaze from her suitcase. She broke into a broad smile when she saw Vega standing there awkwardly with the cellophane bouquet of wilted peach roses in his arms. Her sparkle had returned. If this job was what it took to bring it back, then so be it.

He stepped forward and wrapped an arm around her waist. He leaned over and buried his face in her neck. He felt the pleasing give of her body as she welcomed him. Whatever else had happened in D.C., she hadn't lost her feelings for him. He felt reassured. He took her suitcase from her and pressed the bouquet into her hands.

"What's the occasion?" she asked.

"To celebrate," said Vega. "You got the job, right?"

"Yes. And I turned it down."

"*What?*" Vega stopped in his tracks. People pushed past them in every direction. "But you wanted this."

"I thought I did. But then I got down there and realized that what I really wanted was to have a choice. And I got one. My life is here, Jimmy. Sophia's life is here. *You're* here—"

"I don't want to hold you back."

"I'm glad you said that. Because when I told them my decision, they offered me a position on their advisory board. So instead of relocating to D.C., I just have to fly down two days a month for meetings and be available for occasional conferences. It means we'll have to juggle our schedules a little more, but it's a great opportunity. I won't have to relocate. They'll put me up in a really nice hotel." Adele gave him a tentative look. "So—are you okay with that?"

"On one condition. And it's make or break."

"Oh." She gave him a wary look. "What's that?"

He grinned. "You bring me the mints from your hotel pillow."

"Deal."

Tomorrow was Thanksgiving. Luna and her father would be making a turkey. In more than twelve years of living in this country as a family, they'd never cooked a turkey on Thanksgiving. Luna supposed on some level they'd never felt American enough to do it before. But everything was different now. Her father's order of removal had been rescinded, and Mr. Schulman had turned his case over to Mr. Katz to begin the process of getting green cards for both of them. La Bella Vita gave Papi his old job back. They returned to their apartment. They were gone for only a few days, so it hadn't been re-rented yet. They just had to take all their stuff out of storage.

Luna would be lying, however, if she said that everything was back to normal. Mateo still wet the bed sometimes. Dulce had developed a nervous tic of yanking out her hair. Papi had had to cut it short and make her wear hats to stop the habit. Luna now slept with Mateo's baseball bat under her bed. Papi tried to talk to her about it, but neither of them could find the words for that sort of conversation.

Luna wanted to be the girl she used to be. She wanted to do well in school and become a doctor so she could buy them all a house with a garden just like Mami had always wanted. But she couldn't unlearn what she knew. There was something broken inside of her, something she didn't know how to fix.

When the police finally returned their things from the Gonzalez house, they brought back her mother's begonia. It was dead by then. Luna couldn't stop crying over that plant. Papi remembered how Mami used to take cuttings from plants and make new ones. So they snipped a four-inch piece from the healthiest stalk and put it in water.

Nothing happened for a long time. And then the other day, Luna saw tiny white shoots at the bottom of the stalk. For the first time in a long time, she felt hopeful. A friend of Papi's who worked at the garden center brought them a nice pot and some potting soil. Luna and her father planted the little stalk and set the pot on the windowsill. Maybe, with enough time and patience, her mother's plant would one day bloom again. Papi thought it would.

Luna wanted to see the world the way he did. But she couldn't. She felt like those giant maple trees at her school that had a chain-link fence running through them. She couldn't get rid of the twisted metal inside of her.

She was waiting for the school bus to take her to La Casa one day when she caught a glimpse of those trees across the soccer field. It was late fall now. The trees were bare. Luna could see their trunks easily from the school parking lot, the way the fence sliced right through them, the way they'd grown around it. In the spring, she and her friends gossiped in their cool, deep shade. In the fall, they had leaf fights beneath their graceful branches. Looking up at those trees, no one would ever guess there was sharp metal buried inside.

Luna wondered if life wasn't like that—if people didn't all have, deep within them, some wound they could not heal, one they could only accept and grow beyond. For all their trauma, those trees had flourished.

If they could do it, then maybe so could her family. Maybe so could she.

Acknowledgments

A book is a team effort, and I consider myself the luckiest of writers to have such a wonderful and supportive team behind me. On the research end, I'd like to thank Westchester County Police Captain Christopher Calabrese and Lieutenant James Palanzo for walking me through the finer points of police investigations. (And yes, as promised, I've named the police dog in the book after the Westchester County Police dog, Daisy.)

Thanks, as always, to Gene West, fire investigator, FBI consultant, and storyteller extraordinaire, for his endlessly inventive sense of plot and character. And also to thriller author J. H. Bográn for his eleventh-hour help on some finer points with the Spanish language and culture of Latin America.

My deepest gratitude to my agent, Stephany Evans, for being both a cheerleader and a voice of reason in everything I do. Also thanks to my early reader, Rosemary Ahern, for her many insightful suggestions.

A shout out to Steven Zacharias and the folks at Kensington Books who have put their hearts into this series, from great covers and design work to wonderful marketing. In particular I'd like to thank my editor, Michaela Hamilton, for her editing savvy and attention to detail. My special thanks to her assistant, Norma Perez-Hernandez, for her early enthusiasm for the series and for her tireless work translating all those permission requests! I'm forever grateful.

Thank you always to my husband, Thomas Dunne, my children, Kevin and Erica, and my stepfather, Bill Hayes, for living through all the ups and downs of this crazy writing life. You make it all worthwhile.

Most of all, my gratitude to the men and women whose real-life experiences inspire and inform these stories. I hope to offer a window, however small, into the courage and determination they show every day.